THEY ACTED OUT
THEIR LIVES – AND CHINABERRY
WAS THEIR STAGE . . .

Reeves Douglas – master of Chinaberry. He turned from his cold wife to the sensual love of the slave-woman Josie . . .

Julia – Reeves's daughter. Heiress to a fortune, she wanted only her favourite possession – Darby, the black slave . . .

Darby – whose devotion to Julia was his downfall and who fled from Chinaberry in terror of his life . . .

Travers – Darby's white friend and confidant, who returned with him to Chinaberry and was caught in its treacherous web . . .

THEIRS IS AN UNFORGETTABLE STORY WHOSE SPELLBINDING POWER HAS ALREADY ENTHRALLED OVER A MILLION AMERICAN READERS.

Also by William Lavender in Sphere Books

FLIGHT OF THE SEABIRD
CHILDREN OF THE RIVER
THE FIELDS ABOVE THE SEA
JOURNEY TO QUIET WATERS

Chinaberry

WILLIAM LAVENDER

SPHERE BOOKS LIMITED
30-32 Gray's Inn Road, London WC1X 8JL

First published in Great Britain by Sphere Books Ltd 1977

Published by arrangement with the author's agent
Reprinted 1977 (twice), 1978, 1979 (twice),
1980 (twice), 1984

TRADE
MARK

Set in Photon Times

Printed and bound in Great Britain by
Collins, Glasgow

To my wife Mary –
whose name should have been Patience

PART ONE

AFTER

CHAPTER ONE

The great river rolled with invisible power, fed by the vast intricate system of watercourses that drained the heart of a continent.

In the early morning calm the stream was undisturbed by the movements of life except for a few scavenging gulls that wheeled in silent undulating arcs near the middle, and a solitary skiff, minuscule in the broad dimensions of its natural setting, that nosed its way cautiously down the edge of the sluggish current along the west bank.

Soft clammy-grey mist swirled above the burnished brown, mirror-smooth surface of the water. Silently it yielded, retreating and parting before the gliding skiff, then as silently closing in again behind it, hanging like a shroud over the sullen river.

In the bow of the little craft a black man sat huddled, his elbows on his knees, and stared across the water toward the dark green mass of junglelike growth that formed the near shoreline, as blurred and insubstantial as a mirage in the misty morning air. He looked at the long wavering line of the land absently, without seeing it, dreamily remembering, as he was beginning to do more and more frequently each day, while the skiff slipped down, down the wide river, deeper and deeper into the moss-hung South – and further and further back into the faded past.

I wonder if it's still there, he thought. My God, I wonder if it ever *was* there. It's like another life I lived in some distant past, or somethin' I dreamed about, or read about in a book one time – though the books I've read in the past twenty-one years wouldn't stack up very high, that's sure.

Twenty-one years. He turned the phrase over in his mind, trying to grasp a clear comprehension of that measure of time. Maybe I'm crazy, he thought. Trav says I am, and Trav's been right so damn many times before.

The gentle rhythm of the working oar ceased, and the sudden interruption of monotonous sound pulled his mind away from his private thoughts. He shifted his position and looked back toward his companion in the stern of the skiff.

The white man suspended the oar dripping from the water and scanned the immense solitude around him with a scowl. He had not been working excessively hard – it was mostly a matter of using a single oar as a free paddle and guiding the boat along, nudging it away from snags and sandbars and other obstacles, and otherwise letting it have its head, rather than propelling it. But he well knew that the heat of this day in late June, even with the sun still low in the morning sky, would soon drive away the protective mists and turn the broad surface of the river into a steam bath, threatening to suffocate any man-creature that ventured upon it.

The oarsman squinted off in the direction of the far side, somewhere beyond the range of visibility a half-mile or more to the east. And once again, as he had done many times in the past few days, he tried to shake off a vague feeling of uneasiness, an almost instinctive distrust of this monstrous thing – this mighty, mysterious, silent, slow-moving avalanche of water to which he, born to the high windy desert-dry vistas of the far West, would always be alien.

He searched the face of the black man in the bow of the little vessel, and marvelled at his friend's outwardly casual acceptance of this strange unearthly environment, so disconnected from the solid ground of the real world.

He spoke, and for the thousandth time was startled by the sound of his own voice, unnaturally loud, reverberating across the hard glassy surface of the water.

'D'you know where we are, Darby?'

'Why sure,' came the easy answer. 'We're floatin' down the main highway o' the world.'

'The Father of Waters, right. But does the Father of Waters know where we want to go?'

Darby winced, and frowned in distaste at the other man.

'Trav – anybody who knows anything knows the river's a *she*. People who are only half ignorant might say *it*. Only a God-awful ignoramus calls her a *he*.'

'You're sure about that,' Trav said.

' 'Course I'm sure. She's a woman, Trav – fickle, moody, unpredictable – don't ever let anybody tell you she ain't a woman.'

Trav regarded his companion with quiet patience.

I taught Darby everything he knows about the West, he thought, and some of the things I've taught him have saved his life once or twice. Now it's his turn to lead me into a place he knows about and I don't – his turn to teach me. All right, I'm tryin' to learn. But, God knows, it ain't easy.

He tried again. 'All right, she's a woman. Now that we've settled the important question of the river's sex, can we get back to the question of where the hell we *are*? D'you think we're gettin' into familiar territory yet?'

Darby was scanning the near bank and as far downriver as he could see, not dreamily now, but with concentration. This time his answer was slower, and almost apologetic in its uncertainty.

'Can't tell for sure. River changes all the time, y'know – almost from one day to the next. And I ain't been around here for twenty-one years.'

He continued to inspect the waterway, then suddenly pointed to something near the shoreline.

'See that spit o' sand over there, Trav? It's been there long enough for little sprouts o' trees to start growin' on it, see? But come back in six months, and it'll most likely be gone, trees and all.'

Darby took delight in his admiration for the river; this huge warm thing had been one of the major boundaries of his life in childhood. He had known and loved it from the time of his earliest memory, and splashed and played along its banks almost as soon as he had walked. He remembered the sensuous delight evoked by the cool sticky mud at the lapping edge of the water, in a mysterious way more attractive to a small boy than the water itself. The river held no terror for him, stirred no uneasiness, but seemed to open its arms to him in welcome, like a mother to a wandering son.

He was embarrassed to reveal to Trav his affection for it; he teased it instead, cursed it gently, and called it names.

'Damn tricky ol' river,' he said. 'Nothin' but an ol' whore, tha's all she is. But tricky – you got to be careful with her. You don't show her proper respect, she'll smack you down. She don't give a damn for nobody.'

'I figured that out,' said Trav dryly.

Darby shifted his position to inspect another part of the waterscape.

'Tricky ol' witch,' he murmured. 'Never still, always changin'. She sure will fool you.'

Trav studied his companion intently. 'Hey, Darby – you tryin' to tell me we're lost?'

Darby turned back toward Trav, grinning at him. 'Now, how can we be lost, travellin' down the Mississip'? Ain't hardly no way we can get off the trail, is there?'

'Well, you said yourself it's a tricky river. And I don't mind tellin' you I don't trust it.'

Trav paused, and his irritation picked up steam.

'This ain't no proper river, anyway. A river is a stream o' water where you can stand on one bank and look across to the other. Hell, you can stand on one bank here, and the other side might just as well be Spain. This ain't no river, it's a damn brown ocean. And I never was no sea-farin' man.'

Darby's grin widened as he listened to his friend rant.

'Besides,' Trav went on, 'a hell of a lot has happened since you were here last. It's eighteen sixty-six, you know? A whole damn war has happened. You don't even know whether that place is still *there* or not.'

The grin disappeared from Darby's face. He turned back to his inspection of the passing scenery.

Trav began working the paddle again. In spite of his dislike of these unfamiliar watery surroundings, he had learned quickly the intricacies of handling the rowboat – though at first it had seemed to be alive, and as perverse and ill-tempered as an unbroken colt. Now, after a few days on the river, he had the colt subdued, and was reining it with authority and confidence.

The two men were taking turns working the skiff, though trying always to arrange it so that when passing towns or otherwise coming into view of members of the local population, Darby would be handling the paddle. Darby had conceived this notion, saying that southern locals would consider it more than passing strange to see the white man working while the black man rode in leisure as a passenger – and it was no use arousing either curiosity or hostility in some cantankerous backwoodsman.

Darby studied the shoreline carefully, looking for something – anything – that would make him feel he'd been here before. But the land stubbornly refused to offer up any features that stirred his memory.

Presently he leaned forward, his eyes focusing on something interesting along the near bank.

'Hey, looka there, Trav.'

'What? Where?' Trav searched the shore eagerly, uncertain of what he was supposed to see.

'The moss. The hangin' moss.'

It trailed from the overhanging branches of trees near the water's edge, delicate and gossamer, but as lifeless as withered spiderweb, touching the surface of the river lightly.

Trav glanced at it indifferently and turned away, slightly pained at his friend's excitability.

'It's the first we've seen, you realize that?' said Darby, and added softly, 'We're gettin' down South now, sure.'

The little vessel moved on slowly down the broad waterway. Sometimes it was trapped and mired like flotsam in eddies and shallows; sometimes it caught the sudden thrust of a current just right and shot downstream like a sleek weightless canoe; other times it would heel abruptly and stall with mulish obstinacy, before allowing itself to be manoeuvred past a troublesome snag.

Trav cursed softly from time to time as he navigated the more difficult passages. It seemed to him that the placid surface of the giant river covered a hidden world of malevolent tricks and surprises. A treacherous maze it was, and Trav knew he would never completely master it. That would be the work of a lifetime – and he had no intention of spending more than an insignificant fraction of his life in this place.

The sun climbed higher and the temperature rose with it, and Trav sweated profusely and swore a trifle harder, resenting the heavy, humid southern heat that was so strangely different from the dry scorching heat of the West.

'Damn right,' he muttered. 'We're gettin' down South now for sure. And we can leave again any time you're ready.'

Darby, seeing the grim look on his friend's face, offered to take the oar, but Trav waved him off, saying his turn lasted until noon, and he wanted no special favours, and saying he agreed to come on this damn fool trip of his own free will – though he must have been out of his mind at the time – and he intended to pull his own weight until he could get back to God's country.

'So help me,' he said, 'when I get back to California this time, I'm gonna chain myself to a live oak, and never stray again.'

Trav's grumbling brought the grin creeping back to the other man's face. Darby reached out and scooped up a double handful of the Mississippi River and hurled it playfully in Trav's direction, bringing forth a howl and an answering salvo. Soon they were both dripping wet and relaxed with laughter, and the heat was forgotten for a while.

So they moved on downstream, and at each curve and bend, as a new vista opened before them, Darby searched the landscape for signs of something familiar.

They had come upon the bluffs of Memphis a few days before, and put in at its steep landing, and marvelled at its conglomeration of steamboats and river traffic. Though still suffering from the dislocations of war, it teemed with life; shining black dock workmen, tradesmen, riverboat crewmen, loafers, drifters, and homeless people – these last mostly of the newly emancipated black race, with a bleak bewildered look that set them apart. In contrast, a few prosperous-looking planters and their chattering ladies provided a lingering trace of the old pre-war style of luxurious living with noisy arrivals and departures, surrounded by baggage, servants, and confusion.

It was as if by some minor miracle a handful of charmed people had remained untouched by the savage searing flame of civil war, which, now receded into history by only one short year, had so desolated the land.

After pausing at Memphis briefly for supplies, Darby and Trav had moved on downriver, and now, according to Darby's uncertain calculations and anxious hopes, they were nearing their destination.

By noon the mist of early morning had entirely disappeared, and the details of the passing landscape stood out sharply in brilliant sunlight. The travellers edged their craft in closer to the bank to watch for a convenient landing site, and when they found it, put in to shore for a midday break. After a simple meal they stretched out on the ground for a short rest, taking advantage of overhanging branches for protection from the sun.

Trav, tired from his morning's work, quickly dropped off to sleep. Darby lay back in the grass under a small tree and, with his eyes half closed in drowsiness, stared up into the rich green leaves of summer above his head.

Suddenly he reached up and pulled a tender young leaf off a low-hanging branch, rolled it between his fingers, and examined it closely. He looked up and inspected the small tree above him; its trunk, bark, branches, and general outline.

No, he thought. No, it's not. For a minute I thought it was a chinaberry tree. Haven't seen any o' them out West – guess they don't grow there much. Haven't seen a chinaberry tree in – well, twenty-one years. Twenty-one years in April. That's a long time ago. Good Lord, there are millions o' twenty-year-old people in this world – grown-up people – who weren't even born then.

Trav's right, he thought. I don't know if anything is still there. But, hell, plantations don't get up and walk away, do they?

Had he overshot his destination? An uncomfortable thought. Trav would never stop laughing about that. Hastily Darby dismissed the idea. He had never felt any particular handicap in his lack of education, knocking about the West, but he did wish he had a surer grasp of geographical knowledge.

No, plantations do not get up and walk away, not even after twenty-one years and a civil war. It'll be there, he promised himself, and I'll know it when I see it.

That's not what I'm really wondering about, at all, he thought. What I'm *really* wondering about is – will Julia be there?

For a while he watched a turkey buzzard wheeling silently alone a thousand feet up in the white-hot sky. Sounds and images floated through his mind, spun around, grew vivid, then faded. The drone of insects lulled him in the quiet of the early afternoon.

He slept.

[illegible]

[illegible]

[illegible] Danny [illegible] knowledge.

[illegible]

[illegible]

PART TWO

BEFORE

CHAPTER ONE

In the fresh spring days of April, in the year 1845, there were one hundred and fifty-four people living on the premises of Chinaberry plantation, which sprawled in a roughly rectangular shape over some 1200 acres along the east bank of the Mississippi, in the northwestern part of the state that takes its name from the river.

This population divided naturally into certain well-defined groups and sub-groups. The first and fundamental division was that of race; there were eleven whites and one hundred and forty-three blacks – that is, eleven free people and one hundred and forty-three souls held in bondage.

The whites – those beings who were recognized as *people*, as distinguished from *property* – also divided into two main sections, the gulf between which was, in its own way, almost as profound as the racial division.

On one level was the Douglas family; plantation owner Reeves Douglas, his wife Margaret, their spirited fourteen-year-old daughter Julia, and Margaret's aged and invalid father, Milo Gates. On another level altogether were the hired whites, consisting of overseer Horace Willard and his wife and several children, who lived in a shabby bungalow in a remote area of the plantation grounds, along with two other male hired hands who took room and board with the Willards, and worked as the overseer's assistants.

The plantation's larger category of inhabitants, the black slaves, provided the workpower, the brawn and sinew, the energy and endurance, that made the place into a productive, self-sustaining establishment.

Like the whites, they fell into distinctly different sub-groups, the largest of which was the field hand gang, consisting of seventy-seven people of both sexes, ranging from striplings of eight or nine to the aged and bent. These workers were designated, according to their age and vigour, as full hands, half-hands, or quarter-hands. A smaller group of skilled workers, numbering fifteen, comprised the yard force – specialists like carpenters, mechanics, stonemasons, a blacksmith, even an expert in flower culture.

A still smaller select company of ten house servants formed the domestic staff, which served the Douglas family and maintained the household. The members of this group were chosen with utmost care from the slave population, and were usually the most intelligent – and invariably the most genial and pliable – individuals that could be identified.

The minimally productive members of the chattel work force – children under the age of six, and the very old – were given only light chores around the yards. Several of the ancient and wrinkled elders, deeply sunk in the feebleness of years, had been granted something so unimaginably foreign to their experience that they were hopelessly incapable of coping with it – leisure. Empty idleness, as they waited for death.

In most respects the black people at Chinaberry were typical of the slave population of the South. In one important way, however, they enjoyed an unusual favour of fortune that rendered them the objects of widespread envy among the bondsmen of neighbouring plantations. That was the peculiar quirk in the character of Reeves Douglas that caused him to look with distaste upon the traditional method of punishment – whipping – and to insist upon other less physically brutal means of discipline for his people. This aberrant attitude on the part of the master of Chinaberry was the cause of almost unbearable frustration for his overseers, and a source of ridicule among his fellow planters, who considered it a shocking example of unmanly softness.

Horace Willard, the present holder of the overseer position, had been at the job for five years – a goodly length of service, as overseers went – and during that time had never ceased to argue the question of discipline with his employer, stoutly claiming that it was beyond the power of any mortal man to maintain control over 'the nigger brutes' without the aid of the trusty whip. Nevertheless, the big, burly, ferocious looking Willard constantly undermined his own arguments by managing to operate an efficient well-disciplined gang of field hands. He did this through the expert use of gruff threats, growls, curses, kicks and cuffs, and frequent well-aimed blows with the thick butt-end of his ever present whip – this last tactic, he reasoned, was not using the whip as a *whip*, and thus not violating the letter of his employer's instructions.

Once in a while, under the stress of anger, Willard allowed

himself the satisfaction of an outright violation of the no-whipping rule, reasonably certain that by intimidation he could prevent word from getting back to the master – or, failing that, confident that he could talk his way out of the difficulty with no more than an admonishment from Douglas.

The labour of the field hands, though rigorous throughout the year, increased in volume and tempo relentlessly through the spring and summer, the times of sowing, cultivating, and gathering of crops, and reached its peak in the autumn, the season of cotton picking. Then, as autumn turned to winter, the ginning and pressing of the cotton took place in the gin house, where the mountains of soft white fluff were separated from the seeds and pressed into bales, and delivered to the river landing for transporting to market. The remainder of the wet blustery winter months was then spent in clearing the fields, and preparing for the renewal of the ageless cycle in the coming spring.

With a few exceptions, the black people of Chinaberry lived in small unpainted wooden hovels, square one-room structures with dirt floors, that stretched in a double row along the far side of a series of broad barnyard areas directly behind the grounds of the main house. These little shacks were known collectively as 'the quarters'.

The slaves who enjoyed the privilege of exception to the rule of living in the quarters numbered five. Foremost among them was the butler, the chief of the household servants, a distinguished looking middle-aged man of impressive dignity and intelligence named Moses, who was allotted accomodation in a little room beneath the stairs of the plantation house. Josie, the cook, a handsome mulatto woman about thirty years of age, was second in official rank, but in addition held a special kind of status that was understood by many and spoken of by few. Josie lived in a comfortable apartment that was an annexe to the kitchen house – the kitchen being a separate building immediately to the rear of the main house.

Upstairs in the main house there were two elderly slaves who slept in tiny rooms close by the people whom they served; Margaret Douglas's personal maid, a shrivelled little woman named Sullah, and a silent sombre man named Hector, who was the manservant of Margaret's invalid father, Milo Gates.

Besides these four, one other Chinaberry slave enjoyed

special resident privileges. This was a slender teen-aged boy, who shared Moses's living space, and who was looked upon by the butler with warm fatherly affection, though they were not related.

The boy had been acquired in early childhood – quite by accident – as part of a group of new slaves brought back to the plantation by Reeves Douglas from a trip to the slave markets of Memphis. Because Douglas had made a lot purchase of a dozen human bodies of chattel property, and had paid handsomely, the slave trader had generously thrown in a bonus – a small orphan boy.

Douglas had been pleased; the child was sturdy and bright-eyed, and his chocolate brown skin tone indicated the likely presence of some trace of white blood – a condition that the planter conventionally assumed to indicate the probability of good intelligence.

The boy was brought to Chinaberry and allowed to run free in the house and yards, being looked after in haphazard fashion by Josie and Moses. And as he grew older it fell to his miraculous good fortune not only to escape the hardships of life in the quarters and the brutal labours of the field hands, but to elude the larger burdens of work altogether, except for occasional light tasks put upon him by the butler or the cook.

His life was filled with days of carefree idleness – roaming the deep woods in search of wild grapes and imagined adventure; wandering along the banks of the river and playing in its placid muddy water; sitting by its quiet lapping shore in a long twilight, and wondering what might lie on the other side, to the west where the sun was setting; and in bad weather retreating to a secret place and savouring a cosy bit of shelter – and doing these things almost always in company of a partner, a companion-in-spirit, to whom he was blindly devoted and whose presence by his side through the long sunny days of childhood bestowed upon him a kind of inviolability, a semi-freedom that was inconsistent with his status as a slave.

He had lived in this charmed condition nearly all of his remembered life – becoming aware of its special nature only gradually, as he grew older – because its origin was rooted back in a small, fleeting, accidental moment that occurred soon after he was brought to Chinaberry, and long before he was old enough to comprehend momentous things.

Once, on a summer afternoon just before Julia's fourth birthday, Reeves Douglas had seen his beloved golden blonde child playing with the little black boy of her own age, had watched them running and laughing and chasing each other, and – because the playing together of small children, black and white, was one of the controlled kinds of interracial contact to which the slave-owning southerner held no objections – had been charmed. Then he had been struck with an amusing and whimsical idea: here was an ideal birthday gift for his little daughter.

And so, by simple decree, simply spoken, the boy became from that moment the companion, plaything, personal servant and living property of Julia Douglas. His name was Darby.

CHAPTER TWO

The Douglases of Chinaberry occupied a position of favoured prominence among the local members of the planter class, the aristocrats of the agrarian southern society. James Douglas, the present owner's father, had come to the region from Virginia in 1804, bringing with him a young wife and two small children, a few personal slaves, and a satchel full of money. A younger son of a wealthy family of the Old Dominion, he had sought to console himself over the lack of land inheritance by establishing his own domain and dynasty in the fertile lowlands of the young Mississippi Territory, on the east bank of the nation's great central waterway.

He was a careful and prudent man; he searched diligently for exactly the right location – and his diligence led him to an inspired choice. The land his judgment fixed upon bordered the river on the upper edge of the vast alluvial plain that extended southward from Tennessee to the drowned and trackless marshes at the Gulf of Mexico. It was distinguished by a single topographical feature that rendered it uniquely desirable. That was a low ridge running parallel to the river for several miles, at a distance of two or three hundred yards from the banks. This seemingly insignificant rise formed a natural levee a few critically important feet higher than the dangerously low-lying region around it, and provided life-saving protection from the rampages of the river during flood times.

So James Douglas acquired the property of his choice in a frontier land auction, and set about the double task of transforming the virgin ground into a plantation, and himself into a planter.

His frail young wife Penelope followed him with the dutiful, uncomplaining loyalty that was ingrained in the traditions and training of her people – but she did it with an inner trembling of spirit. She looked with cold fear upon the prospect of leaving behind forever the genteel tidiness and cultured atmosphere of her homeland and taking up the unimaginable hardships of life on the southern frontier.

Penelope Reeves Douglas would spend the rest of her short life longing for Virginia.

The Douglases' five-year-old son, Reeves, would sometimes pause in later years with a fleeting impression of a memory, some shadowy subconscious image from a scene out of his babyhood in a far-off place; the happy gurgling infant girl Amelia would never be troubled by the faintest recollection of the land where she was born.

After installing his family temporarily in the nearest town, James Douglas entered into a period of extended visits to slave markets up and down the river, seeking the manpower necessary for his new property – for after all, he said to his wife, what is the value of land without an ample supply of human brawn to apply to it?

James complained loudly that this was an exhausting business, this collecting of slaves. It was nerve wracking and fraught with risk; a man must look into the dark impenetrable eyes of a strapping black primitive and try to divine, by some miraculous insight, what lies behind them. Is this a reasonable creature, that can be tamed and trained, broken to the plough and furrow like a good mule? Or is it a black tiger, that will snarl and claw and fight back until it has to be killed? Worse yet, will it prove to be a cunning fox, living by its wits, practising black magic and devious deceptions of astonishing subtlety, inventing a thousand little ways to punish and torment its master while remaining always a picture of meek servility? An exhausting and risky business, indeed.

But at length the task was done. The black people were examined, selected, bargained for, purchased, herded away like cattle, and laboriously shaped into some kind of coherent work force, and set to their initial task: clearing a site for the new plantation house.

The chosen spot was a slight uplift of land in the northwest corner of the property, culminating in a low rounded promontory from which a pleasant view of the river and surrounding land could be enjoyed. On this little summit, called Indian Hill by people of the region, Douglas had intended to build his house, but the existence of a local legend intruded on his plans – a story to the effect that the place was an ancient Indian burial ground and the site of all manner of unspeakably savage rites, and that a dire curse of evil would fall upon any who dared profane its sacred soil. Douglas scoffed openly at all this – but quietly altered his plans and settled upon a flat grassy area just south of the hill as the location of his future home.

This matter taken care of, Douglas turned his attention to another problem – a petty annoyance, but one that had to be dealt with. A family of squatters was illegally occupying a small patch of his newly acquired land, in a heavily wooded section at the southern end, close by the river. They would have to be evicted.

The interlopers were foreigners of some sort, he was told, and spoke little English. He surmised they were French, probably, or Spanish – one or the other, no doubt, since this region had been under the control of both nationalities in the recent past. No, he was advised, something much more foreign than that. Swarthy, fierce-eyed, beetle-browed people – better not go near them unarmed, never can tell about such folk.

So one morning at the first light of dawn, with his two most sturdy and trustworthy slaves flanking him, James Douglas quietly walked through the woods to the little clearing where the crude log cabin of the squatters stood. He was armed, as were the men he had brought with him. Roughly he called out to the cabin's inhabitants, he and his lieutenants crouching behind trees with their rifles primed, ready for a violent reaction.

The family came filing out – man, woman, and four or five ragged children, all trembling and fearful, calling out for mercy. Douglas searched their faces, trying anxiously to find some evidence of the expected ferocity that would justify his dramatic method of approach – and could find not a trace.

Though their English was indeed limited, they understood readily that they were to leave, and just as readily agreed, asking only that Douglas do them the favour of caring for the tree they had recently planted before their cabin door, and in which they were just beginning to rejoice, seeing that it was taking on health and growth after a difficult start.

A little chinaberry tree it was, slender and scraggly, entirely unexceptional, dwarfed as it was by the magnificent trees of the forest around it. Hardly a thing, Douglas thought, to inspire such earnest beseeching concern over whether it lived or died.

Looking at it, and at the shabby, gentle people standing before him, Douglas suddenly felt mean and foolish, and wished desperately to extricate himself from this awkward scene as quickly as possible. Gruffly he ordered the squatters to be off the land within forty-eight hours, called his two men, and marched off without another word.

He returned in three days, this time alone, and found the cabin empty and deserted. No trace of recent human habitation could be seen – not a scrap or fragment. Douglas examined the chinaberry tree, and saw that it was parched and wilted; the weather had been unusually dry lately. Before he departed he fetched water from the river and watered the little tree, then left it to its fate, standing in solitude before the lifeless cabin, surrounded by the silence of the wilderness.

Two months later work was completed on basic construction of the plantation house. And when James Douglas brought his wife and children to their new home he announced that the name of the plantation was to be Chinaberry.

The house, painstakingly designed by its owner, was no masterpiece of architectural creativity, following as it did the elementary requirements of frontier serviceability, and taking into account the nonavailability of sophisticated carpentry skills. Like many another frontier dwelling, it was meant to serve first the stark necessity of shelter; gradually, over a period of years, it would expand and take on spaciousness and comfort with piecemeal additions, conforming to the family's growth, and its rate of ascent up the scale of prosperity.

It would be over thirty years after its beginning that the house would reach its finished condition of elegance. When that day came the founder of the house would be seven years dead, the long task finally being brought to completion by the man who was a little boy of five when he stood by his father's side one day and watched in wide-eyed fascination as the original foundations were laid.

So in the course of time the establishment grew and prospered, as did the river valley region in general, slowly evolving from tangled wilderness to orderly fields of crop and pasture.

Two more children, both girls, were born in the new house in its first four years of inhabitancy. Then a few years later came a fifth child – a second son at last, to the delight of the parents – but their delight was turned to grief when this last child died in infancy.

Eventually, following the traditional pattern, the girls were married at appropriate ages to suitable sons of the southern gentry, in ceremonies that filled the plantation house with throngs of lively celebrants, and one by one moved on to become mistresses of their own households.

Both Reeves's younger sisters were destined to help carry on in their generation the steady advance of the American frontier, going with their husbands to establish farms and families, one in western Arkansas, one on the far plains of Texas. The older girl, Amelia, Virginia-born like Reeves, and to whom he was always closest, married a prosperous merchant and settled upriver in the vigorous young town of Memphis.

In equally conventional tradition the boy Reeves grew up to inherit the family property. James Douglas died in 1828, having survived his wife by two years, and Reeves was left as sole owner of Chinaberry at the age of twenty-nine.

In his youth Reeves had been spoiled and pampered by indulgent females – a mother, three sisters, and a succession of black nannies – and as a young man had been something of a dandy. When he inherited Chinaberry many shrewd observers among the local folk confidently predicted that the place would sink into immediate bankruptcy.

But Reeves confounded the experts by turning overnight into a competent and businesslike plantation manager. Under his direction Chinaberry continued to grow, until now, in the spring of 1845, it stood proud and pre-eminent over a wide region.

CHAPTER THREE

A visitor to Chinaberry might approach over either of two possible routes. A narrow dirt road entered from the east, winding through low-grade sandy soil and pine woods from Hanesville, the nearest town, seven miles away. From the west the approach was by way of the river landing, where vessels of various kinds might be encountered, from small skiffs to cotton barges to – on occasion – one of the great ponderous steamboats that plied their trade up and down the wide winding water-thoroughfare from New Orleans to Memphis to St. Louis, and beyond.

The route from the river was the more striking. After disembarking at the landing and passing beneath a tall wooden arch across which the name CHINABERRY was constructed of hand-hewn letters, the visitor followed a little dirt road up the gentle incline of the low ridge and through a dense stand of sandbar willows, and into the open again a quarter of a mile from the river. From that point the great brilliant white bulk of the plantation house loomed with dramatic suddenness into view, a hundred yards ahead.

The road ran past the front of the house, and from it, to the right, a circular carriageway looped around the open grassy area at the foot of the broad veranda steps. Within the loop a tall sycamore tree stood, spreading graceful arching branches over the road. On the other side of the road the rounded outline of Indian Hill rose to an elevation of two hundred feet, the only feature on the landscape exceeding the house in height.

As the visitor approached he would be greeted by the butler, Moses, or by the owner himself, emerging from the cool dark interior of the house with a smile of effusive welcome, to offer him a comfortable cane-bottom chair on the shady veranda, to send Moses off for drinks, and to inquire earnestly after the visitor's health and that of his wife and children and all his relatives – by which time he would know that he was enveloped in an atmosphere in which courtesy and hospitality were not merely pleasant adjuncts to living, but life-sciences of paramount importance, refined and polished to perfection.

Reeves Douglas was tall and trim, a handsome vigorous man in his middle forties, with a ready smile and an open engaging charm, and an enormous enthusiasm for playing the part of genial host – an activity that rivalled the management of the plantation as his principal occupation. He was, indeed, possessed by an insatiable appetite for elaborate social events, planning and staging them with the professional thoroughness of a theatrical director. His constant need for diversions of this kind required him to keep up a diligent search for excuses for them. Anything would do; a birthday or anniversary was considered ideal – preferably within the immediate family, but if necessary the significant dates in the lives of friends or distant relatives could be utilized – when hard-pressed Reeves had been known to have a party in honour of a new-born colt, foaled by a favourite mare.

The master's enthusiasm for a lively social life was not shared by the lady. Margaret Douglas was a quiet, soft-spoken woman, agreeable enough, and at forty-seven still attractive. But there was something vague about her – an aura of aloofness, of withdrawal, that made people uncomfortable – as if her eyes did not quite focus on the object before them, or her mind clearly grasp the subject at hand. She was intelligent, and possessed the impeccable social refinements that qualified her as a leading member of the stratified southern planter society, but she took neither pleasure nor interest in the socializing. She could be depended upon to appear at the proper moment, beautifully gowned and groomed, to move graciously among the guests, and perform the duties of hostess with smooth efficiency – but always with that secret veil before her eyes that protected her from involvement with the world.

Reeves shook his head in dismay over his bewildering spouse, but accepted her peculiarities with resignation, and worked hard at generating enough social initiative for both of them.

So it was that, on this day in April, 1845, the bustling activity of the household slaves began even before first light, a trifle earlier than usual, for besides the endless chores of the normal day, there were additional burdens – special preparations for another of the master's glittering parties, to be held that evening.

Food for a guest list of sixty-five was the assignment for Josie and her kitchen assistants – vast quantities of an overwhelming variety of steaming dishes, each a culinary creation, to make the sturdy banquet table sag under the weight. Other workers, under the expert supervision of Moses, would be busy the entire day, first as a cleaning crew, and later as practitioners of various decorative arts and crafts, for their master liked his parties to be colourful, gaily adorned, and visually stimulating. Outside, in the elegant formal garden along one side of the house, gardeners would be going over the already immaculately manicured grounds and grooming every leaf, every rosebud and blade of grass. Later in the afternoon lanterns would be hung in strategic spots in the garden, along the front veranda, around the carriage loop, and down the front road in both directions, so that the heavy velvet darkness of night would be conveniently pushed back and held at bay until the evening's revelry was at an end, and the guests had all departed.

The occasion for this event was the seventy-eighth birthday of Margaret Douglas's father.

The old man, Milo Gates, was notorious for his cantankerous ill temper, which a fuzziness of mind and memory did nothing to soften. He occupied an upstairs bedroom at Chinaberry, and was seldom seen outside it, having chosen some years before to live as an invalid, and a virtual recluse. His invalidism was a subject of whispered debate among the slaves, and occasionally between his daughter Margaret, who defended him, and her husband, who entertained uncharitable doubts about its genuineness.

In any case old Milo spent the greater part of his waking hours in a rickety wheelchair, which he navigated laboriously and almost ceaselessly across the length and breadth of his closed little world, pausing only now and then at a window to peer out over the plantation grounds with feeble watery eyes that saw little. From this vantage point he squinted and frowned, trying to identify every dim human figure that passed below, wondering what business they were about, and constantly muttering to himself on the subject that dominated his thoughts – the foibles and flaws in the character of his son-in-law Reeves Douglas.

The Gates family had been owners of a neighbouring plantation called Maywood, located several miles upriver. In earlier years Maywood had almost rivalled Chinaberry in vigour and productivity – at least Milo Gates, the master there, considered it a rivalry, and had taken great relish in it. He had been sorely distressed when the Douglas establishment forged ahead, while his own fell upon hard times. Some said the failure of Maywood stemmed from a series of dishonest or incompetent overseers; others were of the opinion that Milo brought all his troubles on himself with excessively harsh treatment of his slaves, a policy that resulted in a runaway rate two or three times that considered normal.

Whatever their origins, misfortunes rained down upon Maywood – not only upon the plantation but upon the Gates clan as well, for of seven children only Margaret and a younger brother survived to adulthood. After her mother had died and her brother Andrew had left home for good and gone to sea, Margaret was left with her father a broken man, rapidly sinking into senility, and the plantation in ruins. She presided alone over the dissolution of the few remaining assets of Maywood, disposed of the land and the slaves – without mercy, separating man from wife and mother from child when necessary, to sell them off as quickly as possible – and closed the doors of the decaying house forever.

She was brought back from the edge of despair by an astonishing and inexplicable reversal of fortune; a sudden courtship, ardently presented by Reeves Douglas, who, the elder Douglas having died recently, was the new master of Chinaberry. Margaret was dazzled and flattered by the handsome bachelor's attentions. He was by far the most sought after young man for miles around, while she was something of a wallflower, and at the age of thirty – a year older than Reeves – already presenting a decidedly spinsterish image. But since love scorns logic, Reeves Douglas offered marriage to Margaret Gates, and she accepted gratefully, looking upon it as a divine miracle, and the saving of her life.

Old Milo saw nothing divine about it, for, though he had been a grudging admirer of Reeves's father, he had little use for the son, whom he considered to be weak and dissolute, and given to sinful ways. He loudly proclaimed his daughter's marriage a disaster, predicted the failure of Chinaberry within five years, and went off to live with distant relatives across the river in Arkansas.

Some years later, when his prolonged and troublesome presence there became unwelcome, he was forced to accept an invitation from Margaret and Reeves to come and live at Chinaberry, which, to his deep chagrin, was enjoying greater prosperity than ever under his son-in-law's direction. The old man came sullenly, took up residence in the upstairs bedroom allotted to him, and withdrew into a shell of bitterness, his humiliation complete.

Around noon on this day of the party preparations, Milo gazed out of his window, squinting his bleary eyes, and noted the somewhat heavier than normal activity around the premises. He rang for his personal servant, an old slave named Hector, the only possession he still retained from the old days at Maywood, and demanded to know what was going on. Hector explained that a party was being held that evening, and that it was in honour of his – 'Massa Milo's' – birthday. Having delivered this information, Hector retreated quickly to avoid the outburst of temper that was sure to follow. It was the third time that day he had been asked and had answered the question.

When Hector had gone the old man fixed his eyes on a large rose in the centre of the floor, part of an old and faded pattern in the carpet that he sometimes stared at for hours, dreaming of his lost youth and wasted life. In a moment he muttered, 'I don't want no birthday party.' His voice rose gradually, as anger grew. 'I got no use for no damn party. I didn't ask for one, and I ain't goin' to one!'

Margaret's maid, Sullah, passed Milo's door, which Hector had left ajar, and, hearing the old man's rantings, looked in on him. 'Is you all right, Massa Milo?' she asked.

Milo lifted his eyes from the floor and gazed at her without expression. 'All my friends are dead,' he said. 'And I nevuh had no friends at Chinaberry, nohow. There ain't nobody livin' that would come to a party to see me, and nobody I would go down the stairs to see.' He shook a stern finger at the maid.

'Don't you come in heah tellin' me I'm havin' a birthday party. I ain't havin' no such of a thing. What's happenin' is, Reeves is havin' a party, that's the truth of it.'

He glared at Sullah, seething with anger. 'Now ain't that the truth of it?' he demanded.

'Yes, suh,' she answered placidly. 'I 'spect dat's de truth of it. But I wouldn't fret about it if I was you. It don't mattuh for nothin'.'

Milo leaned forward, a look of sudden panic on his face. 'Who are you?' he asked. 'Wheah's Hector? Have they done gone and taken Hector away from me?!'

'I'm Sullah, Massa Milo, you know me. Hector's jes' gone downstairs to fetch yo' lunch, and he's gon' bring it up to you d'rectly. Now you jes' try to calm down and keep real quiet, heah? All dat fussin' ain't good for you.' She spoke soothingly, as if to a complaining child, then went out, closing the door gently behind her.

Milo stared at the door for a moment, then shifted his gaze back to the rose on the floor. 'God damn 'em,' he muttered. 'They're tryin' to take Hector away from me.'

When Milo first came to live at Chinaberry a difficult crisis arose involving Hector, which permanently set the tone of the hostility between the old man and his son-in-law.

Hector had been Milo's manservant for nearly forty years, during which time he had suffered a plentiful measure of abuse; a million curses, kicks, and blows, and on occasion, beatings. But during the earlier times, in the better days at Maywood, he had enjoyed one peculiar privilege that few slaves could boast of – he had been allowed access to his master's liquor chest.

Milo held to the quaint theory that the character of 'a good nigguh' is improved by a certain amount of alcohol. 'No good for *bad* nigguhs, mind you,' he would say. 'Makes 'em murderous. But for a good nigguh like Hector it's fine. Brings out the best in 'im.'

Consequently Hector had served his master through most of those years in a state of carefully controlled drunkenness.

The few years spent in Arkansas were trying ones for Hector, for no alcohol was permitted in the house of Milo's host there, a distant cousin who was a Methodist minister, and who preached tirelessly on the evils of drink. When Milo came to Chinaberry and brought his old servant with him, the first thing Hector noticed was Massa Douglas's handsome teak-wood liquor cabinet, standing in a corner of the great main hall of the house. For days Hector looked long and hard at this cabinet. Then one night, in the stillness of pre-dawn hours, he made an attempt to break into it. Reeves caught him at work.

Hector was locked up in a woodshed for the rest o night and all the next day, while the master of Chinab sent for a local slave trader.

'You will be provided with another servant from among my Nigras,' Reeves announced to Milo.

'Hector's my property!' Milo thundered. 'You have no right to dispose of my property!'

'I'll not have a thief in my house,' said Reeves. 'Nor will I tolerate a Nigra who's addicted to drink.'

'Whip 'im if you want to.' Milo said desperately. 'He ain't had a good lickin' in a month o' Sundays, anyway. Do 'im good.'

Reeves looked pained. 'Mistuh Gates,' he said patiently, 'you know very well I don't believe in whipping.'

The old man almost spat in contempt. 'That's the trouble with you. You're soft, you got no spine. You ain't man enough to be a slave owner. What keeps this place goin' with you as master is beyond human understandin'!'

This statement, coming from one whose own plantation had failed miserably, and who now depended on the generosity of the master of this one, struck Reeves as ludicrous. He laughed.

Milo rose from his wheelchair, trembling with rage, his invalid condition momentarily forgotten. 'You sell my nigguh,' he screamed, 'and I'll kill you with my bare hands!' Then he collapsed and fell to the floor, mumbling incoherently.

Moses was summoned; he picked the old man up and laid him gently in his bed.

Margaret intervened, pleading with her husband on her father's behalf, and Reeves relented. Hector was returned to Milo, chastened and repentant, and caused no further trouble. But Milo's distaste for Reeves was from that day congealed into implacable hatred.

The afternoon wore on, and preparations for the evening's festivities reached a peak and tapered off, as all became readiness.

Before going upstairs to dress, Margaret conducted a solemn inspection of the main hall, and the settings on the long banquet table that was always set up especially for such occasions. She was accompanied by Moses, who followed her with respectful attention as she walked slowly through the room, pausing here and there to take note of some small item. At the conclusion of her tour she turned to Moses, and he leaned forward to receive her verdict.

'Everything's very nice, Moses,' she said, smiling faintly. 'As I expected, of course. We can always depend on you.'

He bowed slightly to acknowledge the compliment. 'Thank you, ma'am,' he said, with immense dignity.

Both knew that this little exchange – and the entire inspection ceremony – was the most empty and meaningless of formalities. This party, like every event at Chinaberry, was the creation of Reeves Douglas, and no detail, however insignificant, could have been added or subtracted without his express approval.

She dismissed Moses with another flickering smile, and moved out of the big room through the arched passage that led to the front entry hall, and across this to the broad stairway at its rear. She paused at the bottom of the stairs with a thought, and retraced her steps to the doorway of the main hall.

'Moses, have you seen Julia?'

'She was helpin' me with the table settin's a while ago,' Moses answered. 'But, Lordy, they was gittin' so rambunctious, I tol' 'em, "If that's what you rascals call help, I can do without it." I ran 'em on out o' heah.' He shook his head, chuckling good-naturedly.

'Them?' Margaret asked blankly.

Moses looked at her quickly, surprised at the question. 'Why, yes'm. You know, her and Darby.'

She tossed her head with an involuntary flash of irritation. 'Where did she go?'

'I don't know, ma'am. I 'spect they went out to the kitchen to pester Josie. Y'want me to go find 'em for you?'

'I'm not interested in *them*, I'm interested in *her*.' The tone of her voice was sharp now, with a hard edge of anger. 'You go and find her and tell her I want her upstairs immediately.' She turned away abruptly, and Moses tried to hasten after her with words intended to soothe.

'Yes'm, I sho' will. I'll find her and send her right on up, now don't you fret. . . .'

She was gone, halfway up the stairs, and Moses shook his head and frowned with annoyance at himself for his careless chatter.

At the top of the stairs Margaret encountered her husband,

dressed and on his way down, though it was still two hours before guests were due to arrive. It was the master's custom to receive one or two of his closest cronies in the afternoon prior to a social evening, and to enjoy a convivial hour of relaxed male companionship, during which a prodigious quantity of whiskey would be consumed. Thus, when the main event began, it would be presided over by a host who was already basking in a rosy glow of gentlemanly inebriation.

Reeves greeted his wife cheerfully, and kissed her on the cheek. 'Hello, dear. Everything all set downstairs?' He knew full well everything was, having checked it out thoroughly himself before going up to dress.

'I suppose so,' Margaret answered dully.

'Where's Julia?'

This brought a livelier response. 'That's the very thing I've been trying without success to find out.'

She was cross. That bored Reeves, and he started to move past her down the stairs.

'Reeves,' she said hastily, 'we've got to have a talk about Julia.'

'Of course, dear. Later.'

She took hold of his arm and restrained him. 'Reeves, we've got to settle something, one way or the other, about this ridiculous situation. It just can't go on.'

'What situation, sweetheart?'

'About Julia and that boy Darby.'

'All right, Margaret, we will, we certainly will.' He disengaged himself gently from her grasp. 'But not now. It's time you started getting dressed.'

'It's time your daughter started getting dressed, too, but where is she? Out fooling around like white trash somewhere, with that boy!'

Reeves looked at his wife with a tight-lipped expression, and she read its meaning instantly: *You're raising your voice. Be still.*

'I'll find her,' he said quietly. 'Get dressed.'

He turned and went down the stairs.

CHAPTER FOUR

In the evening the lanterns blazed outside, creating in their flickering smoky-yellow glare a carnival atmosphere around the grounds. Handsome carriages arrived in flurries of creaking wheels and the stamping of horses' hooves from down the east road, while a Chinaberry carriage with a liveried driver made continuous round trips from the river landing, conveying groups of chattering guests to the front steps of the great house.

Moses presided on the veranda steps, resplendent in his formal butler's tails, and met the arriving vehicles. He opened the doors, helped the ladies down – no meaningless gesture, but an act of essential service, for the females in their voluminous skirts were virtually helpless on any surface not smooth and flat – and ushered the guests into the entry hall. There they were greeted by their host and hostess and conducted through the wide arched passageway into the brightly lit main room, where more greetings, between new and earlier arrivals, erupted in a lively new hubbub of hearty handshakes between men, and wholesale embracing among the women.

On several instances young people among the arriving guests greeted the host and hostess with well trained manners, looked around, and inquired, 'Where's Julia?'

Margaret's smile was glassy bright as she answered quickly, each time. 'She's getting dressed, she'll be down in a minute. Poor darling, she was so excited all day long about the party preparations, she simply lost all track of time!'

A pat speech, well rehearsed.

Everyone inquired solicitously about Mr. Gates – after all, the party was in his honour, was it not? Margaret was ready with another carefully prepared speech.

'Dear Papa was terribly eager to join us, but' – here a nervous little laugh – 'I'm afraid it was a tiny bit foolish of us to plan a big celebration for his birthday this year. It's just that he wanted it so, and we couldn't bear to refuse him. But he *is* seventy-eight, you know, and – well, he's a trifle indisposed.'

Exclamations of regret and concern.

'Oh, it's nothing serious, really, I'm sure he'll be all right. But he must remain quiet. He thanks you all for coming.'

Expressions of best wishes for his quick recovery.

'Thank you very much. I'm awfully sorry, he did so much want to come down and join in the fun. . . .'

Mercifully the conversation drifted on to other things.

As the assemblage grew to its maximum size the noise level rose higher and higher, while the slaves assigned to serve at the party moved quietly about, intent on their duties – silent black phantoms in the midst of the loquacious white throng.

Drinks were served, and the guests milled about and formed little islands of conversation, some wandering out into the formal garden, where the last glow of dusk lingered and blended with the amber lantern light to form a pleasant pastel softness. More drinks were served, and the long table was given final touches before the serving of dinner.

Then Julia came down the stairs, crossed the foyer, and entered the big room.

She tried to slip in quietly, without notice, but one of the young people who had inquired about her earlier saw her immediately, and called out, 'Theah she is! Hey theah, Julia!' A hush fell on the room, and all eyes turned in the girl's direction.

The greeting had come from a tall angular adolescent boy who had been keeping a sharp eye on the entranceway, waiting for Julia to appear. He moved toward her, grinning broadly.

'I'm sho' glad you decided to put in an appearance, Julia. I was beginnin' to wonder if you were tryin' to avoid me, or somethin'.' His croaking voice seemed unnecessarily loud in the momentary quiet of the room.

Julia looked at him, unsmiling. 'Thank you very much, Philip,' she said coldly, and went past him into the room, leaving him to turn and stare after her.

Inwardly she had known her attempt to enter the gathering unnoticed could not succeed. The knack for being inconspicuous was something Julia Douglas did not have, under any circumstances. A slender blonde girl of fourteen, somewhat fragile in build, barely pretty – and that a dubious freckled prettiness that hinted only feebly at the possibility of someday developing into beauty – she nevertheless seemed to possess a strange ability to arrest attention. It was a quality that was mystifying even to those who knew her well.

Part of it was the combination of features she inherited in perfect balance from her parents – the pale grey eyes of her mother, containing more than a hint of that faraway, dreamy look that made people pause and wonder; the finely chiselled features and – when she felt like it – the bright easy smile of her handsome father.

There were other things: there was the quizzical, bemused expression, as if she looked out upon a nonsensical world from a secret base of solid self-assurance; there was the cool controlled poise and gracefulness, so uncharacteristic of her age group; and there was, suspended just beneath the surface, a mercurial, devil-may-care mood that was always ready to burst forth at unpredictable times, and transform her instantly from a refined and proper young lady into a wild, free spirit, unfettered by the bindings of convention.

Julia made the rounds of the assembled company, greeted all the guests with faultless aplomb, made excuses for her late appearance with an easy charm that erased all disapproval – or almost all. In her tour she was careful to avoid her mother's dark and smouldering gaze, which followed her accusingly.

The party progressed. Dinner was served and dawdled over for an hour and a half, after which, with his guests herded into the garden temporarily, the master gave a slight nod of his head to Moses, who quickly relayed the signal to a group of waiting servants. They swarmed into the hall and descended upon the long banquet table, clearing, dismantling, and removing it with an efficient dispatch born of repeated experience. The room was further cleared of furniture, except for chairs set around the perimeter of the floor. That done, Moses stepped out and returned shortly with three black men in formal dress, carrying musical instruments – a battered fiddle, a banjo, and a set of ingenious homemade drums. Following directions from Moses, the musicians set up their paraphernalia in a far corner of the great room and waited, their eyes on the butler, who watched his master for the next signal.

The guests were ushered in again; the master-director nodded to Moses; the butler nodded to the members of the little orchestra; the music began. It was jangling, scratchy, out-of-tune, and primitive, and unrestrained by the refined and tempered discipline that marked the sophisticated art of the white man, but rich in the vibrant, pulsating, foot-tapping vitality of country people, and strung taut with the sinews and savage rhythms of Africa.

The guests responded to the music with delight, the younger people seeking out partners for dancing, the older ones taking chairs to form an appreciative audience.

The master beamed. He was pleased with his current production so far. He stood with male companions near the entrance from the garden, conveniently near the liquor cabinet, and engaged in genial conversation. Outwardly he was completely relaxed, but in reality he was poised and alert, his eye moving constantly over the guests, the servants, the musicians, the assemblage in general, ready for the slightest sign of difficulty that might require his attention. From time to time he quietly excused himself to attend to such things. When conversation appeared to be lagging in a group of elderly people in one corner of the room, he immediately moved among them, and with his deft charm quickly revived their spirits. An attractive young lady guest found herself temporarily without a dancing partner; her host was instantly at her side, gallantly requesting the pleasure. An empty glass that needed refilling – even though its owner was already thoroughly besotted – produced a sharp snap of the master's fingers, bringing a servant on the run to take care of the matter.

Between these duties Douglas returned periodically to his knot of friends, slipping back into the stream of fuzzy alcoholic conversation without a trace of discontinuity – but with one eye constantly roving.

'Wheah'd you get the musicians, Reeves?' asked a short stout man at Douglas's elbow.

'Hired 'em over from Pine Grove. They're Jesse Collins's boys.'

The stout man frowned, searching his memory. 'Oh, yes – thought I'd seen 'em someplace befo'.'

Another in the group, a solemn-faced man, snickered with an asthmatic wheeze, and said, 'That's Jesse, all right. Nevuh enough field hands at Pine Grove, but always plenty o' nigguhs fo' entertainment.'

'I envy the man's good fortune,' Douglas said. 'I've searched high and low among my own Nigras for musical talent, but all I can find is damned witch-doctor chants.'

The others laughed, in knowing sympathy.

Douglas went on. 'The only one I've got who has the gift is my man Moses. He plays the banjo like a true artist, and sing – he can make you cry.'

'Well then how come he ain't up theah in the band?' the stout man asked.

'He's my butler,' said Douglas. 'Hell, he's my strong right arm around heah, I can't spare him for such as that.'

'He's a fine 'un, all right,' said the stout man.

The men turned their eyes briefly to appraise Moses, who at that moment was busy preparing a nonalcoholic punch bowl for the benefit of the teetotalling ladies.

'I tell you one thing,' the solemn-faced man said. 'If he b'longed to Jesse Collins he'd be up theah in the band, butler or no butler.'

'Speakin o' fine 'uns, Reeves,' the stout man said, 'you still got that gal Josie?'

Douglas smiled. 'Why, shuah.'

'How is she?'

'Mighty fine.' Douglas gazed placidly off across the room. 'Mighty, mighty . . . fine.' He dragged out the words significantly, and a ripple of leering laughter swept the little group, but was discreetly stifled.

'It's a fact, though,' the solemn-faced man said. 'Jesse Collins can't bring in a decent crop at Pine Grove, but he can put on the best damn nigguh vaudeville show you evuh saw.'

'You're just jealous, Herb,' said Douglas, with a laugh.

Another man spoke: 'Hey, look who's criticizin' somebody else fo' havin' entertainment nigguhs around. You fellas ought to *see* the big buxom yelluh wench Herb brought back from Natchez last month. Herb, I heah tell yo' missus is complainin' the big ol' gal can't do nothin' – nothin' a-tall.'

Herb's solemn face wrinkled with a wicked leer. 'The hell she can't,' he said.

The male laughter exploded in a lusty guffaw, causing ladies to glance quickly in that direction with looks of feigned shock, knowing a laugh like that could arise only from something lewd.

A female guest sidled up to Reeves and touched his sleeve. ' 'Scuse me, Reeves.' Her voice was soft as silk. She beamed a flirtatious smile up at her host, and swept her eyes around to include all the men in the group. 'I hope you-all will forgive my interruptin', knowin' you gentlemen are talkin' about things not meant for delicate ears.'

This brought indulgent chuckles and polite nods from the men, granting her permission to interrupt.

'I just wanted to say, Reeves, I think it's a simply adorable party – but then yo' parties always are.'

She was one of the more conspicuous women at the gathering, one of those who dressed as provocatively as possible, with the object of drawing the attention of men – and in the process incurring the disapproval of other women.

Reeves bowed to her. 'If so, my dear, it is only because of the adorable ladies who grace my house with their presence. Particularly, if I may say so – yourself.' The gallantry of his reply was so extravagant that his male companions recognized it as mockery, and inwardly smirked.

The lady took it as the essence of romantic sincerity, and her eyes fluttered with pleasure. 'Oh, go on, Reeves!' she gushed prettily. 'I must say, though, I have one teensy weensy little criticism of this otherwise delightful party.' She fingered her host's lapel, and pouted. 'You haven't danced with me all evenin'. Not once.'

'Oh, merciful heavens!' Reeves rolled his eyes in horror. 'How could I be so crass?! By all means, dear lady, allow me to correct this dreadful situation upon the instant.' He offered her his arm. 'Will you excuse us, gentlemen?'

They moved away to dance, and the other men watched them go.

'How does he do it?' the stout man said, musingly. 'Reeves could have his way with jest about half the women in this county, without even tryin'.'

'If that's so,' said one of the others, 'how come he's content with one o' his nigguh wenches?'

The stout man shot the questioner a quick look. 'You evuh seen his gal Josie?'

The other man shook his head.

'Thought not,' said the stout man. 'If you had, you wouldn't ask that.' He took a long pull on his drink.

While dancing – and giving his flirtatious partner his complete attention – Reeves collided with someone else on the crowded floor, turned to offer apology, and found that it was his daughter Julia. She was dancing with her tall angular young admirer.

'Oh, excuse me, darling,' Reeves said. 'Having a good time?'

'Yes, Papa,' Julie answered dutifully.

Douglas beamed a hearty smile at the young man, his daughter's escort. 'How are you, Philip?'

'Jes' fine, Mistuh Douglas, I'm – jes' fine, suh.' The boy's words tumbled out in clumsy, embarrassed haste.

'Good!' Reeves and his lady whirled away.

Young Philip Ramsey gazed down at his dancing partner with a look that reflected much admiration, and more perplexity. His eyes remained fixed on her, as hers wandered without apparent interest around the room.

At length he said, 'You didn't sound like you meant that, Julia.'

Her roaming eyes fell on her partner in passing, almost as if by accident. 'Meant what, Philip?'

'About havin' a good time.'

She smiled absently, and offered no reply, her attention straying again immediately.

After another pause Philip said, 'I just can't make you out, Julia. Why don't you enjoy parties? You're always the prettiest girl theah, no matter what. You could have fifty beaus all standin' in line, if you wanted to.' He gave her a smile that he imagined to be irresistibly debonair. 'Of course, *I* wouldn't want you to.'

Julia brought her attention back to him with an effort. 'Wouldn't want me to do what, Philip?'

Philip allowed himself a touch of irritation. 'Honestly, Julia, don't you *listen* when I talk to you?'

Julia allowed herself a trace of ingratiation. 'I'm sorry – it's so noisy in here.'

'It's perfectly cleah, Julia,' he said reproachfully, 'you not only don't like parties, you don't like my company.'

'Dancing makes me tired,' she said.

'Why in the world should it?! You dance marvellously.'

'I do not, and I don't care a fig for dancing.' Her jaw tilted upward in stubborn defiance. 'I'd much rather climb a tree.'

Philip shook his head in despair, realizing the hopelessness of trying to fathom this bewitching, maddening little creature. She looked so frail, so pure and innocent – so simple. How could she contain so much mystery, be so damnably incomprehensible to him?

It must be a sign that I'm becoming a man, he thought suddenly; men are always complaining that women are basically incapable of being understood. And now I see that's true. Yes, obviously that was it. A reassuring explanation.

He looked at the girl in his arms and saw that her attention was gone again. He tried hard to think of something really devastating to say, something that would rivet her pale grey eyes on him for good.

'Honestly, Julia,' he said. 'You're a caution.'

Margaret Douglas, sitting among a group of chattering lady guests, was having almost as much difficulty as her daughter in keeping her attention fixed on immediate companions, but her greater experience in such things gave her an expertise in masking her wandering thoughts. As the ceaseless conversation ebbed and flowed around her, Margaret smiled and nodded instinctively at the right moments, murmured, 'Thank you,' or, 'Oh, really?' or exclaimed, 'Indeed!' – unerringly choosing the correct response, as often judging by the tone of the speaker's voice as by the content of the remark. Occasionally she would honour a comment with conscious attention and specific reply.

All the while she watched the movement of the dancers on the floor, seeing them as a massive undulating blob of humanity, taking no notice of individuals, except when her eyes came to rest from time to time on her husband or her daughter. Then her gaze would linger for a moment in quiet contemplation before moving on.

'My, my, everything's just so elegant, Margaret. You've done it again!' The lady on Margaret's left gushed into her hostess's ear.

The smile and murmured response were automatic. 'Thank you, dear.'

'Yes, I was jus' tellin' Mistuh Parker this mornin', I said, "Mistuh Parker, I jus' can't *wait* till tonight." I said, "You know, evenin's at Chinaberry are always so memorable!" ' The gushing went on.

'That's so kind of you,' Margaret said.

'Tell us yo'uh secret, Margaret,' said an exquisitely groomed lady on the hostess' right. 'How *do* you do it?'

Margaret knit her brows in a rare moment of concentration. She smiled – a devious, enigmatic smile. 'To tell you the truth, my dears, I couldn't possibly manage it without Reeves. He is *so* much help. I'm *shuah* you can't imagine.'

'Oh, really?' said the gushing lady, her eyes round with delight. 'How romantic! I'm shuah *you* can't imagine how fortunate you are!'

The lady who had asked the question looked away without saying more. She had been some years before one of those marriageable young ladies widely regarded as prime candidates to become mistress of Chinaberry, and had been, like many others, astounded and appalled by Reeves Douglas's choice of a wife.

Moses suddenly stood before them with crystal goblets of afterdinner punch on a silver tray, inquiring also if any of the ladies would like another piece of cake. There were protestations of mock horror, and laughing accusations that Margaret was conspiring with her superb butler and her fabulous cook, what's-her-name – Josie – to bring to ruin all the female figures for miles around. But most of the ladies were willing to risk ruin, and accepted, and Moses went off to fetch the cake.

'I declauh, Margaret,' declared the gushing lady, 'the temptations at Chinaberry are *just* irresistible! Every time I come heah I gain five pounds!'

Another lady, sitting somewhat behind Margaret, leaned forward to speak. 'That Josie of yo'uhs is certainly a jewel, Margaret. If you and Reeves evuh consider sellin' her –'

Margaret twisted quickly to face the speaker. 'My dear, don't *think* of it.' Her instant reaction cut off the thought almost before it was uttered. 'Reeves would sooner sell *me* than sell Josie.'

The women around Margaret glanced at her with strained smiles, exchanged furtive looks with each other, sipped their punch, and suddenly became absorbed in watching the dancers.

There came a moment that Moses had waited for; a brief lull in the insatiable needs of the guests, during which by merciful coincidence no one seemed to require service. His skilful eye recognized the opportunity immediately, and he took instant advantage of it. Standing in an inconspicuous spot at the rear of the big room, he allowed the aching muscles that held his back in ramrod stiffness to relax imperceptibly, and at the same time he rocked cautiously back on his heels until he was leaning against the wall behind him, taking some of the weight off his feet. It was not complete rest, but for a precious few moments it was relief. He heaved an inward sigh.

Then he felt a gentle nudge in his side, and looked around and down at Julia.

'H'lo, Moses,' she whispered, and smiled.

It was not the cool impersonal smile of the socially adept young lady performing her duties among the guests, but a soft, sympathetic smile, laden with the secret meanings of affection. Moses returned it in kind.

'Hello, Little Missy,' he said gently. 'You havin' a good time?'

Julia grimaced. 'How can you have the heart to ask?' she said plaintively. 'Haven't you seen me struggling in the clutches of that horrid bore Philip Ramsey? Thought I'd *never* get away from him!'

'How did you manage it?' Moses' voice spoke sympathy while his eyes twinkled amusement.

'Told him I was tired. Told him my feet hurt. Told him it was too noisy in here, too stuffy in here, the music was too fast, the floor was too crowded. *Finally* he got the idea!'

Moses looked over the crowd and spotted young Philip outside in the garden, in animated conversation with another young lady, a demure brunette, who was hanging raptly on his every word.

'I see he done found himself a mo' congenial partner,' Moses said slyly.

Julia looked in that direction. 'Oh dear, he's trapped poor Dorothy Ward now.' She looked closer. 'But she seems to like it. I hope they'll be very happy.'

'You bettuh be nice to young Mistuh Philip,' Moses said. 'I b'lieve yo' papa and mama got theah eye on him fo' to be yo' husband.'

The toss of Julia's head expressed lofty disdain. 'If that's their plan, then you and I know they're in for a disappointment, don't we?'

'Jes' remembuh, he gon' inherit Graystone someday –'

'Moses –' She spoke quietly, in her most even, self-assured voice. 'I have no intention of ever marrying *anybody* for the purpose of bringing together two choice pieces of real estate.'

Moses chuckled. He had mentioned the subject for no

other reason than the delight of hearing the girl's defiant reaction.

He shifted his weight to a straight standing position again, and winced almost imperceptibly.

Julia noticed his discomfort. 'Backache coming on?' she asked. 'You're tired, aren't you, Moses?'

'Why, shucks no, Missy,' he said cheerfully. 'Slaves don't nevuh git tired, you know that.'

Julia regarded him gravely. 'Of course they don't,' she said. 'And they don't ever get sick, or hungry, or hot or cold, or discouraged or miserable. They're just happy and carefree all their lives. Aren't they?'

'Sho'. Till they ready to die. Then they sneak off in the woods to do that, so's not to inconvenience the white folks.'

Julia laughed softly, and touched his sleeve in an involuntary motion of tenderness, common feelings, and understanding. These two, the high-born white child and the middle-aged black bondsman – at the opposite ends of the random chances of human destiny – found it within themselves not only to ignore the awful differences that society stamped upon their stations, but to brush aside as well the conventionally accepted hypocrisy of devoted slave and indulgent master, and to reach across the chasm and clasp hands in a secret pact of equality, and a bond of friendship.

Still, she could astonish him.

'Why don't you sneak out back for a few minutes and rest?' she said in innocent earnestness. 'I'll stand here and take care of things for you.'

Moses looked at her closely and saw that she meant it. In the profound wisdom of his oppressed race he could usually look into and through most white people without difficulty, but this frail blonde child continually took his breath away with amazement. His eyes crinkled with a smile of impish delight.

'Now, tha's a fine idea, Little Missy, sho' is! Massa's daughter gon' take ovuh the servin' duties – tha's a Jim Dandy idea! The folks will look around and say, "Wheah's the butler?" And Massa's daughter, she say, "Oh, he done took a notion to go rest a spell, so I'm fillin' in fo' 'im." '

His lively sense of the absurd always entertained Julia and made her laugh, and she laughed now.

She said, 'I'll just tell 'em, "Moses retired to his room with a headache. He sends his apologies. He said it makes him sick to wait on such stupid people." '

Julia's shoulders shook with a fit of giggles, and Moses fought to stifle a cackle of laughter.

Several guests nearby turned their eyes on this incredible sight: The host's daughter and the black butler – what on earth was going on there?

Moses caught himself, sensing his own carelessness, and quickly pulled himself up to his usual dignified posture.

'Behave yo'self, Little Missy,' he said under his breath.

Julia walked past him and went toward a sideboard nearby on which, surrounded by a disarray of strewn crumbs and globs of icing, the remains of several cakes stood like ancient ruins, sad remnants of past glory. As Moses watched her Julia surveyed this scene of destruction.

'Hours of hot work for Josie,' she murmured, 'and nothing to show for it but this.'

She selected the most substantial section of cake left, and cut a generous piece from it.

Moses came toward her, frowning in disapproval. 'Tha's the second piece o' cake fo' you tonight, Little Missy. You makin' a pig o' yo'self.'

'Sh-h, Moses,' Julia placed the cake on a plate and covered it with a napkin, and gave the butler a look that told him he was being admitted to a minor conspiracy. 'It's for Darby,' she whispered.

Moses averted his eyes to the ceiling, an image of cherubic innocence. 'I didn't see a thing,' he said, and chuckled softly as Julia darted away. Hastily he arranged his face into its expressionless butler-mask, and turned his attention back to duty.

Julia went down the length of the big room toward the arched entranceway, carefully shielding the piece of cake as she threaded her way through the crowd. She had noted that her mother, the only person who might pose a serious obstacle for her, was in the garden, safely out of the way in the opposite direction, so she proceeded with confidence. Near the archway she encountered an elderly lady guest who observed her with curiosity, and inquired where she was going.

'I'm taking a piece of cake upstairs to my grandfather,' Julia said.

The lady beamed. 'How sweet!'

Julia produced an appropriately angelic smile, and moved on. She went out through the arch, crossed the entry hall, and quickly ascended the stairs to the upper floor.

At the top of the stairs she paused. After the bright light and deafening din of chatter in the big room below, she needed a moment to accustom herself to the near darkness of the upper hallway, lit by a single small oil lamp, and to the relative quiet, mercifully soothing to her ears. Then she walked slowly a short distance along the passage, and stopped before the closed and forbidding door of her grandfather's room.

It would be nice if I *could* take a piece of cake to Grandpapa, she thought. Grandfathers should be people you could go and visit, have quiet talks with, and reveal to them confidential thoughts and feelings and small private anxieties, and receive in return a kindly, sympathetic ear, and the balm of sage and seasoned advice.

How vastly unlike this image was Grandpapa Gates – she smiled ruefully to think of it. When she was a very small child, she could remember, he had sometimes taken her on his lap, and talked to her and played with her, his piercing eyes and gruff countenance softened by the charm of her baby prattle. But the mood was brief each time; after a few minutes he would impatiently put her aside. Even these occasional moments of interest seemed to disappear as she grew out of babyhood, until now, in these late years, as senility clouded his mind more and more, he rarely took notice of her at all – and when he did, invariably called her Margaret.

Old Milo was the only grandparent Julia had ever known. It's curious, she thought, how much more sad I feel in not having a warm relationship with Grandpapa Gates than in the lack of it with his daughter, my mother. For an instant she considered knocking softly on his door and peeking in, just to say hello. But no; it was past ten o'clock – he was always asleep by nine.

Then she was struck by a sudden new thought: It's all my fault – I can't expect a feeble old man to come and seek my company. I must go to him, make the effort – enough effort for both of us – and we can be friends. He's lonely and bitter and unhappy, and it's wretched of me not to have tried to make his last years a little brighter – just wretched.

She resolved to do it – starting tomorrow, first thing. I'll surprise him in the morning by taking him his breakfast, she told herself. I'll try very hard. I'll ask him about Maywood – he loves to talk about the old days at Maywood. And I won't argue with him about the blacks. He thinks blacks are animals, but it doesn't matter any more what he thinks – it's too late to matter. I must be kind, that's the important thing. I won't even correct him when he calls me Margaret.

She felt much better. She turned her eyes away from the door of her grandfather's room and her thoughts away from the solitary old man within, and walked with light quick noiseless steps down the hallway in the direction of the front of the house, until she stood before a beautifully carved oaken door. This door was a prized possession of her father's, and guarded the entrance to his personal sanctum, his study, a spacious room that occupied nearly the entire frontal breadth of the house on the upper level.

After a quick glance around the silent and empty upstairs hallway to be sure she was not observed, Julia cautiously opened the heavy door, slipped into the dark room, and quietly closed the door behind her.

CHAPTER FIVE

The cavernous kitchen house at Chinaberry might have suggested to an observer a medieval dungeon, or the boiler room of a steamship. In the centre of the large, dimly lit, square, high-ceilinged room stood its dominant furnishing, and the reason for its being – the huge black iron stove. This object's marvellous resemblance to something fantastically zoological must have been apparent to its manufacturers, for its squat bulging body was supported by appropriately stout squat legs, the lower ends of which were shaped, with accurate whimsy, like giant clawed feet.

Presiding over the kitchen, and controlling the iron monster at its centre, was Josie. She stood before the stove with calm authority, expertly judging from the sound of the inferno within how soon it would need more fuel, constantly gauging the condition of numerous large steaming pots on its surface, and frequently issuing terse orders to her several kitchen assistants.

Josie's pre-eminent status in this domain stemmed from her position as head cook, but in the absence of this official sanction her dominance would have been no less real. She was a striking figure, standing almost six feet tall, correspondingly large of body but with perfect proportions, her smooth skin a shiny milk-chocolate brown, her face round and full, with prominent high cheekbones and liquid black eyes that caught the attention – a close look would reveal that they were slightly slanted. In the full vigour of maturity, about thirty years old – the exact age of a slave was rarely known – she was to all appearances as her master described her – fine.

The high cheekbones and almond-slant eyes added an odd, faintly exotic element to Josie's appearance, and gave rise to an imaginative assortment of legends among the slave community regarding her origins.

One theory held that she was the daughter of James Douglas, her owner's father, the mother being identified as a beautiful girl of mixed Negro and Chinese blood from the prostitute cribs of the New Orleans waterfront. Another story described the mother as a more ordinary mulatto slave woman, and the father as the captain of an oriental pirate ship – again the place being that legendary city of flesh peddling and sinfulness, New Orleans.

There were other tales, with variants, but in truth the authentic particulars of Josie's parentage, like that of many slaves of mixed blood, were beyond the knowledge of any person living. What was known – the only verifiable fact – was that she was purchased by the elder Douglas from a travelling slavetrader about twenty years before, the trader's listing of goods for sale at that time describing her with commendable accuracy as: *Female, age approx. 10 years. Thin & tall. Good bone structure, will grow strong. Colour indicates minimum $\frac{1}{4}$ white. Unruly, needs training. Good intelligence.* The price was three hundred dollars.

It was widely rumoured that over the past few years Reeves Douglas had received a number of attractive offers from neighbouring planters for Josie, the most recent being from one of Douglas's close drinking companions. The amount offered, it was said, was twenty-five hundred dollars. It was turned down without consideration.

The dinner phase of the party was finished, and already a fast fading memory to the pampered guests who had consumed it and moved on to dancing and other diversions. But for the kitchen workers the dinner was not a meal, it was a task, and the task was only half completed when the food was consumed. The hours-long cleanup process was now under way.

Josie's assistants had made repeated trips between the kitchen and main house, collecting stacks of dirty dishes and depositing them on a large table in the kitchen alongside pots and pans, until a great disorderly mountain was formed, awaiting the cleansing and purifying action of hot soapy water.

Josie left the kitchen and started for the big house to offer up one last beautiful cake for sacrifice to those few gluttonous appetites that still remained unsated. As she walked across the small rear yard she breathed deeply of the fresh night air, grateful for this brief respite from the steam of the kitchen. She could hear the babble of party guests inside the big house, their accumulated voices reduced to a gentle drone at that distance, and through the background of sound the vigorous rhythms of the little orchestra twanged and throbbed distinctly.

Josie went up the back veranda steps, and, finding the door to the house closed, stood for a moment in indecision, both hands occupied with the cake platter. Then she became aware of another sound close by, and glanced back over her shoulder. Here in the remote isolation of the rear verandah, another musician was at work with the orchestra.

The teen-aged black boy perched precariously on the banister railing, his feet locked into the turned vertical supports beneath. His knees were spread wide apart, and on the section of railing thus exposed before him his hands worked in a blur of flying activity, slapping an intricate percussive pattern in perfect time to the music from within the house. The boy's eyes were fixed on the planking of the veranda floor, his face a study in total concentration.

Josie crossed the veranda and stood before the young drummer, watching him. His eyes caught her feet; he looked up at her, but his hands did not miss a beat in their rhythmic work. Then he noticed the cake. The drumming ceased – the musicians inside the house were left to carry on alone as best they could – and the boy came off the banister with a finger snaking eagerly toward the luscious creation of culinary art.

'Hey, Josie, gimme a lick o' that frostin'.'

'I'll give you a lick all right, you good-fo'-nothin'.' She twisted slightly to keep the cake out of his reach. 'I done ask you three times to fetch some mo' stovewood to the kitchen, and I ain't seen it yet.'

'I'm goin',' the boy said. 'I'm gon' git it right now. Jes' gimme a little taste o' that frostin'.' His eyes and his poised finger followed the cake tenaciously.

Josie pulled it back farther. 'Keep yo' dirty hands away, Darby,' she said sternly. 'It's fo' the company. Don't you touch it.'

Darby frowned at her, and grumbled. 'White folks in theah stuffin' themselves, while us po' nigguhs starve.'

'You don't look starved to me,' Josie said, suppressing a smile. 'You look like a fat sassy pig.' She crossed the veranda again, to the house. 'Come open the do' fo' me.'

He came around her with an agile leap, and bowed low before her, grinning broadly. 'Sho' I will, ma'am. Be glad to, 'cause I know you gon' save me a nice piece o' that cake, ain't ya?'

'My Lord, boy, why don't you jes' go on in theah and tell all them white folks not to touch this cake, 'cause *you* want it?'

Darby's grin widened. 'You tell 'em,' he said.

'Sho' I will, be glad to.' She mimicked his gallantry of a moment before. 'Jes' open the do' fo' me.'

He pulled himself up to full height – which still left his eye-level several inches below hers – and announced, 'Josie, when I grow up I'm gon' paint myself white and git me a plantation and a bunch o' slaves, and I'm gon' buy *you* from Massa Douglas, and you gon' cook fo' me ev'y single day, and not fo' nobody else.'

He opened the door and bowed again, and she gave way and smiled, unable to maintain her stern countenance. She went in, saying, 'Now go on and fetch me that stovewood, you crazy fool boy.'

'I'm goin', right now,' he said, and as she passed he reached out and deftly slid his finger along the base of the cake, neatly collecting a little mound of frosting. He went back to the banister, climbed back up on his perch, and daintily licked at the delicacy on his finger, while his free hand picked up the drumming rhythm of the music again.

Behind him a wispy figure quietly materialized among the shrubbery bordering the veranda, and a voice whispered, 'Darby.'

He twisted quickly and looked down, startled. 'Julia! Wheah'd you come from?!'

She came out of the bushes and up the veranda steps and stood before him, holding the piece of cake she had smuggled out of the house.

'I brought you a piece of cake, Darby,' she said.

Darby took the plate without speaking, and Julia pulled herself up on the banister and perched beside him, struggling to control her long skirt in that unladylike position.

Darby inspected the cake with a critical eye. 'It ain't chocolate,' he said glumly.

'All the chocolate was gone,' Julia said.

'You know I like chocolate best, Julia.'

She sighed. 'You're terribly spoiled, you know.'

Darby pinched off a bit of cake and ate it. 'White folks gobble up all the chocolate,' he mumbled. 'Po' nigguhs have to take what's lef'.'

Julia giggled, watching him.

He tried another bite. 'I like it, though. It's mos' good as chocolate.'

'What do you say?' the girl prompted.

'Thank you, Julia,' he answered obediently, and quickly demolished the piece of cake, and licked the plate to shining spotlessness. When he was done he balanced the plate on the banister beside him and looked at Julia curiously, 'I said, wheah'd you come from? What you doin' out theah in them bushes?'

'Went upstairs and came down through a certain special way I know to the cellar, and out through the side door,' she said, and, seeing Darby's befuddled look, added in a lower voice, 'There's a little secret stairway that leads down to the cellar pantry from Papa's study. Don't you *dare* mention it – nobody knows about it but Papa and me, and *he* doesn't know *I* know.'

Darby stared at her. 'Now what in the name o' devilment does yo' papa need with a stairway down to that ol' cellar?!' he demanded.

'You said the word,' Julia said slyly.

'What word?'

'Devilment.' She giggled again, and her eyes shone. One of her mischievous moods was upon her.

Darby shook his head and dismissed the puzzle from his attention. When Julia was of a mind to tease him, he knew, there was no way he could fight his way through the mental tangle she would spin for him.

'Anyway,' he said, 'what you come through the bushes fo'? You mos' scared the daylights out o' me.'

'I came through the bushes,' she smiled wickedly, 'to scare the daylights out of you.'

'Thought you was a ha'nt,' he said.

'There is no such thing as a ha'nt,' said Julia severely.

'Ghost, then.'

'No ghosts, or ha'nts, or anything of the sort, by any name.'

'They is, too, I've seen 'em. Millions o' ha'nts up theah on Injun Hill.'

Julia looked pained. 'Darby, don't say "they is." Say "there are." There are no ha'nts on Indian Hill, or anywhere else, so just stop talking nonsense.'

Darby fixed her with a baleful frown. 'Know wheah the wust ha'nts of all is?'

'Are,' she said patiently.

'Down theah in that squatter's cabin in the woods.'

Julia slipped down off the banister and started to walk away from him. 'Guess I'll go back to the party,' she said over her shoulder. 'The moronic chatter in there is better than the idiotic drivel out here.'

'Wait, Julia.' Darby jumped down from his perch and started after her. At that instant the music inside came to a pause, and, after a moment, began again, this time in an unusually vigorous and lively tempo.

Darby's eyes gleamed with a wild enthusiasm. He took both of Julia's hands and said, 'Dance with me, Julia.'

She withdrew her hands, and said stiffly, 'You mustn't act familiar with me around the house, Darby.' She went back to the banister and resumed her seat. 'I'll be the audience,' she said. 'You dance.'

Darby danced. Timidly at first, but gradually with more and more confidence, until his concentration was as intense as it had been in drumming, and he was twirling and stamping in reckless abandon. And Julia was caught up in the spirit of it, and clapped in time to the music, urging him on.

'Dance, Darby, dance!' she laughed in delight.

Neither the dancer nor his audience of one noticed several young party guests – among them Philip Ramsey and Dorothy Ward – who at that moment came strolling around the corner of the house. The strollers stopped, frozen at the sight of Julia and the slave boy. They stared for a few breathless seconds – then, at the gestured urging of young Ramsey, turned and hastily retreated.

Presently Josie emerged from the house, carrying several empty cake platters. She stopped and gazed in astonishment at Darby's dancing performance.

'Darby!' She spoke so sharply that the dancing, and Julia's clapping, ceased abruptly. Ignoring the girl, Josie riveted Darby with a stern frown. 'Did you or did you not fetch me that stovewood?'

Darby gave her a sheepish look. 'Jes' goin'. Jes' on my way.' He ambled toward the veranda steps. As he skipped down the steps and across the yard he muttered, 'White folks play and dance all night. Po' nigguhs work and sweat.' He was dancing again as he disappeared around the corner of the kitchen house.

The woman and the girl gazed at each other in silence. After a moment Julia said casually, 'You're not supposed to order Darby to do kitchen chores, Josie.'

'Didn't order him.' Josie's voice was mild, but firm. 'I jes' ask him to do me a favour, and he said he would. I don't have enough kitchen help durin' party times – it's jes' too much work.'

Julia picked up the plate Darby had left on the banister, and went toward Josie. 'Let me help you with those platters,' she said.

'I can manage,' said Josie, and took the plate from Julia and started down the veranda steps.

'Well, I thought you needed help,' Julia said, following her.

Josie stopped at the bottom of the steps and turned reproachful eyes on the girl. 'It ain't right, Julia,' she said quietly, and Julia looked at her with a questioning frown.

'You ought to be ashamed o' yo'self, leavin' yo' guests neglected while you fool aroun' out heah with Darby. That's no way fo' a young lady to act.'

Julia sighed wearily. 'All right, Josie, don't lecture me, please. I'm going right in this minute, and spend the rest of the evening being a nice, proper young lady.'

'That ain't the wust of it, Julia.'

'What do you mean?'

Josie set the dishes down on a lower step, and stood before Julia and looked hard at her. 'Do you realize what you're doin' to that boy?'

Julia stiffened. She had heard too much on this general subject from her mother lately – but here was an unexpected twist, a new point of view.

'What *I'm* doing to *him?!* What am I doing?'

'You're ruinin' him, Julia. You're a mother hen, keepin' him under yo' wing like a baby chick, so he don't know nothin' at all 'bout what life is like. And one o' these days it's gon' come to an end, and when it does it's gon' hurt him. Hurt him bad.'

'I don't understand you, Josie.' Julia frowned impatiently. 'Darby belongs to me, nothing bad can happen to him. And I've been working on his education – I work on it all the time. Before I'm through with him he'll know as much about the world as any white boy.'

In a conspiratorial tone she added, 'Don't tell anybody I'm educating a slave.'

Josie shook her head as if to brush all this aside. 'Tha's all right, honey, you can teach him about the world all you want, but you ain't teachin' him nothin' 'bout himself.'

Julia shrugged. 'Well, I don't see –'

'Julia –' Josie took the girl's shoulders in her strong hands. 'Darby still thinks bein' a slave is fun.'

With an angry toss of her head Julia pulled herself away from Josie's grasp. 'I see you and Mama are in perfect agreement about Darby and me,' she said icily. 'Except for opposite reasons, of course. Mama thinks it's bad for *me* to be with Darby – you think it's bad for *him*.' She forced a laugh, and withdrew a few steps. 'Maybe you and Mama ought to get together and talk it over. You have *so* much in common!'

'Maybe we ought to, sho' 'nuff.' Josie's voice remained level, as Julia's took on the shrillness of anger.

'Well, why don't you go and talk to her, then? Tell her all about how you think I'm a bad influence on a slave boy!'

'Maybe I will,' Josie said, and bent toward the dishes on the step.

Julia came behind her. 'Good! And maybe *I'll* tell Mama something everybody knows but her. I'll tell her that Papa goes out to your room at night.'

Josie straightened, and looked at Julia for a long moment. A deep sorrowful shadow clouded her eyes.

'I'm a slave, Julia,' she said softly. 'And yo' papa's my mastuh. He's kind to me in his own way, and tha's all that God has given me to know o' kindness in this world.'

Julia bit her lip and looked away, blinking with the sharp sting of shame. 'I'm sorry, Josie,' she whispered. 'I didn't mean it.'

'And don't you worry 'bout yo' mama not knowin' what othuh folks know,' Josie went on. 'She knows.'

Julia stared. 'She does?! Are you sure? How can she endure it?!'

'Why, she endures her burden 'cause she has to, honey, jes' like everybody else endures theahs.'

Josie lifted her eyes toward the lofty bulk of the house, from within which the continuous sound of human sociability radiated like the droning from a beehive. 'Yo' mama's a fine lady, and mistress o' this big house,' she said placidly. 'But you know sump'm, Julia? She jes' as much a slave as me.'

There was a gentle silence between them – then Josie smiled softly, her innately sunny nature coming to the surface. Her exotic eyes shone as she hugged the girl before her, fussed with her dress, and smoothed her hair.

' 'Nuff o' this foolishness! Go on with you, now, and tend to yo' guests. And try to act like a lady for a little while.'

Julia sighed, and smiled. 'I'll try.' She turned and went up the veranda steps. At the top she stopped and looked back.

'Forgive me, Josie,' she said.

Josie laughed. 'Pshaw! I already did.' She took up the dishes and went toward the kitchen house.

CHAPTER SIX

Young Philip Ramsey stood sipping punch with the partner of his second choice, demure Dorothy Ward, and reflected upon the ironies of life. He was aware of his assigned role as a pawn in a large scheme – one that, though it was not of his own devising, he would nonetheless be happy to see brought to fruition. But, he thought wryly, if tonight's experiences could be taken as indicative of a trend, it was clear that the plan was headed for dismal failure – all because of the inexplicably perverse behaviour of a fourteen-year-old girl.

Philip knew that his father and mother were strongly in favour of Julia Douglas as a future daughter-in-law, for reasons having nothing to do with romantic sentiment. The Ramsey plantation, Graystone, situated immediately south of Chinaberry, closely rivalled the Douglas establishment in prosperity, and exceeded it somewhat in ostentatious display. With an instinct derived from generations of estate building – the Ramseys proudly traced their lineage back to English aristocracy – Philip's parents dreamed of the eventual merging of these two great plantations into one gigantic holding that would be unexcelled in magnificence throughout the South.

Their plan required but a single simple event – the marriage of their son Philip to Julia Douglas. It seemed to them a natural match; the accomplishment of the union should be a trifle. With the intuitive vision of a young man in love Philip knew it would be anything but.

The elder Ramseys were not present at the party that evening. They were on an extended visit to New Orleans, buying art works for the adornment of Graystone. But their dream, and their relentless will to accomplish it, was present in young Philip's consciousness as strongly as if they were standing at his elbow.

How infuriating, Philip thought, that even though his parents' ambitions for him coincided by happy chance with his own romantic aspirations, it all seemed doomed by Julia's damnable behaviour.

Now on the other hand, consider Dorothy here. Dorothy

is reasonably pretty, he thought, very sweet, and well equipped with the refinements of cultured society. Besides which, he reminded himself, the Wards are owners of a quite respectable plantation across the river in Arkansas that is only slightly less impressive than Chinaberry or Graystone. Dorothy was, in fact, it seemed to him at the moment, ideally suited to be his lifemate.

Why then, oh why, can't I find her company as exciting as Julia's? Why, he asked himself furiously, must I be so fatally attracted to a wanton creature who flouts the basic tenets of good manners – not because she doesn't know better, but deliberately – ignores and insults her guests, disappears from her parents' party, and dances – for God's sake, *dances* – on the back veranda with a slave boy!

Philip swore under his breath, and demure Dorothy turned startled eyes upon him.

'Sorry,' he mumbled. 'Jus' thinkin' about Julia out theah, dancin' like that. It makes me angry.'

'She wasn't actually *dancin'*,' said Dorothy. 'She was jus' sittin,' and –'

'The distinction is trivial,' Philip snapped. 'Don't try to make excuses for her.'

'Oh, I wasn't!' Dorothy said hastily. 'In fact, I think we ought to tell on her. I know it's horrid to tattle on people, but, after all, it's so – so *strange*. I think it's our duty to inform her parents.'

Philip gazed down into the eyes of demure Dorothy – soft doe eyes, brimming with earnest and sincere concern – and momentarily forgot his anger. She's really very nice, the thought occurred to him again. Why couldn't I be in love with Dorothy, and forget about Julia? The Ward plantation may not be quite as fine as Chinaberry, but what of that, in the face of love? Of course, I must not forget, Dorothy has several siblings and may not inherit outright, whereas Julia, as an only child –

Enough of that, he told himself crossly. Such thoughts are unworthy of a young man in love. He sighed, recognizing the hopeless truth: I adore Julia madly, in spite of everything, and I always will. I should adore her even if she were the daughter of a piney woods pauper. But – perhaps not quite so madly.

'Don't you think we ought to tell her parents, Philip?' Dorothy persisted.

‘It is necessary,’ said Philip with authority, ‘that we deal with Julia directly.’

Julia came down the stairs for the second time that evening, and started across the foyer toward the main hall, looking almost as demure as Dorothy. And for the second time Philip spotted her immediately.

In a hurried whisper he gave Dorothy instructions, then took her by the elbow. ‘Now,’ he said. ‘Let’s get her.’

They hastened down the length of the room toward the archway entrance. With satisfaction Philip noted that Mrs. Douglas was also in the vicinity of the arch, idly chatting with guests.

As Julia entered the room Philip and Dorothy were waiting for her. They gasped in feigned astonishment at Julia’s reappearance.

‘Julia!’ Philip exclaimed. ‘We’ve been lookin’ all ovuh for you! Wheah in the world have you been?!’ Again his voice was much louder than necessary, but this time with a calculated purpose.

Julia hesitated an instant. ‘I had to attend to something.’

‘To what, Julia?’ asked Dorothy, smiling sweetly. ‘To yo’ pretty little slave boy?’

It was a sudden jolt, paralyzing all conversation in that part of the room. Several other young people gathered around Philip and Dorothy.

‘By the way, Julia,’ Philip said, ‘how *is* young, uh – what’s his name?’

Julia gazed at him impassively, without speaking. The space around them was charged with tension.

‘That boy of youhs, Julia,’ Philip persisted. ‘What’s his name?’

‘Digby, or Danby – somethin’ like that,’ Dorothy said to Philip.

‘Darby,’ Julia said quietly.

‘Darby, yes!’ said Philip. ‘How is our young friend Darby?’

Julia remained silent. More young people had gathered around.

‘Why don’t you invite him to the party, Julia?’ Dorothy said pleasantly.

The other young people laughed.

‘Yes, by all means,’ Philip said enthusiastically. ‘Let’s invite him in, Julia. Talent like his should not be wasted on the back veranda.’

The young people laughed again, louder, and grinned at Julia like hounds around a cornered fox.

'Excuse me,' Julia said coldly, and walked through the pack of grinning hounds and away from them, toward the opposite end of the room.

Philip and Dorothy watched her retreat, and the others around them snickered and drifted away, seeing that the little show was over.

Dorothy shook her head sadly. 'All I can say is, I pity the poor unfortunate boy who marries her.' The remark was carefully innocent, but exquisitely pointed.

Philip continued to look after Julia, frowning thoughtfully. 'How is it possible she came down from upstairs?' he muttered. 'She was out back.'

'She's a witch,' said Dorothy. 'She flew into an upstairs window.'

Philip shot an admiring glance at his companion. Yes, he thought, dear Dorothy has resources of which I was not aware. Delightful, really. It is just possible I may learn to adore her madly.

He took Dorothy's hand and they strolled toward the dancing area. Casually he glanced around and saw that Mrs. Douglas was still standing where he had last seen her. As he passed near her their eyes met for an instant. She was pale and shaken; he knew that she had heard all. Behind his facial mask of guileless innocence he smiled to himself with a secret inner pleasure.

So the evening wore on, and little by imperceptible little the party was drained of its verve and energy, and the high pitched babble of an earlier hour gradually diminished into a listless murmur.

And at a certain moment Reeves Douglas conveyed one of his discreet signals to Moses, who transmitted brief instructions to the weary and wilted musicians, who looked at each other in a clear unspoken expression of blessed relief. They played one last number, a placid waltz, then took up their instruments and departed. It was the official notification that the social festivities of the long evening were at an end.

The host took up his station on the front veranda to officiate at the leave-taking ceremonies, which were usually far more elaborate and prolonged than the greetings. Between the intermittent performances of this duty he stood with one of his regular male companions, the two taking advantage of the outdoor air to enjoy large cigars as they talked. The conversation was less animated now than in earlier hours; the atmosphere of jovial ribaldry was gone, replaced by a more sober mood.

Douglas's companion, the stout man, was delivering to his host some observations that he evidently considered to be of serious import. Douglas did not seem to share the speaker's sense of urgency. He puffed his cigar, relaxed and imperturbable as always, and smiled blandly.

'Oh, come now, Fred, you're telling tall tales again,' he said.

'No I ain't, Reeves,' the stout man protested. 'It's true, I sweah.'

Another man joined them at that moment. 'What's true?' the newcomer asked.

'Fred heah's spreading wild rumours about abolitionists,' Douglas told him.

'It's a fact, I tell you,' Fred declared emphatically. 'The damned abolitionists are definitely operatin' in this area now. They caught one ovuh in Hanesville jes' last week. Didn't you heah 'bout that?'

'I hope they hang the bastard,' the new arrival said.

Douglas snorted. 'Hell, every wandering tramp is being taken for an abolitionist these days. It's ridiculous. Nothing but hysteria.'

'Well, all I can say is, you bettuh keep a sharp eye out,' Fred said ominously. 'They're abroad in the land, and they mean to make us bleed. Fust thing you know they'll be stealin' yo' nigguhs right out from under yo' nose.'

Douglas permitted himself a disdainful smirk. 'Have you gentlemen heard about the runaway rate heah at China-berry?'

'Yeah,' Fred grunted. 'We've heard about it.'

Reeves supplied the information, nevertheless. 'One every twenty months, on the average. Not one in almost two yeahs now.'

'Yeah, Reeves, we know.' Fred sounded a trifle weary.

'By far the best record in this county – I'll warrant one of the best in Mississippi,' Reeves went on. 'And why? Because, gentlemen, I treat my people humanely. And they know it. In theah own primitive way, they're sensible – they will not be deceived by lies and false promises. I tell you, it is not easy to run a plantation without the use of brutality, but it *is* possible, and I've found it well worth the effort.'

He smiled his bland smile, and flicked the ashes from his cigar. 'Although I grant you, my overseer, Mistuh Willard, would not agree.'

The other men listened to their host, silent and stony-faced.

'I assure you, gentlemen,' Reeves concluded with lofty smugness, 'my people are well content. The abolitionist will find his efforts unavailing heah at Chinaberry. Unavailing.'

He excused himself, and moved away to say goodbye to a group of departing guests.

Margaret stood just inside, in the foyer, dispensing her farewell amenities from that location. At length Philip Ramsey stood before her, cordially thanking her for a lovely evening. Though Julia was again not present, Philip did not ask about her. Margaret shook the young man's hand, and held it for a moment as she gazed at him with pleading eyes.

'I'm so sorry about Julia's strange behaviour tonight, Philip. Please try to hold charitable thoughts for her. She's not been feeling quite herself lately, for some reason – but I'm shuah she'll be all right again soon.'

'I'm shuah,' said Philip, and smiled reassuringly. 'Please give her my love.'

On the veranda Reeves shook hands heartily with Philip, inquired as to the news of his parents' sojourn in New Orleans, and asked him playfully how he liked being master at Graystone during their absence.

'Fine, suh,' Philip answered readily. 'But I must say, Mistuh Gilbert's been a great help.' Philip's smile was strained; he had in fact been left in charge of nothing at Graystone, the entire management of the place being in the hands of its trusted overseer, Mr. Gilbert.

Presently the alarmist, Fred, gathered his family for departure, and shook hands with his host, and Douglas called jokingly to him as he boarded his waiting carriage, 'Now take care, Fred, watch out for those abolitionists!'

The traffic of carriages that had flowed inward to the house some hours before now came alive again, moving outward, and the midnight air was stirred with the sounds of shouted farewells, the creak and crunch of wheels in the dirt, and the thudding of horses' hooves, as they carried their charges away.

Gradually the activity diminished, and finally, after the last carriage had disappeared into the darkness and the distance, an unfamiliar quiet settled upon the scene. Soon the blackness of night was allowed to close in again, as yard servants made the rounds up and down the road and around the house and grounds, extinguishing the lanterns.

Reeves and Margaret Douglas stood for a few minutes outside their home, listening to the soft natural sounds of the southern night – the numberless unseen crickets ceaselessly broadcasting their busy, mesmerizing little song, and farther away, down toward the river, a stronger and more ponderous pulse, the *basso profundo* of bullfrogs.

Reeves turned his face to the dark sky and sniffed the air. 'Smells like rain,' he said. 'I hope Willard won't have to lose a day's work from the hands tomorrow. They're behind as it is.'

'It's getting chilly,' Margaret said. 'I'm going in.'

She went up the steps and across the veranda, stopped at the front door and glanced back. 'Coming, Reeves?'

'In a minute.'

Margaret went inside and climbed the wide stairs, and moved along the second-floor hallway toward the large rear bedroom she shared with her husband. Her movements were slow and languid, burdened by the weight of physical and mental fatigue. As she passed the closed door of Julia's room she paused, her face grim with the thought of going in to confront her errant daughter. Weariness prevailed; she sighed and went on. Tomorrow, she promised herself. Tomorrow that intolerable situation would be settled, once and for all.

Out in the kitchen house Josie's crew came at last to the end of the long day's work, a day that had lasted from dawn until past midnight. In the big main hall Moses directed several of his assistants in a perfunctory straightening up operation, then put out the lights. The complete cleanup of that scene of mountainous disarray was almost another entire day's work, and would begin in the morning.

The great house was dark, except for one lamp burning upstairs, in the bedroom of the master and his lady.

Margaret undressed and went to bed quickly, but lay with eyes wide open. Reeves came in a few minutes after her, removed his jacket, tie, and shoes, and put on slippers. He fussed with removing his cuff links, then stood before the dresser mirror and became absorbed in a meticulous brushing of his thick wavy hair, handsomely streaked with grey around the temples.

At length he turned and smiled pleasantly at Margaret, and said, 'It went very well tonight, don't you think?'

'It was a disaster. You know it quite well.' Margaret's voice was dull and lifeless.

'Oh?' Reeves registered mild surprise. 'I don't think I understand.'

Margaret sat up in bed. 'It's Julia, Reeves. We've simply *got* to do something about that child. She has humiliated us beyond endurance!'

Reeves frowned in puzzlement, trying to bring to mind his daughter's part in the evening's activities. 'I don't recall seeing Julia doing anything improper tonight.'

'Of course you don't. I'm shuah you didn't notice Julia once the entire evening. You were much too busy paying attention to your drinking companions – and to certain ladies.'

Reeves turned his back on his wife and resumed his grooming operations before the mirror. 'That's unkind, Margaret. I was merely performing my duties as a host. Nothing more.'

He turned back to her, his face brightening with a sudden thought. 'Actually I *did* see Julia – talked to her, as a matter of fact. She was dancing with the Ramsey boy, and as far as I could see, she was on her best behaviour.'

'Really?!' Margaret's face hardened with scorn. 'You were not aware that she didn't appear tonight until long after the guests had all arrived?'

'She's a disorderly child. She was late getting dressed.'

'Or that she came upstairs early, without saying goodbye to anyone?'

Reeves remained unperturbed. 'Well, she was overly tired. It *was* a long day.'

'And of course, my dear husband, you were not aware that your lovely daughter was absent from the party for half an hour during the height of the evening, and that she spent that time out on the back veranda?'

Reeves chuckled indulgently. 'With whom? Young Ramsey?'

Margaret delivered the final morsel of information with a dramatic flair.

'With Darby. With her precious slave boy.'

Reeves stared at her. After an awkward pause he asked, 'How do you know that?'

'Philip Ramsey and some of the other young people evidently saw them theah. I overheard them teasing Julia about it – many others overheard it too, you may be shuah.'

'I see,' Reeves said quietly. He moved to his wife's bedside, and sat down beside her.

'Well, don't let it worry you, Margaret. It occurred to me the other day – it's time we thought seriously about sending Julia up to Memphis to school. I know Frank and Amelia would be glad to have her. It's probably just what she needs.'

Margaret grimaced faintly. 'Your sister Amelia is no more of a disciplinarian than you are.'

'Frank will provide the discipline.'

'Hmph! Julia can wrap her Uncle Frank around her little finger. You know that.'

Reeves gave her his bland smile. 'Well, anyway – I promise to keep a sharp eye on her from now on. Don't fret about it.'

'Reeves . . .' Margaret grasped his hand and pleaded. 'You *must* take that boy away from Julia.'

'We'll see, we'll see.' He took her hand and patted it. 'We'll talk about it further tomorrow. Right now I'm in no mood to be vexed. This has been a splendid evening – I don't want to spoil it.'

Margaret shook her head in exasperation. 'And *there's* one of your main weaknesses, Reeves. You're never willing to come to grips with problems, always want to put them off, put them off – that's precisely why we *have* so many.'

'Oh, come now, Margaret! How many?! He beamed a patient, patronizing smile upon her. 'Do you realize, my love, that we were the envy of everybody at the party tonight, as usual? Literally everybody.'

Her look was cold, glaring. 'I am well aware that *you* are the envy of your male associates, Reeves. It has nothing whatever –'

'We, my angel, *we*. You and I.'

'It has nothing whatever to do with *me*.'

He chuckled benignly, continued to hold her hand, petting and stroking it as if it were a kitten. 'I must tell you something. Do you know what Herb Osgood said about you tonight?'

She stiffened. 'I pray to God, sir, I have not reached such a low station in life as to have come under the lewd appraisal of that, that –'

'That connoisseur of feminine pulchritude?'

She shuddered.

'Believe me, sweetheart, Herb's admiration is a great compliment for any woman.'

'Hmph! Of all your unsavoury cronies, Mr. Osgood is the most shamelessly licentious, the most –'

'But, Margaret, the point is – no man has a more expert eye for the qualities of women. And he said to me, quite voluntarily, he said, "You know, Reeves, your Margaret is the most strikingly lovely lady in the company tonight." '

She sniffed disdainfully – but waited for further details. He attempted to comply.

' "What is the word for her?" Herb said. "Style? Class? Elegance? Whatever, Margaret is a woman of incomparable charm," he said. "Puts all the other ladies to shame." '

Margaret gazed at her husband icily. 'Herbert Osgood is a crude, inarticulate ruffian. He does not talk like that.'

'Oh, I can't recall his *exact* words –' Reeves waved a hand impatiently. 'But that's the *sense* of it. Now be honest – doesn't that please you?'

Her reply came slowly, and was faint with wistfulness. 'It would please me far more, Reeves, if ever in my life I received a compliment like that – from *you*.'

He dropped his eyes, his lips compressed in a twinge of embarrassment. But it was fleeting; he looked up again and smiled.

'The point of my telling you this, my love,' he murmured, 'is that I regard Herb Osgood as the authority *par exellence* on the subject. I thought it hardly necessary to add that I concur in his judgment absolutely.'

'I see.'

He leaned forward and kissed her lightly on the cheek. She sat rigidly still. He pressed her cheeks gently between his fingers, kissed her on the lips. She accepted his kiss passively, without response, and when he released her and sat back, gazed at him stony-faced.

He sighed softly. 'And now to sleep for you, my angel. I can see you are dreadfully tired.' He patted her hand once more and got up.

Her hands fluttered toward him, she looked up at him pleadingly. 'And so must you be, Reeves. Aren't you coming to bed?'

'After a while. I want to read a bit – helps calm me down after one of these exhausting evenings.' He went across the room and took up the lamp.

'Reeves?'

He turned and looked at her curiously.

'Please, don't . . .' She bit her lip and sagged backward in the bed, and her face was contorted with a deep secret pain.

'Don't what, sweet?'

'Don't – stay up too late.'

He moved to the door, turned and smiled his bland smile, murmured, 'Good night, my deah,' went out and closed the door softly behind him.

'Good night,' Margaret whispered to an empty room. She remained sitting up and staring into the darkness for a long time after he had gone.

CHAPTER SEVEN

The house, which a little earlier had rung with laughter and music, now reposed in heavy silence. Reeves walked quietly along the upstairs hall, and as he moved the rays from his lamp threw huge misshapen shadows on the walls and ceiling. At the far end of the hallway he opened the great oaken door to his study, went in, and noiselessly pulled the door closed again.

He stood in the centre of the room for a while, allowing his eyes to probe the dim recesses in all directions. This was his private domain, his sanctuary, in which he took a special pride and pleasure. Here he found the quiet moments of peaceful contemplation that he imagined to be essential to his well-being. It was a spacious chamber, occupying not only most of the frontal breadth of the house, but extending in an L shape some distance back along the side. In a commanding position, at the apex of the L, stood its most significant piece of furniture – a massive mahogany desk.

Reeves set his lamp on the desk and moved to one of the high bookshelves that lined the walls of the room. Scanning the dim titles, squinting close in the feeble light, he selected a book. Then he sat down in an armchair near the desk, opened the volume at a random place, and began to read.

Reeves Douglas was not a man of learning, but he had a deep respectful love of the *idea* of learning, and was inordinately proud of his fine library, which contained nearly six hundred volumes, including, as he liked to say, all of the great classics of world literature. He had collected his library painstakingly and little by little, all his life, and was fond of scanning a page or two in a book and nodding in solemn appreciation of the wisdom contained therein, then putting it back on the shelf with a fresh resolve that, just as soon as he had the time, he was going to read that book, as well as all the others he owned. He believed without question that he would do this. The people who were close to him knew full well that he never would.

In a few minutes the reader raised his eyes from the page

and stared across the room. He sat quite still, listening intently to the sepulchral silence of the house. Quietly he closed the book and laid it on the desk. He rose, went around to the front of the desk, opened a lower drawer and took out a small, soft package of plain brown paper, tied with a bit of pink ribbon. Turning to a velvet smoking jacket hanging on the wall just behind him, he stuffed the little package into a pocket, took down the jacket and slipped it on. Then he took up his lamp again and walked the length of the room to a narrow door, inconspicuous in a far rear corner. He opened the door and revealed a closet, piled high with old trunks, travelling bags, and storage containers. At the rear of the closet, barely accessible, was another, even narrower door. Douglas inched his way past the piles of stored goods, opened the small rear door, and looked through into a tiny stairway that disappeared downward steeply into darkness. Carefully he turned his lamp wick down to its minimum setting, and stepped through the doorway.

In the gradual piecemeal growth of Chinaberry house during the early years, James Douglas had incorporated into its design a certain element of his own whimsical nature. This was a maze of secret chambers and passageways, some leading nowhere, all of vague, dubious or unidentifiable purpose. When the house passed to the ownership of James's more practical-minded son, these passages were either closed off permanently or opened to conventional use – all except one. That was the steep, narrow inner stairway that led from the big front room on the upper floor all the way down to a small chamber about five feet below ground level, toward the rear of the house. This cellar room was also connected by a stepped entryway to the pantry, on the ground floor, and was used as a cool dark storage place for preserved foods. It opened as well to the outside, through a tiny door that led to an excavated landing, from which stone steps led up to an arboured path bordering the garden, along the side of the house.

Reeves emerged from the house at the cellar landing, went up the stone steps, and walked along the path toward the rear yard. Moving as quickly and silently as a ghost, he crossed the yard and stepped up onto the rough-planked porch of the dark kitchen house, pushed the door open, and went inside.

The great black monster stove stood silent and slumbering, though still warm from its fiery work of the earlier hours. Douglas set the lamp on the stove and crossed the kitchen to a closed door at the far side. He knocked softly.

After a moment the door opened a cautious crack, then wider, and Douglas gazed into the dark liquid-soft almond eyes of Josie. She was wearing a housecoat of plain coarse material under which her large breasts and well-rounded hips lost some – not all – of their striking prominence. Her thick black hair was pulled back tight and bound at the back with a piece of brightly coloured cloth, and on her ear lobes a pair of blue stones gleamed in the dim light. She was tall, her wide-set slanted eyes almost on a level with the man's, and she stood in perfect dignity, and returned his gaze.

He inclined his head slightly, with impeccable formality. 'Good evening, Josie.'

She nodded gravely. 'Evenin', Mastuh.'

'I hope I'm not disturbing you. I know you've had a long day.'

'Not at all, suh. I am always happy to see Mastuh.'

'I was wondering if I might visit with you for a little while.'

She nodded again, and replied with solemn graciousness. 'It would give me pleasuah, suh. Mastuh is welcome to my little dwellin'.'

She opened the door wide, and stood with lowered eyes as he stepped inside. Then she closed the door swiftly, and slid a bolt in place.

Douglas stood in the centre of the tiny room and gazed around. It was gloomily dark, illuminated only by a single candle on a table by the bed, in one corner, and in the corner opposite, by a modest blaze in a narrow fireplace.

'Ah!' he smiled. 'You have a fire.'

'These spring nights are chilly, Mastuh. I like to be warm.'

He winked at her. 'I know you do. Cold is not for my Josie – she's a hot-blooded woman.'

She allowed her eyes to meet his, and the hint of a smile played on her full lips, shattering for an instant the veneer of dignity, and was gone again.

She touched him on the arm. 'Take yo' coat, suh?'

He gave her his jacket, and she hung it carefully on a peg by the door. Then she motioned him toward the only other large piece of furniture in the room besides the bed – an old tattered armchair, facing the fireplace, its thick textured upholstery showing the wear of decades.

'Sit down, Mastuh. Make yo'self comf'table.'

'Thank you, Josie.' He sank into the chair with a deep sigh, and put his feet up on a small footstool before it. 'Ah-h-h.'

She leaned over him in solicitous attention. 'Cup o' warm milk, Mastuh? To soothe the stomach?'

'If you recommend it.' He watched her through half closed eyes as she took a pan from the hearth and poured steaming milk into a mug, and brought it to him.

'Lovely. Thank you.'

Josie knelt at his feet, deftly loosened the ties of his shoes and slipped them off, and rubbed each stockinged foot between her hands vigorously. She glanced shyly at the man. 'Good fo' tired feet,' she said.

'Um-m. Indeed it is.' He sipped his milk, cradled the warm mug in his hands, and sighed again. 'You're so very kind, my deah.'

Josie pulled a small wooden chair close to the armchair, and sat prim and straight beside him.

Douglas gazed musing into the fire. 'So you see how life is, Josie. The king comes to the humble thatched-roof hut of the peasant, and finds there vastly more warmth, more comfort, more contentment, than in all the vaulted chambers of his castle.'

'Yes, Mastuh.' She regarded him with a look of blank serenity.

He turned his eyes on her, and bemusement crossed his face. 'You know – sometimes I wonder why it gives me such pleasure to talk to you, Josie. I often think you haven't the faintest notion what I'm saying.'

Her reserve fell away somewhat, and she gave him an open guileless smile. 'I'm ignorant, suh. But I love to heah Mastuh talk. 'Specially 'bout rich lofty things.'

He chuckled. 'Rich lofty things! You may be ignorant, my love, but you're wise, so wise – you understand far more than you admit. You are the most prized of all my possessions.' He reached out and patted her on the knee.

She lowered her eyes to her hands, folded in her lap.

He leaned forward suddenly, studied her more closely. 'Those earrings,' he said. 'Are they the ones I brought you from Memphis last yeah?'

'Yes, suh.' She touched a finger to one of the turquoise ornaments in fond feminine vanity. 'They's so pretty. I jes' love 'em.'

'An excellent choice I made, if I do say so. They set off your eyes delightfully.'

For a moment her face became animated. 'I jes' love 'em so much. I wish I could weah 'em all the time, 'stead o' jes' in my room.'

'You cannot.' He spoke with sudden sharpness. 'You nevuh can, you know that.'

'Yes, suh. I know.' She was subdued instantly.

He smiled, and laid his open hand softly against her cheek. 'Ah, Josie. Don't be sad, my wondrous one. It is for *me* to be sad, that I own such a precious jewel, yet I cannot weah it on my arm, for all to see.'

As he spoke he let his hand glide down along the contours of her neck and throat, and down beneath the housecoat to a great soft breast, covering it, squeezing it gently, rubbing the nipple with a feather-light touch of the thumb. 'My jewel,' he murmured. 'My wondrous one.'

Josie closed her eyes, pulled the upper folds of her housecoat somewhat apart to give him room, placed her hand over the hand that held her breast, and stroked it, pressed it against her flesh.

'We will go to bed soon, my love,' he said quietly.

'Yes, Mastuh.'

Abruptly he withdrew his hand and sat back in his chair, sipped from his cup of milk, and smiled at her.

'But first I have another present for you.'

Her eyes opened wide in suprise. 'A present, Mastuh?!' Hastily she pulled her housecoat closed again.

'In my jacket pocket.'

She flew to the jacket, fished in the pockets, drew out the little brown paper package, and turned her eyes questioningly to her benefactor.

He nodded.

She smiled with childlike excitement. She rubbed the package with her fingers, pressed it, poked it, weighed it carefully in her hand.

He watched her, amused. 'Well, open it.'

'I want to guess,' she said coquettishly – then, 'No! I *can't* guess!'

She tore the package open, and gasped, as the soft folds of

a sheer nightgown fell in a slender cascade from her hands. She held the garment up to the firelight, stared in wonder at the smooth weightless pale blue fabric, bordered with exquisite lacework, of transparency so delicate that her fingers were clearly visible behind it.

'Oh, Mastuh! What *is* it?'

'A nightgown, silly goose. Pure silk, I'll have you know. Imported.'

She frowned, uncomprehending.

'I mean it came all the way from Europe, across the sea. There's nothing so fine as that in America.'

She shook her head slowly and stared at the exotic treasure, and her expression reflected a mixture of joy and awe. 'It's so *nice*!'

'Go on,' he said, 'put it on. Only when you see how it caresses the skin, can you understand *how* nice.'

She smiled uncertainly, started to open her housecoat, stopped and gazed at Douglas with eyes gone abruptly grave again.

'Mastuh, don't look, please,' she said.

He threw back his head with a burst of laughter. 'Josie, my girl! I know your splendid body better than I know the back of my hand!'

Her expression remained unchanged. 'Mastuh, don't look.'

'Oh, all right!' He turned a little in his chair and fastened his eyes on the opposite corner of the room, and chuckled to himself.

Then she was standing before him, and the firelight behind her captured the magnificent brown body in a silhouette of dreamlike softness, radiant in the shimmering blue veil. Douglas's jaw dropped. He set his cup on the floor, reached out and laid his hand around her leg behind the knee, just below the hem of the garment, and stared in astonishment at the miracle of transformation.

Josie watched him as he roamed over her body inch by inch with his eyes – over the wide rounded hips, the extensive bushy black pubic region, the gracefully curved waist that led up to the fine prominent breasts – and when he reached her face she smiled down at him. She moved her shoulders and hips in a slow languid undulation, and made the silk slide lightly on her skin, and rolled her eyes with voluptuous pleasure toward the ceiling.

'Makes me feel wicked,' she said.

He held his gaze on her as if gripped in a hypnotic spell. 'Oh, Josie, my wondrous one. You are so –' There was no perfect word. 'So ravishing.'

He put both hands behind her knees and moved them caressingly upward, raising the silken gown. On his feet then he continued higher, sending one hand up and down the back and pulling her close to him, finding a breast again with the other hand, and her lips with his own. Her arms wound around him, and they stood locked together, rocking gently, for a long time, while his tongue probed deep within her mouth. She threw back her head finally, and gulped air convulsively, and his lips fed on her throat.

'Now, Mastuh?' she whispered, at last. 'Now?'

'Yes, Josie. Now.'

He slipped the gown off over her head and tossed it on the bed, and took one step back from her, and held his arms slightly away from his body. It was a cue. She unbuttoned his shirt, pulled it off and draped it over the armchair. She opened his trousers, loosened his underwear, and pushed his clothing down to the floor, kneeling as she did so, and he stepped out of them naked. Then from the kneeling position she raised her face to the level of his extended erection, caressed it with her fingers, her lips, and her mouth, as he stood rigidly still and looked down at her with his hand on her head.

His breathing became laboured as she worked. He perspired, he quivered, at last he clutched at her. 'All right, Josie. Enough.' He bent down and pulled her away from himself, and brought her to her feet. 'To bed now.'

'Yes, Mastuh.'

She lay on her bed, arms and legs sprawled, and he came over her and nestled on the broad soft cushion of her body. Under his gaze her dark eyes sparkled, and the turquoise earrings gleamed.

'How beautiful with jewels,' he murmured. His hand went to her breast again immediately and fondled it, while he kissed her repeatedly with caressing little movements of the lips, and looked into the remarkable almond eyes with a profound sadness.

'Ah, Josie, my jewel, my beauty. Do you know how it tortures me to keep you hidden away? The most marvellous woman in the world is mine, and I cannot breathe a word! Can you imagine what an anguish it is, that I can't boast about you, display you to my friends? Those fools! They think I use you the way they use *their* women – forcing you down and mounting you like an animal. They can never know that you are my beautiful, my wondrous, my adored. . . .'

Josie's head swayed gently from side to side as if to music. Her eyes were drugged. 'Oh, Mastuh – I love to heah that magical talk.'

He continued to press her lips with short tender kisses, and caress her body with his hands. Her long legs opened wider, and came around him. Her hand groped, and guided him into herself.

He moved at first very slowly and deliberately, and spoke with whispering softness in her ear. 'Josie, Josie – that God might grant me the power to make the world over to my liking! I would have you gowned and jewelled, and standing gloriously beside me for all the world to see.'

She moaned softly. The rhythm increased, and she moaned more deeply, and said, 'Oh, Mastuh, Mastuh, Mastuh. . . .' over and over again.

And afterward, long afterward, they lay quiet, his head on the great breasts that were shining wet with perspiration. She gazed at the low ceiling above them with wide tranquil eyes, and at her side she fingered an edge of the blue nightgown, and gently stroked the smooth silken cloth.

He sighed with deep weariness, and said, 'Let the king rest a bit. Then he will bid you farewell, and return to the cold hard castle.'

CHAPTER EIGHT

In the night some hidden power in the atmosphere stirred; the weather changed, grew restless. On the western boundary of the plantation gusty squalls ruffled the unseen surface of the wide river, and the treetops along its banks.

Old Milo Gates raised himself with grunting effort in his bed, supported himself on a fragile elbow, and gazed in cloudy confusion around his dark room, trying to puzzle out where he was. He called once, 'Alice!' – the name of his long dead wife. A feeble croak, heard by no mortal being. Then he lay back, panting, and staring in terror at some awful vision hanging in the air above his bed.

The first faint traces of dawn crept into the sky with a sombre ash-grey tint, signifying a cloud-hung day coming, and the likelihood of rain. The darkness was diluted by infinite fractions of degrees. It retreated reluctantly, clinging to the dense woods at the edge of the fields after the open ground was imbued with the soft half-light that was neither pure night nor yet day. Slowly the buildings and other major features of the plantation became dully visible, emerging like phantom ships in a shallow sea of mist that had rolled over the land from the river during the secret hours of the night.

A long double line of human figures moved out of the shadows between the two rows of shanties that comprised the slave quarters. The field hands were on their way, trudging down the narrow dirt road that led toward the fields of cultivation, and toward another long day of labour. And gradually, with inaudible beginnings, the sound of a soft rhythmic chant arose from the midst of the marchers, punctuating their silent padding steps. They moved along with senseless, unhurried, automatic motions, like zombies – men, women and children, most carrying hoes and rakes and other implements over their shoulders, all eyes fixed on the ground, each person following the heels of the person ahead, and all contributing to the soft mournful song that seemed to be their only source of momentum.

At an intersection of roads a hundred yards from the quarters a solitary white man on horseback sat motionless, watching the approach of the work gang. As the lead members of the lines drew near the intersection they increased the tempo of the chant and the walking pace by the slightest discernible degree, turning the corner and heading down the second road. The workers did not look at the white man as they passed by him, but their awareness of his presence was evident. A curious bow developed in the lines, moving the path of progression to the opposite edges of the roadway, cutting the corner of the turn, and leaving the maximum possible clearance between the marchers and the horseman.

Horace Willard, overseer of Chinaberry, sat stiffly erect in his saddle and inspected the procession as it moved past him. He was a man of middle age, large, heavy, and muscular of build, with a florid face from which small blue eyes glittered like points of steel as they roved expertly and without rest over the field hands, briefly examining each individual, missing none. In his right hand the overseer held a whip, wound in a neat, tight coil.

Turning the corner last, at the tail end of the lines of labourers, were the children, called quarter-hands, roughly between the ages of eight and twelve. Among them were two or three women who, in addition to their regular duties, had the responsibility of supervising the fledgling workers.

As soon as the lines had snaked past him and completed the turn, Willard stood in his saddle and yelled out, in the manner of a platoon sergeant, 'Halt!' The marchers stood in their tracks, and the chant-song died abruptly.

Willard spurred his horse into a trot and moved down to the head of the lines, reined to a stop there, and turned his attention to a tall black man in the lead. The overseer pulled a gold watch from his pocket and consulted it, frowning.

'Eighteen minutes from call to move out, Nate,' Willard said crisply. 'Three minutes too long.'

The tall man gazed up impassively. 'Yas suh,' he said without expression.

'The second time this month,' Willard continued. 'You want to draw extra duty on Saturday nights, Nate?'

'Naw suh.'

'Then you look to yo' duties durin' the week. Git them hands out on time, you heah?'

'Yas suh.'

'All right. Any absentees?'

'Yas suh. Five.'

Willard put away his watch, shifted in the saddle, and took a small notebook out of his pocket. 'Who are they?'

'Ol' Abner, he took'n down in he back ag'in,' said Nate. 'And Lucy, she gittin' de pains fo' to hab her baby –'

'That's a damn lie,' Willard growled, scribbling in his notebook. 'She ain't no more'n seven months along. Who else?'

The overseer listened impatiently to the rest of the sick list, and made notes accordingly. This was the first of his daily moments of frustration – the report of absentees among the field gang. He was required to make a list of names of those slaves claiming incapacitation, and to report it directly to Mr. Douglas, who would visit the quarters and, guided by some secret insight of his own, decide upon the validity of each claim, either issuing instructions for care and remedies to be administered, or ordering the malingerer back to work.

The worst thing, in Willard's view, was not that Douglas was far too lenient in his findings, allowing many outrageously false claims of illness to stand. It was that the judgment of these claims was outside the authority of the overseer. This arrangement set a crippling limitation upon him – a boundary beyond which his power did not extend, and behind which the cunning black folk could take refuge. And it galled.

After noting the absentees named by Nate, and the man's brief unscientific description of each one's ailment, Willard snapped his notebook shut.

'All right, five shirkers today. They'll be dealt with.' Secretly he was pleasantly surprised. The usual daily number of missing workers – shirkers all, he automatically assumed – was around eight or ten.

Willard pulled his horse around and rode slowly back up the line, making a closer inspection of the hands, all of whom stood quietly, their dark unfathomable eyes fixed on the overseer, awaiting his next command. Halfway up the line he stopped and looked hard at a young man.

'Ollie, wheah's yo' hoe?'

'Handle broke yestiddy, Mars Willard,' said the young man.

'You damn fool, why didn't you report it?'

Ollie gazed stolidly at the overseer. 'I fergit,' he said.

Willard was off his horse instantly, and swinging the thick butt end of his leather whip with a dexterity almost too swift to see. The blow was solid and well aimed, and Ollie went down without a sound, clutching his head with both hands, and twisting his body in the dirt to evade further attack. The people around him hastily stepped back out of the way, the blank expressionless masks of their faces not changing by as much as a flicker.

'You'll work today on yo' hands and knees,' Willard said with unruffled calm. 'And this evenin' you git that hoe ovuh to the blacksmith and git a new handle on it.'

Ollie got slowly to his feet, his eye on the alert for any further movement of the overseer's whip hand. 'Yas suh,' he said dully.

It was a routine incident; the overseer had administered discipline without anger, and the culprit had received it without visible resentment. Willard swung back into his saddle and moved on, displaying no further interest in the chastened slave.

At the tail end of the line he stopped before the group of children, and addressed a stooped and wrinkled old woman in their midst.

'Ellie, make them quarter-hands keep up, damn it! They're always fallin' behind.'

The old woman's rheumy eyes squinted vaguely toward the overseer, then fell away. She answered in a thin quavering voice. 'Yas suh, I try.'

Around her the bright round eyes of children stared up in silent awe at the great white god on horseback.

Willard stood in his saddle again, and issued another command. 'March!'

Nate at the far end started off, and the procession resumed, moving at the same deliberate trudging pace as before.

'Move it along now, damn it!' Willard snapped. It made no difference.

Presently the soft doleful chant-singing began again, and faded gradually, as the long lines of labourers moved on and away down the rutted dirt road toward the distant fields.

An hour later the day was full born. Grey clouds rolled

from horizon to horizon, and the blustery air was heavy with the threat of rain.

In fields some two miles southeast of the plantation house the hands were at work. Horace Willard, sitting in the lofty eminence of the saddle, walked his horse leisurely up and down the adjacent road and surveyed the workers with unrelenting vigilance, and glanced occasionally at the threatening sky. His coiled whip hung as a silent warning at his belt.

It was the rule at Chinaberry that, on the morning after a party, the house servants were allowed to remain abed an hour later than usual. So it was that the dank grey light of this day found the big house still wrapped in quiet.

One of the first to stir was old Milo's man, Hector. His master was usually awake and demanding service at first light, every day, and if Hector was not in attendance instantly, the old man would not hesitate to bellow for him in full angry voice, and disturb the entire household.

The wrath of his tyrannical owner stirred no fear in Hector's breast, as it had in earlier days. The punishment that Milo was now capable of delivering – the feeble cuffs, the abusive, ill-tempered curses and insults – were as harmless as the fluttering of butterfly wings. What filled the old servant with constant dread was the displeasure of Massa Douglas. The lord of the house tolerated Hector's presence in it for only one reason – to keep peace with his belligerent old father-in-law. But on more than one occasion the younger man's patience had been worn dangerously thin by Milo's obstreperous behaviour – and more than once Hector had felt a terrifying possibility that he would be sacrificed, purely as a gesture of spite. His existence was precarious – this Hector knew full well.

And so, as the chill light of this early April morning pervaded Milo's bedroom, Hector rose from his pallet in an adjoining alcove, stretched his creaking bones painfully – for he too was ageing now – padded quietly into his master's room and approached the high overstuffed bed.

He looked down at the ashen face, started to speak, paused, and wondered stupidly at the meaning of the wide open eyes staring without sight at the ceiling. He spoke softly, and was startled as he spoke at the strange tremor in his own voice.

'Massa Milo? Is you all right, suh?'

Then he gasped and stepped back, stared for a long breathless moment, then turned his eyes upward in supplication, and trembled with terror at the awesome reality of death. He trembled not for the unceremonious departure from the world of this man whom he had served faithfully for over forty years, and whom he hated with a deep secret passion.

He trembled for himself.

PART THREE

AFTER

CHAPTER ONE

Robert B. Travers, western man, part-time wanderer, part-time gambler, part-time wrangler, full-time adventurer, was in his middle thirties, tanned and weather-beaten from his outdoor life, lean and muscular-hard, and known to his friends, who were few, as Trav.

His friends were few because Robert B. Travers was gifted – or cursed – with an uncommonly acute sensitivity to sham and hypocrisy, and made a game of mentally categorizing the several generic and countless varietal forms of human posturing whenever he saw them, which was almost as often as he was in human company, and took no pains to hide his sardonic amusement therein. Consequently, though he also possessed an easy relaxed manner and an air of worldly poise that was attractive to men and women alike, he had so far in his rootless existence found that close personal friendship was a will-o'-the-wisp, forever eluding him. One person in his life formed an exception to this rule – the black man, Darby, his present companion.

They had been gangling youths when they had first met on the western trails years before. Trav at that age had been brash and cocky, with the sparkle of impudence in his eye. He was amazed at the gentle soft-spoken black boy, who possessed a quiet self-assurance that seemed inconsistent with his youthful innocence. Darby's colour set him apart; he needed a friend, that was certain. Trav was attracted to the idea. He elected himself, and had held the position ever since. And somewhere along the way, the carefree boyish association had ripened into a lasting, deeply committed friendship on both sides.

But friendship took its toll, Trav had discovered. Darby was surely the only person in the world who could have persuaded him to forsake the wide, burning bright horizons of the far West, his home country, and embark on this strange pilgrimage to the distant steaming lush valley of the lower Mississippi, in quest of the elusive phantoms of old memories.

Trav shook himself awake in his napping place on the western bank of the great river, perspiring and cursing because the earth had treacherously turned in the past hour, the cool shade in which he had drifted off to an early afternoon nap had shifted, and his face was exposed to the direct attack of the merciless southern sun. He sat up and gazed off across the wide water that to his western mind seemed to be the eastern edge of the world. It looked no friendlier than it had an hour ago – or a week or so ago, when he had stood on a low bluff in northeastern Arkansas and beheld it for the first time, and had been struck dumb by its serene immensity. He glanced toward his companion, a few yards away.

Darby was sitting cross-legged on the ground, steadying his right elbow on his knee, and squinting along the gleaming barrel of a revolver. His target was a noisy jay in a small tree just beyond the spot where Trav was sitting.

Trav remained stone still; the projected line of fire was two feet above his head.

With one eye shut, lips pursed in concentration, Darby took aim, and pulled the trigger. The weapon emitted a sharp metallic click as the hammer descended on an empty chamber. As if on cue, the jay squawked in ridicule, and took flight.

The gunman blew imaginary smoke from the muzzle of his revolver, and favoured Trav with a thin smile.

'Have no fear, *Señor*. The man-eating monster that was about to sink its cruel talons een your hide has fallen veectim to my deadly aim. Once again *El Bandido Moreno* has saved your life.'

Trav was unimpressed. He yawned mightily, and leaned back on his arms and closed his eyes.

Darby examined his gun, polished the barrel against his sleeve, and admired its gleam.

'Hey, Trav, maybe we ought to break out the ammunition and have a little target practice once in a while.'

'No ammunition,' Trav said firmly. 'The first thing you'd do is shoot yourself in the foot.'

'I ain't fired this cannon in so long I don't even know if it still works.'

'It works,' Trav said. 'All you have to do is wave it around and say, "Do not trifle weeth me, *Señor*. I am *El Bandido Moreno*." '

Darby chuckled.

'But don't pull that on any o' these Mississippi River Rebs,' Trav added quickly. 'They jus' might not take it too kindly.'

Darby stuck the pistol inside his shirt, sniffed the air, and said cheerfully, 'Le's git movin', friend. The wind's a-blowin', the river's flowin', and time's a-goin' to waste.' He scrambled up and started for the skiff, which was pulled up halfway out of the lapping water nearby.

'You writin' a song or sump'm?' said Trav.

Darby leaned down beside the boat and inspected a recently carved legend near the bow, and scraped at it with his finger-nail. The fresh inner wood exposed in the carved area stood out clearly against the dark weathered exterior of the old skiff. The inscription read: *El Bandido Moreno.*

Trav continued to recline in his place, still lethargic from sleep, and Darby glanced back at him and said, 'Come, *Señor.* Eet ees not healthy to keep *El Bandido Moreno* waiting.'

'All right.' Trav got up slowly. 'Stop admiring your handiwork, and let's go.'

They pulled their little craft into the water, and got aboard. Darby, manning the oar this time, swung the skiff around and nudged it out into the ideal path of progress, two or three hundred feet from shore, and headed downstream.

Darby's mood continued cheerful. 'Know sump'm, Trav? I got a feelin' we're almost there.'

Trav settled himself comfortably in the bow of the boat, using some of the baggage for a head rest, and regarded his friend with cool detachment.

'Know sump'm, Darby? I got a feelin' we're gonna paddle right down to the mouth o' the river, right on out into the Gulf of Mexico and halfway to South America, and you're still gonna be sayin', "We're almost there, Trav, we're almost there!" '

'You got the general idea, pal,' Darby grinned. ' 'Cept you got the destination wrong. I aim to paddle this here scow all the way to Africa. I jes' wasn't gonna tell you yet.'

'My dumb luck,' said Trav, 'to go boating with a damned crazy African.'

'The truth is,' Darby said, 'I'm on my way to claim my ancestral inheritance, a million-acre plantation on the banks o' the Congo River. The main crops there are sugar cane, rum, and nigger babies. I figure I'll import some white folks from America to be my slaves, though God knows they ain't worth their keep – lazy, ignorant, natural-born thieves, every damn one.'

Trav grinned at Darby, and trailed a hand pleasantly in the water, enjoying the bantering mood.

Suddenly he jerked his hand back and sat bolt upright. 'What the hell's *that?!*'

A small wrinkled reptilian head protruded a few inches from the water barely an arm's length away, and gazed at the human intruders with cold ancient eyes. A second head appeared, a third – then half a dozen or more, on both sides of the boat.

'My God!' cried Darby, his eyes wide with mock horror. 'It's the terror of the Mississippi! Vicious man-eatin' river serpents!'

Trav groped for something to use as a weapon, and picked up a spare oar.

'Goodbye, ol' friend,' Darby declaimed. 'We're done for!'

'I ain't goin' without a fight!' said Trav, and swung the heavy oar mightily, bringing it down flat on the surface of the water with a resounding smack, and sending a spray of water in all directions.

Darby tried to duck, was drenched in spite of it, and fell over backwards, howling with laughter. Trav searched the water's surface, holding his weapon poised to do battle. The man-eating river serpents had vanished.

Trav turned frowning at Darby, who was wiping water from his face, and still laughing.

'I just saved your life,' Trav said. 'And all you can do is laugh.'

Darby resumed working the skiff, and grinned at his companion. 'Trav, if you're gonna get all hysterical about a few li'l ol' harmless turtles, I guess I won't be able to take you with me to Africa, after all.'

'Those brutes were harmless?!' Trav croaked indignantly. 'Those brutes could snap your arm off!'

'Harmless as lambs,' Darby said placidly.

Trav put down the oar and returned to his position of rest. '*You* know they're harmless,' he snorted. 'Do *they* know it?'

At that moment they were startled by the hoarse bellowing blast of a steamboat whistle, rolling across the water. The wide squat vessel ploughed its churning furrow downstream a quarter of a mile behind them, its position marked by a billowing plume of black smoke. It was headed directly toward the little skiff, the only other piece of human traffic within sight on the broad expanse of river.

Trav sat up and stretched to look, then picked up the oar again, and glanced at Darby. 'Shall we let 'em pass? Or shall we fight 'em?'

'You're too tired to fight a steamboat,' Darby said. 'You're all tuckered out from fightin' them man-eatin' river serpents.' He manoeuvred the skiff sharply around and headed it shoreward, to give the steamer a wide respectful clearance.

Trav put the oar back in its place and returned to his own reclining position. He watched Darby, admiring the easy way his friend handled their little vessel.

'Um-m, I do love to watch you work,' he said teasingly, and stretched out in comfort.

These two friends had spent boisterous years together in and out of saloons and brothels and gambling halls, the noisy lusty towns and the wild lonely quiet places of the West, working as horse trainers and wranglers and wagon train drivers and at odd jobs, earning just enough to stay modestly solvent, and managing by some miraculous alchemy to stay alive, though they knew they could confidently expect to reach a peaceful old age.

Neither had ever fired a shot in anger. They always carried weapons; here in the South they kept them concealed, but in the West they wore them prominently displayed according to custom, well-oiled and apparently ready for instant use – it was compellingly necessary in that wild and turbulent land, where the average man felt naked without his gun – but the arms they carried were always empty of ammunition.

They had developed a belief that it was possible to cope with the challenges of the society of men without the punctuations of gunfire, and had resolved to put this philosophy into practice. They did not flaunt their pacifism, nor advertise it – in the minds of most men it would have put them in a category with old women and infant babes – but for fifteen years they had managed to live by their private code. They lived perilously, but they lived.

It was a heady life – reckless, exciting, and full of vibrancy. But in the past few years a mellowing had set in. They had begun to tire of adventuring, and to yearn for something of more lasting value to pour their life-energies into. They had worked more, played less, and begun to save their money diligently.

Then one crisp winter day they had stood on a low hill in the great central valley of California, and looked out over tawny fields rolling toward the foothills of the glittering snowy Sierras to the east. This was prime ranch land before them, richly endowed with the nutrients of the earth, well watered, and blessed with a climate that was close to perfection. It was available; it would cost most of their present savings and half of what they could hope to earn for a number of years. They talked it over, in low, serious tones.

'It can't be beat,' said Trav, his eyes roving admiringly over the land. 'There's nothing else we can get our hands on that'll touch it for quality.'

'It'll wipe us out,' Darby said, frowning.

'Wrong. We've been wipin' ourselves out all these years. It'll give us somethin' to build on, a goal to strive for. It won't wipe us out. It'll save us.'

'You think we're ready to be saved?'

Trav grinned and clapped his friend on the shoulder. 'How old do you reckon yourself to be now, pal?'

Darby frowned vaguely. 'Julia always used to say she and I were the same age, and I figure she'd be thirty-five now.' He reflected briefly, and added. 'Not would be. Is.'

'Well, I'm goin' on thirty-seven,' Trav said. 'And I'm tired o' livin' in smelly bunkhouses, and sleepin' in wagons, or in bedrolls on the cold hard ground, and roamin' around from one place to another like big dumb buffalo, grazin' on the plains. We're big boys now, Darby. It's time we lived in a *house.*'

Darby looked at the beautiful golden land, decorated with occasional olive-green masses of live oaks, and was willing to be convinced.

He pointed. 'Seems to me right over there would be a great place for a ranch house,' he said. 'In that flat area, between those two big oaks.'

'Well, I'll be damned!' Trav slapped his thigh and beamed. 'Just exactly what *I* had in mind!'

Darby took a deep breath, struggling with the weight of momentous decision. 'Sure is pretty land, all right.' Finally he said, 'I guess you're right. It's time we lived in a house.'

'Not just *any* ol' house,' said Trav. 'A ranch house. Ours.'

So they shook hands on it, and the course was set.

'We'll go fifty-fifty all the way,' Trav said. 'And we've got more'n enough for the first instalment right now. Let's get movin'.'

'Uh, jus' one little thing, Trav,' Darby said hesitantly. 'One little trip I got to take first.'

'Where to?'

'Mississippi. Back to Chinaberry.'

Trav flung an oath across the landscape. 'What?'

'Gotta go visit the old home-place,' Darby said flippantly.

'You're crazy!'

'Got to, Trav.'

'How do you know there's anybody left there at the "old home-place"?!'

Darby's grin flashed. 'Southern plantation folk don't go roamin' around from one place to another like buffalo, the way us low-class western people do. When they build them a place, they stay there.'

Trav snorted.

Darby was suddenly serious. 'Got to go, Trav. Got to see Julia one more time, before I settle down.'

'Darby,' Trav said patiently, 'it's over two thousand miles from here to Mississippi. Julia's dowdy and dumpy and middle-aged and has ten kids by now. And she wouldn't even know you. You'd hate yourself for a fool.'

Darby tried to listen, but didn't hear. 'I wonder if Moses is still around,' he mused. 'He'd be old now. But I bet he's there. And I bet he's spry.'

'And what about her husband?' Trav went on doggedly. 'She's probably married to one o' those Confederate Colonels – big hero, personally blew the heads off three or four thousand damn yankees durin' the war. What's he gonna do when he sees a black buck, come to pay a social call on his lady? Invite him to dinner?'

Darby shrugged, without interest.

Trav's last question was, 'What about our ranch?'

'We'll make the first payment, and get the papers, then go. It'll wait for us.'

'You're a damn fool,' Trav said, and turned away. '*I'll* make the first payment, and start to work. And if you don't come back, I'll go it alone.'

Darby looked across the rolling California hills for a long moment. 'I got to see Julia again, Trav,' he said quietly.

'Wish you'd come with me. Don't know if I can make it by myself.'

Trav turned and glared at him angrily. 'Why? *Why* do you have to see Julia again?'

Darby met his friend's gaze with steady eyes. 'I promised.'

Trav shook his head in the futility of incomprehension.

'Got to, Trav,' Darby said. And Trav knew it was settled.

They made an initial payment and secured title on their land, then rode away from it, Trav taking a long forlorn backward look as they went. They acquired three sturdy young horses – two to ride and one to carry supplies – and moved southward down the central California valley and around the lower end of the still snowbound Sierras, then struck east to pick up the Old Spanish Trail, and followed its endless meanderings through the orange-red rock temples and high mesas and blinding-bright sandy vistas of the southwestern desert. They arrived in Santa Fe, a familiar watering place from their earlier trail riding days, and stopped to renew old friendships. Then they continued on along the great thoroughfare of migration and trade, the Santa Fe Trail, already in the eighteen-sixties worn with traffic and history.

All during those first days of travel Darby had kept the rocks and canyons and hillsides along the way echoing with his laughter and singing. He was blissful and carefree, leaving the planning and navigating to Trav, who was the acknowledged expert on the geography of the West. But since Trav had never been east of the boundary of Missouri, the eastern terminus of the trail, it was agreed that when they entered the Mississippi Valley the leadership of the expedition would pass into Darby's hands.

So they followed the old trail slowly across the wide treeless wilderness, negotiated the parched wastes of the Cimarron Crossing, and arrived at length upon the Arkansas River, and bathed in its waters with delight, admiring the first substantial stream they had seen in weeks.

At this point they turned away from the trail and followed the Arkansas southeastward, and shortly thereafter entered the realm of the old Confederacy. Soon they left the river and headed directly east, Darby calculating that the Arkansas would lead them too far south.

Trav laughed about the uncertainty of Darby's geographical knowledge. 'Are you sure we'll know the Mississippi?' he asked, and it was Darby's turn to laugh at geographical naivete.

'When you see it,' said Darby with a grin, 'you'll know it.'

In the South they put their guns away. A show of arms in a land that was still smouldering with the passions of war and the humiliation of military defeat would have no protective value whatever, they reasoned – on the contrary, it would invite challenge. In Darby's case, it would absolutely guarantee it.

They proceeded without difficulty, striking the river a short distance above Memphis. Standing on an overlook there and trying to make out the low-lying cloudy-blue vagueness of the far shore across the massive muddy current, Trav was seized with an urge to give it up at last, turn back and go home. He recovered himself, and persevered.

They sold their horses in a village a few miles downstream, bought a good-sized skiff, ancient but solid, and launched themselves on the final southward floating leg of the journey.

At first Trav was tense with apprehension on the unfamiliar watery highway, and reflected with a tinge of regret that he had never been a religious-minded man, for now would be a good time to enjoy the solace of piety and prayer.

Darby settled into a serenity of spirit, as placid as the broad waterway. During brief leisure moments of twilight in their evening campsites, he worked with slow meticulous care on cutting letters into the bow of the skiff. His efforts did not achieve graphic excellence, but when he stepped back at last and observed his finished work, he was pleased. Then the good ship *El Bandido Moreno*, bold and valiant, was christened with a cup of muddy Mississippi River water.

After a few days on the river Trav was beginning to feel relaxed, and was developing some degree of skill at handling the skiff – but no sooner did his confidence revive than fresh misgivings arose.

As they proceeded southward and penetrated the deep southern territory Darby's spirits began to falter, to be replaced more and more frequently with a sombre brooding moodiness that made him seem withdrawn and uncommunicative. It was a facet of Darby's nature that Trav had not often seen, and it filled him with a vague uneasiness.

The cause of it, Trav was convinced, was the unseen

looming proximity of the place that was their destination, and the wraithlike figures that floated dimly through Darby's mind, inhabiting his remembrance of that place. It seemed to Trav that the attraction Darby felt was growing stronger, like the pull of gravity, as they approached its source. And it was not pure attraction, Trav felt sure – there was a repelling element present as well. The force was dual, ambivalent, self-contradictory, clutching at Darby from two directions at once – the opposite halves of some grotesque double-headed monster, one face soft and alluring, the other poisonously evil. Twin devils, struggling for dominance: imagined love, and remembered terror.

The blast of the steamboat whistle rocked them again, this time much closer, and with a deep intensity that could be felt as well as heard. The ponderous steamer rumbled past them fifty yards away, and they scanned the human figures walking the deck and leaning against the railings, and instinctively waved a greeting, and received jaunty waves in return; travellers of the world extending a friendly gesture of recognition to fellow travellers, secure in the knowledge that they would never be called upon to make good that expression of friendliness, that the passing strangers would be gone in a moment, never to be seen again, and their salutation in the same moment forgotten.

The men in the skiff watched the steamer move noisily on down the channel, revealing as it went past them its mighty stern wheel, pounding the water and transforming it into an angry swirling maelstrom of churning foam and clouds of spray. Shortly the bow waves rolling outward from the ship sloshed against the skiff, and rocked it rudely. Then all was quiet again.

Darby absently resumed working his oar, but watched lingeringly as the stern-wheeler receded into the distance downstream.

'We used to play a game, Julia and me,' he said, after a while. 'Anytime we heard a steamboat, we'd run to the river, fast as we could go. All the boats goin' downriver were hers, and the ones goin' upriver were mine. We'd count for days, for weeks, I reckon, to see who could get the most steamboats. Lots o' times we'd sit on the bank with our bare feet splashin' in the water for hours, jus' waitin' for one to come by.'

Darby smiled with fondness upon this small treasure retrieved by accident from the dusty recesses of memory. Trav noticed the distant look in his friend's eyes, and knew that the jocular mood was over for the day.

The spell was deepening.

CHAPTER TWO

In the afternoon they worked their way around a wide bend in the river and saw ahead of them a long slender promontory, jutting from the west bank. Approaching this landmark, Darby studied its contours intently, his eyes roving restlessly up and down the irregular shoreline.

'If that's what I think it is . . .' he murmured, and increased the pace of his paddling a subconscious degree. Trav watched, and could feel the subliminal beginnings of excitement stirring in his companion.

They rounded the point, and on its southern side a long, low sandy cliff came into view. At the far end of the cliff the mouth of a little creek emerged from dense woods and emptied its shallow current into the river. A mile farther southward the buildings of a small human settlement could be seen.

Darby stood in the skiff, holding his oar horizontally for balance and climbing onto the seat. He studied the surroundings in all directions. Then he looked down at Trav, excitement now gleaming brightly in his eyes.

'See that sandy cliff over there, Trav?' he said, pointing. 'I know it. It's crumbled a lot, and lower than it used to be, but I recognize it. And that little creek over there – that's called Fox Creek. And down yonder –' he pointed to the settlement downstream – 'that's Tolliver's Landing.'

Trav followed Darby's gaze in that direction. 'Tolliver's Landing,' he repeated. He frowned with an effort of recollection. 'Oh, yes – I've heard you mention it. That's the place that's right across the river from –' He looked quickly back to the other man.

Darby was staring across toward the thin, hazy, blue-green line that marked the opposite shore.

'We're here, Trav,' he said quietly. 'Over yonder's Chinaberry.'

Trav too stood in the skiff and strained his eyes toward the far side of the river. He tried to think of something appropriately dramatic to say, in recognition of a memorable moment.

'Can't see a thing,' he mumbled, and sat down again.

''Course you can't,' Darby said impatiently. 'The east bank's a mile away, and the house is a quarter of a mile back from the river.' Nevertheless he continued to gaze intently across the empty sheet of water, as if by sheer effort of will his vision could penetrate the haze and the distance.

After a while he sat down, and looked hard at Trav. 'Well, shall we start across?'

Trav glanced at the sky, and frowned. 'It's gettin' late. Better camp on this side tonight, and cross in the morning.'

'How come?' Darby demanded. 'We can make it before dark easy. Let's go.' He prepared to get the skiff underway again, but Trav's low voice made him pause.

'Hold on, Darby. We better take the time to ask a few nosy questions at Tolliver's Landing first, don't you think? To see if we can find out *exactly* how things stand?'

Darby frowned thoughtfully for a moment, then nodded. 'Guess you're right,' he said. He headed the boat in toward the west bank, and the narrow strip of beach along the base of the sandy cliff. 'We can camp here tonight, then stop by Tolliver's Landing in the morning. How's that?'

'Good,' Trav answered, and was relieved.

High clouds rolled across the sky from the west, hastening the departure of the late afternoon light, and it was almost dark when they put in on the bare sand strip below the cliff and quickly made camp. They prepared their evening meal over a small fire and ate in silence, and afterward Trav cleaned up while Darby secured the skiff for the night and broke out their bedrolls. With an expert glance at the sky, Darby pulled out oilskins as well, for protection against rain.

He worked rapidly in the last dim light before darkness closed in, but paused frequently to look up and down the lonely strip of beach where they had pitched camp. The soft murmuring of little Fox Creek nearby could be heard plainly in the quiet of dusk.

'Yeah, I remember this place very well,' Darby said. 'We used to come here once in a while to go fishin', Moses and me.'

Trav looked up in mild surprise. 'You mean you were allowed to go places like that?'

'Moses was. An' sometimes he let me tag along with 'im. Slaves weren't all alike, y'know. Now Moses, he was a privileged character. He went lots o' places. He ran the plantation household, and I mean to tell ya, in his own way he was just as much a slave driver as any white man.'

Darby chuckled softly, in reminiscence. 'Him and Josie – privileged characters.' His eyes roamed off across the darkness on the river.

'They were my friends,' he said, more to himself than to Trav. 'It'll be good to see 'em again.'

He paused in his work, and his face was suddenly clouded. 'Trav – what if nobody's there?'

Trav's reaction was a patient, sardonic smile. 'Seems to me I recall askin' you that same question back in California, several months ago. Seems to me I recall you gave me some kind o' sassy answer, and –'

He broke off, seeing the troubled look in Darby's eyes. He fixed his friend with a look of sharp suspicion. 'Tell me sump'm, Darby. You're not thinkin' o' this little venture in terms of – homecoming, are you?'

Darby laughed softly. 'You couldn't hardly call it home – a place you left the way I left Chinaberry.'

They worked for a while in silence. Darby carefully prepared two spots for sleeping, brushing away stones and laying out the bedrolls. Trav finished the camp cleanup and put out the smoking embers of the little fire.

'Well, let's not worry about it now,' Trav said lightly. 'Things always seem much better in the light of morning.'

Nothing more was said. They crawled into their bedrolls, stretched their weary muscles gratefully, and lay still, each wrapped in his own silent contemplations.

You bet your sweet life you can't call it home, Trav thought. That's why we've got to do a little nosing around at Tolliver's Landing first, before we go barging over there and maybe walk right into something we can't get out of.

He was thinking of a certain aspect of this undertaking they almost never spoke about, but which lurked like a shark in a tropical sea, just beneath the surface of their minds. It seemed to Trav that Darby faced something more than the likelihood of disappointment or disillusionment in his return to Chinaberry. From the scraps of information he had gleaned over the years from Darby about his early life – distorted images and unrelated fragments of scenes and events, only half real, perhaps, half imagined – Trav saw a chilling possibility. Darby might be greeted with charges that had lain in the books and in the backs of people's minds for twenty-one years, waiting.

Criminal charges. Just possibly, a charge of murder.

During the early hours of the night a gentle rain fell intermittently, substituting for short periods its soft spattering sound in place of the nocturnal serenade of frogs and crickets. Sometime after midnight the skies cleared, and the river lay suddenly gleaming in the cold glow of a nearly full moon.

Darby lay awake, and stared up into the night, his mind restless and feverish. He watched the moon, suspended serenely in its slow celestial orbit, and sensed the quiet turning of the mother planet beneath it. After a while he sat up, and looked over at his companion. Trav lay still, in a deep sleep.

Darby climbed out of his bedroll and walked slowly along the narrow beach. After going a short distance he stopped, moved forward a few steps, and let the river touch his bare feet, and gazed down at the gentle lapping of the water, shimmering in the soft moonlight. Soon he walked on aimlessly up the beach a little farther, and sat down at the edge of the water on a piece of smooth grey driftwood, the ancient skeleton of what was once a tall pine tree in Wisconsin. He watched the kaleidoscopic reflections of the moon's image on the slumbering river, and raised his eyes slowly, following the glittering path they made across the surface, toward Chinaberry. The fragments of moonrays leaped and danced so gracefully on the face of the dark water that it seemed to Darby that some sweet, angelic music should be playing their accompaniment – but there was none. The silence was as high and as wide as the great vaulted space above him.

Another chance memory discovered: suddenly he recalled how Julia used to try his patience by bidding him be still and listen to the silence. He could never comprehend what she was talking about. Now he knew.

Far out in the middle of the river the reflected shaft of moonlight became muddled, diffused, and lost in dismal grey-black mist, and Darby strained his eyes and every nerve and muscle and molecule of consciousness to the utmost to see beyond the dark veil, but could not.

And down along the delicate dancing moonbeam path

came soft sounds that echoed faintly off the sky and the water and caressed his ears tenderly, and made him cold.

A girl's voice, sobbing and tremulous in anguish, called to him, and pulled him with a force as deep as the magnetism of the earth.

'*Darby, come back! You belong to me! Come back, Darby, come back. . . .*'

PART FOUR

BEFORE

CHAPTER ONE

There had been a series of blustery squalls of rain that struck at irregular and unpredictable intervals during several days following the night of the party. Overseer Horace Willard scanned the sky constantly, scowled, and cursed the capricious weather, which was forcing the loss of valuable work time for the field hands in these critical early spring days of cultivation.

The big house at Chinaberry was subdued and sombre with the outward trappings of mourning. And the people who had entered the spacious main hall in an atmosphere of gaiety on the evening of the party, who had eaten and drunk at the bountiful table, and laughed and flirted and gossiped and danced, all returned three days later, wearing black, their facial expressions carefully arranged and set in the appropriate mould of sombre melancholy, to attend the funeral of Milo Gates.

Mixed in their mournful manner, too, were traces of something sheepish and shamefaced, as though the realization was just dawning that the celebration three nights before had supposedly been in honour of old Milo's birthday. All knew that the occasion had been fraudulent, that the cantankerous old man had loathed his son-in-law the genial host, and detested all forms of social frivolity. Few had made the effort to extend congratulations to be conveyed to Milo, alone in his self-imposed exile upstairs; none had sought an opportunity to convey greetings in person.

Now the hypocritical revellers assembled again, in stiff and shameful embarrassment, and many thought they sensed the ghost of the old departed misanthrope watching them, and chuckling in devilish glee.

The sullen grey weather added to the dismal mood, as the day of the funeral dawned.

Margaret Douglas, calm and dry-eyed, had moved with uncharacteristic efficiency in taking charge of the arrangements, while Reeves had quietly faded into the background, in a curious reversal of their usual roles. It was Margaret's parent who was dead; it was her occasion. She assumed the responsibility with a kind of secret, subdued relish, and an interest in detail that was altogether lacking in her under normal circumstances.

The Douglas family cemetery had been established thirty years before on the far side of the low rise of ground known as Indian Hill, just north of the plantation house. The gently rounded summit was the spot on which Reeves's father, James Douglas, had wanted to build his plantation house, but had lost his zest for the idea when he heard the local legend attributing an evil Indian curse to the place.

Years later, in grief over the death of his youngest child and second son, James had thought again of this lonely isolated area, undisturbed by any earthly sounds except the whispering of wind in the thickets of birch and hickory and dogwood that grew on its slopes, and the endless gentle twittering of songbirds that nested there. He decided it would be an ideal site for a burial ground – surely a curse that might bring evil upon the living would allow peace to the dead.

So in 1815 the cemetery was laid out on the shadowy north side of the hill, with two-year-old Roger Douglas the first to be buried there. In 1826 the infant's mother, pale, patient Penelope Reeves Douglas, gave up her wistful longing for her native Virginia and came quietly to rest in the second grave on Indian Hill beside the Mississippi. Two years later the grave of James, her husband, became the third.

Now, on this April day in 1845, the fourth grave was ready.

Red Jake, the plantation blacksmith, whose duties included grave digging when the occasion required, gave his newly completed work a careful last minute inspection, then withdrew with his three muscular assistants and stood waiting for the slow procession that would shortly wind along the circuitous little road through the woods and up the slope to the burial ground.

Red Jake – so named because of a mysterious reddish tinge to his hair – was one of the craftsmen among the Chinaberry slaves, and took fierce pride in his work. He had measured the new grave several times to be sure that it would accept without a hitch the massive pine coffin for which it was intended. It was a fine grave, Red Jake thought, and he waited for the burial ceremony with real pleasure, confident that afterward his master would bestow upon him well earned compliments for his excellent workmanship.

The black folk convened first, and formed a wide half-circle around the grave site some distance back; they would be the outer ring of mourners. In the front ranks stood the aristocrats of the slaves, the house servants, and foremost among them were the elite, Moses and Josie. Between those two, trying to be inconspicuous, stood Darby.

The boy had been advised by Moses to put on his other shirt – the clean one, the one he kept tucked away under his bunk for special occasions – for the funeral was indeed, Moses assured him, a special occasion. Moses had further instructed the boy on the proper behaviour at white folks' funerals, emphasizing that it would be at the very peril of his life to appear to be anything other than grief-stricken throughout the proceedings.

After the slaves came the plantation's white employees, forming a tight little knot on the side of the grave opposite the black people; Horace Willard, stiff and uncomfortable in starched shirt and necktie, with his lean, muscular, rawboned wife, and the two hired hands, youthful brothers Frank and Walt Elwood. These four stood in awkward isolation, not a part of the social microcosm of the Douglases and their friends, yet rigidly aloof from the blacks – suspended in a lonely no-man's-land between two worlds.

Then the main procession: the creaking, lurching wagon that bore the great pine coffin; following immediately behind it, on foot, Reeves, Margaret and Julia, and the presiding minister – a paunchy, waddling, hellfire-and-brimstone backwoods preacher with fiery eyes and heavy hanging jowls, the Reverend Jarvis – wheezing and panting from the walk up the gentle hillside; finally the respectful assemblage of friends and neighbours from the surrounding countryside, all impeccable in sombre attire and solemn attitudes.

After everyone was in place, Red Jake and his assistants lifted the coffin out of the wagon and placed it over the open grave, suspending it there by means of ropes held taut. All was in readiness. Reverend Jarvis hastily wiped his perspiring brow one last time, and stepped forth to intone his chosen words in the sonorous ringing voice for which he was locally famed.

The black people, many of whom would not have recognized old Massa Milo if they had met him face to face, were grateful for this or any other event to break the numbing routine of their days, and cheerfully threw themselves into their well understood roles, assuming expressions of heart-rending grief, and from time to time emitting piteous wails and moans.

Darby had stared in disbelief as Red Jake and his helpers had struggled to move the huge coffin into place over the yawning grave. He recalled Massa Milo as a thin wasted little man, and marvelled at the tremendous size of the pine box that had been constructed in the plantation's carpentry shop to house those meagre earthly remains.

Then, remembering his instructions from Moses, Darby cast his eyes downward and composed his features in what he imagined to be a look of inconsolable mourning. Surely, he thought, if Massa Douglas looks this way and sees how heartbroken I am, he will be reminded that I'm a good boy, and will feel kindly toward me.

Darby had a vague understanding of the precarious nature of the life he led, and felt occasional anxiety about what the great and mighty Massa Douglas might be thinking of him. He did not dream that his mortal enemy and the principal threat to his security was not so much the master, but the lady, now standing veiled and quiet at her husband's side.

While Reverend Jarvis delivered the eulogy, Darby yielded to the temptation to sneak a quick timid glimpse of the big ruddy-faced man, and to wonder at the source of all the resounding dramatics with which the preacher commended old Milo's soul to heaven. Then he stole a glance at Julia, and was dismayed to see that she was red-eyed from weeping. It seemed to Darby that poor Julia was the only person in the entire company present who was feeling something real there on the hillside that day. She looked so sad that Darby was seized with a desire to run to her and take her hand, and whisper words of comfort.

With a shock he realized that his eyes were no longer properly downcast, but staring boldly and directly at the Douglas family. And Massa Douglas's restless, constantly alert eyes were roaming in his direction. Instantly Darby fastened his eyes on the ground, and resolved to concentrate on keeping them there.

At length Reverend Jarvis, choked with emotion at his

own eloquence, brought his ceremonial oration to a tearful end. Red Jake waited nervously for his cue, received it, motioned to his assistants, and the four brawny men gently lowered the coffin into the grave, Red Jake feeling an inward satisfaction as he noted how smoothly and neatly the article fit into its earthen repository.

After the ritual was completed the black folk moved away first, and trooped quietly back down the hillside road to return to their regular daily chores, the field hand gang herded along by overseer Willard's two assistants, the Elwood brothers.

Final respects were paid, final handshakes exchanged and a few parting remarks of comfort and condolence murmured, and the gathering dispersed. The mourners retraced their steps down the little forest road, back to their waiting carriages and rivercraft, to return to normal living with remarkable quickness and ease, removing all vestiges of the tiresome melancholy expressions from their faces, and even indulging here and there in a discreet joke and an occasional subdued chuckle.

Reeves remained behind at the burial ground for a few minutes to give words of instruction to Red Jake and his men regarding the final phase of the work, the filling and covering of the grave. Be sure it is well filled and thoroughly packed down, he told them, and then more dirt added. Nothing is so unsightly, nor more degrading to the noble spirit of Man, he declared, than a sunken grave. He remembered to confer a gracious compliment on Red Jake and his crew for the fine craftsmanlike grave digging job; he knew how Jake thrived on words of praise, and how he particularly liked being called a craftsman – and Reeves did it gladly, for it was true.

Then, his mind free of responsibility for a brief while, Reeves walked a short way up the slope and stood for a few minutes gazing at each of the other three graves in the old family plot – those of his parents, and that of the child who had been his only brother, and who today would have been a man of thirty-two, had he lived. Briefly Reeves tried to bring to mind the faded images of his father and mother, how they had looked, how their voices had sounded – tried, with strangely little success. He wondered idly what his brother Roger would have been like as a man. He thought of these lost people fondly, but without strong feeling.

The graves were neat and well tended, he noted. He

nodded with approval and turned away, cast a final glance around the little cemetery, and felt, all in all, a sense of satisfaction. Even the treacherous weather had chosen to be reasonably co-operative on this solemn day. Although the ground was soggy and the skies grey and threatening, no rain had fallen, and once in a while a stray shaft of sunshine had broken through long enough to catch a few droplets of water clinging to foliage, and turn them into sparkling jewels.

It had gone quite well, Reeves thought, and smiled inwardly. It was not at all unlike the good feeling he experienced when a party came off with smashing success. He reminded himself to congratulate Margaret on her excellent management of the event.

All the others having gone, Reeves started back toward home alone, and immediately found himself enjoying the brief solitary walk. What a pity, he thought, I don't have the time to get out and walk over my land more often. He realized with a fleeting twinge of shame that, before this occasion, he had not been up to the little cemetery on Indian Hill in, perhaps, two or three years. He smiled wickedly to himself, thinking: now that my vinegary old father-in-law has joined the company there, I doubt seriously that the frequency of my visits will sharply increase.

Reeves glanced around in the damp shadowy forest as he walked, looked up at the misty slant of light through fresh fragrant branches overhead, took a deep breath, and felt content.

Suddenly a discordant thought struck him, intruding upon his feeling of serenity and spoiling the mood. It was a thought that had been temporarily brushed aside in his mind by the distraction of the funeral, but it came rushing back now, and as it did Reeves's contentment vanished. The ceremony had not been quite complete, not perfect in every detail, after all. For one person who should have been there – standing, in fact, in a kind of place of honour and weeping bitterly, as befitting a devoted servant of forty years – had been shamelessly and conspicuously absent.

Hector had not been seen since the morning of Milo's death. He was listed on the plantation books as a runaway.

CHAPTER TWO

The first awful rumour that had spread like grass fire through the quarters at Chinaberry the morning after the party was that Hector had murdered his old master.

Reeves had called an assembly of his plantation people, and with tight lips and hard voice told them that he was prepared to lift his lifelong ban on whipping; anyone guilty of spreading that wild and malicious tale would be put to the lash. Also, he informed them, anyone caught harbouring or aiding Hector would not only be whipped, but would be sold down the river. The black people listened in stolid silence, saw that Massa Douglas was more genuinely, deeply angry than they had ever seen him – and took careful note of it. To be sold down the river – an unimaginable terror.

Reeves was angry – but behind his anger there was something else. Secretly he was hurt by Hector's action. The master of Chinaberry took great pride in the low runaway rate among his people; with a stab of embarrassment Reeves remembered his smug boasting about this at the party. And now Hector had spoiled that beautiful record. Well, never mind, he consoled himself – technically Hector was not really one of his people at all, he belonged to Milo. So, strictly speaking, the Chinaberry record remained unblemished. Still, Reeves felt injured, and was grimly determined to apprehend Hector at no matter what effort and expense, and to sell him off to one of the local slave traders for whatever few dollars he might bring.

And as he nursed his wounded pride it did not occur to Reeves to reflect that he had always intended to sell Hector off the minute old Milo was gone, anyway, that Hector had probably known this full well, and that the knowledge of his impending fate must have been what had driven the old slave to his desperate action. Had he been confronted with this line of thought, Reeves would have been astonished, indignant, and more hurt than ever.

The day after Milo's interment the sunshine burst forth in unobstructed radiance, burned off the mist and dampness of the days of gusty rain, and beamed down in splendid life-giving warmth, and the fields, the crops, and the forest received it gladly.

Around ten o'clock in the morning of this day, when the plantation and all its people were securely back into the pattern of their daily routines, young Frank Elwood, one of overseer Willard's white assistants, walked hurriedly up the little side road that led from the barnyard area, entered the rear yard of the big house, and approached the steps of the veranda. He paused there and looked around nervously, as if uncertain what to do, then went up the steps, across the veranda, and knocked timidly at the back door. After a moment he knocked again, a bit more solidly.

Moses appeared, looked at the visitor with no visible evidence of recognition, and said, 'Yes?'

'Wanna see Mistuh Douglas,' Elwood drawled.

Moses continued to gaze at the young man. When he spoke his manner was rigidly formal, and contained a trace of haughtiness. 'May I tell him what it's about?'

Elwood fidgeted in irritation, and considered saying something abusive to the haughty black man, but thought better of it. 'Tell 'im it's about Mistuh Talbot.'

Moses's eyes narrowed slightly, in an involuntary reflection of hostility. 'Wait heah,' he said curtly, and turned and disappeared into the interior of the house. Young Elwood stood on the veranda, shifting his weight back and forth from one foot to the other.

Reeves was in the formal garden at the side of the house when Moses brought him the message, and came rapidly around the corner and approached Elwood from behind. He stopped at the bottom of the steps. 'Yes, what is it, Elwood?'

The young man started, wheeled around, and stared, open-mouthed.

In times of stress Reeves was given to self-pity, and at this moment he marvelled at his hard lot in life. Why is it, he wondered, that it is apparently beyond the bounds of possibility to find white hired hands who are possessed of sufficient intelligence to remember their own names with certainty? His face was set in grim patience as he waited for young Elwood to recover his presence of mind and deliver his message – if he could remember what he had come to say.

Frank Elwood whipped the cap from his head and descended the veranda steps, nodding rapidly several times, in an earnest display of obsequiousness. As assistant to the overseer, he might have occasion to speak directly to the plantation owner perhaps once or twice a year, and he approached such an event with undisguised nervousness.

'Mistuh Douglas, suh, Mistuh Talbot's heah. He down by the barn with Mistuh Willard, wantin' to speak with you, suh.' His voice was high-pitched and squeaky. He delivered his little speech as rapidly as he could, and stood gripping his cap and nodding his head repeatedly.

'Did he bring the dogs?' Douglas snapped.

'Naw, suh. Didn't bring no dogs.'

Douglas swore vehemently, and brushed past Elwood, causing the hired man to step back in alarm. Reeves strode rapidly across the yard and down the road toward the barnyard, and young Elwood followed at a respectful distance.

Henry Talbot was a swarthy, greasy man, dirty and ragged, with an unkempt black beard and beady narrow-set eyes that peered from under the wide brim of a scruffy felt hat. He was an example of what the genteel folk of the planter class referred to distastefully as 'po' white trash' – those backwoods folk, hopelessly mired in poverty and ignorance, to whom the humanizing effects of education, leisure, breeding and manners were totally unknown. Reeves Douglas would no sooner sit down to dinner with a man like Henry Talbot than he would with one of his own slaves.

But Talbot enjoyed one possession that from time to time rendered him the most sought-after man in the county among the wealthy planters who would otherwise disdain his company. That was a pack of ferocious dogs – bloodhounds, he called them – that were kept in a large wagon especially equipped for the purpose, with a sturdy cage built on its flat bed. In their kennel on wheels the hounds were thus ready at any time to be transported to the grounds of a planter who had need of their services. The discovery of a slave being missing from any plantation within twenty miles of Talbot's small rundown farm usually resulted in the quick dispatch of a messenger on the run, requesting the rental of the dogs.

Talbot's animals were good at their work – bloodily, horrifyingly good. Their reputation was great, and their services were expensive. The defection of a slave – even one of little value – was regarded as a calamity, not only by the culprit's owner, but by neighbouring slaveholders as well. It was agreed that the runaway impulse was an infectious disease; one incident could quickly start an epidemic, especially if the fugitive was not immediately caught and severely punished.

The news of a runaway, then, might bring anguish to the eyes of many people, of both races – it invariably brought a thin smile of gratification to the lips of Henry Talbot, tender of hounds. Talbot's grubby little farm was neglected because its owner had found a much better way to make a living.

And business had been good lately. Reeves knew this, as he hurried toward the barnyard, from the visitor's manner. Talbot was leaning lazily against a fence post, chatting with overseer Willard, and he stayed in that casual position until the last possible moment. When he finally stood forward to greet Douglas he did not bother to remove his hat, which perched on his head at a jaunty angle. Reeves was well aware that when Talbot was in need, he would snap to instant respectful attention at first sight, hat in hand.

Reeves dispensed with the hypocrisy of social salutation as he came up to the man, and asked crisply, 'Wheah are the dogs, Talbot?'

'How do, Mistuh Douglas?' said Talbot cheerily, and grinned, revealing rotten teeth.

'Wheah are the dogs?' Reeves repeated.

'Ovuh to Graystone, suh. Took 'em ovuh theah yestiddy. Gilbert ovuh theah's been havin' right smart o' trouble with one o' the nigger gals runnin' off to the woods at night, meetin' a man. Gilbert thinks maybe it's a buck from Chinaberry she's been meetin' with.'

'That's a damn lie,' Willard growled. He bristled, sensing his reputation as custodian of the Chinaberry slaves being questioned. 'Ain't none o' our niggers goin' out o' the quarters at night, I'll guarantee it!'

Talbot threw a brief uninterested glance at Willard, then continued, to Reeves. 'Gilbert was wonderin' if maybe ye'd look into the mattuh, Mistuh Douglas?'

'Yes, yes, all right,' Reeves said impatiently. 'What about the dogs?'

'Gilbert's a no'count overseer,' Willard muttered. 'He ain't no damn good for nothin'. How come Ramsey leaves that place in the hands of a damn fool like that is beyond me!' Willard turned away, fuming.

'The dogs, Talbot?' Reeves said grimly.

'They caught the gal, jes' fo' dawn this mo'nin',' Talbot said. 'I got word little while ago. Chewed her up purty bad, they say. They's good dogs, damned if they ain't!'

Reeves averted his eyes from the evil grin. 'The question is, when can you have them *heah?*'

'I'll git 'em to ye by three, fo' 'clock this afternoon, maybe sooner. They'll do the job fer ye, too. They's good dogs, I swar.'

'All right. Bring them as soon as you can.' Reeves turned to Willard.

'Horace, I've got to go into Hanesville today, on some other business. I'll be back as soon as I can, but if the dogs arrive in the meantime, you get on with the job. You know what to do.'

Willard nodded.

'I'll tell Moses to fetch you a few articles of Hector's clothing,' Reeves continued. 'You go on up to the house after a while and get them, and have them ready for the dogs to, uh – get familiar with.'

Willard nodded again. His eyes glinted with secret anticipation.

Without looking at Talbot, Reeves turned and strode away.

'Uh, Mistuh Douglas,' Talbot called after him. 'About the price, suh. . . .'

Reeves paused and looked back, frowning. 'Ten dollars,' he said. 'Ten dollars, isn't it?'

Talbot's hat came off for the first time. He twisted it in his hands as he talked.

'Well, suh, I got me a couple mo' dogs, now. Good 'uns, too, I'll tell ye – pure-bred bloodhounds, jes' like all the rest. I won't have no mongrel dogs in my pack, naw, suh! Nothin' but pure-bred bloodhounds. Mighty costly to feed 'em, too. I swar, them hounds eat a heap – that is, when they ain't chewin' on black meat!'

The sickening grin, revealing blackened teeth – absurd, like an ill-fashioned jack-o'-lantern.

Reeves breathed deeply. 'All right. Twelve dollars.' He turned and walked rapidly away, not waiting for confirmation. He took several more deep breaths, trying to rid himself of the feeling of suffocation that always gripped him in Talbot's presence.

The tender of hounds raised his hat and waved it gallantly at Douglas's back.

'Good day to ye, suh,' he called, and grinned again.

CHAPTER THREE

Darby sat hunched on the top railing of the wooden fence that enclosed the chicken yard, and observed without interest the aimless wandering and scratching and pecking going on below him. His perch was ideal for his purpose – which had nothing to do with watching chickens – because it gave him an unobstructed view of the big house, a hundred yards distant, and at the same time afforded him an obscure and sheltered position, where his idleness would not be readily noticed. He did not regard himself as truly idle; he was busy doing what he had been doing a lot of lately – waiting for Julia.

The four days since Massa Milo's death seemed like an age, empty and endless. Julia had been deeply stabbed with grief by the experience, Darby knew. She had come to seek him briefly the first day, handwringing and tearful, to tell him how she had resolved only the night before to start spending more time with the lonely old man. Then she had turned away, inconsolable, and disappeared into the house, leaving Darby standing mute and helpless. He had not seen her again until the burial, where she had seemed to be distraught with grieving still, and oblivious of all else.

Darby's heart was swollen with sympathy for her; he longed to offer comfort, or at least cheerful distraction – if only she would come out of her shell of seclusion.

He watched the scampering chickens, and raised his eyes from time to time to scan the house. He had a clear view of the rear and side exits, and was ready to leap off the fence and go running to Julia the moment she chose to appear.

A little while earlier he had watched with intense curiosity when young Frank Elwood had come hurrying up to the house with some kind of message for Massa Douglas, who had then rushed away to the barnyard. Darby had slipped off his perch and trailed along, and, lurking expertly out of sight behind the barnyard fence, had listened in on the conversation between the master and Mr. Talbot, the dog man.

Troubled and brooding, he had returned to his observation

post at the chicken yard, and temporarily shifted his sympathy from Julia to the old slave who had run away. Poor Hector, he thought. They're goin' to turn the dogs loose on 'im. Poor, poor Hector.

He wondered what he would have done in Hector's position. Is it better to run away, or face being sold to a slave trader, and ending up on a sugar cane plantation in Louisiana? It was said among the blacks that being sent to the sugar cane fields was a sentence of death. But if you run away, where do you run to? How long can you live, hiding in the woods, even if the hounds don't come and find you, and tear you apart?

He had tried to discuss these questions with Moses the night after Hector's disappearance, and had found that usually wise man to be curiously lacking in practical helpfulness. Running away, Moses had declared, is never a good solution to any problem. Darby had countered with the remark that running away *might* be a good solution, if running away is the only solution available. Moses had shrugged, and said that you've just got to make the most of whatever conditions the Good Shepherd, the Lord, saw fit to impose upon you in life.

The Good Shepherd? It's all right for Moses to talk about the Good Shepherd, Darby thought. His life ain't so bad. Or me – I've been lucky, havin' Julia to look after me. But what shepherd would put upon his flock the terrible burdensome lives the field hands led? Or the fix old Hector was in right now? What kind of a good shepherd is *that?*

These are bad, wicked thoughts, Darby told himself. He gathered his resolve to thrust them out of his mind, and went back to watching the population of the chicken yard.

It was a tiresome vigil. The clucking fowl displayed little in the way of intelligence or personality to render them interesting. Darby pulled a sliver of wood off the fence railing and flicked it spinning toward the nearest hen. The bird ran squawking in alarm across the yard.

'Dumb chicken,' Darby muttered.

A patch of bright yellow caught the corner of his eye. He looked up quickly, and saw Julia standing on the rear veranda of the big house. She was dressed in a pretty yellow frock, which, with her pale skin and shining blonde hair, gave her an aspect of pure brightness. At the sight of her Darby's spirits leaped within him. She was looking for him, naturally, and he cursed himself for not having seen her the instant she came out of the house. He was off the rail fence in a flash and running toward her, all dark and weighty philosophical ponderings forgotten.

'Heah I is, Julia!' he called. He skidded to a stop at the bottom of the veranda steps, grinning up at her.

The girl regarded him gravely, and walked with slow deliberation down the steps.

'Darby,' she said in a low voice, 'around the house you address me as Miss Julia.'

Darby's grin did not falter. 'Yes'm,' he said cheerfully. 'Heah I is, Miss Julia.'

She grimaced, still dissatisfied. 'And for heaven's sake, will you please pay attention to your speech? "Heah I is" – really! I've taught you better, and you *know* better. Say "Here I am." '

'Yes'm.' Darby's cheerfulness remained unaffected. He assumed an expression of immense and solemn dignity, like the one he had often seen Moses employ when functioning as butler. 'Here – I – am – Miss – Julia.' His intonation was deadeningly mechanical, but his pronunciation flawless.

'Now you be careful about that,' Julia said sternly. 'I won't have you talking like a field hand.'

'Yes, ma'am. I mean, no, ma'am.' His grin was back in place.

Julia started to walk briskly across the yard, and Darby followed like a puppy. She stopped suddenly, and placed a finger on her chin, thinking, and Darby hovered at her side, dutiful and attentive.

'Now, let me see – what shall we do today?' she said musingly, half to herself.

Darby pondered. 'How 'bout goin' to Indian Hill pool, and catchin' tadpoles?'

It was one of their favourite places – a small shallow spring-fed pool, half hidden by rock outcroppings part way up the west slope of Indian Hill, from which a tiny brook ran gurgling to the river.

Julia wrinkled her nose in distaste. 'I don't feel like tadpoles. I think –' She hesitated, then made a decision. 'I think we'll pick wild grapes today.'

Another of their popular haunts was a giant cottonwood tree, far down in the woods near the river, in which an ancient wild grapevine sent its gnarled tentacles, thicker than a man's arm, twisting and climbing sixty feet from the ground.

Julia turned to the boy and issued a crisp order. 'Darby, go and fetch two pails from the kitchen house.' She walked away from him.

Darby's eyes grew round with excitement. He called, 'Yes, ma'am!' and ran in leaps and bounds toward the kitchen house to get the pails, inwardly exulting in the knowledge that everything was all right again, at last.

A sudden thought struck him, and made him pause for an instant: the grapes don't get ripe until July or August – now, in April, the old vine isn't even yet in bloom. Impatiently he thrust the knowledge out of his mind. That don't matter, he told himself, don't matter a little ol' bit. Ain't no need to remind Julia o' that. Everything's all right again – that's all that matters.

By the time he caught up with her again, with the two pails banging against his legs as he ran, she was a hundred yards down the little dirt road that led southward from the big house toward the fields, and the woods beyond. He came up beside her, and she looked at him with a sharp frown and said, 'With decorum, Darby.'

He had no notion what the word meant, but easily understood the tone of her remark, and responded, in his Moses-dignity voice. 'Yes, ma'am. *Heaps* o' decorum.'

So they walked along sedately, like an elderly couple on their way to church.

The road led them past the smoke house, where meat was hung and cured; past the blacksmith shop, where Red Jake supervised a crew of busy workers; past the stable; past the gin house, quiet now, but the centre of feverish activity at cotton baling time; past a huge barn that formed, along with several other buildings like it, the perimeter of a wide enclosed barnyard, fragrant with the pungent odours peculiar to animal habitations; and finally, on beyond the man-made structures of the plantation and out toward the open fields.

Ahead of them and off to their left Darby could see the hands at work, spread out across several hundred-yard-square areas of cultivation. And on the little road, which was adjacent to the fields, he saw Horace Willard sitting militarily erect on his horse, watching the workers.

Darby stopped short. Julia walked a few steps farther, then stopped and looked back at him.

'What's the matter, Darby?'

He walked slowly up to her, his eyes fixed on the man ahead. 'Le's cut across the field, Julia,' he said, nodding toward a fallow field to their right.

'What in the world for?'

'Short cut.'

Julia frowned impatiently. 'It's nothing of the kind, Darby. What are you talking about?'

Then, following his gaze, she noticed Willard. 'Oh, is *that* what's bothering you? Mr. Willard?'

'Well – I'd jes' soon not go past him.'

Julia laughed. 'Don't be ridiculous, Darby. Who's afraid of a silly ol' overseer?'

'I am,' Darby muttered. He hurried to catch up, and switched to walk on the other side of Julia, so that she would be between him and the man on horseback.

Willard showed no signs of being aware of them as they approached, and Darby entertained a wild hope that they might somehow walk past him unnoticed. But at the last moment the overseer turned his head and gazed at them.

'Good morning, Mr. Willard,' Julia said.

Willard put a finger to his hat and nodded almost imperceptibly. 'Mornin', Miss.' It was the absolute minimum that could pass as a greeting.

Willard's gaze shifted to Darby. The boy stared straight ahead and went past as quickly as he could without breaking into a run. He could feel Willard's cold gaze boring into him from behind, though he did not dare to look back. He was grateful that Julia moved on, without pausing for further conversation. Some distance farther on, the road made a sharp turn to the right, mercifully removing them from the overseer's field of view, and Darby was able to relax again.

Soon they passed the house where Willard and his family lived – a low rambling bungalow, set a little way back from the road. As they approached the spot where a path led off toward the house, they noticed a child, a pudgy boy of five or six, who was clinging to the crosspieces of a sagging wooden gate at the head of the path, and watching them. The boy's mouth hung open, his eyes were squinted almost shut – whether from an impediment of vision or the innately suspicious nature of his backwoods breed, couldn't be told – and he stared fixedly and without expression at Julia and Darby as they went past.

'Hello, Gene,' Julia said pleasantly, and received no answer.

For an instant Darby looked directly into the eyes of the silent boy, and felt a familiar chill, seeing there the same pinpoint glints of ice-hardness he always saw in the eyes of the overseer.

After they had walked on a little farther Darby said, 'Jes' think – someday little Eugene'll be a grown-up man like his pa, and be a overseer someplace. I bet he'll lick the slave folks from mornin' till night. Won't he be happy!'

Julia sniffed. 'He won't be working at Chinaberry. Not if *I* have anything to say about it.'

Soon the little dirt road left the cultivated fields behind, and began to struggle against the encroachment of wild vegetation. Gradually it became less distinctly a road, finally being reduced to the dimensions of a footpath that wound through dark green woods, leading toward the river.

Julia led the way along the path, and in a few minutes stopped and stood still. Darby waited patiently beside her. Julia looked around in all directions, examining their surroundings with careful attention. They were completely alone.

Suddenly she uttered a tiny gasp and clutched at Darby's arm. 'Oh, look!'

He followed her gaze, expecting to see the movement of some small wild creature in the brush. Then he remembered a danger, and tensed his muscles in anticipation – but was not quite quick enough.

The sharp jab of the girl's fingers in the side of his rib cage caught him unprepared. He gasped and staggered back, dropping the pails he carried, and broke into convulsive laughter, groping to grab the attacking hand. It was Julia's favourite ploy when she felt in the mood for romping. Darby was notoriously ticklish, and an easy victim, and it delighted her to exercise endless ingenuity in catching him off guard.

She was off and running, calling over her shoulder, 'Race you to the chinaberry tree!'

Darby watched her flying down the wooded path, her yellow hair and yellower dress trailing behind her, and felt a surge of deep joy. He retrieved the pails he had dropped and raced after her, yelling exultantly, 'Gonna git you!'

They ran through the forest with reckless abandon, their eager young bodies gratefully releasing several days' accumulation of pent-up energy. Julia climbed over a fallen log that blocked the path, leaped over a shallow brook, and ran on, laughing, and casting quick glances behind her as she went. Darby's running ability was so superior to the girl's, handicapped as she was by her long twisting skirt, that he found it necessary to control his speed as he bounded after her, not wanting to overtake her too quickly, and cut short the fun. At length he judged the time to be right, and contrived to catch her in a smooth spot covered with thick grass that would safely cushion her fall, grasped her fragile shoulders in his outstretched hands, and with a victorious yell pulled her to the ground. They collapsed and tumbled and came to rest in a tangle of arms and legs, and lay there breathless, panting, and choking with laughter and exuberance.

'I win!' she cried joyously. 'You pulled me down, and that's against the rules, so I win!'

'*I* win,' he countered, between gasps for air. 'You tickled me and got a head start, and *that's* against the rules!'

'No it isn't,' she said severely. '*I* make the rules, and I say *I* win!'

He grinned and gave up – and so it was settled, as their competitions were always settled, by her proclaiming herself the victor and his good-natured acceptance of defeat. One way or another, he knew, she always won every game – and he was content that it should be so.

Rested and in a quieter mood they lay side by side on the soft spring grass, and felt the gentle April morning warmth, and listened to the drowsy insect drone and the whispering trees of the forest.

Julia lay flat on her back, arms stretched above her head, her yellow hair spread luxuriously, and turned her face with closed eyes to the sun. Darby rested on his side with his head propped on an elbow, and gazed at the bright girl beside him.

In a moment Julia felt a tiny movement near her head, turned to look, and saw that Darby was winding his fingers in a strand of her long tresses. He smiled at her sheepishly.

''Scuse me, Julia.' He withdrew his fingers. 'Yo' hair's so soft and pretty. I like to touch it.'

She smiled permission. 'You may, if you like.' She turned her face back to the sun and closed her eyes again. There was no further sound from the boy. But after another moment she suddenly felt self-conscious, became aware of a tingling in her body that came from something other than the warmth of the sun. She tried to ignore it, but couldn't; the feeling grew, demanded investigation. She opened her eyes and looked at Darby.

He was leaning closer toward her, and his eyes were fixed in a hypnotic stare on the front of her dress, on the twin protrusions of her hard little breasts. A quick flash of excitement leaped within her, and she was astonished by it. She stretched her arms farther above her head, inhaled deeply, and thrust her bosom a subtle degree higher, and wondered at the strange pleasure her own actions gave her.

Darby shook himself free of his trance as he realized she was watching him, looked away quickly, pulled a weed and began to chew on it, and stared at the ground.

She reached out and tweaked his ear, to make him look at her. He looked, smiled shyly, and dropped his eyes again.

''Scuse me, Julia,' he said again, very softly.

'Do you like to look at me, Darby?'

He took the weed from his mouth and studied it with minute attention. 'Oh –' He shrugged. 'Sometimes.'

'You can look at me all you want. I like for you to. Out here in the woods, that is – never around the house.'

She watched him, waiting for him to raise his eyes again. But he had developed a sudden absorbing interest in the structure of weed stems.

'Darby, have you noticed how I'm beginning to be – different?'

He nodded.

'Do you like that?'

He threw down the weed and gazed off across the treetops. 'Julia – do you think you gon' git big, like Josie?'

She considered the question gravely. 'You mean – here?' She touched a hand to her breast.

He swallowed hard. 'Yeah.'

'Probably not. Just medium-size, I guess. More like my mother.'

He nodded, and pulled another weed. She took it out of his hands and threw it away.

'Darby, you didn't answer me. Do you *like* it?'

'Oh, yes. I like it, Julia. You gittin' *so* pretty. I'd like to – to –'

'To what?'

He hesitated for a moment. 'To see you.'

She stared at him. 'You mean – *see* me? You mean – without any *clothes on?!*'

He nodded. He was beginning to gaze at her boldly. She decided a touch of moral indignation was called for.

'Darby! Really!' She sat up abruptly and turned her back on him.

'You said I could look at you all I wanted to.'

'Well, my heavens – I didn't mean – *that* way! I couldn't *dream* of it!'

'Once you did, Julia. 'Membuh? When we was little? I looked at you and you looked at me –'

'That was different. We were just children then.'

'But I want to learn about things, Julia.' He tried pouting a little. 'You always sayin' you tryin' to educate me – guess you don't really mean it.'

'That's true!' she breathed. 'That's very true, you're right.'

He watched her slyly, and waited.

She turned partially toward him. 'All right, then. I will.'

'Now?'

'Of course not! At the squatter's cabin.'

'Why not now?'

'Not *outdoors*, Darby! That wouldn't be *decent!*'

He understood, nodded in agreement. He rolled onto his stomach and cupped his chin in his hands and gazed up at the girl, and his eyes were bright with admiration for her intellect.

She got up and brushed her skirt, and he scrambled to his feet and stood waiting to follow when she was ready.

'I'm lucky to have you, Julia,' he said. 'To make me learn things.'

She heaved a patient sigh. 'But sometimes you *are* a trial!'

He grinned.

So they walked on, quiet and pensive, down the forest path, and between them there was something strange and exciting and indefinable that hadn't been there before.

And both their hearts were beating a trifle faster because of it.

CHAPTER FOUR

After a while they stepped out into a small meadowlike clearing, a golden sunny opening in the midst of the cool greenness of forest growth. The little clearing seemed to be enclosed and isolated from the world, enveloped in a quiet distinctly deeper than that of the surrounding wilderness. At its grassy centre stood the chinaberry tree.

It was not a large tree, rising no more than thirty feet to its topmost point, with a crown that was dense and curiously flattened, producing an exaggerated effect of wide horizontal dimensions. Its branches, resplendent in new spring growth, spread in a broad graceful umbrella-shaped curve that created an inviting circle of deep shade beneath.

Beyond the tree, at the far edge of the little clearing, could be seen Julia's favourite retreat – though Darby did not share her affection for it – the silent ruins of the old squatter's cabin. It was a basic rectangular structure of thick pine logs, now half submerged in a profusion of weeds and wild bramble, moss-grown, and hoary with age.

Julia went to the chinaberry tree and stood with her back against the trunk, and gazed up into the foliage overhead. Darby came and stood next to her, and followed the direction of her eyes upward.

'It's like a umbrella,' he said.

'That's right,' Julia said. 'Some people call it the umbrella tree.'

They stood still and quiet, savouring the cozy feeling of safety in the shelter of the arching branches.

Darby said, 'Wish it would rain, so we could stand under this good ol' umbrella and keep dry.'

Julia laughed, and darted away, and ran to the squatter's cabin.

She stopped at the cabin doorway and waited for Darby, who started to follow, but stopped, and called to her in sudden alarm, 'Julia! What about the ha'nts?!'

Julia gave a saucy toss of the head, and disappeared into the cabin.

After a moment Darby approached cautiously, leaned forward and peered in through the doorway. 'Julia?'

No answer. He stepped up to the threshold and stuck his head into the dark interior and called again, his voice tremulous with anxiety. 'Julia, wheah are you?'

'Boo!' She materialized out of the darkness in a burst of bright yellow, and laughed as Darby yelped and leaped backward.

'You silly,' she said. 'There are no ha'nts. Come on in here.'

Darby shook his head and muttered ominously, 'You gon' be sorry. Ha'nts gon' git you one o' these days, you wait and see.' But he followed her, putting one foot tentatively across the threshold, then stepping inside.

The interior of the cabin was one large room, through which broad bands of sunlight slanted down through the holes in the roof, catching silvery glints from spider webs, and creating isolated patches of brightness on the hard-packed dirt floor.

Built into the wall opposite the door was a low rough-hewn wooden shelf that might have served the original inhabitants as a work surface or a sleeping place, but now served Julia as a bench. She sat very still and waited until Darby's eyes became accustomed to the gloom. As soon as he saw where she was she patted the bench beside her, indicating that he should come and sit there.

'Be quiet,' she whispered. 'Listen to the silence.'

The silence in the cabin was deep indeed, deeper than the silence of the meadow. They remained quiet for a few moments, Julia listening raptly, and Darby pretending to, and watching the girl in wonderment.

Presently he ventured to speak again, gently. 'Julia?'

'Yes?'

'I know you felt real bad about yo' grandpa. I wanted to tell you I was sorry.'

She looked at him with soft eyes. 'Thank you.'

Darby wanted to say more, to tell her how touched he had been by her grief at the burial, and how he had wanted so much to go to her and comfort her – he wanted to tell her, but he couldn't think how.

And presently he gave it up, and allowed his mind to drift back to a subject of more immediate and personal interest. He stole a glance at Julia. She seemed lost in reverie. He waited a bit, for what he judged to be a decent interval, then quietly edged a little closer to her.

'Julia? Can we do it now?'

She turned a vacant look on him. 'Do what, Darby?' she said perversely.

'*You* know. Gittin' me educated.'

'Oh. All right.' She folded her hands in her lap. 'You go first.'

'What?!'

'First I'll look at you, then you can look at –'

'No!'

'Darby, don't be quarrelsome. You must do as I say. You go first.'

He glared at her in what was as close to defiance as he could muster. 'Julia, *you* int'rested in educatin' *me*, *I* ain't int'rested in educatin' *you!*'

She cast her eyes wearily upward in resignation. 'Oh, all right. If you'll *just* stop saying *ain't* so much!' She looked at him sharply. 'Do you promise not to breathe a word to anybody? Not *anybody?*'

He placed his right hand over his heart and recited a sacred oath. 'Cross my heart, 'fo' God, and hope to die, double-die, triple-die!'

'You understand, Darby, this is *not* a game. It is for the very *serious* purpose of furthering your education.'

He nodded solemnly. 'I unduhstand, Julia. Education.'

She was satisfied. She stood up and turned her back to him, swept her long hair up in her arms and held it on the top of her head. 'You can unhook me, then.'

He was stunned by her casual tone. 'Do – what, Julia?'

'Unhook me. See those little hooks down the back of my dress?'

He got to his feet and bent forward, making an inspection. 'Oh – yeah.' He stood there, twisting his hands together, and staring at the back of her neck.

'Well, go on. Unhook them.'

He began to fumble with the hooks. 'I don't know how to do it,' he announced almost immediately.

'Start at the top, silly. It's much easier.'

He tried at the top. It was no easier. He snorted and grunted.

'Oh, good heavens, Darby!' She slapped his hands away. 'See, like this.' She reached behind her neck and undid several hooks. 'Now you finish it.'

He went back to the task with an intense frown of concentration. Beads of perspiration stood on his forehead, and his hands trembled.

She sensed his feelings, smiled to herself and said gently, 'Don't be nervous, Darby.'

Finally it was done. Without hesitation Julia pushed the dress down off her shoulders and slipped her lightweight petticoat down with it, and after a swift rustle of fabric stood clad in nothing but thin cotton panties. She draped her clothes carelessly on the wall bench, whisked off the panties and tossed them onto the other garments, and turned to face Darby in shining virginal nudity.

He took an uncertain step back, reached down and behind him to find the bench, and sat down, open-mouthed, his eyes mesmerized by the tender pink girlish flesh that he had so often tried to summon to his imagination – and now understood how woefully unequal to the task his imagination had been.

Julia smiled and stepped closer to him. Her face was serene. She let her arms float outward from her body, and stood still, for inspection.

Darby swallowed hard, and gripped the edge of the bench. He hadn't suspected he'd be so shaken by what was supposed to be a casual educational experience; it was alarming. He tried to take in everything quickly, fearing that the opportunity would be fleeting. It was an intoxicating feast, and he wished he could partake of it at his leisure, for hours. He forced his eyes to move constantly, trying to resist the temptation to linger long on vital areas – the delicate young breasts, with the rosy nipples growing in their centres like budding fruit; the soft downy sand-coloured cushion of the pubic area, so mysteriously, powerfully fascinating – for fear that Julia would be offended.

After several tours of the body his eyes finally met hers, and stopped there. He felt he should say something, to make some comment appropriate to the educational aspect – but he was speechless, his mind paralyzed.

'Well?' she said. 'What do you think?'

He nodded thoughtfully, gulped, wiped his brow on the sleeve of his shirt. At last the power of speech returned. 'You, uh – you don't have much hair. I got lots more'n you.' It sounded dumb; he squirmed with embarrassment.

'Really? Let's see.'

He stared up at her without moving, wishing he hadn't said it.

'Come on, let me see.'

'You'll laugh at me,' he mumbled.

'No, I won't. I promise.'

He compressed his lips and gripped the edge of the bench, and struggled with indecision.

'Come on, Darby. Don't be bashful.' Her voice was soft and coaxing.

He stood up and quickly slipped off his shirt. He loosened his trousers, paused for an instant to take a deep breath and gather fresh courage, and shoved his clothing down. Then he returned to a stiff straight posture, and stared unblinking at a point in infinite space.

Watching him, Julia had noticed the odd protrusion at the front of his pants – but before she had time to speculate on it the skinny black body was revealed, the rigid penis had been freed from all constraints, and seemed to leap from the lower edge of the boy's abdomen straight toward her.

She recoiled. A hand flew to her throat; she sucked in her breath and let it out slowly. 'Oh-h-h! Darby! It's so . . .'

He brought his eyes back from infinity and dared to look at her. 'What's the mattuh?'

'It's so – *big!* I mean – how do you carry it *around?!*'

He glared at her in sudden annoyance. 'It ain't *always* this big, Julia. Only when it's, when it's – jes' once in a while.'

'Oh.' She stared at him fixedly, making no effort to disguise the direction of her attention, as he had done. 'You're right,' she said at last, matter-of-factly. 'You *do* have more hair.'

Darby's brow was glowing with perspiration again, but he stood his ground bravely, and endured the frank appraisal. And then unexpectedly his confidence returned. He felt a surge of bravado, and a trace of vanity. He arched an eyebrow at the girl and said, 'You wanna touch it, Julia?'

She uttered a little gasp of astonishment and horror. 'Oh – no!'

'You welcome to,' he said offhandedly.

'No. No, thank you.' She began to lose her poise, to wilt, to try to hide her own body with her hands. She reached hastily for her panties.

Feeling vaguely victorious, Darby stood naked for a carefully calculated moment longer, then stooped and pulled up his pants. He went to the bench and sat down, near Julia, and watched her as she dressed.

'Julia? Could *I* touch *you?*' His eyes drifted down to her breasts and stopped. 'Jes' – theah?'

She paused in the act of pulling up her petticoat, and looked at him in alarm. 'Oh, *no*, Darby, you mustn't! I mean – it's not that I'd *mind*, but . . .' She sat down next to him, the petticoat bunched at her waist, her upper body still bare.

'You see – and this is very important for your education, so listen carefully – if a man touches a woman's breast she's liable to become uncontrollably excited. She might become wild with passion, maybe even swoon dead away in sheer ecstasy.'

Darby stared. 'In *what?* What's *that* mean?'

'Well, it means –' she searched for the right words – 'it's what happens when a man touches those certain places on a woman's body. Suddenly they can't control themselves, they become maddened – both of them. Sometimes they almost lose their minds. . . .' She shrugged helplessly. 'I just can't explain it exactly – but it's very dangerous. You have to be *terribly* careful.'

Darby was awe-struck. ''Fo' God, Julia, I wouldn't want anything like *that* to happen!'

'Of course you wouldn't.' She slipped her petticoat up in place and hastened to put on her dress, and stood again with her back to Darby. 'Hook me up, please.'

After they were completely dressed she faced him and looked into his eyes with a deeply solemn expression. 'You must put all this out of your mind, Darby, do you hear? Put it out of your mind *utterly*. Don't think about it again until you're at least twenty years old.'

'How long will that be, Julia?'

'About six years. I'll tell you when.'

He blinked, but nodded obediently. 'All right, Julia. I won't think about it ag'in till you tell me to.'

'Good.' She sat down on the wall bench and folded her hands primly in her lap. 'Come sit down, now, and let's talk about something more – respectable.'

He sat down next to her and gazed out through the doorway of the cabin to the bright sunny meadow, and worked mightily at the task of shifting his mental machinery to some other subject. Oddly, none seemed of much interest – but at length it was accomplished. He began to look around the gloomy interior of the old cabin, at its log walls and roof beams, all dark and dismal with the effects of age and exposure and abandonment, as massive and silent as the walls of a medieval dungeon.

'Julia, tell me 'bout the folks that built this place.'

Julia smiled. 'I've told you hundreds of times.'

'Tell me ag'in. I like to heah 'bout 'em.'

'Well, this cabin was built by a squatter family, a long, long time ago.'

'When? How long ago?'

'No one knows exactly. It was even before my grandpa came here, and that was forty years ago.'

'You mean Massa Milo?'

'No, not Grandpa Gates. Grandpa Douglas. When he bought this land he found the squatters living here.'

'What's squatters, Julia?'

She had expected this question next, and was ready with the answer.

'Squatters are people who roam through the wilderness until they see some land they like, then they just build a house and live there.'

'That sounds good,' Darby said. 'I'd like to be a squatter.'

'It's not good. Sometimes they work hard for years and years to make a home for themselves, then suddenly somebody comes along and tells them they have to move, 'cause they're trespassing. That's sad.'

Julia gazed around the old cabin, and tried to sense some faint lingering presence of its long departed inhabitants.

'Especially if your home is as nice as this.'

'What you talkin' 'bout?' said Darby scornfully. 'This place is cold and gloomy. Ain't no good for nobody – 'cept maybe ha'nts.'

Julia laughed gently. 'You're wrong, Darby. It's warm and friendly and cozy. I'd like to live here myself.'

She saw that the boy was staring at her in disbelief, and went on insistently, 'I would, I really would. I think it would be a lovely place to live.'

Darby got to his feet and walked away from her, muttering, 'Julia, sometimes I think you ain't right in the head!'

He went to a far corner of the room, where, on a smooth section of one of the wall logs, some carved letters, worn and weathered, could barely be seen. Julia watched him as he looked at the carvings, and ran his fingers over them curiously. He had done this many times before, and she waited, knowing that next he would ask her to explain the strange characters carved in the wood.

Their visits to the deserted cabin had become a formalized ritual over the years, and varied only in details, never in substance. Darby would always hang back at first, protesting, and predicting dire results from disturbing the 'ha'nts' that dwelled in the cabin. Later, feeling more at ease, he would examine the old carving on the wall with wonder that never diminished, and beg Julia to tell him about the mysterious people who had lived in this place, long ago.

He turned to her now, true to form, and asked earnestly, 'What's these letters, Julia?'

Julia came and stood beside him, and lightly ran her fingers over the inscription. 'They're Greek letters. The squatter family was Greek.'

'What's Greek, Julia? Some kind o' Indians?'

'No, silly. They're from a country called Greece, far across the sea.'

'What sea? The Miss'sippi?'

'No, the Atlantic Ocean. Goodness sakes, Darby, the Mississippi isn't a sea, it's a river.' She heaved a gentle sigh of exasperation. 'Honestly, you're so dumb, sometimes I think it's hopeless trying to educate you!'

He looked at her with genuine sympathy. 'Don't give up, Julia. Keep tryin'.'

Julia again examined the letters on the wall, admiring the meticulous workmanship of some unknown woodcarver.

'You know, Darby, Greece is an ancient country that had a wonderful civilization thousands of years ago, even before Jesus lived. Isn't that amazing?'

Darby frowned. 'If them Greeks got such a wonderful country, how come they comin' over heah foolin' 'round in *our* country?'

'They were immigrants, I guess. They had a perfect right to be here, same as anybody else.'

'What's –'

Julia anticipated the next question, and went on quickly. 'Immigrants are people who leave their native land, and come to seek new homes in this country.'

'Oh, yeah,' Darby said, nodding. 'My folks was immigrants from Africa, huh?'

'Well – no, not exactly.' Julia pondered how she was going

to explain the distinction. Then she caught sight of the sly gleam in Darby's eye, and saw that he was teasing.

Darby's keen, untrained mind was such a chaotic tangled mixture of ignorance, knowledge, naivete and wisdom, that it sometimes baffled Julia hopelessly.

'Darby, do you want to hear about this, or not?' she said crossly.

'Yes, ma'am, I sho' do.' He composed his features to reflect serious attentiveness.

'Well, then, tell me what this carving says.'

Darby raised his eyebrows and his voice, indignantly. 'Now, how in tarnation do *I* know what it says?! I ain't Greek!'

'I'm not Greek,' Julia corrected.

'Ain't neither one of us Greek.' The mischievous gleam danced in his eyes again.

'Come on, Darby,' the teacher coaxed her pupil. 'You know what it says. Tell me.'

Darby stared at the inscription and pondered mightily, to no avail. He shook his head. 'What it say, Julia?'

'It says: "God Bless This House." '

Darby frowned at her sceptically, then demanded, as he always did, 'How in the dickens do you know *that?*'

Julia was ready and eager for this question. 'My Uncle Andrew told me. He told us both, don't you remember?'

'Oh, yeah, I remember.' Darby smiled at this pleasant recollection. 'But how did *he* know? He ain't no Greek, neither.'

'Uncle Andrew has been all over the world,' Julia said proudly. 'He knows everything.'

Andrew Gates, Margaret Douglas's younger brother, was the only child besides Margaret of the brood at Maywood plantation that survived into adulthood. He had been a wild and dissolute young man who lived only for pleasure, the more reckless the better, and took no interest in the business of the plantation, thereby incurring very early the ready wrath of fiery-tempered Milo.

When his mother died suddenly Andrew was heartbroken. When Maywood collapsed in failure soon after, it caused not a trace of sorrow in the young man; plantation life was not for him anyway, he declared. He packed his satchel, announced his intention to become a sea captain, and set out for New Orleans, leaving his sister Margaret to cope with their difficult father alone, and salvage what she could from the bankrupt estate.

Andrew had not been heard from since, until one day – in the summer when Julia was nine years old – he had suddenly appeared at Chinaberry.

He was a big, strapping, handsome man in his middle thirties, his thick blond hair burnt and bleached by the sun and wind of three oceans and a dozen climes, and his speech inflected with the tongues of South America, India, and the lands of the Mediterranean. He wore the attire and demeanour of a seafaring man – not a captain, but a mate. The plantation blacks, heedless of such trivial distinctions, immediately dubbed him Cap'n Andrew.

When Margaret saw her dashing younger brother again she felt forgiveness welling up in her, and welcomed him warmly. Reeves was cordial, but distant, fascinated by but not quite approving of this rakish black sheep of the Gates family. Old Milo, recently launched in his voluntary exile in the upstairs room, refused to see his errant son at first, relented only after tearful pleadings from Margaret, then greeted Andrew curtly, and had nothing more to say.

Julia was enchanted beyond measure. Andrew swept his little niece off her feet in a great bear hug – and her heart was his.

And then – this was talked about in the slave quarters of Chinaberry as long as they were inhabited – Cap'n Andrew caught sight of Darby hovering nearby, was told that he belonged to Julia, approached the shy little black boy with a hearty smile and held out his hand, saying, in a booming voice, 'How d'you do, Darby?'

The boy stood frozen, staring, not knowing how to react.

'Shake!' said Andrew, and reached for Darby's hand and shook it vigorously. And another heart was his.

The next few days were pure heaven for the children. The world traveller took little interest in the staid polite society of his sister and brother-in-law and their friends, instead spent endless hours taking long rambling walks through the woods and along the river with Julia and Darby.

He was a born talker, and had an inexhaustible supply of salty yarns and incredible tales of narrow escapes from pirates, and desperate struggles against the terrible forces of nature at sea, all of which he delivered with vividly dramatic re-enactment, keeping his two young listeners wide-eyed, and their heads spinning. His speech was heavily spiced with exotic place-names and abstruse shipboard jargon; nautical terms flew from him like sparks from a grinding wheel, as he talked, and talked, and talked –

'We were rounding Cape Horn, beating to windward under close-reefed topsails,' he roared. 'The weather was fine – but suddenly a great blithering sou'wester rose like the end o' the world, and bore down upon us!' He gestured wildly, and his audience was gripped in breathlessness.

'We hove to on the starboard tack, sent down the royal yards, and unrove the gear! I threw the downhaul over the windlass, and jumped between the knight-heads out upon the bowsprit!'

'My gracious!' little Julia exclaimed. Darby was transfixed.

At night the children dreamed of stinging salt spray lashing a rolling deck, and great white sails embracing the ocean wind – next day they were ready for more.

Andrew allowed them to reveal to him what they imagined to be priceless secrets, their favourite haunts – the pool on Indian Hill, the great grapevine in the cottonwood tree, and the ultimate prize, the squatter's cabin. He dazzled them with his erudition by explaining that the strange inscription carved on the cabin wall was Greek – not only that, had translated it for them.

Abruptly his visit was over. His ship was due to leave from New Orleans in a few days, he said, bound for Brazil. He walked with his young friends one last time, to say goodbye. He shook hands with Darby again, kissed the tearful Julia, and told her he would come to fetch her one day, and take her on a voyage with him on his beautiful ship – it was a promise.

Then, with a hearty laugh and a wave, he was gone.

Julia and Darby stood in the old cabin now, gazing at the carvings, and thinking of that great golden-bronze man.

'Julia, d'you think Cap'n Andrew will come back sometime, and take you on his beautiful ship, like he said?' Darby asked.

'I don't know, Darby. I hope he will.'

'Hope he'll take me too,' Darby said, wistfully.

CHAPTER FIVE

Julia walked slowly around the rectangle of the cabin's interior.

'Lots of times I think about the people who lived here,' she said. 'Sometimes I wonder if it was right of Grandpa Douglas to make them leave, after they'd worked so hard to establish a home.'

She stared at the dirt floor as she walked around, frowning in thought.

'Once in a while I argue about it with Papa. He says Grandpa was absolutely right. It was not their land, Papa says, and it's a sin for people to work land that doesn't belong to them.'

She stopped before Darby and fixed him with a searching look. 'What do *you* think, Darby?'

The boy considered the matter carefully. 'Well – yo' papa's a smart man. I 'spect he's right. 'Course, 'cordin' to that, them darkies up yonder workin' yo' papa's fields be 'bout the sinfullest folks that ever lived.'

Julia's eyes opened wide in astonishment; the astonishment turned to delight, and she laughed. 'That's *right!* Wait till I use *that* argument on Papa!'

'Jes' don't tell 'im wheah you got it!'

Their unrestrained laughter degenerated quickly into giggles, and a mood was shattered and forgotten.

She poked a finger in his ribs again, bringing forth a yelp. 'Race you to the grapevine!' She flew out of the cabin.

Darby leaped after her, stopped at the doorway, and yelled, 'Ain't no use goin' theah, Julia!'

She paused in her flight and looked back, puzzled. 'Why not?'

'Ain't no grapes yet. It's only April!' There was scorn in his voice.

'Oh dear, I forgot!' She fumed at him. 'Why didn't you tell me before?'

He sauntered up to her, casual, smug and superior. 'Julia, you're so dumb, I figure it ain't no use tryin' to educate you.'

This provoked a fresh assault upon his ticklish rib cage, quickly reducing him to helpless gasps, as he tried to defend himself.

The sudden blast of a steamboat whistle rolled over them from a distance, and echoed through the forest. The scufflers were instantly frozen, listening.

'Mine!' yelled Darby. 'It's goin' up!'

'You're crazy, it's going down!' Julia streaked away, with Darby right at her heels.

The narrow path plunged through dense foliage as it wound toward the river, a hundred yards distant. The runners threaded their way at perilous speed, dodging low-hanging limbs and evading the clutches of prickly branches as they went. At a small bare area on the river bank they emerged from the woods, and looked frantically up and down the broad waterway. The whistle sounded again, from far across the river, near the west bank. Julia caught sight of the distant steamer, and jumped up and down in delight.

'It's downriver! It's mine, it's mine!' she shrieked, and clapped her hands. 'That's nineteen for me, and twenty for you. One more and I'll have you tied!'

'Tha's all right,' Darby grinned. 'One more and I'll have you beat.'

His confidence was empty posturing; secretly he knew that providence in its divine wisdom would contrive to send two more downriver steamboats in succession, rightfully bestowing upon Julia the winning total of twenty-one.

They waded in the shallow water along the river's edge, sat on a log and dug their bare feet in the mud, and improvised some competition out of the question of who could squeeze the largest globs of the heavy, sticky substance between their toes. Quite naturally Julia appointed herself judge of the contest, and soon declared herself the winner.

Tiring of that, they cast about for other fun-making ideas.

Julia said, 'I know. Hide your eyes and count to a hundred.'

Darby made a sour face. 'Aw, Julia, I don't wanna play that. I can't evuh find you.'

'I won't go very far,' she said. 'Just down the path a ways.' She backed away from him, and, poised for flight, commanded, 'Hide your eyes.'

Darby obeyed, and called out, 'Don't go pullin' no tricks!'

The trail they had used to reach the river made a sharp

right-angle turn at the bank, and meandered some distance through junglelike undergrowth at the edge of the water. Julia started to run down the path along the river, but turned and retraced her steps, and scampered noiselessly back up the trail in the direction they had come, toward the old cabin.

With his eyes shut tightly Darby chanted in a loud voice: 'Five, ten, 'leventeen, twenty, twenty-five, fo'ty, fo'ty-five, eighty, eighty-five, fifty, fifty-five, ninety, ninety-five, ninety-six, ninety-eight, ninety-nine, hunnerd! Comin', ready or not!'

He opened his eyes and looked around, then ran down the path along the river, guessing that Julia had gone that way. Immediately he found it necessary to slow down to a walk, and pick his way along carefully, for here the little-used path was more than ever densely overgrown, with ground foliage reaching upward and becoming entwined with tree branches from above.

Darby paused and looked around, calculating that in these difficult surroundings Julia would not have travelled far. His eyes roved from left to right, searching for a tiny flash of yellow somewhere, that would give her away. He walked on a little farther, stopped again, and this time stood quite still and listened, putting his ears to work to aid his eyes in the search. Except for the undercurrent of soft natural sounds, the chirping gossip of birds and the drone of insects, all was quiet.

Darby smiled as he thought of Julia saying, 'Listen to the silence.' She's a funny one, he thought, all the time talkin' 'bout crazy things like listenin' to silence. She's a funny –

He heard a sound. A small sound, muffled and insignificant, down to his right, from the direction of a huge tangled mass of vines and bushes at the edge of the river. He turned to face that way, and listened intently. As he was beginning to doubt that he had heard anything, he heard it again. It was too faint and indistinct to be identified, but definitely not a natural sound, and clearly coming from the interior of that large clump of vegetation.

He crept forward to the edge of the thick green mass, and sank to his hands and knees to penetrate it. Silently and with careful stealth he inched his way along, his vision blocked by leaves and small branches that brushed against his eyes. The going was torturous, and he wondered at Julia choosing such a difficult hiding place. It was strange. It was unlike her.

Suddenly a new thought flashed across his mind, and brought him to a stop.

Hector. The runaway was hiding somewhere – probably right here in the deep woods, the natural place for a runaway to go.

An enormous moral problem loomed. What do I do if I find Hector, he asked himself. Do I tell Massa Douglas? If I did, Massa Douglas would appreciate it, and like me. No. I couldn't do that. Angrily he rejected the idea.

But if I know where Hector is and don't tell, I'll be in terrible trouble myself. Maybe I jes' better go 'way, and leave him alone.

His mind was darkened and troubled – but then a light shone through, a solution presented itself.

I'll persuade Hector to come back on his own. That's it. If he don't, Mistuh Talbot's dogs'll find 'im anyway, and tear 'im to pieces.

Again he heard something – close by now, and distinct. A soft cough, deeply bass, decidedly male. It was Hector, all right. He knew it now.

He opened his mouth to speak, but the sound froze in his throat. The foliage ahead of him came alive with a quick flurry of agitation, branches were pulled back and parted, and Darby gasped and stared, trembling, into the bearded, grizzled face of a white man.

He struggled desperately to overcome the paralysis of fright, tensed his muscles, and prepared to leap to his feet and fly. But another surprise obliterated that impulse.

The man's broad face crinkled with a smile. He spoke, in a voice deep and gruff, but kindly. 'Don't be afraid, my boy. I won't hurt you.'

He held the branches back to make a passage for Darby. 'Comin' through?'

Darby drew back, silent and staring.

'I was just sittin' here wishing for a bit o' company,' the stranger said pleasantly. 'Glad to have you join me, if you like.'

He waited a moment and, receiving no response, said, 'Well, suit yourself.' He lowered the foliage back in place and disappeared.

Darby crouched, very still, wondering what to do. The man was evidently friendly, but frighteningly alien. There was something strange about his speech – broad and rustic it was, but oddly unlike the soft languid drawl of the white people Darby knew. The boy was torn between curiosity and fear.

Curiosity prevailed. He crept forward, cautiously parted the leaves and branches, and peered through. He saw a small clearing, no more than fifteen feet wide, enclosed on the landward side by the dense undergrowth, and bordered on the far side by the river. In the centre of the bare area the bearded man sat on the ground, his back propped against a log. His head was bent over some work he held in his hands – a complex task involving the lacing of a leather satchel with rawhide thong. Near him a skiff was pulled up and moored, halfway out of the water.

Darby gazed around, wide-eyed and wondering. He and Julia had roamed these woods for years – they had never seen this beautiful spot, nor suspected its existence.

The man glanced up, caught Darby's eyes staring in uneasy fascination, and smiled again.

'Never any rest,' he said, cheerily. 'Always some repair work to do.' He watched Darby closely. 'Wish you'd come and sit a spell. Sure would enjoy a little human company.'

He turned back to his work briefly, then looked up again and gazed at Darby. 'Or don't you know how to talk?'

Darby squirmed, feeling silly. He climbed out of the bushes and stood in the little clearing, and said, in a firm voice, 'Yes, suh. I know how to talk.'

'Good!' The man's voice boomed enthusiastically. 'Come sit down. Tell me about yourself. What's your name?'

Darby sat down on the log – not too close to the stranger – and kept himself poised for instant flight.

'Darby, suh. Darby's my name.'

'Darby. Good.' The man nodded, and went on with his work. 'You belong to somebody around here, Darby?'

'Yes, suh. I b'long to Miss Julia Douglas, at Chinaberry.'

'I see. Chinaberry's a big plantation, I hear. That right?'

'Yes, suh, sho' is.' There was unconscious pride in Darby's voice. 'This heah's Chinaberry land we're sittin' on.'

The stranger looked up, smiling. 'I know.'

He worked a few moments in silence, grunting as he pulled the rawhide lacing through holes in the leather satchel. Then he looked back at Darby.

'By the way, my name's Rutledge. Matthew Rutledge.' He held out his hand to the boy. 'I'm pleased to make your acquaintance, Darby.'

Darby was taken aback, but recovered quickly, and responded. 'How do, suh.'

They shook hands, and Darby felt a surge of manly pride. He recalled how he and Julia had just been talking about her Uncle Andrew a little while before – now, because of Cap'n Andrew, he was equal to the occasion when this stranger became the second white man in his life to offer him the courtesy of a handshake.

After another short silence, Rutledge said, 'You a runaway, Darby?'

The casual question startled the boy. 'No, suh! I ain't no runaway!' His answer was emphatic, and a trifle indignant.

'Ever thought of runnin' away?'

'No, suh. I wouldn't run away from Miss Julia. She's kind and good to me.'

The man paused in his work and looked closely at Darby. 'You mean you don't *mind* bein' a slave?'

'Well –' Darby frowned, hesitating. 'Yes, suh, I reckon I mind. But I been lucky, bein' Miss Julia's slave.'

'Yes. I suppose you have.' Rutledge continued to gaze at the boy, studying him.

'But, you know, lad, there are places out yonder where people like you don't have to live in slavery. They can be free, just like everybody else.'

'Up north, suh?'

'Yes, and out west, too. There's a lot happenin' out there, and a lot more goin' to happen in the comin' years. Big things. Excitin' things.'

Rutledge put his work aside, and turned to face the boy.

'For instance – I operate a tradin' post, way out on the western border o' Missouri, where the Santa Fe Trail starts, and the Oregon Trail. Ever heard of 'em?'

Darby shook his head.

'They're the routes for traders to Mexico, and emigrants bound for Oregon and California. We outfit expeditions, repair wagons, and provide packers and drivers – hired men, that is – for the wagon trains. We need good workers out there, and we pay 'em well. And we don't care what colour a man's skin is.'

Darby's eyes had lit up with recognition at the sound of one of the words he had just heard. 'Yes, suh, I know all about emigrants,' he said eagerly. 'But I don't know nothin' 'bout none o' them places –' He tested on his tongue one of the strange place-names Rutledge had used. 'Cali – Cali – fornia. That sounds like a good place.'

He tried it again. 'California.'

He leaned forward, with a thought, and asked, 'Suh, is that anywhere near Greece?'

Rutledge chuckled. 'I reckon not! It ain't anywhere near Mississippi, either.' He waved a hand westward. 'D'ya have any idea what's out there, lad?'

Darby lifted his eyes toward the far side of the river. 'Lots o' wild Indians, I reckon.'

'They *seem* wild, mostly because they're tryin' to protect what they've got. And you can't blame 'em. What they've got is millions o' square miles of beautiful virgin land. Prairies and plains, broad rivers, great mountain ranges with snow shinin' on top all year round, and canyons and valleys with clear rushin' streams, and best of all –' he scooped up a handful of dirt and sifted it through his fingers – 'best of all, fine, fertile soil, just achin' to be tilled.' The man's eyes shone with bright fervour as he gazed intently up at Darby.

'Riches, my boy. Riches beyond measure, far greater than men's foolish dreams o' gold and silver and such like. The greatest treasure of all is land. And it's out there, lad, just waitin' for settlers, for people like your Miss Julia, for people like me.' He tapped Darby lightly on the knee with a finger, and smiled. 'For people like you.'

Darby stared at the man.

Rutledge leaned forward, and said in a low, soft voice, 'Darby – would you like to go there with me?'

Darby continued to stare, without answering.

'It won't be easy, lad. You'll meet with bad men, and suffer hardships and peril. But you'll have freedom, and someday – you'll know it was worth it.'

In the distance, far up the path, the sound of Julia's voice, calling: 'Darby? Darby, where are you?'

Darby stood up. 'I got to go now, Mistuh Rut – Rut –'

'Rutledge.'

'I got to go now, suh. Tha's Miss Julia callin' me.'

'Want to go with me, Darby? Say the word, and we'll push my boat in the water right now, and be gone.'

Darby sat silent, mesmerized by the seductive words, by the man's clear handsome eyes and warm smile.

'Say the word, Darby.'

'I – I couldn't run away from Miss Julia, suh.'

Julia called again. Closer.

'Think it over, lad,' Rutledge said. 'I'll be here for a day or two. You'll know where to find me.'

'Yes, suh.' Darby started to turn away.

Rutledge grasped him by the wrist, and held him in an iron grip. His voice was low, and suddenly hard. 'Don't give me away, Darby.'

'No, suh. I won't.'

'Swear!' The pressure on Darby's wrist tightened.

'I sweah, suh. I sweah I won't!'

Julia's voice sounded again, from nearby. It was shrill, and edged with anxiety. 'Darby, where are you?!'

'Good luck, my boy,' Rutledge whispered. He released his grip on Darby's wrist, and the warm smile returned. 'I hope we meet again.'

Darby nodded mutely, turned and plunged into the brush, and fought his way back to the path, driven by a compelling urge to hurry to Julia.

She stopped and waited on the path when she saw him, with hands on hips, her worry turned instantly to anger.

'Darby, where have you been? You're not very funny!'

He stood before her shamefaced and apologetic. 'I jes' remembered,' he said. 'I was s'posed to be lookin' fo' you – and all the time I thought *you* was lookin' fo' *me!*' He put on his most foolish grin.

Julia glared at him. 'I'm surprised at you, Darby. Sometimes you act so idiotic!'

Darby hung his head. 'Reckon you're right about me bein' dumb, Julia,' he said meekly.

Then he brightened quickly. 'Want to go hide again, Julia? I'll find you this time, sho'.'

'No,' she said crossly. 'I don't want to play anymore. I want to go home now.'

She took him by the arm and pulled him along up the path.

CHAPTER SIX

They retrieved their empty and useless pails at the squatter's cabin, and walked back toward home in silence. Julia, in an ill-tempered mood, walked ahead rapidly. Darby trudged along behind, a troubled look on his face, eyes fixed on the ground.

I *am* dumb, he told himself. I should 'a' warned Mistuh Rutledge 'bout the dogs. They gon' turn Mistuh Talbot's dogs loose to hunt fo' Hector – Oh, Lord, I should 'a' warned 'im – *why* didn't I warn 'im?

A wild, exciting idea suddenly struck him with the impact of physical force. He stopped, and stood still.

I got to find Hector and take 'im to Mistuh Rutledge. Hector will be saved – Mistuh Rutledge will take 'im out west. But how'm I gon' find Hector? Wheah can I even start to look –

Julia called him. 'Darby, come on, stop your dawdling!' She was impatient and annoyed, and Darby hurried on.

They emerged from the woods and walked again past the rickety wooden gate of the Willard house, and were relieved to see that the little boy Gene was no longer there.

They went on to the sharp turn that pointed the road northward through the cultivated fields toward the big house, made the turn – and then Julia stopped abruptly. Darby came up beside her and looked at her, wondering.

'Something's wrong,' she said.

There was a shout in the distance ahead, then another – a man's voice, high-pitched in agitation. They saw Walt Elwood, the older of the two Elwood brothers, running toward the fields from the direction of the plantation barnyard. Overseer Willard was not in sight, but as Elwood came closer Willard's stallion bounded out onto the road from a side path that led along a line of bushy trees bordering a field. Willard reined his horse, and Elwood ran up to him, shouting something in an excited torrent that Julia and Darby could hear but could not understand. Willard snapped some brief reply to Elwood, and spurred his horse to a full gallop, away and up the road toward the barnyard area. Three or four blacks, members of the field gang, had come up on the road, but scattered as Willard's thundering horse bore down upon them. Elwood ran toward them, yelling harshly and waving a pistol, and they leaped cringing back into the field. By now a crowd of blacks had gathered at the roadside, craning their necks and chattering in curiosity. Elwood turned and glared at them, brandished his weapon, and shouted, 'Now git, you bastards! Git on back to work, damn it, 'fo' I plug two or three of ya!'

The hands quickly dispersed and spread out again over the fields, and Walt Elwood stuck the gun in his belt and walked slowly along the roadway, hands on hips and scowling ferociously, playing the role of overseer with relish.

Julia walked rapidly toward Elwood. Darby trailed after her, hanging back and struggling with a vague welling-up of fear, and called to her, 'Wait, Julia, be careful!'

She paid no attention, but hurried on, and Darby followed at a distance.

When Walt Elwood noticed Julia approaching, the scowl on his flabby face immediately disappeared, and was replaced by a broad grin. He nodded to her, and drawled pleasantly, 'Mornin' to ya, Miss Julia.'

Elwood was about twenty-five, two or three years older than his brother Frank, but his short stocky build was already spreading in the middle, producing a decided waddle in his walk, and making him seem middle-aged.

'What's happening here, Mr. Elwood?' Julia asked, trying not to seem anxious.

'Aw, nothin' much to speak of, ma'am. My brother Frank done found that ol' runaway little while ago, danged if he didn't! Mistuh Willard's gone to take care o' things, since yo' pa's away. He done lef' me in charge o' the hands.'

Elwood quickly scanned the fields with his fierce scowl, demonstrating his competence at wielding the authority of the overseer.

'You – you mean Hector?' Julia's voice quivered. 'Where was he found?'

'Yes'm, Hector. My brother Frank, he done found 'im up in the rafters in the barn. Can you beat that? Way up in the danged ol' rafters, right under the roof!'

Elwood shook with giggles as he slapped his thigh in appreciation of this amusing tidbit.

'Dad-blame, wouldn't you know it?' he went on. 'Jes' soon's yo' pa sent fo' Mistuh Talbot's dogs, the ol' coon turns up right smack in the barnyard! Can you beat that?!'

He scowled briefly at the field hands again, then turned back to Julia, resuming his amiable manner.

'I tell you one thing, Miss, I knowed it all the time – if they's a dang soul can find a runaway, it's my brother Frank. I sweah to goodness, if he ain't the smartest, sharpest-eyed son-of-a-gun you evuh –'

'Excuse me, Mr. Elwood.' Julia flew toward the barnyard. Darby was at her heels instantly, appearing out of nowhere.

Elwood scratched his head in befuddlement as he watched them go.

It was three hundred yards, and this run was not for fun.

Julia arrived at the heavy planked gate of the barnyard and almost fell against it, clinging, and gasping in exhaustion, with Darby right behind her, whispering, 'Easy, Julia, easy!'

They found the gate fastened shut with a knotted rope. The barnyard appeared to be deserted. Julia struggled with the rope, trying to loosen it, then Darby took it from her.

From inside the barn a sharp sound reached them, distinct and unmistakable – the searing impact of a lash across bare flesh.

Darby's stricken eyes met Julia's. 'Don't go in theah!' he hissed.

'I must, *I must!*' she said fiercely.

The rending sound came again, and they both flinched. Darby got the rope loose and pulled the gate open, and Julia ran toward the barn. Darby stayed where he was, and crouched low, and looked about with a wild irrational fear. He felt that he, too, was a fugitive.

Willard had laid on the lash for the third time, and was drawing back for the next stroke when Julia flung open the barn door and rushed into the dark interior of the barn. She regained her composure with an intense effort of will. When she spoke her voice was firm, controlled, and ice-cold.

'Put down the whip, Mr. Willard.'

The overseer paused, his arm upraised.

Frank Elwood was standing next to Willard, with a pistol

in his hand. He gaped at the girl in open-mouthed astonishment.

Hector stood in the centre of the hay-strewn barn floor. He was stripped to the waist. His back, which was turned toward his assailant, was crossed with three bloody-wet and glistening streaks from the lashes. He was not bound, nor physically restrained in any way. He stood with head lowered, gaunt, haggard, silent and resigned, accepting his fate without protest or resistance.

Willard stood as he was for a long moment, eyeing Julia with narrowed eyes. Then he lowered his arm, and the whip trailed limply on the floor.

Julia stepped toward the overseer, her eyes unnaturally bright and flashing with fury. 'Mr. Willard, my father does not permit the whip. You know it very well.'

Frank Elwood said, timidly, 'Miss Julia, ma'am, you shouldn't be in –'

'Be quiet!' she snapped. Her eyes remained fixed on the older man.

Willard adopted a mild, casual tone. 'Well, now, Miss Julia, I jes' nevuh have understood exactly how yo' pa expects me to maintain any discipline –'

'He expects you to employ humane methods, not brutality.'

Willard could not resist a smirk of amusement at this. It fed Julia's anger.

'He also expects you to have sufficient intelligence to distinguish between field hands, who are your responsibility, and house servants, who are not. You have no right to administer any punishment whatsoever to this man, Mr. Willard, and you will be punished for it yourself!'

The overseer stared at her, as if uncertain how to react. Something about the fiery intensity of the girl wiped away his amusement. Slowly he pulled his whip up into neat coils.

'Take 'im away, Frank.' He addressed his assistant. 'Lock 'im up in the back room of the gin house.'

'Yes, suh.' Elwood put away his gun and stepped to the prisoner's side, grasped him by the arm and started to lead him away.

'And then, Mr. Elwood,' Julia commanded, 'you go to the kitchen house and tell Josie that Hector needs food and water and bandages for his injuries, and you see to it that she has access to him.'

Elwood glanced at Willard, seeking guidance. He got none. He nodded meekly to Julia. 'Yes, ma'am.'

He pulled at Hector, and the old slave stumbled out with his jailer. The prisoner's head remained slumped on his chest. He had not once raised his eyes.

For a moment Julia and Willard looked at each other in silence, and the space between them crackled with hostility. Then Julia turned abruptly and walked out of the barn. Willard followed her slowly.

When she reached the road Darby emerged from behind the fence and fell in step beside her. They walked rapidly away toward the house.

Willard came to the gate and stood there watching them, his face dark with rising anger at the realization that the girl had humiliated him in front of young Elwood – and in front of a slave.

His courage returned. He yelled after her, 'It'd be a heap bettuh, Miss, if you'd stay in yo' pa's house and tend to yo' mannuhs, 'stead o' traipsin' around with a nigger boy in the woods all day, like a tramp!'

Julia walked on, taking no outward notice of this, but her cheeks burned with anger. Darby kept close to her, his eyes fastened on the ground.

By the time Julia reached the rear yard of the plantation house she was raging inside. She headed for the house, muttering under her breath. 'Just wait till Papa hears about this!'

Darby had slackened his pace, and was lagging behind. He stopped at the yard gate and called to her. 'Julia?'

She turned to him with impatience.

'Don't tell yo' papa.'

'Why not?!' she demanded hotly.

'I – Mistuh Willard might – git us in trouble.'

Julia snorted contempt. 'I certainly *will* tell Papa! You think I'd let that horrid man get away with *that?!*'

'Yo' papa ain't home, anyway,' Darby said. 'I heard 'im say he was goin' to town.'

'I know that, but just as soon as he comes home –'

'Julia – I been thinkin'.' Darby took a few steps toward her. His face was so grim and sombre that Julia walked back to meet him, and looked at him in concern.

'If I evuh had to work fo' Mistuh Willard, I'd run away myself, I sho' would.'

Julia smiled. 'Oh, Darby, you'll never have to worry about anything like that –'

'And if I ran away, I wouldn't hide in no dumb barn, no ma'am! I'd run far, far away, where nobody could evuh find me. I'd run to some place like – someplace like –' he delivered the name carefully, to be sure he got it right – 'California.'

Julia came closer to him, and looked probingly into his eyes. It was not a customary experience for her to be mystified by this boy. It was unsettling.

'Darby, what's gotten into you?' she asked gently. 'What in the world do *you* know about – California?'

He turned partially away from her, and gazed off across the plantation grounds.

'I heard some folks talkin' one time. I heard 'em say theah ain't no slavery out in the west. They say every man is free out theah.'

He glanced at her quickly, then looked away again. 'Maybe I'd like to go theah someday.'

She laid her hand on his arm, pulled him around to face her, and fixed him with intense, solemn eyes.

'Darby, listen to me. I'm making you a promise. You don't have to run away to find your freedom. When I'm grown up and mistress of Chinaberry, I'm going to set you free. I've already decided that.'

Darby looked down at his feet, stolidly, without response. Then he raised his eyes to her and said softly, 'Cross yo' heart?'

'Cross my heart,' she said.

And to fix the moment in both their memories, to record her promise indelibly and seal it, she put her arms around his neck and held him in a close embrace.

On his way back from his conversation with Willard and Henry Talbot at the barnyard that morning, Reeves had stopped at the stable and instructed the attendant there to have one of the boys saddle his horse, Mollie, and bring her around to the front of the house.

Mollie wasn't shod, the attendant told him. Would Massa take another horse this time?

Douglas swore. Horseback riding was not one of his favourite occupations – but on his fine young sorrel mare Mollie it was at least endurable. She was lively and spirited, yet gentle, and as responsive to the touch as an amorous girl – just the right combination of qualities. They got along well together, he and Mollie.

'That horse should have been shod early this morning,' the master growled at the cowering attendant. 'What do you do around heah, sleep all day?!'

Grumbling, he agreed to accept another horse, and continued on to the house.

In a little while a horse was brought, and Douglas came out, mounted, and rode away, heading down the road that led east from the plantation toward the town of Hanesville, seven miles away. After travelling a mile or so he reined to a halt, and grimaced with irritation.

The horse wasn't right. Reeves knew he could face a fourteen-mile round trip only on Mollie, no other mount.

And another thing troubled him – I'd better be on hand when Talbot brings the dogs, he thought. I'm not absolutely sure Willard will handle the situation properly. The business in town was routine; it could wait until another day.

He pulled the horse around and returned home.

The rest of the morning he spent in his study, leafing through his books, and fretfully contemplating the relentless stream of problems that seemed to plague him without cease. Around noon he walked downstairs and out to the front veranda to have a breath of fresh air. The place was quiet; Margaret had gone to spend a day or two visiting at a neighbouring plantation, and had taken her maid Sullah and several other household servants with her.

Reeves strolled along the front veranda to the corner of the house, and stood by the railing there, leaning against a post and gazing out over his dominion. He was a man much envied by his peers, he reflected. A magnificent estate, a gracious wife, and a lovely daughter – though he regretted not having more progeny, to be sure; Margaret had nearly died at Julia's birth, and could bear no more children – all in all, he was bountifully blessed, undeniably.

And yet it seemed to him he should be more pitied than envied. The management of the plantation was an endless burden. The gracious wife was gracious only in public – privately she was dour and complaining, constantly and unmercifully gnawing at him over trifles. Thank God, he thought, I can occasionally retreat unto the comforting balm of Josie's fine yielding body.

And Julia –

He caught sight of his daughter at that moment, walking rapidly up the little road from the rear fields toward the house, her black boy, everlastingly present, tagging along behind her. Reeves sat down partially, one leg up on the banister railing, and watched Julia as she started into the rear yard area, stopped, and went back a few steps and stood there engaged in some sort of earnest conversation with the boy – what's his name? – Darby. He shook his head in quiet wonderment. What in *God's name* does an intelligent girl like Julia find to be forever conversing with an ignorant slave boy about?

Still another tiresome problem suddenly intruded: Margaret is after me to take that boy away from Julia, and I know she won't give me a minute's peace until it's done. Too bad. I know Julia's behaviour is exasperating at times, but I hate to make her unhappy. She's really not guilty of anything worse than childish foolishness – still, Margaret's probably right. In practical matters, she usually is.

He heaved a sigh of immense weariness. Problems, problems, never-ending. Even Julia has to be a problem, in her own sweet, stubborn way. Seems to me everywhere I turn there's another –

Suddenly he slipped off the railing and stood stiffly, staring, his thoughts and muscles paralyzed by what he saw. He squinted, looked harder, and concentrated his entire will on fixing the image clearly. His mind searched for an explanation: was it a trick? – an optical illusion of some sort, a peculiarity of light refraction? – was he the victim of hallucination?

None of these, he told himself. What you are seeing is clear enough. Your daughter and that boy Darby are embracing.

Reeves felt himself trembling. Swiftly he turned and went back into the house.

When Julia came in a few minutes later he was waiting for her.

'Oh, Papa!' She rushed toward him, eagerly. 'I'm glad you're here. I thought you'd gone to –'

Her voice trailed off, as she looked more closely at her father. Suddenly she felt a chill of mysterious apprehension.

'Go to your room,' he said grimly. 'Do not come out until you've been told. Your dinner will be brought to you.'

Julia opened her mouth to protest, but her father's terrible look stifled the words in her throat.

Silently she retreated from him, shaking her head, turned and went upstairs to her room.

CHAPTER SEVEN

Late in the afternoon Henry Talbot arrived with his dogs. The large flat-bed wagon on which their cage was mounted creaked and rattled as he drove it into the Chinaberry grounds, past the main house and down the little road toward the barnyard. Its cargo, six great hulking brutes with massive jaws and deep-set, yellowish eyes, lay quietly, lulled by the movement of the vehicle.

A pair of tired old mules pulled the wagon with listless indifference, Talbot maintaining motion only through constant vocal agitation and loud slaps with a short whip. The man's saddle horse followed along behind, its bridle secured to the rear of the wagon.

After he had gone past the house and had progressed fifty yards down the road toward the barn, Talbot heard his name being called from the direction of the house, and pulled the mules to a halt. He turned to see overseer Willard hurrying to overtake him. Several of the dogs, disturbed by the cessation of the wagon's motion, got to their feet, yawned, and stared at the man approaching. Willard gave the cage a wide clearance as he walked past it.

'How do, Mistuh Willard,' Talbot said. 'Got the dogs heah, y'see.'

'Won't need 'em,' said Willard curtly. 'Runaway's been found.'

Talbot slumped in the wagon seat, his hairy face darkened with disappointment.

'Well, damnation, if that don't beat all!' he mumbled. 'When'd you ketch 'im? Wheah was he?'

Willard ignored the questions. 'I jes' been talkin' to Mistuh Douglas,' he said. He reached in his pocket and brought out some folded money. 'He says fo' me to give you this.' He handed the money to the man in the wagon. 'It's six dolluhs,' he said. 'Half price.'

Talbot took the money without thanks and stuffed it into a shirt pocket, and drawled, 'Well, now – they's jes' one little problem.'

'What's that?' snapped Willard, impatient to be done with it.

'I figured on goin' into Hanesville this evenin'. I can't git mah dogs home now, it's too late. Can I leave 'em heah? Pick 'em up in the mornin'?'

Willard shot a worried look at the caged animals.

'They's already fed,' said Talbot. 'They'll jes' sleep in the cage. Be no trouble at all.'

'Well – all right,' Willard said. 'Park the wagon 'round back o' the barn. I'll have one o' the boys put yo' mules up.'

Talbot tipped his battered hat and grinned. 'Much obliged to ye.'

He gave his reluctant mules a slap with his whip and yelled, 'Giddyap!' With grating protest the wagon creaked into motion.

Reeves dined alone that evening. He was sombre and withdrawn, and did not raise his eyes from his plate throughout the meal. Usually the master of the house amused himself at table by engaging in genial bantering conversation with Moses as the butler went about his serving duties, but tonight a heavy silence filled the dining room.

Moses did his work quietly and efficiently. He guessed that his master's uncommunicative mood was due to the struggle going on in the man's conscience over the question of what to do with Hector, at that moment lying in captivity in the darkness of the gin house.

His guess was far off the mark.

Reeves ate lightly and without appetite, rose abruptly after finishing, and spoke for the first time.

'Moses, I have work to do in my study tonight. I do not wish to be disturbed.'

'Yes, suh,' said Moses, and began to clear away the dishes.

'Except that I'm expecting Mr. Willard at eight o'clock. Show him in when he comes.'

'Yes, suh.'

Reeves paused at the doorway, turned and delivered one more instruction.

'And just before that, about ten minutes until eight – I want you to bring the boy Darby to my study.'

He waited for the usual automatic response. Moses stared at him without answering.

'Do you heah me, Moses?'

'Yes, suh.'

Reeves left the room, and the butler stood gazing after him.

At ten minutes before eight Moses slowly climbed the stairs, with Darby at his side. At the top they turned and faced the great carved door of the master's study, at the front of the upper hallway.

Darby gazed at the awesome door, his mind numb with fear, his heart pounding.

'I don't know what it means,' Moses said, softly. 'I jes' don't *know* what it means.' He took Darby by the elbow and moved him gently forward.

Darby looked hard at the door to Julia's room, across the hall. He tried to pierce the closed and silent barrier with his thoughts, to reach the girl hidden behind it.

Where are you, Julia? Come out, I need you.

Reeves looked up from his desk and called, 'Come in,' in answer to the soft knock. The great oaken door opened, and Moses said, 'I brought Darby, suh.' Darby stepped timidly across the threshold. Moses laid his hand for an instant on the boy's shoulder, in a silent message of comfort and encouragement, went out and closed the door behind him.

For a moment – for what seemed like an age to Darby – the master gazed at him in silence. Then, with a gentleness of voice that surprised the boy, Douglas said, 'Come heah, Darby,' and motioned to the area immediately before the desk. Darby stepped forward, stood rigidly still, and stared straight ahead.

Douglas continued to look him up and down, observing every detail. He leaned forward and spoke again.

'Let's see – how old would you be now, Darby?'

Darby tried to recollect that which he had never known. 'I – I don't rightly know, suh. I 'spect I'm 'bout –' he started to say ''bout the same age as Miss Julia' – but something whispered in his mind that it would be better not to mention her.

'I jes' – don't rightly know, suh.'

'About fourteen, I'd say,' Douglas mused. 'As I recall, you're about the same age as Julia.'

Darby blinked. 'Yes, suh – I reckon so, suh.'

Douglas went on with his close scrutiny of the boy, and seemed pleased by what he saw. 'You've certainly grown up well, I must say. Straight and strong. That's good.'

He leaned back in his chair, and took on a relaxed and chatty air.

'Tell me, Darby – I'm afraid I haven't been watching your development very closely – have you been keeping busy around heah?'

'Oh, yes, suh.' Darby's answer was quick. 'I help Moses 'round the house. An' I help Josie in the kitchen lots o' times. An' I help –' He hesitated.

'Yes?'

'I help Miss Julia.'

'You help Miss Julia. I wasn't aware that Miss Julia did anything that required assistance. What do you help her with?'

'I, uh – I run errands fo' her, suh.'

Douglas rubbed his chin thoughtfully as he gazed at Darby.

'Seems to me that's hardly enough to keep you employed. A big strong boy like you. Almost a man.'

His eyes narrowed suddenly as he leaned forward and looked at Darby with a closer intensity.

'Tell me something, Darby. Have you evuh been with a woman?'

Darby stared. 'Suh?'

'A woman. Have you evuh lain with a woman?'

Darby's mind groped for an appropriate answer. What does he want, he thought – what does he *want* me to say?

Douglas smiled disarmingly. 'You know what I mean,' he said. 'After one of those Saturday night fiddling and dancing sessions in the quarters, when everyone's hot and sweating and feeling good – haven't you evuh slipped away in the darkness with one o' the females?'

Darby stammered, searching for a way out of the question. 'I, uh – I – don't go 'round the quarters much, suh. Miss Julia don't like fo' me to 'sociate with –' It was the wrong answer, he suddenly knew. He bit his lip and choked off the words.

The master's smile vanished. 'No, of course not,' he said dryly. 'Julia wouldn't approve of that, naturally. If I'm not mistaken, it's been Julia's intention to make you into a gentleman.' He laughed softly.

Beads of perspiration stood out on Darby's forehead.

'Well then, tell me this, Darby –' Douglas got up and walked leisurely around the desk, and stood over the boy. 'Have you evuh felt – desire? Let me put it this way – have you evuh felt desire for a *white* female?'

Darby stiffened with shock. But this time he had no trouble knowing the correct response.

'No, suh, no, suh! I nevuh had no idea like that, suh, 'fo' God –'

'Good! See to it that no such thoughts evuh enter yo' mind.'

Douglas placed heavy hands on Darby's shoulders, held him firmly, and leaned down toward him, fierce eyes boring into the boy's.

'For the union of white flesh and black flesh is a ghastly sin. It is blasphemy, it is outrage against the sacred laws of God, and so hideous in His eyes, that He will hurl down thunderbolts of wrath upon those who are guilty, and damn theah miserable souls to the fires of Hell forevuh!'

His voice climbed from husky depths to a peak of shrill impassioned intensity. 'Do you understand me, boy?!'

Darby quivered and trembled, helpless in the man's grasp. 'Y-yes, suh. I understand, suh.'

Douglas withdrew his hands abruptly. He walked back behind his desk and sat down, his manner again cool and casual.

'Believe me, boy, I speak to you for your own good.'

'Yes, suh,' Darby said weakly.

There was a knock at the door. Douglas called, 'Come in.'

Moses opened the door and started to speak, but Horace Willard strode into the room without waiting to be announced.

'That will do, Moses,' said Douglas. The butler stole a quick searching look at Darby before he closed the door.

Willard stood in the centre of the room and waited. He glanced around, his eyes passing over Darby, pausing in surprise, and narrowing in shrewd private conjecture as to the possible meaning of the boy's presence there. Darby stared at one corner of the master's big mahogany desk, and kept his eyes fixed on that point.

Douglas chose to keep the overseer waiting. Aimlessly he studied some papers on his desk, and appeared to be deep in thought. At length he glanced toward Darby again.

'I'll have more to say to you in a few minutes, Darby. Wait outside the door. Don't move until I come out.'

'Yes, suh.' Darby turned and went quietly out, and closed the door behind him.

In the silent and deserted upper hallway he stood for a moment as if in a trance. Then he sank down to the floor with his back against the wall, clasped his hands around his knees and sat there, staring vacantly into the gloom, unable to think.

Willard stood before the desk and glared down at his employer, lips set tight, ready for another one of their frequent verbal duels. Impulsively he decided to take the initiative.

'I s'pose Miss Julia's been tellin' tales on me,' he said. 'Prob'ly complainin' that I used the whip on Hector.'

Douglas fixed a cold look on the overseer.

'Julia's been in seclusion since early this afternoon. I have not talked with her. I *have* been out to the gin house to take a look at Hector, and I don't need to be *told* you used the whip, I could see that for myself.'

Willard laughed, and the laugh dripped scorn. 'I stroked 'im lightly, two or three times. Didn't even git warmed up.'

'You know my rules on that, Willard. I don't like it, and I won't have it.'

'But you like the good crop yield you been gittin' the past few yeahs, don't you, Mistuh Douglas? You like Chinaberry bein' the best damn plantation in three or fo' counties – you like that, don't you?' A cool insolent smile played around Willard's mouth.

'That is beside the point, suh.'

'Beside the point, suh?!' Willard leaned over the desk, growling.

'You reckon them black bastards work and sweat out theah in the fields 'cause they *love* you, Mistuh Douglas? I got to tell you somethin', suh – them black devils don't love you, not one little bit. They serve you 'cause they're driven to it. And theah ain't but one thing in the world can drive 'em, one thing only. Feah. Nothin' else will do it!'

Douglas leaned forward in turn, his jaw set in anger.

'In the first place, Willard, if extraordinary discipline is required for a hand, it will be administered only on my specific authority. It is not for you to take upon yourself.'

Willard opened his mouth to reply, but Douglas hastened on.

'And in the second place, suh, if I may have the audacity to point it out, Hector is not one of yo'r hands –'

Willard exploded with exasperation. 'Good God, man, if you don't even believe *runaways* ought to be punished, how in hell –'

'It is not yo'r responsibility, Willard. When I want you to take on additional authority I'll let you know. Meanwhile you stick to yo'r job, which is managing the field hands. And you do it, suh, without the whip.'

Willard snorted, and looked away.

Douglas got up and walked a few paces, hands clasped behind his back, then retraced his steps.

'But that's not what I wanted to talk to you about tonight,' he said, and his manner was calm again.

'You know, you've often complained that I keep the choice Nigras for the household, and send you the inferior ones. And, I must admit, as a rule I've done that. But now I'm goin' to make an exception.'

Douglas continued to pace, eyes on the floor, as he talked.

'I have in mind the boy Darby,' he said. 'As you may have noticed, he's strong, straight and healthy, a fine young specimen. Bright, too, one o' the brightest Nigras we have. But he's goin' to waste heah in the house. And it's a shame to waste good manpower, I'm sure you agree.'

Douglas stopped in front of Willard and looked directly at him. 'Therefore, I'm turning him ovuh to you. I assume you can use him?'

Willard stared at his employer, dumbfounded. 'You mean –' he gestured toward the door. 'Miss Julia's boy, theah?'

'We're making some changes,' Douglas said crisply. 'He is no longer Miss Julia's boy.'

A slow smile crept over Willard's face. 'In that case, suh, I can use 'im. I sho' can.'

'That boy's training has been sadly neglected,' Douglas said. 'I want him to learn the meaning of discipline.'

Willard nodded solemnly.

'But I warn you, Willard,' Douglas snapped. 'No whip. Just firm discipline.'

Willard nodded again, and his smile returned. 'Yes, suh, I understand perfectly. Just firm discipline.'

For one of the few times in his years of service at

Chinaberry, Horace Willard addressed his employer with something akin to respect.

Darby sat huddled and motionless on the floor, his back against the wall, his head bowed and resting on his arms. Occasionally he raised his eyes and stared through the murky gloom of the upper hallway toward Julia's room. He wanted to run to her door and pound on it, and tell her that in some strange and terrifying way he was being threatened. She would do something, surely she would help him somehow –

But he dared not move.

The massive door of the master's study opened, and Douglas and overseer Willard came out. Douglas carried a lamp, and held it high as he and Willard stood and regarded the boy at their feet. Darby peered up at the two men, looming tall as gods above him. Desperately he searched their faces.

Douglas spoke quietly. 'Darby, it seems to me we haven't done right by you. We've prevented you from reaching your full development, keeping you around the house, and under the thumb of a girl. So I'm transferring you to the field hands. The healthy outdoor work will do you good, make a man of you.'

Douglas smiled – his patented, pleasant, genial smile.

'You go along with Mr. Willard, heah. He'll acquaint you with yo'r duties. You work hard and be obedient, and you'll find –'

A door slammed with a startling slap of sound in the hallway behind them. The men turned quickly, and Douglas extended his lamp in that direction. Julia appeared in its circle of light.

She was inhumanly pale, as fragile as a floating spectre in her nightgown, and staring with wild eyes at her father.

'Papa!' The word was breathed, but carried the penetrating intensity of a screech.

'Julia, I ordered you to remain in yo'r room –'

'Papa, what are you *doing?!*'

Now he advanced upon her, and the hard core of ruthlessness that lay beneath his geniality came rushing to the surface.

'Damn you!' He hurled the curse at Julia – but inwardly he cursed himself. His shallow, orderly mind recognized no justification for a dramatic crisis here, perceived no pathos; he saw only an appalling erosion of filial obedience, caused, no doubt, by years of neglectful permissiveness on his part. He felt he had to restore paternal authority now, immediately, or suffer the unthinkable – humiliation in the haughty eyes of Horace Willard.

'Get back in yo'r room!' he roared. With his free hand he lunged wildly at his daughter, and she gasped and retreated, cowering. Douglas strode rapidly after her, paused at her door, and turned to Willard. 'Go,' he snapped. 'Take the boy with you.'

He went into Julia's room and closed the door.

Darby remained huddled motionless on the floor. He felt the cold eyes of the overseer on him; he looked up. In the dim light the man's face was blotched with dark shadows, seemed twisted, distorted, diabolical. Darby shuddered.

'On yo' feet, boy,' Willard said quietly.

Moses stood halfway up the stairs, with a lamp in his hand. His broad expressive face was slack-jawed, his eyes glazed with anguish. Incredulously he listened to the heavy sound of Willard's boots as the overseer came stomping past him down the stairs, gripping Darby by the arm and pulling him along. Moses did not turn to follow them with his eyes, but heard the front door open as they went out, and the door slam again with a shuddering thud.

In the quiet that followed he became aware of the low growling tones of the master's angry voice in Julia's room. The sound was muffled through the closed door, and hard to understand. Moses listened intently, straining his ears to the utmost; for the first and only time in his life, he eavesdropped.

'It's not fair! Darby's mine, you *gave* him to me!' Julia cried out, her voice shrill and tremulous in a sudden outburst.

'I made a mistake, Julia. A tragic mistake. And now it must be corrected.'

'No, no! It's not fair!' The girl's voice rose toward hysteria, and her father's became correspondingly more stern.

'Be silent, Julia, I command it! You may choose a new personal servant from among the Nigras tomorrow – a *maid*.'

'I won't! I don't want a stupid old –'

'That is final, Julia. Now be silent!'

'No, no, no!' Julia screamed. 'I *hate* you!'

The sound of a slap – and Moses winced. Then there was nothing but the girl's soft, half-stifled sobs.

Moses looked blankly at his hand, the hand that held the lamp. His knuckles ached intensely from his iron-hard locked grip on the lamp handle. With an effort of will he relaxed his fingers slightly, turned and went slowly down the stairs. He paused at the bottom and listened again – to the sound of Julia's door opening and closing, and footsteps retreating to the rear of the upstairs hallway, and the soft opening and closing of the master's bedroom door. Then all was still and quiet.

With bowed head Moses made his way to his own little room under the stairs. He set the lamp on a small table and sat down on his bed, and gazed with dull and heavy eyes at the narrow bunk that had been Darby's, against the opposite wall.

He remained that way for a long time.

CHAPTER EIGHT

The man and boy walked in the darkness and in silence until they reached the circle of light from a lantern that Willard had left hanging at the barnyard gate. The overseer opened the gate, pushed the boy through, and closed the gate behind them. He glanced at Darby; his expert appraisal told him that the boy was docile, too immobilized with shock to make an effort to escape or resist.

He said, 'This way,' and took the lantern and moved off across the barnyard, and Darby followed obediently.

Willard led the way around the huge barn to the back, rounded the corner, and approached the big wagon cage that contained the animals that were Henry Talbot's livelihood. He hung the lantern on the end of the wagon chassis, and turned to Darby.

When he saw the dogs Darby stopped in his tracks, and stood still, staring.

'Come ovuh heah, boy,' Willard said to him. 'I want you to take a good look at these hounds. They're mighty interestin'.' His tone, like Douglas's had been a little while before, was surprisingly pleasant. He almost smiled.

Darby remained where he was. Willard went to him and took him by the shoulder, not roughly, and pulled him toward the wagon.

'Come on,' he said. 'Come and look.'

The dogs had been sleeping in a great heap of tangled hairy bodies, but, stimulated by the light and the sound of voices, were stirring and getting to their feet, one by one. Huge leggy beasts, all black, or black mottled with red and tan – with pale yellowish deep-set eyes that gave them an occult expression; long limp ears, and folds of loose wrinkled skin that suggested venerable age; and cavernous jaws lined with great gleaming teeth that were prominently displayed as the animals yawned and grunted and dripped saliva – they gradually came out of their torpor of sleep and became animated.

Darby gazed at the dogs with the fascination of horror.

Willard looked at them with a mixture of admiration and disdain.

'Bloodhounds, Talbot calls 'em,' Willard said. 'But they ain't nothin' but mongrels, most of 'em. They might 'a' had bloodhounds fo' granddaddies, that's about as close as they come. But they're mighty good at what they're good fo', like trackin' beah, or fox –'

He glanced down at Darby with a sly grin. 'Or niggers.'

The man's manner was casual, relaxed, and conversational. It baffled Darby, filled him with foreboding. He tried to turn away. Willard held him.

'Listen,' the man said. 'Maybe you'll learn sump'm.'

The dogs began to grow restless, to whine, and pace in their cage.

'Now, heah's the thing about these dogs,' Willard said. 'They're gentle, or they're mean, dependin' on how hungry they are. Talbot told me they was fed this afternoon, but Talbot's a damn liar, everybody knows that. Ain't no tellin' how long them dogs –'

Darby tried to turn away again, but Willard seized him, roughly this time, and pulled him back.

'Hold still, damn it!' he growled. 'You niggers always think white folks try to keep you ignorant. Well, I'm tryin' to learn you sump'm, so pay attention!'

He grasped the back of Darby's head and pointed it forcibly in the direction of one of the largest dogs, in a corner of the cage. 'Now jes' look at that big ol' black bastard, theah. Jes' *look* at them teeth! Evuh see anything like that? He's the leader o' the pack, you can tell – the biggest and strongest.'

He leaned down close to Darby. 'How 'bout that? The biggest one, the leader o' the pack – is black. Now don't that make you feel good?' He chuckled softly.

With a sudden twist Darby broke away, and ran for the barn. At the barn door he grappled frantically with the latch – then the breath went out of him as Willard's heavy body pinned him against the rough wooden boards.

'You don't want to leave now,' Willard said calmly. 'I'm jes' gittin' to the good part. Come on back.'

He twisted the boy's arm around and behind him and up tight, and pulled him stumbling back toward the dog cage.

The animals were becoming excited. They whined and growled and moved about nervously, nipping at each other, and pushing against the bars of the cage. The wagon creaked with their movements.

'Looka theah!' Willard said reproachfully. 'You done got them dogs all riled up, with yo' runnin' around. Now I 'spect they gon' have to have some exercise. The po' critters ain't had no exercise since they tore up a nigger gal ovuh to Graystone, early this mo'nin'.'

He pulled tighter on Darby's arm, and the boy sucked in his breath with pain. Willard leaned down and whispered, close to Darby's ear. 'Le's give 'em a little exercise. What d'ya say?'

He released Darby's arm, and with the other hand grasped the back of the boy's shirt, at the neck, and yanked violently. The thin cotton shirt ripped readily and came off.

Darby reeled and fell to the ground, and Willard stood over him, holding a section of the torn shirt.

'Now pay close attention,' Willard said. 'It's very interestin', how this works.'

He moved over to stand near the cage, and the dogs' agitation increased. Teeth flashed and growls grew louder as the beasts thrust their slobbering muzzles through the cage bars. Willard ignored them as he continued his lecture.

'Now, let's say you want 'em to track down a certain party. How d'you let 'em know who you want 'em to track? Very simple.' He held up the remnant of Darby's shirt. 'You give 'em a good whiff o' the certain party's scent.'

Willard moved a little closer to the dogs and gingerly thrust the piece of cloth into the cage. The beasts pounced on it as if it were a living thing, and tore at it wildly, snarling and snapping with vicious eagerness. The cloth was quickly reduced to shreds. Darby crouched on the ground, watching, and struggling with panic. In desperation he found his voice.

'I ain't done nothin' wrong, Mistuh Willard. Why you want to turn the dogs on me?'

Willard walked slowly toward the crouching boy. 'I told you, I want you to learn sump'm tonight. Everybody needs a little education once in a while, even niggers. Two things I want you to learn. One is how the dogs work – that's important to know.'

He stood over Darby, towering like the Angel of Death, his huge frame silhouetted against the flickering light from the lantern behind him.

'The other thing I want you to learn –' He leaned down,

and his shadow fell across Darby's upturned face – 'is how unhealthy it is for a nigger boy to git friendly with a white girl.'

Darby was shaking his head frantically. 'No, Mistuh Willard, it ain't fair! I ain't done nothin' wrong, 'fo' God, suh, I –'

'What d'ya mean, it ain't fair?!' Willard boomed. 'I'm gon' give you five minutes' head start. Now ain't that fair? You can cover a lot o' ground in five minutes.'

He pulled a large gold watch from his pocket, opened the lid, and studied it. Then he looked down at Darby and smiled.

'Whenevuh you're ready,' he said pleasantly.

Behind him the dogs growled and whined and leaped at the cage bars, yearning to be out and at the chase.

'I – I don't understand, suh,' Darby said weakly.

Willard pointed to a small wire gate in the far corner of the barnyard fence. Beyond it was the darkness of an empty field, not presently under cultivation, and beyond that, a quarter of a mile away, the deeper velvet darkness of the forest.

'That way,' Willard said. He looked at his watch. 'You have five minutes – startin' – now.'

Darby tried again to protest. 'No, Mistuh Willard, please. I can't –'

'You're wastin' yo' time, boy. Yo' five minutes has started.' He jerked his head toward the corner gate. 'Git goin'.'

Darby looked toward the gate, then at the snarling dogs, fighting to get out of their cage, then back at the man standing over him, gazing placidly at his gold watch. His muscles seemed paralyzed, though his eyes roved with the desperation of a hunted animal.

'Git goin'!' Willard roared, and Darby's muscles came to life. He sprang up and raced to the gate. Reaching it, he worked at the latch with clumsy trembling hands for a moment, and at last swung the gate open. As he did so his eye caught a glimpse of a tall object leaning against the fence a few feet away – but his panic-stricken mind registered nothing.

Wildly he plunged out into the field beyond the gate, ran toward the black mass of the woods in the distance, stumbled in the darkness, and fell. He lay still on the bare ground, panting, and tried to think of what to do – but his mind seemed curiously disengaged, unable to rivet its attention on the problem.

Rest a minute, he told himself. Pretty soon I'll be able to think. He laid his head on his arm, face down, and struggled to gain control of his mind.

Then through the grey blankness a simple image formed – an image of the bearded man, Mr. Rutledge, sitting on the ground beside the river, lacing a leather satchel and chatting in his warm, comforting way. Gotta make it to the river, a voice said to him. Gotta find Mr. Rutledge.

He thought of the awful distance he would have to cover; the long meandering way through the woods, across the brook, past the squatter's cabin, and on, farther and farther, into the deep dense jungle along the river, difficult to penetrate in broad daylight, but at night, in the blackness of night – a wave of despair swept over him.

I can't make it, he thought. Not in five minutes – less than that by now. The dogs'll have me before I'm halfway. Gotta try anyway, the voice kept saying. Get up and try. But he lay still, and the foggy grey blankness covered his mind again.

After a moment he looked up. Through the open gate in the barnyard fence a hundred feet away he could see his tormentor, Willard. The man was strolling up and down, looking at his watch, and counting off the time. Darby could not see the dogs from where he was, but he could hear them, snarling their impatience.

Then he noticed something else. A small insignificant protrusion, extending several inches above the top of the fence, a few feet from the gate. He looked at it for a moment, absently, not knowing what it was – then another image leaped into his mind. Something he had seen in a flashing glimpse, without realizing it, in his headlong rush from the barnyard – now registered in a picture of vivid clarity.

A long-handled spade, leaning against the fence, just inside the gate. Its heavy iron blade was half-buried in the soft ground where it stood. Its rough hand-hewn handle was as thick as his wrist and tall as a man – the rounded end of that handle was the object visible just above the top of the fence.

From this image sprang a plan of action, and from the plan came strength, and resolve. And miraculously the helpless despair fell away, and was replaced with a feeling of control, of ability to act in his own behalf. A feeling of power.

His muscles responded. Swiftly and silently he leaped to his feet and ran back to the barnyard fence and crouched in the shadows just outside the gate.

From this position he could barely see Willard, slowly pacing, studying his watch. He knew that when the time was elapsed and the man turned to the wagon cage to release the dogs, a cumbersome iron latch would have to be manipulated – this would require a few seconds of concentrated attention. He knew that during those few seconds Willard's back would be turned toward the open gate, twenty yards away. And he knew that from where he crouched the big iron spade could be reached in one quick leap.

Willard consulted his watch frequently, with growing impatience. He muttered to himself, and cursed under his breath. The dogs were getting too noisy in their eagerness for release and for action; he was worried that the sound might carry in the still night air to the big house, and reach the ears of the master.

He shook his watch, and swore again. He had not realized how long five minutes was.

Oh, well, four and a half minutes – good enough, he decided. He snapped the lid of his watch shut, put the timepiece in his pocket, and turned to the dog cage.

As he worked at the latch the dogs sensed that their moment was at hand, and leaped and clawed at the cage, and slobbered from their open-hanging mouths like demons possessed.

'Shut up, you bastards!' Willard growled, as he struggled with the rusty latch. As soon as the dogs bounded free of the cage and hit the trail they would become eerily silent, and remain so until they had cornered their prey. Then their vocal outburst would be hideous to hear – but that little scene, Willard reasoned, would take place far down in the woods, safely away from the house.

Because of the noise of the animals Willard did not hear the soft footfall behind him; he could not have told why he glanced around suddenly, in time to catch in the corner of his eye the swinging glint of the spade, arcing in the air. He whirled, instinctively throwing his hands up for protection – and the knuckles of one hand thudded against the wooden spade handle a split second before the iron blade crashed into the side of his head.

In the shivering half-moment of consciousness remaining to Willard he saw the boy's face – a face that had always been full of timidity and fear toward him, now grim, distorted with physical exertion, and set firmly in determination. He felt a sharp pain – not from the wound in his head, but, ludicrously, from his rapped knuckles. As he sank to his knees his fading mind registered one clear concept: astonishment.

He was dimly aware of the unpleasant jarring sensation as his head struck the ground, then was aware of nothing more – not of the boy standing over him, staring down, transfixed in horror; nor of the deep red stain soaking the ground under his head; nor of the deafening din of the dogs, now leaping and howling in their cage in a pandemonium of frustration and frenzy.

CHAPTER NINE

Reeves Douglas sat up in his bed, cocked his head in attention, then got up hastily and made his way across the dark room to the window. He leaned out, squinted uselessly into the darkness toward the barn area, and listened intently.

'God damn dogs!' he muttered. He reached for his trousers, fumbling in the darkness, and cursing softly. As he started downstairs he saw Moses standing in the entrance foyer below, ready with a lantern.

Douglas fumed and grumbled. 'Damn that Willard, letting Talbot leave those fool dogs heah overnight. Typical high-handed decision of his – I would nevuh have allowed it!'

He took the lantern from the butler, and started for the front door. 'Come on,' he snapped, and went out, and Moses followed.

Julia had been lying in her bed for what seemed like hours, alternately weeping and dry-eyed, torn with anguish over her father's unexpected display of rage. It was a facet of his nature she had never seen before, and it horrified her.

Over and over she reviewed recent events, roaming in her memory, trying to discover the probable cause of these sudden and catastrophic developments. The best she could do was the tenuous theory that the initial impetus had been provided by her behaviour at the party a few nights ago, the night before her grandfather's death. But all that seemed so long ago now, so remote.

Or perhaps, this afternoon – could it be that her father had somehow overheard her promise to Darby that she would set him free someday? Curiously, the idea that he may have seen her embrace the boy did not occur to her.

She remembered how Darby had looked at that moment – strong, manly, and surprisingly tall. Then she pictured him again, huddled on the floor in the hallway, a frightened and trembling child, with her father and Mr. Willard standing over him.

Her mind's eye turned away from this agonizing scene, and was confronted immediately by another, not less so. The spectacle in the barn – the crushed and broken old man, Hector, standing silently with head bowed, resigned to whatever punishment his white keepers chose to mete out. She had intended to go and see about him later, to make sure that he had been fed, and that his injuries had been treated – but it had not been possible, since she too was confined. She imagined him as he must be at this moment, slumped in a corner in the chilly damp darkness of the gin house, old, weak, suffering, helpless in his ignorance, without a friend and without hope.

The tears welled up in Julia's eyes, but angrily she brushed them away, and compressed her lips tightly with a firm resolve not to cry anymore. She had always hated to cry; even as a small child she had stubbornly resisted it as much as she could, preferring to take pain or disappointment with tight-lipped defiance, rather than with tears.

I'm sick of silly crying, she told herself. Women have been crying for thousands of years, and it has accomplished nothing. I am going to *do* something, I am going to make myself into a person who must be reckoned with. When I see wrong-doing, when I see cruelty and injustice, I am going to *resist*. I am going to *fight back*.

She felt her fists clench in angry determination. It was a good, warm feeling.

And as she savoured this sensation her vision expanded, and spread outward from the narrow personal confines of individuals like Darby and Hector, and embraced, instead, an entire oppressed race. It's so simple, she thought. So beautifully simple. It is not people like my father who are to blame, nor people like Mr. Willard. They are thrust by accident of birth into the roles of masters and drivers; they are as unwitting and helpless as the miserable wretches who are their victims.

What is to blame is slavery. The great hairy stinking beast, slavery, that has lived among us all our lives, and eaten away our souls, white and black alike. Slavery is wrong. It is worse than wrong, it is pure, undiluted evil. It is poisonous to the human spirit. And it must be attacked and attacked, and attacked again, until it is done to death.

Something that had lain entrapped beneath the surface of her mind for years, struggling to break through, succeeded.

She said it to herself, aloud: 'Slavery is wrong.' And she knew, consciously and completely, for the first time in her life, that this was true.

The suddenness of the revelation took her breath away. She raised herself on one elbow, and stared into the darkness with shining eyes. She felt elated; she felt buoyant, as if she were rising and floating on the surge of this strange and wonderful knowledge that washed in upon her like a cold and cleansing wave from the sea.

Gradually she became aware of the sound of the dogs. It was an unpleasant rasping sound that floated in on the night air through her open window from somewhere off in the distance, and she realized that she had been hearing it for some time before becoming conscious of it. She wondered vaguely what it could mean.

Then she heard her father's bedroom door open, heard his heavy hurrying footsteps along the hall and down the stairs, dimly heard his deep voice as he spoke to Moses, and then rapid footsteps again, followed by the opening and closing of the front door. She held her breath and listened longer. All was silent in the house. The sound of the dogs seemed to have grown louder.

Then a sudden sharp rattling sound made her gasp and clutch at her bed covers. A small hard object had clattered against her window casing, and fallen to the floor inside her room. She slid out of bed and flew to the window, reached down and picked up a pebble.

She leaned out of the window and looked down. Something told her that Darby must be there – but she could see nothing except the dim shadowy mass of a small tree in the garden below.

She called out in a whisper, 'Darby? Where are you?' She saw him then – or imagined she saw him – step out from beneath the tree.

'I'm heah, Julia.'

The sound of urgency in his whispered response from the darkness below struck Julia with a shock.

'I'm heah, but I got to go. I came to say goodbye.'

'What do you mean? What's happened?!'

'I hit Mistuh Willard with a shovel. Maybe kilt him. I got to run away now. I'm goin' out west and be a free man.'

Julia's voice rose in frantic distress, the whisper

abandoned. 'Darby, you're mad, you can't! You'll be killed by Indians!'

'I got to go, Julia. I ain't got no time. I'll see you again someday, I promise. Goodbye, Julia.'

The sound of his voice receded to the farther side of the garden – he was already on his way.

'No, no! You can't, Darby! Come back, do you hear?!'

'Someday I will, Julia. I promise.'

Then faintly and from a greater distance she heard him again.

'Goodbye, Julia.'

'No, Darby, no!' She choked with sobs, clutched the side of the window and leaned far out, and sent her pleading voice trembling across the empty darkness.

'Darby, come back! You belong to me! Come back, Darby, come back!'

She heard him no more.

For a time she stood weeping quietly beside the open window, her vow not to cry anymore forgotten, and gazed through a blur of tears at the constellations hanging low in the sky to the west. Then she stumbled blindly back to her bed and fell into it face down, numb with despair, and closed her eyes tightly, as if to shut out the rest of the world forever.

CHAPTER TEN

He ran at nearly full speed, encouraged to find that his eyes had become accustomed to the darkness enough so that the faint starlight gave him a dim perception of the ground. He skirted widely around the barnyard area, from which the yelping and howling of the dogs continued unabated, and around the quarters and other outbuildings of the plantation, and headed for the nearest point from which he could enter the woods.

He knew from the sound of the dogs that they were still in their cage, and took comfort from the knowledge that if someone let them out, they would have to track him all the way to the house before doubling back in the right direction.

He made it to the woods with surprisingly little difficulty, but pulled up at the edge of the dark forbidding wall of forest, panting and limp with fatigue.

There was no path through the woods from that point, but he reasoned that if he could manage to hold a straight course directly toward the river, he would come out not very far from Mr. Rutledge's campsite.

No time to rest. He turned and plunged into the forest.

After going a short distance he stopped again, appalled at the suffocating darkness that suddenly enveloped him, like a cloak thrown over his head. Running was out of the question now – he'd have to move slower.

Even so he collided immediately with a tree, and took a painful jab in the face from a low protruding branch. He moved on, keeping his arms up and his hands spread in front of his face for protection.

He fell down three times in a few minutes, the third time crashing heavily against a fallen log and spinning off onto the ground, wrenching a shoulder. He lay there for a moment and stared up into the canopy of blackness above him, and yielded to his aching body's desperate need for rest. But the churning fear inside him, and the compelling urgency of his desire to reach the strange, kindly, bearded man at the river, would not permit it. He forced himself back to his feet, and went on.

He fell again and again, losing count of the number of times, taking bruises and lacerations across his face, neck, and bare chest and shoulders. Pain burned his body – but slowly a blessed numbness crept over him. He felt the stickiness of blood on his skin, and tasted it in his mouth, but the awareness of pain faded. Only weariness remained.

He had no conception of time, and after a while no further sense of direction. He paused and tried to take his bearings, turning his eyes in every direction, but saw nothing but the awful and infinite darkness.

Suddenly he held his breath, cocked his head and listened. The sound of the dogs had ceased. Was he out of earshot? It couldn't be. Someone must have arrived on the scene, there in the barnyard. Had they quieted the dogs? – or had they released them to do their work?

Panic rose in his throat. He lurched and stumbled on recklessly, thrusting all sensation of weariness out of his mind, forsaking caution.

Gradually he became aware of a new sound. He stopped to listen, and recognized the soft gurgling of the little brook, just ahead. Heartened, he summoned his strength and hurried on toward that gentle, comforting babble. He walked down the middle of the shallow stream bed then, using sound as a guide in place of sight, and accepting sticky mud gladly in exchange for the clawing punishment of briars and bramble.

Some small wild creature scurried suddenly in the underbrush nearby, and startled him. In daylight the forest was a pleasant, friendly, familiar place – he had spent many hours of his life in it, and thought he knew it well. But at night – it was alien, threatening, sinister. A shiver went through him. He went on doggedly, pushing his feet through the sluggish water.

At length the brook led him into a partially open space; he stood on the path that he and Julia often used. He was near the squatter's cabin, and not far from the river. For an instant he allowed himself a feeling of relief in being at least securely oriented in his location. Leaving the little stream, he walked along the path now, but moved slowly, his legs stiff and heavy, and unwilling to respond.

The weariness was killing. It was an agonizing, unreasonable weariness, of a kind he had never known before, making every step an ordeal that required a separate and distinct effort of will to undertake. He found himself lulled with an almost overpowering desire to stretch out on the soft grassy ground and sleep.

Got to rest, jes' for a minute, he told himself. Jes' *got* to.

But he kept going. He knew that if he gave in to the urge to sink to the ground he would not get up again.

The path led him through the little meadow where the old cabin stood, silent and ghostly, and strangely luminous in the starlight – it shamed him that he was afraid to look at it – and on into the dense tangle of woods that bordered the river, where the darkness became total again, as he knew it would. But he managed to stay on the path, feeling his way along, and forcing himself to keep moving, though his leaden muscles refused to respond to his urging of speed.

He came at last to the point where the path made a sharp turn southward, parallel with the river. Ahead, through a narrow break in the foliage, he could see it – he could barely make out the flat, broad, grey-brown open space of water. Though almost invisible in the faint night-glow, it seemed resplendently beautiful, more so than it had ever been before.

He tottered, panting heavily, and grasped a branch beside him for support, and gazed with admiration and wonderment out over the magnificent watercourse that he hoped would be his pathway to deliverance. Once more he indulged himself in a feeling of relief, almost of elation.

I'm makin' it, I'm makin' it, he told himself – but suddenly a chilling new thought clutched at his mind.

What if Mr. Rutledge ain't there? He said he'd stay a day or two, but he could have changed his mind. Oh, God, what if he ain't there? Exhaustion pressed down upon him with a staggering weight; he shook his head frantically, trying to keep his thoughts clear and his resolve firm. Go on, he urged himself, don't stop now. Go on. He turned toward the part of the path that led into the deepest jungle-mass along the edge of the river, sucked a gulping breath into his tortured lungs, and gathered his draining strength for the final stretch.

Then he heard the dogs.

Just one short yelp, not loud – it could easily have gone unnoticed – but he froze, and listened, and he heard it again, from somewhere up in the woods behind him. They were coming.

His skin crawled with horror. Panic rose again, this time overwhelming all reason.

He screamed, 'Mistuh Rutledge!' and hurled himself forward in the darkness. Wildly he ran, twisting and stumbling, with no further thought or hope of control, or the conserving of failing energy.

'Mistuh Rutledge, where are you?!' he screamed, as loudly as his hoarse quavering voice would deliver it, and plunged blindly on, waving his arms in a frenzied and futile effort to fight off the evil vegetation around him, and the cruel punishment of thorns and branches and tentacles of vines that reached out from all sides to flagellate his torn and bleeding body. The forest – the forest that he had loved all his life – was his major enemy now; it struck viciously at him like a thousand seething serpents; it tore at him, tormented him, tried to grasp and hold him for the dogs.

The struggle was useless. He was surrounded, imprisoned, impaled in his tracks. He stood in the midst of the strangling jungle, and knew he was off the path, with no idea which way to go, and no more strength to move, even if he had the knowledge.

He was lost.

With a last particle of energy and gasp of breath he called out once more. 'Mistuh Rutledge!' It was a despairing cry, empty of life, and could carry no distance.

He heard a dog yelp again, closer, and sank down to the ground in the merciful release of defeat, and closed his eyes.

At first he could not imagine what was happening when he felt strong hands slide under his arms, grasp him firmly and lift him up. He thought he was dreaming.

Then a soft gruff voice sounded close to his ear. 'It's all right, lad. I've got you.'

'Mistuh Rutledge.' His lips moved, voicelessly. He felt himself being lifted off his feet and carried like a child, and he twisted his head away in shame, and sobbed convulsively, and warm tears came.

He was deposited in a hard wooden cavity – he felt dampness under him, and a rocking motion – he knew that he was in Mr. Rutledge's skiff.

'The dogs!' he whispered fiercely, and strained upward. 'The dogs are comin'!'

He was astounded to hear the man laugh. The strong deep bass voice boomed out heartily. 'Dogs, hah! Do not fret yourself about dogs, my lad. Man is superior to dogs!'

The skiff shuddered repeatedly as Rutledge threw his belongings into it, evacuating his campsite.

'Do not fret yourself about anything,' the booming voice said. 'We're on our way.'

He pushed the skiff off and leaped into it, and Darby grasped the sides and held on tightly as the little craft rocked wildly before settling itself free-floating in the water.

Then quiet. Marvellous, eerie quiet. There was no sound except the gentle lapping of water against the bow of the skiff, and the muffled rattle of Rutledge's oars, working with firm steady rhythm.

Darby lay back and looked up at the stars imbedded in the deep black vaulted space above him. He tried to speak, could not find his voice, swallowed hard, and tried again.

'I'm in terrible trouble,' he croaked. 'I hit Mistuh Willard. Maybe kilt him. I didn't mean to, 'fo' God –'

'Hush, lad,' Rutledge said sharply. 'Don't talk now. Tell me later.'

Darby lay still. Soon his exhaustion submerged him in a feverish condition of half-waking, half-sleeping. He stirred slightly, resisting, and the protective numbness began to fall away, and the searing pain lurking in his bloody lacerated body advanced and grew relentlessly.

He opened his eyes and frowned in confusion, trying to determine where he was – then remembered. He shook his head, struggling, constantly struggling, to keep his mind clear.

He thought of Julia. Did I say goodbye to Julia, he wondered. I can't remember. I hope so. Julia, Julia – I'm sorry.

With an excruciating effort he twisted himself, lifted his head and looked over the side of the skiff, out across the tranquil surface of the river, back toward the dark dimming line of the east bank, far off now and dissolving into nothingness.

He felt himself slipping. The murky darkness was suddenly splashed with lurid colour; the spangled starlit water grew unendurably dazzling, spun crazily, and exploded without a sound. Frantically he clutched at the side of the skiff, and opened his mouth to cry out – but his hands had lost their grip, his voice was gone. He slid slowly, gently downward into the vortex of unconsciousness.

The last thing he heard was Julia's call, reverberating inside his head, behind his eyes, penetrating the depths of his being and piercing his heart.

'Darby, come back! You belong to me! Come back, Darby, come back. . . .'

PART FIVE

AFTER

CHAPTER ONE

Tolliver's Landing, Arkansas, in the summer of 1866, consisted of a number of homey and harmonious elements: one rotting and dilapidated plank wharf that clung precariously to the steep hard-packed slope of a levee along the west bank of the Mississippi River; the main street – the only thoroughfare of consequence – a dirt road that ran westward from the river in an ambitious imitation of a broad avenue for a quarter of a mile before giving up and becoming a quiet country lane; two business establishments – one a high-roofed barnlike structure with a tall sign on its gable that read ELY'S FEED GRAIN & GEN'L STORE, and the other, across the road from the store, a combination stable and blacksmith shop; several ruined and abandoned buildings paralleling the river southward from the landing; beyond these a cluster of shabby makeshift shanties, the habitations of Negroes; and finally, on the landward side of the wharf, a small freight storage building, from which extended the only other sign in town, a worn weather-beaten board that proclaimed, in barely legible letters:

TOLLIVER'S LANDING
THE PRIDE OF ARKANSAS
POPULATION 415

If a visitor, scanning the drowsy little hamlet, should trouble to voice his scepticism of the sign's statistical information, he would receive a ready explanation at the general store: 'Well, suh, that sign was put up by the town's founder, Abraham Tolliver – old Abraham, Senior, that is – way back in the eighteen-thirties. You understand, suh, this was a hustlin', bustlin' town in those days, yes, suh – 'peared for all the world to have a mighty fine future ahead. But that was way back yonduh, long befo' the waw. The ol' Miss'sip's run a lotsa watuh past heah twixt then 'n' now.'

The speaker would be Ely Griffith, proprietor of Ely's

Feed Grain & Gen'l Store, and the community's most articulate spokesman. Ely would shake his head sadly whenever he said, as he often did, 'That was long befo' the waw.' It was as if the Civil War was the sole justification for the failure of every dream that ever died in the breast of a southerner in the nineteenth century.

Ely Griffith was a thin stoop-shouldered little man, grey-haired and elderly, but possessed of a mercurial quickness of movement and speech that belied his age, and his southern heritage. As proprietor of the general store he not only presided over the principal establishment of commerce and trade within a thirty-mile radius on the west side of the river, but was also the unofficial host, master of ceremonies, and arbiter of all disputes in a lively social arena.

The area around the little pot-bellied iron stove that occupied the centre of the worn plank floor in Ely's store was the home ground of the men's club, social centre, and town hall of Tolliver's Landing and the surrounding countryside. From early morning until dusk, six days a week, the store was hardly ever without two or three idlers, who lounged in the creaky cane-bottom chairs that Ely provided for his customers' convenience and droned endlessly, their voices rising occasionally in eruptions of argument that threatened the musty tranquillity of the setting, until Ely was obliged to crack his apron at them and shoo them off the premises, scolding like an angry schoolmarm.

There were occasional legitimate customers, too, who were not members of the permanent male forensic society – people from the houses along the main village road, and from farmhouses farther out, come to buy staples for their kitchens, and perhaps a tool or a piece of cloth; and now and then, in this latter time since the war, a Negro from the shanties down by the river, who would enter on soundless catlike feet, to buy a nickel's worth of snuff or molasses, and inquire of Ely, with soft voice and lifeless eyes, if he knew of any employment to be had.

This last phenomenon – blacks wandering about seeking employment – was one of the strange new aspects of life in the post-war period, and took some getting used to. It seemed unnatural, to whites and blacks alike. The blacks themselves, in one year of freedom, had gone from initial wild-eyed jubilation to uncertainty, to bewilderment, disappointment, and sullen despondency, realizing that misery wore many disguises, took forms other than the grim shape of slavery – chief among these being poverty. True freedom was a theoretical abstraction, seemingly impossible to grasp.

Ely had a handyman in steady employment around the store, a short, stocky middle-aged black man named Oscar. He had been a freeman even before emancipation, the son of a slave who had managed to purchase his liberty from a kindly master in Vicksburg in the 1820s. Oscar had been hired as a boy of sixteen to come to this outpost in the Arkansas Territory, to work in the store. He had been there ever since.

After the war, when a distressingly large unemployed black labour force suddenly sprang into being, Ely tried to find extra work, and occasionally hired one of the local ex-slaves on a short term basis, to assist Oscar. But Oscar made it clear that he needed no assistants. He had always looked down from a position of haughty superiority upon slaves, declaring with unconcealed contempt that they were a lazy, shiftless lot, and couldn't be trusted.

'Them no-good slave nigguhs ain't wuth spittin' on, much less payin' wages to,' he would say to Ely, his ebony brow creased with a disapproving frown. When one of them was temporarily put in the position of working under Oscar's despotic supervision, the wretch would soon wonder if he hadn't been better off as a slave.

The second ranking member of the General Store cracker barrel society, after Ely Griffith, was a great, puffing, huge-bellied giant of a man who was almost always present, who sat on a sturdy wooden bench reserved for him because Ely's flimsy cane chairs were not built for his gargantuan bulk, and who issued forth pronouncements of opinion on all subjects with the ponderous sonority of rolling thunder, in a voice so deep that the man's loose-hanging jowls shook when he spoke.

The esteem this man enjoyed in the community stemmed not from accomplishment, nor from intellectual superiority – he was in fact regarded as a trifle slow-witted, even by local standards – but from his name. He was a Tolliver. He was Abraham Tolliver Junior, and to all who knew him – to his friend Ely Griffith and other cronies at the store, even to his carping shrew of a wife – he was known as Junior.

One of the small astonishments awaiting any stranger who might happen to spend time in Ely's store was the spectacle of Junior Tolliver's ancient servant and former slave, Tully, peering into the store from the front veranda, and announcing in scolding tones to his employer, 'Mars' Junior, Miz Ethel wants you home right dis minute, or she gon' come take a stick to you!'

And Junior Tolliver would stare at the old man as if unable to fathom what he was talking about, and Tully would frown sternly and say, 'Come on, now, Mars' Junior. I ain't gon' tell you ag'in.'

One of the other white men – Ely himself, or perhaps Jud Watkins, another charter member of the group – would say, 'You heard 'im, Junior. Go on, we don't want Miz Ethel comin' round heah bustin' up things with her broomstick.'

A ripple of gentle laughter all around, every time, as if this were an original joke, freshly created – and Junior Tolliver would get reluctantly to his feet and waddle out, grumbling, with Tully leading the way.

Judson Watkins was the third member of the trio, along with Ely Griffith and Junior Tolliver, that made up the charter membership of the General Store Men's Club and Debating Society. He was a relative newcomer, having lived in the region only a brief ten years, and was thus the lowest ranking member of the Select Three.

Jud was a farmer – he always took great pains to emphasize that his place, consisting of a hundred and sixty acres of tolerably good land just south of the village, was a farm, not a plantation. There was a profound difference, much more fundamental than the mere factor of size, and Jud was always ready to point it out to anyone who cared to listen.

A farm, he explained, was a place worked by its owner and his family. The success or failure of the farm was directly related to the ability and willingness to work of the people who owned and lived on it. A plantation, on the other hand, was a penal institution, where the work was performed by prisoners – stubborn and recalcitrant black slaves, whose every grudging step had to be forced at the point of a gun or the crack of a whip, because their interest in the prosperity of their white masters was absolutely nonexistent. Moreover, declared Jud, the Negro was naturally born inferior, both in physical and mental capacity – any damn fool ought to be able to see that. Not only would he never be a good worker – he *could* not be. It was no use trying to force him to do what he was incapable of doing.

'I would nevuh be a slaveowner,' Jud would growl, 'for the same reason I wouldn't own a mule with a broken leg, or a cow that won't give milk – because I don't want no goddamn useless property that ain't wuth its keep.'

These three, Ely, Junior and Jud, were the three permanent members of the general store social clique. Though other locals came and went frequently, and were treated with courtesy, there was always a subtle unspoken distinction between them and the regulars, an inner exclusiveness that enclosed the principal trio, and could not be violated.

It was in 1860 that Abraham Tolliver Junior abandoned his given name.

Politics was one of the staple subjects of conversation at the store, especially so during the decade preceeding the Civil War, when the long simmering controversy between pro- and anti-slavery forces began to boil and rage across the land. In 1858 Tolliver had begun to read of political waves being made by an upstart country lawyer in Illinois named Abraham Lincoln. This Lincoln had been put up as a candidate for the U.S. Senate by the newly formed Republican Party, and was involved in a series of debates with the incumbent in the office, Senator Stephen A. Douglas. Tolliver read humorous descriptions of the tall, ugly, gangling nonentity from Illinois who aspired to a high seat in the temple of government, and chuckled with glee. The chuckles soon died in his throat – for the things that other Abe was saying aroused no amusement.

Tolliver huffed, and read, his great voice husky with anger: ' "A house divided against itself cannot stand." ' He shook his newspaper irritably, and glared at his listeners. 'This is from a speech by that maniac Lincoln, boys. Jes' listen to this!

' "I believe this government cannot endure, permanently half slave and half free. I do not expect the Union to be dissolved . . . but I do expect it will cease to be divided. It will become all one thing, or all the other."'

'Hm-m, them's pretty strong words,' said Ely. 'Jest how does this Lincoln fella propose to bring about this all-one-or-all-the-other thing?'

'How?! I'll tell you how!' Tolliver shuffled the pages of his paper, searched briefly with his finger, and cleared his throat for another momentous delivery. 'Senator Douglas says heah – now jes' listen to what Senator Douglas says.

' "Mr. Lincoln advocates boldly and clearly a war of sections, a war of the North against the South, of the free States against the slave States – a war of extermination – to be continued relentlessly until the one or the other shall be subdued, and all the States shall either become free or become slave."

'That,' Tolliver cried dramatically, 'is how the fiend proposes to bring it about! Well, if it's waw they want, by God, suh, it's waw they shall –'

'Oh, calm down, Abe,' Ely scolded. 'Lincoln won't git nowheah with that kind o' prattle. Every reasonable man knows the only right way is for folks in the North to mind theah own business, and let folks in the South mind theahs.'

'Every reasonable man, yes! But this Lincoln is a madman and a fool, I tell you!'

Jud Watkins spoke up. 'Beg to differ with you, Abe. This heah Lincoln may be mad, but he ain't no fool. He knows this country has got to git rid o' the damn wuthless niggers, or it ain't nevuh gonna amount to a hill o' beans.'

'You ain't nothin' but a damn fool yo'self, Jud!' Tolliver bellowed. 'It's easy for *you* to say we ought to git rid of 'em, since you ain't *got* any – but what do you suggest we *do* with 'em?'

'Load 'em on barges and float 'em down the river –'

'Stop talkin' nonsense, Jud! We *need* the nigguhs, they're the only source o' labour we got!'

'Keep yo' voices down, boys,' Ely said, 'or I'll throw you both out o' heah.' He went off to wait on a paying customer.

The voice of Abe Lincoln continued to ring out across the land like a clarion call; his name grew on the nation, and rage grew in the breast of Abe Tolliver. In April, 1860, an unthinkable thing happened. Lincoln was named to carry the hopes of the young Republican Party in quest of the presidency. And in November, the ultimate unthinkable – he was elected.

When Abe Tolliver read the news the paper in his hands shook, and a crimson apoplectic passion flamed in his face. He rose, slammed the crumpled paper on the floor, and thundered, 'By God, I sweah I'll wring the neck of the man who evuh again dares to call me by that accursed name, Abe!'

'What shall we call you?' asked Jud Watkins calmly.

'Any other name in heaven, earth, or everlastin' hell but that!'

Ely Griffith approached the towering, trembling hulk of a man, patted him gently on the shoulder, and said, 'All right, we'll jes' call you Junior. Now sit down, Junior, 'fo' you have an attack. Me and Jud would play the dickens tryin' to carry you home.'

Tolliver sat down. And from that moment on he was known as Junior.

So the deadening, mesmerizing tranquillity of life in that backwater corner of the land was swept away by the terrible winds of war. The little group of friends in Ely's store shuddered at the news of the fall of New Orleans in the spring of 1862, shuddered again at the word that Memphis was taken in early summer.

For another year they huddled in a daze of fear as Federal troops moved up and down the river, as the assault on Vicksburg, the last pocket of Confederate resistance on the waterway, intensified.

Inevitably, Ely's store was raided and stripped clean of all goods by the hated blue-clad Union troops. After several months, when things seemed quiet, Ely bravely attempted to reopen – and was immediately looted again, this time by patrolling Confederates.

Ely boarded up what remained of the store, to await the coming of peace.

In July, 1863, Vicksburg fell, and the Mississippi was completely in Federal hands. Although the war raged on elsewhere for nearly two years more, for the people along the river the fighting was over, the galling potion of defeat measured out. The long painful struggle to recover lay ahead.

Now, in the balmy days of early summer, 1866, one year and two months after the agonizing death of the Confederacy, the old cronies gathered again, nearly every day, around the pot-bellied stove at Ely's Feed Grain & Gen'l

Store. They spoke of the old times with nostalgia, and of the war years almost fondly – as if that period had been a lively and colourful chapter in ancient history, remembered from school days.

It seemed reasonable to them to hope that tranquillity had returned to the land.

CHAPTER TWO

After a night that began with light intermittent rain, the June morning came up clear and crisp, with a coolness that was uncharacteristic of the season. Oscar decided to take advantage of the weather, and haul some boxes of goods from the storage building on the wharf up to the store, a distance of a hundred yards. He was returning to the store on his second trip, pushing a heavily laden wheelbarrow, when Junior Tolliver's horse and buggy arrived, and Junior slowly and carefully lowered his great bulk to the ground, tied his horse, and started up the steps of the store veranda.

Oscar sang out a greeting in a hearty, gravelly voice. 'Mawnin', Mars' Junior. Nice day, ain't it?'

'Nice day, Oscar, nice day.' Junior puffed laboriously up the half-dozen steps. 'Hope we git a little mo' o' that gentle rain. Fine fo' the crops.'

'Sho' is, suh, sho' is.' Although burdened with a heavy sack that he had just swung up on his shoulder, Oscar walked rapidly past Junior on the steps, crossed the veranda, and held the door open for the big white man to enter.

Twenty minutes later, returning from his third trip to the landing, Oscar went inside the store, where Junior was settled on his bench as usual, and Ely was up on a ladder, busy placing stock on a high shelf. There was an early morning hush in the store; the day's rambling stream of conversation was not yet flowing.

On his shoulder Oscar again carried a sack, which he dumped noisily on the counter. He looked up at his employer on the ladder.

'Mistuh Ely, they's a skiff headin' in to de landin',' he said.

'Who is it?' Ely asked.

'Strangers. White man an' a nigguh. Nevuh seen 'em befo'.'

Ely paused in his work. Junior Tolliver looked up from the old newspaper he was reading and gazed at Oscar with interest.

'They's some kind o' queer writin' on the skiff,' Oscar went on. 'Some kind o' foreign words. Can't make it out.'

Ely came down off the ladder and headed for the front veranda, and Junior rose from his bench and followed. Even the routine arrival of local people was enough to bring the store company out front to watch; by no means could a stranger land at the wharf unobserved.

Darby stared intently at the place ahead as he nosed the skiff in across shallow water. The dilapidated little hamlet looked familiar, and yet strange at the same time, and vaguely disappointing.

The only person in sight as they drew near was a black man, who was loading sacks of goods from the little warehouse building at the wharf onto a wheelbarrow. Darby saw him standing there staring for a moment out at the approaching skiff, looked more closely, and recognized him.

He leaned forward and whispered to Trav, 'I know who that is. That's Oscar. He works at the general store. He's always been a freeman, never had nothin' to do with us lowly slaves.'

As they came closer, they saw Oscar hastily close and lock the storage room door, take up his wheelbarrow, and hurry away.

The bow of *El Bandido Moreno* bumped gently against a wharf post. Trav secured the skiff with the mooring rope, then he and Darby climbed rickety steps to the rough-hewn planking of the wharf deck, walked to the landward side, and surveyed the landscape. Oscar had disappeared inside the general store. A mangy, emaciated dog wandered listlessly across the dusty roadway – otherwise, no stirring of life could be seen.

Trav studied the carved wooden sign extending from the landing warehouse. ' "Pride of Arkansas," it says here. "Population –" ' He turned to Darby with a look of astonishment. ' "Four hundred and fifteen?!" '

Darby gave him a wry grin. 'They don't jus' count *people*, Trav. They count cows and horses and chickens . . .'

Trav was looking now in the direction of the store. 'Well, we've seen one native – and there's two more.'

Darby followed his gaze and saw two white men standing on the store veranda, observing them.

'Recognize those characters?' Trav asked.

Darby studied the men in the distance. 'The big heavyweight must be Abe Tolliver Junior.'

'Tolliver, like in Tolliver's Landing?'

Darby nodded. 'Son of the fella who started the place. And the little grey-haired man is probably Ely Griffith, the storekeeper. Try to concentrate on him if you can. He's fairly decent, as I recall.'

'How would *you* know?'

'He gave me a piece of candy once, when I was here, taggin' along with Moses on an errand. I must 'a' been about –' Darby extended his hand, palm down, indicating his three-foot height at the time. 'Small thing – he wouldn't remember it. But it was a big thing to me.'

'All right, I'll go up and make their acquaintance, and see what I can find out,' Trav said. 'Let's have a last minute check. Who am I?'

'Mister Travers, rancher from California. And my employer.'

'What am I doin' in the South?'

'You're on business.'

'What kind of business?'

Darby lapsed into a primitive black dialect. 'Lawsy, Massa, Ah don' know nothin' 'bout white folks' bizness. Ah'm jes' a po' ol' nigguh –'

'All right!' Trav cut him off impatiently. 'What's your name?'

'Daniel Ross,' Darby answered crisply. 'Sometimes known as Dangerous Dan. Sometimes known as *El Bandido Moreno*.'

'Never mind all that. It's Daniel Ross. You're the son of a freeman from Pennsylvania who went west way back when. You've never been in the South before in your life. Right?'

'If you say so, boss.'

Trav looked skyward in mock exasperation, started to walk away from the wharf, paused after a few steps and looked back.

'Don't get into any arguments, Dangerous Daniel. See you later.'

Darby smiled and flipped his hand in a jaunty unmilitary salute. Trav walked on up the road toward the store, and Darby stood looking after him. Darby's face was suddenly sombre.

Ely and Junior stood on the veranda of the store and watched the stranger approach.

'He ain't a southerner,' said Junior shrewdly. 'If he's one o' them goddamn Yankee carpetbaggers, I'll send 'im on his way, 'fo' he knows what happened.'

'You'll do nothin' o' the kind, Junior,' the storekeeper snapped. 'You go and sit down and hush up. I'll take care o' the customers around heah.'

Junior snorted.

Trav came up to the front steps of the store, stopped there and looked up at the men on the veranda.

'Mornin',' he said pleasantly.

'Good mornin', suh,' Ely responded, and stepped forward.

Trav came up the steps, and extended his hand. 'My name's Travers. Bob Travers.'

They shook hands, and Ely replied cordially.

'How 'do, Mistuh Travers. I'm Ely Griffith. I run the sto' heah. And this is –' He turned to introduce Junior Tolliver, but the big man was just disappearing inside the store.

'Uh – come on in, Mistuh Travers.'

Inside, Junior Tolliver was seated on his bench with his face buried in an old newspaper. Ely walked up to him and said, in a loud voice, 'Junior, say hello to Mistuh Travers heah. Mistuh Travers, Mistuh Tolliver.'

Junior glanced up and extended a limp hand toward the visitor, making no move to rise.

'Pleased to meet you, Mister Tolliver,' Trav said.

Junior grunted, and returned his attention to his paper.

Ely glared at Junior for a moment before turning to Trav, and waving him toward one of the cane-bottom chairs. 'Sit down, Mistuh Travers, and I'll bring you a cool drink o' well watuh.'

'Thanks,' Trav said, and sat down. He glanced toward Tolliver. The great round man was motionless, deeply absorbed in his newspaper.

Ely returned with a dipper of water and handed it to Trav, saying, 'I can see you're a travellin' man, Mistuh Travers, and we're always happy to welcome travellers in our midst. Gives us a chance to heah news from faraway places, and git a fresh viewpoint, so to speak. Ain't that right, Junior?'

'Oh, to be shuah,' Tolliver said dryly, and glanced briefly at Trav. 'To be shuah.' He went back to his paper.

'Much obliged to you, sir,' said Trav, as he handed the dipper back to Ely. 'That's mighty fine water.'

' 'Course it is. Finest watuh in the state, right heah.' Ely put the dipper away, and drew up a chair near Trav. 'That's why Mistuh Tolliver Senior chose this spot for a settlement. Ain't that right, Junior?'

Junior's mumbled response was, 'I've heard it said.'

Ely crossed his legs and settled himself for a long informative session of conversation. He fixed his eyes on Trav in close scrutiny.

'Well now, Mistuh Travers. Pardon me for bein' personal, suh, no offence. But I can't he'p noticin' from yo' speech that you ain't southern. Sho' do hope you'll pacify our natural friendly curiosity, suh, and inform us wheah you're from, and wheah you're headed.'

'Be glad to,' Trav said. 'I'm from out west. California.'

'California. You don't say!' Ely's eyebrows rose in lively interest. 'You heah that, Junior? California!'

Junior did not choose to react.

'I'm on a sort of combination business and pleasure trip, you might call it,' Trav went on. 'My business is ranching – cattle raising. I'm lookin' to see what the situation might be here in the South, as far as potential market is concerned – that sort o' thing.'

'Well, now, that's mighty interestin', mighty interestin' indeed,' Ely said.

Trav continued. 'I've never been in the South before, and I know I have much to learn. In fact, that's why I'm here this morning – to see if I can get some particular information from you gentlemen.'

'Why, shuah!' Ely bubbled with enthusiasm. 'You tell us some stories about California, and we'll tell you some about this area.'

Trav shrugged. 'I don't have any great stories to tell, Mister Griffith. Not much time, either – my friend's down at the landing, and I don't want to keep him waitin' too long. So if I could just ask you a couple of quick questions –'

'Friend?' Tolliver put down his paper, and regarded Trav suspiciously. 'We jes' saw yo' nigguh with you. Whea's yo' friend?'

'That's him,' Trav said readily. 'That's my friend.'

A heavy silence descended. Ely and Junior exchanged a look.

'Now I know the solution to our problem heah in the South,' Tolliver said to Ely, his voice a deep indignant growl.

'What we ought to do is ship all our unemployed freedmen to California, so each one can find himself a white "friend." That must be nigguh heaven out theah.'

Trav leaned forward, holding the big man in a steady gaze. 'You may be interested to know, Mister Tolliver, that some years ago, when California first joined the Union, its legislature came very near passing a law to exclude black people from the state altogether. It failed, but just barely. And the chief reason it failed was that the Californians got so riled up about the influx of Chinese, they didn't have time to worry about the blacks anymore.'

'How interestin',' Tolliver muttered. His narrowed eyes bore into Trav. 'Jes' what is yo' point, Mistuh Travers?'

'The point is, there are probably more people like you in California than there are like me.'

'If that's true, suh, then why didn't the damn fools do one thing or the other – establish slavery, or, failin' that, exclude the blacks?'

'Because, Junior, there are just enough people like me there to make a *big* difference.'

Tolliver's jaw dropped. There was something about the inflection this stranger put on the word *Junior* that touched a nerve.

'By God, suh, you're insolent, suh!' he thundered.

Trav slumped in his chair. Something Darby had told him once flashed suddenly through his mind: You can always tell how angry an old-fashioned southern gentleman is by the number of times he calls you *sir*. When he calls you *sir* twice in the same sentence, you're in trouble. Ruefully he recalled the sardonic advice he had left with Darby: *Don't get into any arguments, Dangerous Daniel.*

'My apologies, Mister Tolliver,' he said meekly. 'No offence intended.'

Tolliver glared at him in sullen silence. Ely responded on his friend's behalf.

'Pay no mind to Junior, Mistuh Travers. He was jes' naturally *born* to argue. Now, then – what was it you wanted to ask us?'

About time, Trav thought. He shifted his attention gratefully to the storekeeper. 'Well – I was wondering if you could tell me anything about a plantation somewhere around here. Place called Chinaberry.'

Ely and Junior Tolliver exchanged another quick look.

Trav saw that their faces were suddenly masks, blank and guarded. Tolliver broke the silence.

'Jes' what connection did you have with Chinaberry, Mistuh Travers?'

'Oh, no particular connection. An acquaintance of mine toured the river some years ago, and mentioned it to me as one of the places he found interesting.'

'What was the name of yo' acquaintance?' Tolliver demanded.

'Oh – I can't recall, exactly. Never was much good at rememberin' names –'

Ely slapped his knee noisily. 'Junior, you ought to be ashamed – you're lettin' yo' suspicious nature get the bettuh of yo' good mannuhs.' He leaned back comfortably in his chair. 'What did you want to know about Chinaberry, Mistuh Travers?'

'What about the family that owned it – Douglas, I think their name was – are they still there?'

'What's left of 'em.' Ely shook his head sadly. 'An ill-starred family, the Douglases. Very ill-starred.'

'Theah's a local legend of long standin', Mistuh Travers,' Junior Tolliver said darkly, 'to the effect that an evil curse –'

'Oh, don't waste the gen'leman's time with that nonsense, Junior!' Ely said with irritation. 'He's interested in facts, not legends!' He turned back to Trav. 'The history o' Chinaberry has been troubled, it's true. But then, so has the history o' this whole region.'

Ely shook his head again, in reflection. 'Chinaberry was a fine plantation once, a great plantation. Back in the days o' Reeves Douglas, it was some place! I was nevuh theah more'n two or three times, and then only to deliver some goods Mistuh Douglas had ordered, or some such reason – 'course, not bein' a member o' the planter class, I was nevuh theah socially atall –'

'*I* was a member of the planter class,' said Junior Tolliver, 'and *I* was nevuh theah socially either.'

'But it was a splendid place in those days,' Ely persisted. 'Everything fine and gracious about the ol' South was contained in places like Chinaberry, Mistuh Travers. All gone now, o' course. All gone.'

'Ruined by the war, I suppose?' Trav suggested.

'No, suh!' Junior Tolliver barked. 'The waw had nothin' to do with it, suh. Chinaberry was ruined long befo' the waw.'

'What happened?'

'The madwoman!' Tolliver growled. 'The madwoman happened, that's what happened.'

'He means Julia,' Ely said. 'Reeves's daughter, Julia – she inherited the place when her pa died, 'bout six or eight yeahs befo' the waw –' He looked thoughtfully at Tolliver. 'What yeah did Reeves Douglas die, Junior?'

'B'lieve it was 'fifty-fo'. But her ma was still alive then. The madwoman didn't inherit till she figured out a way to git rid o' her ma –'

'Now don't start *that* ugly talk again, Junior!' Ely rasped.

'Well, it was jes' mighty damn peculiar, how Julia brought her villainous friends in theah and took ovuh aftuh her pa died – and then jest a yeah latuh her ma conveniently died, and left her a cleah field to do her mischief!'

'Margaret Douglas had been ailin' fo' yeahs – what's so peculiar about her dyin'?!'

Junior opened his mouth to reply, but Ely stormed on. 'Theah was no reason under the sun to think Julia had anything to do with her mama's death – no reason but vicious, low-down meanness, and you know it, so jes' hush up with that damn foolishness!'

Junior glowered in the face of Ely's anger, but did as he was told.

Ely turned to Trav. ' 'Course, it can't be denied, Julia Douglas always was a strange 'un – even when she was a child, she was peculiar. Nevuh seemed to fit into polite society, they say. A real misfit.'

'Misfit?!' Tolliver exclaimed. 'She was crazy as a howlin' banshee, from the day she was born!' The big man huffed with indignation. 'Come to think of it, though, it ain't so strange that Julia turned out crazy, 'cause her pa was a little touched in the head, too. Reeves Douglas had some preposterous notion that he could operate a big plantation, with lots o' slaves, without usin' the whip fo' discipline!'

'Seems to me like he done pretty well on that principle,' Ely said.

Tolliver looked pained. 'Now, you know that ain't so, Ely! 'Twas Willard that done it –' He delivered a hasty explanation to Trav.

'Douglas had an overseer by the name o' Horace Willard – best damn overseer that evuh worked in this area. He managed to keep the Chinaberry nigguhs in line, and made that place pay, *in spite* o' Reeves Douglas and his idiotic notions.'

'Well, I can't say, nevuh bein' a slaveholder myself,' Ely said.

'Think back, Ely,' Tolliver demanded. 'Wasn't it right aftuh Willard's time that Chinaberry started to go downhill? Wasn't it?! When Douglas lost Willard he lost his prosperity.'

Ely sighed heavily, and looked toward Trav. 'I nevuh did envy slaveholders, Mistuh Travers. Nothin' but torment and trouble. I'm glad I nevuh owned a slave.'

'Huh!' Tolliver grunted in contempt. 'You and Jud, always yappin' about how you wouldn't own slaves. But slaves was our livelihood heah in the South. How *else* we s'posed to work our land?!' Turning his fierce gaze on Trav: 'The reason the South is prostrate today, Mistuh Travers, is not because the goddamn Yankee bastards *whupped* us – it's because they *took away our labour force!*'

Trav shook his head solemnly, trying to look sympathetic.

'Do you realize, Mistuh Travers, the amount of property they stole from us when they took away our slaves? Two billion dollahs' worth, at a conservative estimate, suh. *Two billion dollahs – stolen!*'

'Shocking,' Trav murmured. He had no intention of being drawn into another useless debate; he turned toward Ely.

'About this fellow Willard, Mister Griffith,' he said. 'What happened to him?'

'Well, now, that's a good question, what happened to 'im,' Ely said. 'The way I understood it, Douglas had a young male slave in his household that was gittin' sassy – jest a young boy, but a troublemaker. He gave 'im to Willard for the field hands, and the boy attacked Willard –'

'It was Julia's slave,' Tolliver put in. 'Douglas wanted to git 'im out o' the house, 'cause Julia was makin' a pet out of 'im.'

'Oh yes, that's how it was,' Ely said, nodding. 'That was way back yeahs ago – Julia was jest a young girl then.' The old locked-up recollections were gradually loosening and opening.

'So then, this boy snuck up on Willard one night, and bounced a shovel off his skull, and ran away. Funny thing, they nevuh did find that boy. Douglas had a pack o' dogs roamin' up and down the river fo' somethin' like two weeks.

The only thing they could do was track 'im to a certain spot on the river bank, and that was all. He must 'a' tried to swim across, and drowned.'

'About Willard,' Trav said doggedly. 'What happened, was he killed?'

'Naw!' Ely snorted. 'Wasn't even hurt bad. Jest a little gash in his scalp, was all.'

Trav tried hard not to breathe a sigh of relief.

'You wouldn't say that if you'd been on the receivin' end o' that shovel, Ely,' said Tolliver. 'I saw Willard once aftuh that – he had a great ugly scar. His wife told me he was nevuh again right in the head.

'And theah was this one strange thing about it,' he went on, to Trav. 'Douglas up and fired Willard, like it was all *his* fault. Mighty peculiar.'

Ely continued. 'Well, after that, Julia got real wild. Her parents couldn't do a thing with her, couldn't manage her atall. She started rantin' and ravin' about the injustice of slavery – they say she even went to the slave quarters and told 'em they ought to rebel, and all kinds o' crazy fool things like that. Her folks finally shipped her off to Memphis, to live with her Aunt Amelia up theah, but evidently that only made her worse. Her aunt let her run loose, I reckon, 'cause word got back that Julia'd taken up with some kind o' secret society. A long time latuh we found out it was abolitionists.'

'Can you imagine it?' muttered Tolliver, shaking his massive head. 'At seventeen or eighteen yeahs of age, a high-born southern girl, surrounded by luxury, and every advantage of culture and refinement unduh the sun . . .' He trailed off, overwhelmed still, after long years, with the incomprehensibility of the phenomenon of Julia Douglas.

'Anyway, when her pa died suddenly some yeahs latuh, Julia came home,' Ely went on. 'She was a grown woman by then, o' course. Her ma was ailin' and invalid – fact is, nobody evuh thought she'd outlive Reeves – so Julia took ovuh runnin' the plantation.'

'Runnin' it into the ground,' Junior mumbled.

'Well, suh, you nevuh saw anything like it. Julia brought some o' her wild-eyed friends with her, and they set up what they called a communal society, or somethin' like that. Folks said they was livin' in sin, men and women all togethuh. 'Course, the local people was scandalized – but they didn't know then about Julia and her friends bein' abolitionists.'

'Julia's mama knew it, though,' Tolliver said. 'And it was more'n she could stand – what with her daughter's sinful way o' livin', and bein' an abolitionist, besides. It killed her.'

Ely started to protest. 'Now, Junior –'

'That's what I was sayin' befo'!' Junior declared hotly. 'Jest as sho'ly as I'm sittin' heah – jest as sho'ly as if she'd plunged a knife in the po'r woman's breast – Julia killed her mama!' His eyes burned with dramatic fire.

Ely shrugged. 'Well, anyway,' he said to Trav, 'Julia had this one partic'lar special friend –'

'Lovuh,' Tolliver corrected.

'Fella by the name of – Hollingsworth, wasn't it, Junior?'

'Charles Hollingsworth,' Junior simpered the name disdainfully.

'Yes, that was it. Sort of a thin, mousy, pipsqueak of a fella, from Kentucky. Claimed to be a schoolteacher. Him and Julia proceeded to set up a school fo' the black folks – kids, adults, everybody. They maintained the Nigras had a right to a little education, same as anybody else.'

Tolliver rumbled with indignation. 'Education! In the name o' Jesus, what fo'?! Why, we should 'a' known what they was up to – we should 'a' put a stop to it, right off!'

'Well, be that as it may,' Ely said, 'folks 'round heah *did* finally start to catch on to what was takin' place. The last few yeahs befo' the waw the Chinaberry crop production fell way off, and people noticed that a lot o' the best fields ovuh theah jes' warn't bein' cultivated no mo'. The Nigras seemed to be disappearin'.

'Then one time a night patrol intercepted a couple o' wagons up on the road to Memphis. Turned out to be some o' Julia's communal friends, and about twenty Chinaberry Nigras. The white people claimed they had bought the slaves, and were goin' home with 'em to Tennessee. They had a lawful bill o' sale from Julia Douglas to prove it, so the patrol let 'em proceed. But aftuh that, everybody pretty well knew what was goin' on. Julia was shuttlin' her Nigras north to freedom, a few at a time, through that secret society she was mixed up with – somethin' like that Underground Railroad, or whatevuh they called it.'

Ely shook his head, and chuckled softly. 'You know, even if you don't approve o' her, you got to give the woman credit. What she did took spunk!'

'All right, Ely.' For once Tolliver's voice was calm and

even. 'Everybody knows you've always been sweet on Julia Douglas. But git on with yo' story. You're about to come to the good part.' A sly grin crept across the broad face.

Ely turned a stern frown on Tolliver. 'That's an evil thing to say, Junior. Ain't nothin' good about cold-blooded murder, and it's sinful to call it such!'

Tolliver snorted loudly, and picked up his newspaper. 'You sound jes' like a woman!' he muttered.

Ely was on his feet, his old voice shrill and quavering. 'Considerin' the courage and bravery Julia Douglas showed all those yeahs, I consider that a compliment!'

Tolliver emitted another contemptuous snort, and retreated behind his paper, giving up the contest.

Trav remained still and quiet. We're gettin' there, he told himself. Just be patient. Hope Darby's holdin' out all right.

He studied his nails, and waited.

CHAPTER THREE

Darby stood at the end of the wharf and watched until Trav had gone inside the store with Ely Griffith. He continued to stand for a few moments, gazing up and down the empty dirt street, and felt a shiver of apprehension.

This may be the end of the line, right here, he thought. Trav will be back shortly, and when he comes he'll know something definite, good or bad. It may be only a few minutes until I find out that Chinaberry is no more, that Julia's long gone from there – and that'll be that. Funny, after comin' all this way. . . .

He shrugged and turned away, and walked slowly back along the landing. He went all the way to the other end of the long planked platform, stepping carefully to avoid places where the ancient boards had partially rotted through. At the far end he crossed to the river side and walked back in the opposite direction. There he paused, leaned on the railing and looked down thoughtfully at the little skiff, *El Bandido Moreno*, seemingly right at home, bobbing placidly alongside several local craft in the turbid water below. It felt strange to him to be there – to walk as a free man along those old planks, where, as a boy bound in slavery, he had walked with timidity and fear a few times, long ago.

His mind roamed back over the intervening years. He thought of Matthew Rutledge – as he often did, and always with a feeling that bordered on reverence – of that gentle and kindly but immeasurably brave man who was the true authentic hero and idol of his life.

He thought of his first, early days under Rutledge's tutelage, as an apprentice harness maker in the big bearded man's wagon supply post in western Missouri, on the eastern terminal of the trade road to Santa Fe, and that other long luring westward route that would become known around the world by a name that stirred the blood – the Oregon Trail. Those early days were so full of strange and exciting sights and sounds and experiences that he often lay awake in his bunk at night, unable to sleep for sheer exhilaration. For the first time in his life he worked, and worked hard – the throbbing of muscular fatigue after a day's labour was one of the countless things that were new to him – but after the initial shock had worn off he knew the joy of being a person in his own right, and doing a useful job. It was an orderly, rigorous, and disciplined existence, and didn't seem at all like what he had imagined freedom to be. But, whatever it was, it was good.

His thoughts wandered on back further into the past – to that moment when he had lain drowned in despair and close to death in the forest, and Matthew Rutledge had picked him up and put him into the skiff and rowed away across the dark water in the night. That event had formed an image in his mind; it was a vast and awesome crevice in the earth that divided his life into two distinct, profoundly separate parts. Now, as he walked along the brink of the crevice, he thought that the other, earlier side should seem close, the terrain familiar – but it was not so. It was farther away and more hidden in mist than it had ever seemed before.

All right, he told himself, when Trav comes back and says to me, Forget about it, Darby, nobody's there, we might as well start back – I'll go willingly. I won't let myself be disappointed.

Still, he dreaded the moment when Trav returned from the store.

He resumed his strolling. After making two leisurely trips up and down the length of the wharf, he sat down on a low wooden bench that stood at the south end of the little warehouse building. He glanced up the street toward the general store. No sign of Trav yet. No sign of anything. He rested his head against the boards of the building wall behind him, and let his gaze drift aimlessly down the little rutted alley of a road that paralleled the river.

Human figures registered in his sight. He jerked his head up and opened his eyes in instant alertness. Two black women moved up the road, in the direction of the main street. One elderly and stooped, the other young, tall and erect – both moved with slow deliberateness, each balancing on her head an enormous bundle.

Laundresses, probably, Darby thought, as he watched them come closer. Takin' the washin' back to the white folks. At least they're workin'.

He let his head drop back against the wall again, and closed his eyes. The women would immediately know he was a stranger; he did not want to make them nervous by watching them. When they had progressed to the point on their route closest to him he raised his head and looked again. The older woman's eyes were fixed on the ground, but the wide round eyes of the younger were turned full on Darby, openly curious, and it seemed to him, warm with hospitality.

It lasted only a moment – then the women turned away from him and started up the main street. Darby watched the gentle undulating movements of the younger woman's strong supple body as she climbed the slight grade of the road, the burden balanced with miraculous grace on her head. Darby watched her longingly, and spoke to her with breathless earnestness in his mind.

Oh, I would like to follow you, Mama. I would like to follow you, and lift your burden down and take your hand and lead you. I would like to lead you deep into the quiet woods, Mama, and make a bed for your fine body on the sweet summer grass, and lie there beside you and look far down into your eyes and talk to you softly about many things – oh, so many things I'd like to talk to you about, Mama.

He rolled his head back against the wall again, and gazed dreamily off across the bright morning sky, and sighed.

'That's a lie, Mama,' he muttered aloud. 'There's only one damn thing I'd like to do with you – and it ain't talk.'

He closed his eyes and sighed again, and a soft glowing daydream formed in his mind, filled with shimmering images of women he had known at one time or another, in one way or another – women who had occupied small impermanent corners of his life.

Women of the pioneer wagons, on the western trails. Tall and clear-eyed, sturdy of limb and strong of heart, and fired with an unquenchable spirit of independence.

Indian girls, as shy and elusive as birds of the brush – fierce in the chase, tender in the hand.

Women of the brothels. Gliding with sensuous ease through the saloons and dance halls of dusty western towns, and the incredible perfumed parlours of the San Francisco waterfront – expertly provocative, often unattractive, but mysteriously desirable. Enigmas of the human species.

Spanish girls. Senoritas with flashing black eyes and flowers in their hair, the vital rhythms of guitars and castanets living in their movements.

Darby smiled to think how, in many of those western scenes, his dark skin had been a source of fascination and wonderment, and a decided sexual attraction.

Then – another image, separate and quite different from the rest, coming from a special secret pocket of his memory reservoir: a shining blonde fourteen-year-old girl in a pretty yellow dress, running through the April woods, her flying hair lifted by the soft breeze, light trailing behind her like the afterglow of a shooting star.

He felt himself grasp her by the shoulders and pull her down laughing to the earth, with careful gentleness, not to hurt, and filled with a wonderful sense of joy. He had discovered then – and remembered with agonizing clarity now – that her slender body next to his had generated a wild, mysterious excitement.

We loved each other as children, Julia. And we could have loved each other as man and woman, but the world would never have let that happen. Never, never, never. . . .

A dull ache of longing and loneliness burned in his throat.

There was a soft bumping sound from somewhere down along the wharf – and reality returned with a jolt. Darby opened his eyes and looked around quickly.

A swarthy, grizzled white man in a crumpled felt hat was tying his skiff at the wharf next to *El Bandido Moreno*, and frowning in dour curiosity at the canvas bags and other paraphernalia of travel in the unfamiliar boat, and then at the carved letters of the name on its bow.

Didn't hear him comin' at all, Darby thought. Must 'a' dozed off – got to do better than that.

He studied the man for a few seconds, and made a quick expert appraisial. Local farmer. Considers himself a great fisherman. He'll go up to the store and tell his buddies about the twenty-pound cat he almost pulled in. But first he'll give *me* a hard time, just for the fun of it.

While the fisherman busied himself collecting his tackle and tying his skiff, Darby let his head drop back against the wall again, and pretended to be asleep.

The man thumped heavily along the wharf and stopped in front of Darby. With the toe of a boot he delivered a sharp kick to the sole of Darby's upturned and extended shoe. 'Hey! Sambo!'

Darby opened his eyes and squinted up in feigned surprise

at the man before him. *Well, well. Sambo. Haven't heard that term of endearment in some time.*

'Speakin' to me?' he said.

'Ain't nobody else heah but you and me, Sambo,' the man said. ' 'Course I'm speakin' to you. And you stand up when I do, you heah?'

'Why, certainly,' Darby said blandly. 'Be happy to.'

He stretched his arms and legs and got leisurely to his feet. He was several inches taller than the fisherman.

'And, permit me to correct a mistaken impression you evidently have.' He took a small step forward. 'The name is Ross. Daniel Ross.'

The man frowned fiercely, and stepped back. 'You tryin' to git sassy with me, boy?'

'I'm tryin' to be as courteous as I can. Are you?'

'You ain't southern. Wheah you from? Who you travellin' with? That yo' boat ovuh theah?'

Darby pondered. 'Well, in the order you asked – No, I ain't southern, I'm from California. I'm travellin' with a fella by the name o' Travers. He's a white man, by the way – I can save you *that* question. We're in the South on business, the exact nature of which Trav – Mister Travers – could tell you more about than I can. And yes, that's our skiff. We agreed that I'd remain here and keep an eye on it while Trav – Mister Travers – went up to the store to make inquiries. We figured he'd have a hell of a lot better chance o' gettin' straight answers to questions than *I'd* have, y'see.'

The white man stared; Darby smiled brightly and went on.

'Now, in connection with the name engraved on the bow o' the skiff – I noticed you lookin' at it with some interest a minute ago. It's *El Bandido Moreno*' – Darby gave it the crisp, lilting, authentic pronunciation. 'That's Spanish, meanin' *The Dark Bandit*. It's a title I acquired as a result o' some horseplay out in Santa Fe, a number of years ago. Only a joke – but it makes kind of a nice name for a boat, don't you think?'

The man took another step back, and his expression took on a trace of uneasiness. 'Are you tellin' me you're a *bandit?*'

Darby shrugged. His smile continued to beam, warm and amiable. 'Out in Santa Fe mothers tell their children, "You better be good, or *El Bandido Moreno* will git you!" ' He chuckled gently. 'But then, you know, mothers will tell their kids all kinds o' crazy things.'

The fisherman clutched his fishing gear, adjusted his hat, and backed away from Darby. 'Guess I'll be goin' on,' he mumbled.

'Nice talkin' to you,' Darby said pleasantly.

The man walked away rapidly, crossing the road and heading in the direction of the blacksmith shop. Several times he threw quick nervous glances back over his shoulder.

Darby stood watching, and marvelled at the sudden hasty retreat. Maybe I overdid that bandit stuff a wee bit, he thought.

CHAPTER FOUR

Ely had to leave his seat to take care of one of his infrequent legitimate customers, and the conversation in the store hovered in suspension until he returned. When he sat down again he stared vacantly at Tolliver's newspaper barrier, then at Trav, and said, 'Now, wheah was I?'

'You were sayin' somethin' about murder, Mister Griffith,' Trav prompted.

'Oh, yes.' Ely nodded, recapturing his train of thought. 'Well, one time – it was jes' befo' the outbreak o' the waw – that fella Hollingsworth, the schoolteacher, started up the north road with another one o' them wagonloads o' Chinaberry Nigras. They nevuh got to wheah they was goin'. The next day somebody came across the wagon in a ditch, turned ovuh and burned. Couple o' days latuh they found Hollingsworth's body. It was floatin' in the river, shot full o' holes. They nevuh did find out what became o' the black folks, and they nevuh found out who did the deed, neithuh. T'tell the truth, they nevuh tried real hard to find out.' Ely shook his head solemnly. 'They say po'r Miss Julia was terrible grieved about it. Terrible, terrible grieved.'

Tolliver lowered his paper a few inches to hazard another remark. 'Now tell 'im about the rest o' "po'r" Miss Julia's" brave, courageous friends, Ely.'

'I nevuh said *they* was brave and courageous,' Ely snapped. 'Though they did no worse'n most people would've. They packed up and skedaddled out o' theah fast, and left Julia alone.

'But she carried on, jes' the same. She only had a few mo' Nigras to smuggle out, and she went right on with it, till they was all gone – all 'cept two that stayed with her, the old man named Moses, who used to be her pa's butler, and a young light-skinned gal. She got threats, she got insults, she had outbuildin's on the place burned – she even got shot at once or twice.'

Ely paused, frowning thoughtfully. 'But somehow – I don't know what it was – her enemies must 'a' been a little bit afraid o' her in some strange way. No real harm evuh came to her.' He shook his head in wonderment. 'It's jes' downright unbelievable. I wouldn't 'a' bet two cents on her chances to survive, but she did. She finished her work. Then the waw broke out, and she was gone.' Ely snapped his fingers. 'Jes' like that, she was gone, overnight. Chinaberry was deserted.'

'Gone?' Trav said, frowning.

'Not permanently, suh.' Tolliver lowered his paper again and re-entered the conversation. 'We couldn't be *that* fortunate. Ely says he don't know how she survived, but I can tell you, suh, the country people 'round heah know – they're wise in such things, they know. It's part o' the curse on that place – I started to tell you about it befo', but I was rudely cut off, you remembuh.' Tolliver leaned toward Trav, his eyes hot with mysterious knowledge. 'She's not jest a madwoman. She's a witch. She is *no mortal human!*'

Having delivered this, Junior gave a vigorous nod of emphasis, and his great jowls shook. A faint smile flickered briefly on Trav's lips, in spite of his efforts to suppress it.

Tolliver's sonorous voice grew deeper. 'Laugh if you like, suh, go ahead and laugh. You're an outsider, you know nothing o' these mattuhs!'

Ely exchanged a look of patient understanding with the outsider, and resumed his story.

'Well, we all thought we'd seen the last o' Julia Douglas, madwoman, or witch, or whatevuh. But danged if she didn't come back. She showed up last winter, as sudden as she had left, with her two faithful Nigras still with her – ol' Moses, and the young light-skinned woman.

'The house is a wreck, o' course. It was occupied durin' the waw by Yankees, then by Confederates, then by Yankees ag'in, finally by bands o' thieves and deserters and riff-raff – theah's nothin' left but an empty shell. But Julia's livin' theah ag'in, and scratchin' out a livin'. How she does it, God only knows – nobody but her and the two Nigras. Up to now, far as I've heard, nobody's bothered her. Everything's nice and peaceful.'

Ely paused and gazed reflectively at the back of Tolliver's newspaper. 'Come to think of it, Junior – *that's* the good part o' the story.'

The sound of footsteps intruded, falling heavily on the front veranda. Ely and Junior looked up curiously; Trav, his back to the door, twisted around quickly in his seat.

A large, burly man stood scowling in the doorway of the store. He wore no shirt, and his muscular build was overpoweringly evident in massive chest and bulging biceps. In the crook of one arm a rifle rested. The man squinted into the interior of the store, and called out, 'Hey, Ely, y'all havin' any trouble in theah?'

Ely jumped up and walked rapidly to the door. 'Naw, we ain't havin' trouble,' he said brusquely. 'What's the mattuh with you, Hurley?'

The bare-chested man stared dully at the storekeeper for a moment. 'Jud Watkins said he thought mebbe you had trouble.'

The fisherman came quietly up the steps of the store and peered over Hurley's beefy shoulder. 'Ever'thing all right, Ely?'

'Why of course everything's all right. What the devil's gotten into you-all?'

Hurley broke into a high-pitched, sniggering laugh. 'I don't know what's gotten into *Jud*. He came 'round sayin' y'all's got *bandits* or sump'm.' He grinned in Jud's direction. 'You been nippin' too much o' that nigger moonshine, Jud!'

Another shrill laugh, and Hurley slung his rifle over his shoulder and went off down the steps.

Ely loosed his scolding tongue on Jud Watkins. 'What's the meanin' o' this foolishness, Jud? We're jes' bein' sociable with a gen'leman from California, heah. Is that any reason to raise a fuss?!'

Jud stepped into the store, and his eye fell on Trav. 'You Mistuh Travuhs?' he demanded.

Trav got to his feet and eyed the new arrival carefully. 'That's right.'

'You sho' got a sassy nigger down theah at the wharf.'

Trav frowned. 'Sassy? In what way sassy?'

'He tol' me he was a bandit out west. That true?'

Trav shook his head, and forced a laugh. 'Oh, that's just a joke. Daniel's a little loony, but he's harmless. Pay no attention to him.'

'Humph! He's gon' git his black ass shot, talkin' the way he does.' Jud stalked to the rear of the store, and helped himself to a dipper of water.

Ely followed him, inquiring about his fishing luck.

'Almost got a whoppuh,' Jud said sullenly. 'Must 'a' been twenty pounds. But the bastard slipped off.'

That's about enough, Trav thought.

He called out, 'Thanks for your hospitality, gentlemen.' He nodded to Ely and to Junior Tolliver. 'Happy to have made your acquaintance. Good luck to both of you.' He started for the door.

Ely came forward again quickly, protesting. 'Aw, wish you wouldn't rush off, Mistuh Travers. We ain't hardly had time to talk atall yet.'

'Got to move on,' Trav said. 'Maybe I can stop by again on my way back west.'

'By all means, do that,' Ely said. 'I'd take it amiss if you didn't.' He led Trav toward the door, saying, 'I'll come out with you and show you wheah Chinaberry is.'

'Uh, Mistuh Travers,' Junior Tolliver called, and Trav turned to him. 'Good luck to *you*, suh. And remembuh – tread very carefully.'

Trav smiled, and nodded. 'I'll do that, Mister Tolliver.'

Trav and Ely walked out into the road in front of the store, and Ely pointed off toward the east, across the river.

'Y'see that little mound stickin' up yonder?'

Trav scanned the hazy blue-green horizon in the distance, but could make out nothing definite. He nodded vaguely.

'That's Indian Hill. It's on the north boundary o' the Chinaberry property. You'll find what's left o' the landin' jes' below that, to the right. Theah's a little road that leads up to the house, which is 'bout a quarter of a mile back from the river.'

'Thanks,' Trav said, eager to depart. He extended his hand toward the storekeeper.

Ely gazed down toward the wharf, where Darby could be seen, slumped motionless on the bench beside the warehouse. 'One othuh little thing, Mistuh Travers,' he said, in a lower voice.

'This heah's Arkansas on this side o' the river. Most of Arkansas was in Federal hands fairly early in the waw. In spite o' what Junior might tell you, this state was nevuh one hundred percent *in* the fight. But 'cross yonder –' Ely waved a hand toward the far side of the river – ' 'cross yonder is Miss'sippi. That's a whole othuh world ovuh theah. That's the very heart o' rebellion country. Junior was tellin' *you* to tread carefully – but it's yo' – uh – friend – who ought to be warned.'

'Of what, in particular?'

'Well, things like vagrancy laws. The Black Code, they call it. Nigras have to be employed, and can't wander about without written permission from theah employers. If they do they're liable to be arrested. *Any* white man can arrest 'em, it don't have to be an officer. So tell yo' friend –'

'In other words,' Trav said, 'the black people are not free *yet*.'

Ely's smile seemed to contain a trace of embarrassment. 'Well – I guess you'd have to say that. So tell yo' friend to stick close to you. And tell 'im to be careful with his little jokes.'

'I'll give him the message.' Trav smiled, and extended his hand again. 'I appreciate all your help, Mister Griffith.'

'Oh, don't mention it. You stop by anytime. I'd love to heah mo' about California.'

They shook hands, and Trav turned and walked toward the wharf.

'Oh, Mistuh Travers?' Ely called, and Trav stopped. Ely started to speak, paused and looked back toward the store, then walked forward to overtake Trav. He came up very close, wanting to say something, for the first time awkward and hesitant.

'When you see Miss Julia Douglas,' he said softly, 'I wish you'd give her my kindest regards.'

'I will,' Trav said.

He moved on down the slope toward the landing, and Ely went back to the store.

CHAPTER FIVE

Darby was on his feet as Trav came down the road to the landing. He searched his friend's face anxiously, steeling himself for bad news. Trav's expression was blank, told him nothing.

'Let's go, Daniel,' Trav said crisply. He went past Darby and walked rapidly along the wharf toward the steps. Darby followed.

'Is she there, Trav?' Darby asked the question timidly, almost in a whisper.

Trav went down the steps and untied the skiff. 'She's there. I'll tell you the whole story while we cross.' He climbed into the skiff.

Darby stood still, staring after him.

'Well, come *on*, Daniel,' Trav said imperiously. 'Let's go.'

Darby came to life, scrambled into the skiff, took up the oars and went eagerly to work, quickly manoeuvring the little craft out and away from the wharf. He watched Trav intently, and his hands trembled imperceptibly as he worked.

As they left the western shore behind and inched toward the broad open water of midstream Trav relayed to Darby as best he could the conglomeration of opinions, hearsay, conjecture, gossip, folklore and fact that he had heard at Ely's store, trying to arrange it in the re-telling into some semblance of form and order. Darby listened hungrily, intense and solemn-faced.

'So Julia's there,' he breathed. 'And Moses.' He frowned, trying to imagine it. 'But the other woman – they say she's young?'

Trav nodded.

'Then it's not Josie. Josie's gone.' Darby shook his head, and went on grimly with the task of rowing.

By the time they reached the halfway point of the crossing, Indian Hill had grown from an almost imaginary bump on the eastern horizon into an unmistakable landmark, its partially bare summit rising two hundred feet above the deep green texture of the wooded land along the river's edge.

Trav took the oars for the second half of the crossing, and Darby sat hunched in the bow, gripping the edge of the boat with unconscious tension, his eyes probing the landfall ahead. When they were two hundred yards from shore he spotted the crumbling and weathered remains of Chinaberry landing – a jumble of old timbers and beams, and a single surviving vertical post. He pointed out the location to Trav, who corrected his course accordingly. Darby's grip on the edge of the skiff tightened. Journey's end ahead.

They closed the distance in silence, and in a few moments stood, weary and perspiring, on Chinaberry land. The fresh crispness of the morning had disappeared; now the sun beat down ferociously from high in the burning sky. *El Bandido Moreno* had made the crossing in just over half an hour.

The travellers had come from the Sacramento Valley of California in fifty-two days.

They examined the ruins of the landing, of which nothing remained in place except several log pilings, embedded in the soft mud. Around these, other water-soaked and rotting pieces, once parts of a careful and orderly construction, were strewn like the debris of an ancient shipwreck. A few yards landward from the muddy shore stood the solitary upright post, the remaining member of what once had been a pair of supports for a graceful wooden arch, across which letters formed by short tree-limb sections had spelled out CHINABERRY. In a pile of moulding trash a short distance away, the broken remains of the arch could be seen, discoloured and barely recognizable.

One object in the vicinity seemed to be a part of the present day, rather than a relic of the departed past. That was another skiff, beached well out of the water and secured by a rope to one of the old pilings. It was somewhat smaller than *El Bandido Moreno*, but meticulously well kept and in fine condition, obviously in regular use.

'Must belong to Moses,' Darby murmured. 'Nobody but Moses could keep anything that spotless.'

Trav secured their skiff, and followed Darby up the narrow road that led away from the landing and into a dense thicket of sandbar willow. The little road, once a busy thoroughfare of plantation traffic, now barely survived as a pair of dim parallel tracks in knee-high weeds, almost completely drowned in the deep shadows of the willow thicket.

All was deathly still and silent in the heavy humid noonday heat, and the intruders respected the silence, and walked along slowly and warily – wary of what, they could not have told.

As Darby walked along the old ruined road a swarm of wispy, transparent images danced soundlessly in and out among the drooping trees, leaping out at him, tugging at his sleeve, and fluttering tantalizingly in the corners of his vision.

He and Julia had flown with dusty bare feet up and down these ruts a thousand times, chasing each other, playing hide-and-seek, and racing to the landing at the sound of a distant steamboat whistle, to chalk up a downriver boat for her, or an upriver one for him. There used to be a path beginning about here, in the middle of the willow stand, he remembered, that led up along the western slope of Indian Hill to an unexpected treasure, and one of his and Julia's favourite places in the old times – the pool; cool and shadowy, secluded, private, a miniature paradise for secret-loving children. The path is gone now, apparently – no, there it is, very faint but still there, a few steps farther along. Old memories play tricks, mixing up their details in mischievous confusion.

Darby tried to imagine how the path used to look, all along its twisting way. Above the pool, he remembered, it continued on to the top of the hill, presenting a challenge to sturdy young legs. He could feel again the ache in his lungs from running at full speed up the winding trail, either chasing or being chased by the girl with yellow hair.

He hadn't liked going to the top. There were ha'nts there, and evil spirits, he'd tell the girl – ha'nts because of the family burial ground on the north slope of the hill; evil spirits because the old Indian legend proclaimed their presence. Julia would laugh and gently scorn him, and try to teach him better, just as she always did. She had been tireless in her determination to pull him up out of the mire of ignorance and superstition, working against both the mores of her social order and his own undisciplined fun-loving temperament.

He had been born with nothing, the son of slave parents whose identity was unknown to him, parents who themselves had nothing, not even hope, and who could give to him only the breath of life and no more. That blonde girl, on whose charity he had depended, had been born with the finery of a prosperous and orderly world spread before her like gifts for a princess; all that could be coveted could be possessed with the snap of dainty fingers.

In the security of her own birthright she had been solicitous of *his* well-being. And yet – he had escaped into an exciting, almost carefree existence, while she had endured years of strife and embattlement, in peril of her life, and surrounded by hostility and hatred.

He smiled to himself as he thought of it – a wry, grim smile, devoid of amusement. *Life, you are a jest. Fate is a treacherous lady.*

They came to a certain turn in the little weed-drowned road, and Darby quickened his pace slightly, for just ahead, he knew, the dense willow thicket would end, and they would emerge into openness. He came up to that point of emergence and stopped, and Trav came up beside him. Across a ragged open field that once had been a broad tailored lawn, stood Chinaberry house.

Ely Griffith had said there was nothing left but a shell; even so the sight was unexpected, and struck Darby with the force of shock. He stood as if in a trance, gazing mutely at the scene, while Trav stood quietly at his side.

The house had long since lost the gleaming whiteness that Darby remembered, no paint remaining except forlorn peeling shreds, the bare wood beneath cracked and ashen grey from weathering. Most of the huge high windows that in happier times allowed the interior of the house to be awash with streaming daylight were boarded up; in contrast, the front doorway was a great gaping hole, the heavy handsome door that had graced the entrance having been ripped from its hinges on some violent occasion, leaving ugly scars in the woodwork.

Only isolated sections of the veranda banister remained standing. What was left of the ornately carved intricacies that had added a touch of delicacy and grace to the massive house front now seemed a bizarre caricature. Boards were broken through and missing in the veranda floor and front steps, adding common hazard to the total effect of decay. Abundant weeds grew insolently high around the base of the house and through the holes in the front steps.

The house was grim, sullen, and desolate on the silent

landscape, a monument to ravagement and ruin. Yet, by some miraculous combination of heroism and obstinacy, it continued to stand, like a great wounded beast that refused to die.

One feature of the scene remained unchanged from the old times. The magnificent sycamore tree that had spread its heavy branches protectively over the grassy area enclosed by the circling carriageway in front of the house still stood as before, like an island in a turbulent stream, its graceful serenity unaffected by the powerful flow of years.

Then they saw the girl. She was standing in an area at the side of the house that was once the formal garden, enclosed by high hedges. It was now completely open, and appeared to be serving as a vegetable garden.

The girl had evidently been picking garden produce, putting it into a heavy cloth bag that she carried. She was of mixed blood, with creamy light milk-chocolate skin, young – perhaps twenty – with a full ample figure that would have been dumpy on a shorter frame, but because of her tall, straight-backed carriage, gave a well-proportioned, statuesque appearance.

She stood motionless, staring at the two strangers who had suddenly appeared – and it seemed her stillness was an effort to remain unobserved herself; when she saw that she had been seen, she flung the bag over her shoulder and moved with long graceful strides out of the garden and disappeared from view behind the house, throwing a quick apprehensive glance back at the intruders as she went.

'Beautiful,' Trav murmured.

'Wonder who she is,' said Darby.

It was the first exchange of words between them since leaving the river landing.

Darby began walking again, slowly and hesitantly, going nearer the house. Trav followed a little way behind, and stopped under the sycamore tree, squatting there to rest and take advantage of the shade, and to wait for Darby to make contact with the people in the house. It was Darby's affair from here on.

Darby approached to within twenty feet of the front steps, and paused there. Easy, he told himself. They're skittish and scary, and you can't blame 'em. They know you're here, so wait till they've had a chance to look you over. He stood quietly for a few moments, then started forward again.

'Stop wheah you are! I got a gun!'

The gruff male voice rang out commandingly from the dark interior of the house, and rooted Darby in his tracks.

He was about to call out, to identify himself, when the girl suddenly reappeared. She was framed in the wide front doorway, and her skin seemed even lighter now, against the darkness behind her. She walked out on the veranda, and stood at the top of the steps. Her dress was a thin cotton rag, tattered and worn, but her bearing was imposing and haughty, and when she spoke her voice was cultivated, her speech the speech of a southern lady.

'May I help you? Are you looking for someone?'

Darby kept his eyes fixed on her, and smiled – he hoped it was a disarming, reassuring smile – and took another step forward.

'Don't come any closer,' she commanded. 'What do you want?'

'Well, I – I was hopin' I might see Julia,' he said hesitantly.

The girl's large luminous eyes narrowed in suspicion. 'Do you mean Miss Douglas?' she said coldly.

' 'Scuse me,' Darby said meekly. 'I always called her Julia when we were children.'

The girl frowned, bewildered. She looked beyond Darby to Trav beneath the tree, and back again to Darby.

Moses emerged from the house. He came around the girl and stood gazing intently down at Darby. In his hand was a large heavy stick, which he grasped firmly and held in readiness as a weapon; Darby could see that this was his 'gun.' He was slightly stooped, and somewhat stouter than Darby remembered, his skin deeply lined and wrinkled, and his hair completely silver. But his eyes were clear and his step was as firm and sturdy as ever. Slowly he began to descend the steps with his eyes fixed on the other man. And a glimmer of recognition dawned.

'Can it be?' he said, very softly, as if to himself. 'Can it be?' He came close to Darby and searched his face.

Darby trembled with a desire to shout the old man's name and grab him in a vigorous bear hug. Instead he said gently, 'Hello, Moses.'

'Sweet Jesus,' the old man murmured, and tears welled in his eyes. He flung his stick to the ground. 'Sweet Jesus be praised, it's Darby.' He grasped the younger man's arms in his two hands, as if to test the corporal reality of what he saw, and said again, 'It's Darby.'

'Yes, Moses. It's Darby.'

'Oh, miracle of miracles, blessed miracle!' Moses cried, and said once more, for the first time with certainty, 'It's Darby!'

They clasped each other, both shaking and choked with emotion. Darby spoke with difficulty, managing only a half-whisper. 'I'm glad to see you, Moses.'

After a moment Moses turned, still clasping Darby tenaciously, and called to the girl on the veranda. 'Luanna, come heah! It's Darby, honey, it's my boy Darby!'

The girl was already down the steps and approaching, looking at Darby in a new way, her haughty defensiveness forgotten. 'Darby?' She spoke the name with a trace of awe, and stood still and stared at him in childlike wonder.

Moses reached out and took her by the arm and pulled her closer. 'This heah's Luanna, Darby. She's Josie's child – you 'member Josie. You see the resemblance?'

Darby nodded. The girl's eyes, a striking feature even at a distance, at close range compelled immediate attention. They were at once dark and luminous, and faintly almond-shaped – the same mysterious qualities that had characterized her mother's. Darby and Luanna gazed at each other in silence while Moses chattered on, driven by excitement and joy.

'Lawd, I can't believe it! Darby! So many yeahs it's been – and us nevuh knowin' whethuh you was livin' or dead. Oh, Lawd, Lawd. . . .' He touched Darby again, on the arm, on the shoulder, and gently patted him on the cheek. 'I'm sho' glad I nevuh gave up believin' in miracles, 'cause this is the best and biggest one of all!' His voice broke.

Luanna smiled and held out her hand to Darby. 'I've heard you spoken of all my life, Darby, so many times. Meeting you is like coming face to face with a legend.'

'Luanna was born the yeah aftuh you lef' heah, Darby. She was Josie's girl – yes, I tol' you that, didn't I? We lost po'uh Josie yeahs ago – Luanna's an orphan now.' Moses' face clouded with sadness when he said this – but he did not stop to dwell on it; he was in no mood for sadness now. He looked closely at Darby again, to make sure that it was really he. 'My, my, Darby, I tell you, Julia won't be able to b'lieve this.'

He squinted into Darby's eyes, and frowned suddenly. 'Darby, wheah in tarnation you *been* all these yeahs?' he demanded.

Darby smiled. 'Missouri. California. And lots of other places in between. I'll tell you all about it.'

Moses shook his head, unable to fathom it. 'I tell you, Julia ain't gon' b'lieve it. She was not to be consoled aftuh you run away, not fo' yeahs and yeahs.' He glanced quickly toward the house. 'Lawd, I'm 'fraid she gon' fall down in a dead faint when she sees you now.'

Darby followed the direction of the other man's look. 'Is she inside?' he asked.

Moses nodded. 'She and Luanna live in the big room upstairs in back, that used to be her mama's and papa's bedroom. She's workin' up theah now, tryin' to fix it up a little. The house was ruined, you can see.' Moses's eyes became melancholy. 'Julia's weary, Darby. When you see her you'll know. Life ain't been very good to her.' He smiled suddenly. 'But she's still Julia.'

With an effort Darby tore himself away from these thoughts, and turned to look for Trav. He was still under the sycamore, watching and listening. Darby beckoned, and Trav came toward the others.

'Moses, Luanna –' Darby said, in introduction, 'I want you to meet Bob Travers. Trav's my friend – you can trust him.'

'We're pleased to make yo' acquaintance, Mistuh Travuhs,' Moses said, as they shook hands.

'My pleasure, Moses,' Trav said. 'And, jus' call me Trav.' He swept his eyes quickly to Luanna, to include her in the remark.

She smiled, but lightly brushed aside his invitation to informality. 'We welcome you to Chinaberry, Mister Travers,' she said with cool dignity.

Darby's mind strayed back to thoughts of Julia, and his eyes returned to the house.

'Do you think it would be all right if I went in – alone?' he said to Luanna, then looked from her to Moses, not sure to whom he should address the question.

Luanna hesitated, and looked to Moses. He answered. 'I think it would be fine.'

The others watched as Darby approached the house, went up the steps and across the veranda, hesitated for an instant, and entered. Moses's gaze remained fixed on the empty doorway, his brows knit in thought.

Luanna turned to Trav. 'Come up on the veranda where there's shade, Mister Travers. You can rest, and I'll bring you a cool drink of water.'

She smiled with cordial ease – though her formality remained firm – and Trav smiled in return, feeling the comforting warmth of hospitality.

'Thanks, I'd appreciate that,' he said, and meant it. He remembered with surprising pleasure the good well water given to him by Ely Griffith, that morning.

I've heard it said about southerners, he thought – they may not have a damn thing to offer you but a cool drink of water, but they'll offer you the cool drink of water in a way that'll make you think it's the elixir of the gods. He followed the girl toward the veranda.

Moses came along behind them, walking slowly and absently, continuing to stare at the open doorway where Darby had gone in.

'Lawd, Lawd,' he murmured. 'What a miracle.'

CHAPTER SIX

Darby stood in the entrance foyer of the house, transfixed. The deterioration outside, which had jolted him, was superficial compared to the dismal ruin that confronted him here.

The interior was gutted. Bare walls, gashed, ripped and mutilated in an astonishing variety of ways, from bestial actions, from negligence, and from obscene, malicious vandalism; bare floors – in some sections no floor at all, where boards had been pulled up as a convenient source of firewood, or for who knows what.

To Darby's left was the vast silent space that had been a temple of social glitter, the main hall – what was once elegant and spacious, now, in desolation, an awful cavern of emptiness. The windows in the great room were all boarded, creating an eerie midday darkness that intensified the effect of total gloom. To the right was a little parlour that had been a much favoured retreat for Margaret Douglas in the old days, where she had often sat doing needlework – now empty, dust covered and dark, except for a great jagged patch of daylight through a gash in an outer wall, marking some unrecorded moment of violence in the past.

Straight ahead, the wide staircase. A hazardous thing to negotiate now, for, in addition to the inevitable broken steps, the entire banister railing was gone.

Darby's eyes drifted upward from the murky twilight at the bottom of the stairway to the landing above, almost lost in darkness. Old memories stirred. He felt the pain in his arm from the iron grip of Horace Willard, and the awful pounding of terror in his chest, when the overseer pulled him stumbling blindly down those stairs that night long ago.

He took a few soft steps toward the staircase, trying not to disturb the heavy silence. Ancient boards creaked under his feet – and were answered, it seemed, by faint echoing noises in unseen beams somewhere in the darkness above him. If I still believed in ghosts, he thought, this is the place where I'd find 'em. Oh, how I used to pester Julia with those everlasting ha'nts of mine. . . .

Something moved at the top of the stairs – a wispy, nebulous movement, just catching the corner of his eye. He looked up quickly, and stared at the wraithlike vision of the pale blonde woman standing there.

For a breathless moment she gazed down at him in silence.

'Who are you?' she asked. Her voice was soft, elusive, unreal, floating down to him from a mountaintop.

It was Julia, surely – the same curious mixture of delicacy and firmness. Julia the woman, refined and distilled from Julia the girl – something was added; something was missing – the uncanny combination of strangeness and familiarity stunned him.

Darby put his foot on the stairs and moved up to the second or third step and paused there, and spoke her name quietly, like a question.

'Julia?'

Her hand flew instantly to her throat. She sucked in her breath sharply, and her face seemed suddenly contorted with anguish.

'No, don't!' she whispered fiercely.

She took one step downward on the stairs and stopped, and swayed slightly. Darby moved up quickly toward her, but she flung out her hand protectively, stopping him half-way.

'Don't – don't play tricks,' she said huskily. 'Who are you?'

'Don't you know me, Julia?'

She stared at him, motionless, her arm still held out before her. 'Come closer,' she said.

He went up the stairs very slowly, as if approaching a bird in a bush, keeping his eyes riveted on her face and trying not to make any suddden moves that might frighten her. When he stood two steps below her he stopped and lifted his hand to touch hers, but she withdrew her hand quickly, and continued to stare at him.

She was tall, it seemed to Darby – or perhaps it was an illusion created by the angle of the stairs. The face was the same, and different – the finely chiselled features, the clear cool grey eyes, the pale rose-petal complexion, all unchanged from girlhood; the facial bones more prominent now, the cheeks faintly sunken, tiny wrinkles lacing the outer edges of her eyes, and the worn, weary look that Moses had warned him of, all unfamiliar – the legacy of toilsome years.

And more: She was something more than the sum of her parts, something personal, subjective, and intimate, not apparent to just anybody, surely, but for Darby unmistakable, and as permanent as remembrance. She was beautiful. She was Julia.

After a moment her hands came forward, not defensively, but reaching out to him. A wan smile tugged feebly at the corners of her lips. She stepped down one step, put her hands lightly on his shoulders, and said weakly, 'Darby. . . .'

He came up beside her then, and the illusion of tallness was altered somewhat; though her eyes were almost on a level with his, she seemed suddenly small again, slender, supple and girl-like. They came together in a tight embrace.

'Darby – you've come back,' she whispered.

Luanna slipped in the front doorway, and Trav and Moses followed her. They stood in the foyer, gazing up at the two people on the stairs.

Julia sensed their presence and looked down toward them past Darby's shoulder, and called, 'Moses, look! Darby's here!' Her voice was suddenly alive and vibrant with excitement.

Moses hurried up the stairs, and Julia turned and held out her hand to him. Her eyes glistened.

'Moses, did you know? It's Darby! He's come back to us, Moses!'

'I know it, Little Missy, I know it!' the old man blurted, coming up to them. 'It's a miracle, ain't it?'

'Look at him, Moses, just *look* at him!' she cried.

'I'm lookin' at *you*, Little Missy. I ain't seen yo' face shinin' so with happiness fo' a long, long time.'

Darby gazed mutely at Julia, at Moses, and back again at Julia. He tried to speak, but could not.

'Lawd, Lawd, look down on us today!' Moses intoned, with head thrown back. 'Jes' look at us – we are three happy chillun!'

His old voice quavered. He opened his arms and encompassed Julia and Darby within them.

In the foyer below Luanna turned to Trav and smiled, her own eyes damp and shining. 'Let's go out on the veranda, Mister Travers,' she said in a whisper. 'You sit on the steps and rest a while, and I'll bring you that cool drink of water.'

Luanna went outside again, and Trav moved to follow her,

pausing in the doorway long enough to cast another glance at the people on the stairs. They were clinging soundlessly to each other, all three together, their voices choked and silenced by their inexpressible joy.

Trav's face was solemn as he gazed up at them for a long thoughtful moment. I have a feeling, he said to himself, this is going to be more complicated than I thought.

He slipped quietly out.

CHAPTER SEVEN

The old friends, Julia, Darby and Moses, spent their first hours together in a daze of breathless marvelling at the incredible fact of their reunion. Darby's reappearance had been astonishing; the disclosure that his journey had brought him all the way from California aroused speechless amazement. The eyes of Moses and Julia remained fixed on him, spellbound. A medieval knight returned from half a lifetime of absence in the crusades could not have excited greater wonderment.

Because of the stop at Tolliver's Landing, Darby had arrived with some knowledge of Julia's life in the intervening years, although he knew the source of information was questionable, its accuracy suspect. They would eventually go over it all again together, and their common memories from the earlier years as well. Meanwhile, since she knew nothing of his condition and whereabouts during the long period of separation, Darby determined to give Julia first turn at questions. But she was not immediately moved to detailed questioning; her mind seemed overwhelmed with the miraculous reality of his presence.

'They tried to tell me you were dead,' Julia said to him. 'But I knew better. Moses and I both knew it wasn't so, didn't we, Moses?'

'We didn't know nothin',' Moses said, chuckling. 'We jes' hoped.'

'*I* knew it wasn't so,' Julia insisted. 'I knew it because Darby's trail led to a place by the river where there had been some kind of campsite.'

'That didn't prove a thing,' Moses said stubbornly.

'Someone had obviously taken him away – whether to freedom or to slavery elsewhere, couldn't be told, but *somewhere*.'

'Maybe he tried to swim the river and got drowned,' Moses suggested.

'No, he didn't,' said Luanna with a light laugh. 'Because he's here, you see?'

Julia looked at Darby, and her face shone with the triumphant vindication of her years of faith. 'I knew it because I *had* to know it,' she said quietly. 'Without that I couldn't have gone on.'

'You sound pretty shuah o' yo'self *now*, Little Missy,' Moses said. 'But I 'member very well, you wasn't so shuah at first.'

He went on, to Darby: 'I tell you somethin' – Julia didn't come out o' her room fo' a week after that night you ran off. Josie and me, we'd take turns sneakin' food up to her. Mars Douglas tol' us not to do it, but we done it anyway. Mars Douglas had them ol' dogs runnin' up and down this plantation, uprootin' every rock and log in the woods, and stickin' their slobbery noses into every nook and cranny. It was awful.'

Julia stared at Darby, gripped again by memories that she had often fought desperately to put out of her mind.

'Every moment, every hour of every day, I sat waiting,' she said. 'Waiting for the shout to go up outside – that would mean the dogs had found you, and had torn you to pieces. I wanted to be alone in my room when I heard it.'

They were silent for a moment. Across the chasm of years the horror of that time still haunted them.

Moses continued: 'Mars Douglas finally went and banged on Julia's doah and ordered her to come out, and she said she wouldn't. And Mars Douglas tol' me to bust down the doah and drag her out. I tol' him no, I wouldn't. He yelled at me and said he'd have me whupped. I said go ahead. He said by God, he'd sell me down the river. Then Julia came out.'

'And then –' Julia said, her eyes burning into Darby's, 'Papa searched my room, looking for you.'

She suddenly smiled. 'After that I began to feel like living again. *That's* when I knew you'd gotten away.'

Julia conducted the newcomers through the house, speaking of things that used to be here, things that had once been there, and pointing out details of interest, particularly to Trav, with all the chatty, cheerful aplomb of a tour guide in a museum. The evidence of violence, vandalism and destruction all around her she mentioned only casually, or took no notice of whatever.

Upstairs, she led the visitors into the large room at the front, which had been her father's study. The great oaken door to this room was surprisingly still in place, though its elegantly carved surface bore countless mutilations – doubtless the work of men who in some mysterious way were enraged by the sight of beauty. The windows here, as in the other unused rooms of the house, were boarded, producing a dank and gloomy darkness, in defiance of the brilliant daylight outside.

The little group stood before the place in the back of the big room where old dust-covered boards were nailed over what appeared to be a very narrow doorway. Trav expressed curiosity; Julia explained that her grandfather Douglas had had a penchant for secret passageways, false panels, and mysterious trapdoors, and had built a number of such bizarre features into his house – much to the distress and annoyance of his poor wife. Nearly all of these contrivances had been done away with very early; most had never been used at all – only this one. It had amused her father to preserve it, and use it on occasion, Julia said. She did not elaborate.

Darby walked slowly around the room, remembering how he had felt that night, standing in a cold sweat of fear before the great white master's desk, and wondering what his fate was to be. He stood in the spot where he had stood before, and stared at the place in the dim murkiness of the room where Mr. Douglas's face had been, looking up at him – a bland and genial mask, behind which lurked sinister and terrifying intentions, doubly terrifying to the trembling boy because they were unknown. And then Mr. Willard had come in. . . .

He turned away. 'Let's get out o' here,' he said to Julia. 'I never was very fond o' this room.'

Julia smiled and took his arm, and led the way downstairs and outside.

The old kitchen house that had once been Josie's domain, behind the big house, was a burned out ruin, with nothing surviving but one wall and the stone hearth on which the monstrous black stove had lived. Farther away, those few of the plantation's outbuildings that were still standing were skeletal ruins only. Where the slave quarters had been nothing remained but a few piles of crumbling brick, vestiges of old foundations. The area was grown up in a tangle of weeds and brush, almost completely reverted to a natural state.

What was left of one of the barnyards nearest the house had been partially rebuilt by Moses, and there a small chicken yard had been established, and next to it, an enclosure that was home for a highly prized possession, a cow.

In the late afternoon they went off to take care of the farmyard chores, Darby and Trav watching with interest, their aid politely but firmly declined, while Julia, Luanna and Moses went about feeding the chickens, gathering eggs, and milking the cow, all sharing the work on an equal basis.

Toward evening Julia and Luanna busied themselves in what used to be the pantry, now converted into a kitchen by Moses's ingenious carpentry talents. At length, in the lingering twilight of summer evening, a meal of unadorned simplicity but of surprising abundance was served – a thick vegetable stew, steaming from an iron pot, corn bread, cheese, butter and milk, and a rare delicacy, brought out for a special occasion – wild plum preserves.

The man of this house was Moses now, and he sat at the head of the table that he had built himself, out of scrap lumber collected wherever he could find it. Chairs, too, he had built, and a wide work surface for the kitchen, as well as other odds and ends of furnishings. His creations were rough and primitive and lacking in beauty, but sturdy and serviceable, and all constructed of salvaged material – scrap wood, remnants of old packing crates, even floating debris pulled from the river – nothing escaped being put to use.

With the food on the table, the women quietly lowered their heads, and Darby and Trav, seeing this, quickly did the same. Moses said grace, with an eloquence born of artless simplicity.

'Lawd, our hearts are full of joy tonight. A long lost child has returned to us from distant lands. A new friend has come to join our little circle. We have food on our table, and shelter over our heads. And best of all, we have our love for one another. For these things, Lawd, we thank Thee. Amen.'

Later they sat outside on the veranda steps, under the dark velvet blue sky of early evening. Moses brought out an ancient and battered banjo, and strummed softly and hummed, and produced a gentle music of astonishing lyricism.

A mood of subdued soft-voiced serenity descended upon them. And after a few minutes, at Julia's quiet urging, Darby began to talk about that part of his life unknown to her, the years following his headlong flight from Chinaberry.

CHAPTER EIGHT

'At the beginning there was Mister Rutledge,' Darby said. 'I have to tell you about Mister Rutledge because without him I wouldn't have made it.'

He related how he had come upon the strange man at the river's edge quite by accident that last day he and Julia had been together, when they had been playing hide-and-seek. And he went on to tell, as best he could, the events of that terrible night, remembered as a tumbling kaleidoscope of hallucinatory sensations, leading to merciful oblivion in the bottom of Mr. Rutledge's skiff, in the middle of the dark placid river.

'When I woke up it was almost dawn,' he went on. 'We were landin' at a camp in some deep woods, somewhere on the other side o' the river. There were some people there – two other white men, and about twenty runaway slaves, huddled together and too scared to move. The other white men made fun o' Mister Rutledge for bein' gone a long time and then comin' back with only one runaway.

' "Tha's all right," Mister Rutledge told 'em. "The one I got's a prize." He kind o' grinned at me, and winked, and I felt good – I could tell he liked me.

'We stayed there one day and night, and the day after that the slave folks were divided up into three groups, and loaded into wagons. The three white men each took a wagon, and all went their separate ways. I was glad I was with Mister Rutledge, but I wasn't much glad about the accommodations. Us runaways had to be concealed under big piles o' hay in the wagons, and that's where we stayed durin' the daylight hours every day for about a week, stuffed and cramped and half chokin' to death from the heat and the hay in our faces, out insides churnin' with sickness and our outsides takin' a good beatin' from the wagon constantly grindin' over rutted roads –'

He smiled wryly, remembering. 'That's when I began to think I'd made a mistake to run away. I almost wished I was back in the woods with the dogs after me.

'At night we'd get off the roads and camp in woods, and Mister Rutledge would let us out and feed us, and give us a chance to get a little exercise. Then, one blessed day, we didn't have to get under the hay anymore, we could ride out in the open. That was a great feelin' – the world looked all brand new and wonderful. Pretty soon we were all laughin' and singin' and havin' fun, and Mister Rutledge told us to calm down and be quiet, or we'd have to get back under the hay again.

'We were in Missouri then, Mister Rutledge said. Nearly every evenin' he'd stop at some farmhouse along the road where the folks were friendly, and would feed us, and sometimes give us clothes.

'Finally we got to a place called Westport, on the Missouri River, way out on the western edge o' the state. That was the end o' the line. Across the river was Indian territory.'

Moses had long since put down his banjo; the audience was rapt and still. Darby leaned back on his elbows, and continued.

'Westport, Missouri was one hell of a place. I'd never seen so many different kinds and colours o' people in my life. White, black, red – it was a livin', breathin' rainbow.

'Indians! I was amazed – Indians all over the place. Some half naked like savages, some in buckskins, and some, believe it or not, dressed up in suits, smokin' big cigars, jus' like rich white men.

'Spanish men, Mexicans, traders from Santa Fe – Westport was one o' the main terminals for trade on the Santa Fe Trail. People from the East – settlers, families of emigrants headin' west. The Oregon Trail was beginnin' to be a busy road, too.

'And blacks. Some slaves, some runaways, and lots o' freemen – the first natural-born free blacks I'd ever seen, besides old Oscar, over at Tolliver's Landing.

'Mister Rutledge had a shop up the river a few miles, at a little settlement called Big Bend – nothin' much there but a tradin' post and several shops that catered to the wagon trains, and a ferry. Mister Rutledge's place was situated on a big plot o' flat ground right alongside the river, near the ferry, where the wagons crossed to hit the trails west. It was a wagon repair and harness-makin' shop, and it was a beautiful place, all shiny and clean and efficient. There was another white man who worked there, fellow by the name of Archie Billings. He was an old grey-haired man, very quiet and gentle – he looked after the place while Mister Rutledge was away.

'Mister Rutledge had found employment in various places along the way for the other black folks in our group, but me he took on with him to his shop, and put me to work as an apprentice harness-maker. Well, I got along fine, and learned real fast, but after a while I began to get a little restless. Mister Rutledge practically never let me out o' his sight. I couldn't even go out o' the shop and down to the river, unless I was with Mister Rutledge or Mister Billings.

'I complained. I told Mister Rutledge I used to have a lot more freedom as a slave at Chinaberry than as a freeman, workin' for him. Mister Rutledge smiled and said I was doin' fine in my work, and within a year I'd be a full-fledged expert harness-maker, and then, if I didn't like workin' for him I could find employment lots of other places. In fact, he said, I was free to go any time I felt like it – he was keepin' me close by him mainly for my own protection. There were men out there, he said, who made a profession out o' grabbin' people like me and sellin' 'em back into slavery.

'Well, that shut me up. I quit my complainin' and got down to work, and pretty soon I was beginnin' to enjoy it. I'll never forget the day Mister Rutledge sold my first piece o' work. A buggy harness I'd made – it was on display in the shop, and a man came in and bought it. Paid four dollars for it, and after he'd gone Mister Rutledge came to me and gave me two dollars, sayin' we were gonna share fifty-fifty. Before I had a chance to feel it good he took it back – he'd save it for me, he said. I was too young to handle money – I'd lose it sure.'

Darby shook his head and chuckled at the pleasant remembrance. 'Two dollars – my first wages! At that moment I started to think of myself as a free man.'

With a glance in Julia's direction, Darby continued.

'You'll be glad to know, Julia, that Mister Rutledge didn't neglect my education. In the evenin's we'd sit together, and he'd drill me on my letters and numbers, and give me readin' assignments. He owned three books – a collection of Bible stories, an old almanac, and a copy of *The Last of the Mohicans*. I read all of 'em through, cover to cover.'

For a brief moment Darby fell silent, musing, before going on. 'He was a lonely man, Mister Rutledge. I came to realize after a while that I was more to him than just an employee in his shop. I was something like a foster son.

‘He’d been married in earlier years, had come from Pennsylvania and gone to Texas to settle, with his young wife and little baby son – they were some o’ the first American settlers let into that area by the Mexican government, back in the eighteen-twenties. He had staked out a piece o’ land and just about had a cabin built for his family, when his wife and child took sick with some kind o’ fever, and died. First the baby, then the wife, within a few days of each other.

‘Mister Rutledge lost all interest in bein’ a pioneer – his heart went right out of it. He buried his wife and baby on the plain, and walked off and left his unfinished cabin, without lookin’ back. He wandered around for a while, and finally settled in Missouri, but he never married again.

‘He opened that wagon shop in Big Bend, and it prospered, but pretty soon it became a second interest for ’im. His first was fightin’ slavery – it was the only subject he could get really excited about.

‘He took to leavin’ his shop in Archie Billings’s hands every year, and goin’ down south and collectin’ runaway slaves, and any others he could lay hands on, and smugglin’ ’em out. Dangerous business. He’d leave every spring, and people would figure they’d never see ’im again – but in a month or two he’d be back, with a wagon load o’ black folks. The time he picked *me* up – that was his fifth or sixth expedition. After that he stopped makin’ trips for a while – I think it was because he developed a kind o’ fatherly feelin’ toward me, and didn’t want to go off and leave me till I was old enough to take care o’ myself.

‘Well, when I got to be about eighteen years old I started to get restless again, and this time it was the real thing. I’d heard stories about the adventurous life on the trails, and I wanted to be a part of it. The war with Mexico was over, and the traffic on the Santa Fe Trail was buildin’ up again fast. And the Oregon Trail was gettin’ so busy it seemed like half the population of the United States was headin’ west. There were jobs available on the wagon trains – they needed men bad, and they couldn’t afford to be too choosy about what colour they were. I wanted to go.

‘Mister Rutledge didn’t like the idea. He told me trail life would not be adventurous and exciting at all, the way I thought. It would be nothin’ but back-breakin’ work, drudgery, and hardship. I told him he’d done a good job teachin’ not to be afraid o’ work. I’d be in constant peril of

Indians, he said, and what's worse, unscrupulous white men. There was somethin' else besides, although he didn't come right out and say it – he'd miss me, and be lonely again, after I went. And I knew I'd miss him, too.

'But he was wastin' his breath – I had to go. I got myself a job as a wagon-master's helper on a big train headin' out for Oregon. Mister Rutledge came to see me off, and he gave me a big fat envelope with all my saved-up wages in it – and more, besides, I discovered later. He also gave me a piece o' paper that he said he wanted me to keep. It was a statement, signed by him, sayin' I was his heir. If anything happened to him I was to be owner o' the shop. I thanked him, and we shook hands. He said he had to get back to the shop, and walked away real quick, so I wouldn't see the tears in his eyes. Or maybe he jus' didn't want to see the tears in mine.

'That was the summer o' 'forty-nine.' Darby paused, and stared broodingly at the ground. 'That was the last time I ever saw Mister Rutledge.

'It was a year before I got back to Big Bend, and when I went to the shop I found old Archie Billings in charge. He said Mister Rutledge had taken up his old hobby again, goin' down south and collectin' fugitive slaves, and bringin' 'em back. He had already made one trip that spring. Archie said, and had just left the week before on another one.

'Well, I was pretty disappointed. There was nothin' to interest me in Big Bend, with Mister Rutledge not there. I hung around in the shop with Archie a couple o' days, then hired out on a tradin' train goin' to Santa Fe. It was on that trip that I met up with Trav – he was workin' caravans between Santa Fe and California at the time. We got acquainted in Santa Fe, and decided to team up. I told him about Mister Rutledge, and we hatched a plan to go back to Big Bend and try to get 'im to go into a three-way investment with us, on a small tradin' expedition of our own.'

Darby took a deep breath, and continued, more deliberately.

'When we got back to Big Bend the next summer, not only was there no Mister Rutledge, but no Archie Billings, either. And there was a big new sign on the front o' the shop, that said *Lawson & Company, Trail Outfitters*. I thought I was dreamin', thought I was in the wrong place or somethin' – surely there was some mistake. But no, up the road about a hundred yards was another business, Peterson's Blacksmith Shop, right where it had always been. I went to see Mister Peterson, and asked him what had happened.

'He told me Mister Rutledge had never come back from his second trip south, the year before. Rutledge had been askin' for it all these years, Peterson said, and everybody figured he'd finally gotten what was comin' to 'im. He said old Archie Billings had started to suffer from bad health the past winter, and had sold the shop to a Mister Lawson and some other people.

'I said, "Sold the shop?! What the hell do you mean, sold the shop?! It wasn't his to sell, damn it! Mister Rutledge can't be declared dead, just' like that – not by a damn sight! And if he was, the shop would be mine. He left it to me, and I've got a piece o' paper to prove it!"

'Well, Mister Peterson scratched his head, and shuffled his feet, and said he couldn't see how *that* could be, 'cause Archie Billings had a bill o' sale showin' he bought the property from Rutledge. I demanded to know where Billings was, and Peterson said Archie had gone to live with a daughter, back in Ohio, or Indiana, or some place like that – he wasn't sure just where.

'Then he looked at me real hard, and said, "Hey – you wouldn't be tryin' to pull somethin' funny, would you, comin' 'round claimin' Rutledge's property, jes' 'cause you worked for 'im once?" He squinted his eyes up real meanlike, and he said, "That ain't a healthy way for a nigger to act."

'All at once I knew somethin' bad was goin' on. Trav was standin' next to me, and he took me by the arm and pulled at me and said, "Come on, let's get out o' here."

'That saved me. If he hadn't done that I would've hit Peterson sometime durin' the next three seconds. There were several white men standin' around, watchin' and listenin' – that would've been the end o' me.'

Darby shook his head, frowning, and lapsed into silence. Trav took up the story.

'We talked the situation over that day, and far into the night,' Trav said. 'And we decided *I'd* take over investigatin' the matter, while Darby kept out of sight. If it was really dirty work, they wouldn't hesitate to wipe him out before he could make a fuss.

'Next morning I went around to Lawson's to see what I could find out. Lawson was a smooth, well-groomed gentleman in a fancy business suit, who had a bunch o' tough-lookin' thugs workin' for 'im. He told me he'd heard about how my nigger partner had tried to make trouble over at Peterson's the day before – most unfortunate, he said. Most unfortunate, also, that a nice young fellow like me would choose to associate with niggers – but, of course, he said, that was my own affair.

'Lawson was very polite and pleasant. He poured me a drink and offered me a cigar, and he assured me that legal papers existed showing the transfer of the property from Rutledge to Billings, and from Billings to his own company. Those papers were in the custody of the sheriff. He urged me to go and see for myself, even told me exactly how to get to the sheriff's office.

'I told him I sure *would* see the sheriff, because my partner had a piece of paper from Mister Rutledge that appeared to be in direct contradiction to all that. Well, that's fine, he said, but he'd appreciate it if in the meantime I'd convey a message to my partner. I should tell my partner that if he showed his face around that shop he'd never be seen alive again. Very simple message – I should be able to remember it all right, he thought. I told him I'd sure try, and I left.

'I went straight to the sheriff's office, and there I had another educational conversation. The sheriff was a short squat little man by the name of Frank Jenkins. Yeah, he knew all about that young fellow Darby. Runaway slave, wasn't he? I said I didn't know anything about that – all I knew was, Darby was apparently bein' cheated out of some property that was rightfully his.

'Jenkins started to laugh. He laughed and laughed, and he said, "Are you serious? Do you think a runaway slave could come in this town and claim the property of a deceased white man, and get away with it?"

'I said as far as I was concerned Darby was a free man, and as far as I could make out nobody knew for sure that Rutledge was dead – and the sheriff grabbed me by the arm and said, "Wait a minute." He went into another room and came back with a copy of an old newspaper, and handed it to me. It was a Memphis paper, and it was dated in July of the previous year. On the front page was a story about an abolitionist who had been caught with a group of runaway slaves in western Tennessee, and had been shot and killed. The victim was identified as Matthew Rutledge, of Big Bend, Missouri.

'While I was tryin' to digest that, the sheriff brought me two other papers to look at. One was a bill of sale transferrin' the shop from Rutledge to Billings. It was dated in May, eighteen-fifty. The other was a new deed to the property, all pretty and proper, with everything all written out in gorgeous script – "the third of February, in the Year of Our Lord One Thousand Eight Hundred and Fifty-one" – and so on. This document transferred ownership from Billings to a group called Lawson and Company. There were about half a dozen signatures of shareholders in the company, the first bein' Harold Lawson. Among the other names I recognized two. One was James Peterson, the blacksmith. The other was our stalwart sheriff, Frank Jenkins.

'This Jenkins was almost as nice and polite as Lawson had been. He said I could keep the newspaper – he had other copies. And he suggested that I tell any runaway slave that I might happen to run into that Big Bend just wasn't the healthiest place in the world for 'em, especially if they had aspirations to be property owners.

'I took the newspaper to Darby and showed it to him. I said I was pretty sure the whole thing was a fraud. If Billings had taken ownership of the shop in May of 'fifty, then he was already the owner when Darby had been there talkin' to him, the year before. He hadn't said a word about it. I said, "Darby, d'you think they forced Billings out? Or d'you think he was in on it from the beginning?" Darby just shook his head. He didn't seem much interested in the question. I was pretty mad by then. I said, "Darby, d'you want to fight this thing? We could pool our savings and hire a lawyer."

'Darby just sat there and read the newspaper story about Mister Rutledge bein' killed. He looked at it for a long time, readin' it over and over. "Mister Rutledge knew what he was doin'," he said. "He always knew what the dangers were, and he accepted the risk. That's the way he was."

' "Well all right," I said. "But, damnation, we can't let those bastards get away with this property steal."

'Darby looked at me, and said, "They *did* get away with it, Trav. They're right, I *am* a runaway slave. I ain't got no rights."

' "To hell with that," I said. "They don't deserve to have it without a fight. Somehow we ought to fight 'em."

'Darby got up and walked back and forth a couple o'

times. “I don’t give a damn about the shop,” he said. “And I don’t give a damn about Billings. The only thing around here I cared about was Mister Rutledge. I would’ve fought for *him* till I died. But he’s past fightin’ for now.”

‘Then he crumpled up the newspaper and threw it away. “Let’s get out o’ here,” he said. “Let’s get back west as soon as we can.”

‘And we did – we left the next morning. And we haven’t been back since.’

Trav had come to the end of his narrative. In the pause that followed Darby reached in his pocket and pulled forth a worn leather pocketbook. Engraved on it were the initials D. R., in gold gilt. Darby held it up for the others to see.

‘Mister Rutledge gave it to me.’

‘D. R.?’ Julia said questioningly.

‘My name is Darby Rutledge,’ he said. ‘I’ll bear it proudly, as long as I live.’

There was no more talk. Moses picked up his banjo again, and strummed a soft lazy tune. Out of the darkness a cool night breeze stirred, moving in from over the river.

Julia laid a soft hand on Darby’s arm. ‘Let’s go in now,’ she said.

Darby and Trav were given the one empty bedroom upstairs that was in minimally usable condition.

‘Good,’ Trav said. ‘It faces east. We like to wake up to the mornin’ sun.’

Julia and Luanna retired to their spacious room at the rear, which had been the bedroom of Reeves and Margaret Douglas; Moses still occupied the little cubicle below stairs that had always been his, having good-naturedly scorned Julia’s frequent urging that he renovate a more comfortable room upstairs for himself.

Darby and Trav remained awake for a while, made restless by the unaccustomed indoor sleeping environment. They lay in their bedrolls on the floor in the dark, and talked in low tones.

‘What d’you think, Trav?’ Darby asked.

‘They’re nice people. Good people.’

‘I knew you’d think so.’

‘Julia’s quite a lady, very impressive. Very strong-willed, I imagine. She’d have to be, to do all she’s done. I suppose she’d dominate any man who took up with her.’

Darby frowned in the darkness toward the other. 'I'd argue with you on that.'

Trav yawned and stretched. He was uninterested in arguing. 'And that Luanna,' he murmured. 'There's somethin' that could keep you awake all night, jus' thinkin' about it.'

'*It?*' Darby said sharply. 'She's a person, not a thing.'

Trav chuckled softly. 'Right.' He yawned again, and turned over.

Darby lay awake for a few minutes longer, staring up into the darkness. Slowly he became aware of stars, visible above him; straining his eyes, he made out the dim outlines of several gaping holes in the ceiling.

This old house is in bad need o' some fixin' up, he thought. This house is – let's see – somethin' over sixty years old. I guess it's got a right to need fixin' up. But, sixty years ain't so terribly old, for a house. What *is* the lifespan of a house? For how many years is it young and vigorous, and forward-looking; at what age does it become feeble and doddering, and sit dreaming of the past? When death comes, how does it die – pathetically, or with pride and dignity?

Listen to the silence. In darkness his ears were ultra-sensitive. But there was no silence; the old house made noise. It creaked and groaned like a ship on a rolling sea; it complained softly of the aches of venerable age.

As he sank toward sleep Darby was visited by a stray thought that slipped suddenly into his mind, and jarred him back momentarily into wakefulness. He raised himself on one elbow and gazed around in the darkness, uselessly, unseeing.

This is the room that had been the closed and forbidding domain of Julia's grandfather, the terrifying old man, Milo Gates. He had lived the final decade of his life in this room, in voluntary exile, railing with bitter invective at every human figure that dared venture within his range. And this is where he had died.

Darby smiled to imagine what the former occupant of the room would think of the present ones. Talk about ha'nts . . . He turned toward Trav. 'Pay no attention to that grindin' noise you hear.' he whispered. 'It's just ol' Mars Milo, turnin' over and over in his grave.'

He was answered by a gentle snore.

CHAPTER NINE

The next day Darby and Trav slipped easily into the placid routine of life at Chinaberry. The severely spartan simplicity of it posed no problem, being in spirit completely harmonious with their style of life on the western ranges, where the maximum comforts that could be hoped for were no more than the elemental essentials of existence.

Julia and the others were not self-conscious about their inability to offer more bountiful hospitality; they shared the little they had with easy cheerful graciousness, with no strain or awkward apologetic gestures.

And it was enough; it was good.

Darby slept unaccustomedly late. When he came downstairs at mid-morning he found the house empty. He went out on the rear veranda and blinked in the bright sunshine, and sat down on the steps. In the distance he saw Julia and Luanna, on their way back from chores in the chicken yard. When the women saw him they waved and hastened toward him, smiling good morning. Julia moved more rapidly, and strode ahead of Luanna. It seemed to Darby, watching them, that Luanna hung back deliberately, in deference to the other.

'Hello!' Julia called to him, 'Ready for breakfast?' She pulled off a large sunbonnet she was wearing, and shook her bright yellow hair loose. She seemed vivacious, pink-cheeked and exuberant. Luanna smiled softly at Darby as she came up to the steps, went past him, and continued on into the house.

'Mister Travers has gone with Moses to take the cow to pasture,' Julia said. 'They'll be back shortly. We've gotten our chores done early, so we can spend the rest of the day relaxing, in honour of your arrival.' Her eyes sparkled with enthusiasm.

'Now, you just sit still,' she said, and bustled past him to go inside. 'I'll fix you something to eat.'

Darby smiled his thanks, and sighed contentedly. He felt like a gentleman of leisure – and it was a rare, strange, and comfortable sensation.

After he had eaten he sat for a while at the table and talked with Julia and Luanna. They spoke of Trav. Darby tried haltingly to convey to the women some faint impression of the kind of close camaraderie and unspoken loyalty that existed between himself and his friend, but stopped short, embarrassed, and afraid of sounding silly.

Luanna said. 'You're lucky, Darby, to have a friend like Mister Travers. He's a good, good man.'

'Mister Travers seems to be an intelligent, perceptive person,' Julia said stiffly. 'Obviously he recognizes worthiness in human character when he sees it. I have great respect for him.'

Darby stared at his coffee cup, musing for a moment. 'Seems like all my life I've been helped along by some pretty nice people,' he said. 'First you, Julia – then Mister Rutledge, then Trav. I've been lucky, no question about it. Damn lucky.'

Soon Trav and Moses returned to the house, conversing in easy geniality, like old friends. Immediately Julia began to organize the little group with the efficiency of a schoolmarm.

'All right, everybody, this day shall be given over to pleasure and relaxation. And since you're the cause of the special occasion, Darby, you shall name the diversion. What suits your fancy, honoured Sir?'

Darby pondered only briefly. 'Is the squatter's cabin still there, Julia?'

Her eyes shone with joy at his choice. 'Almost exactly as you last saw it,' she said, smiling.

They walked together, all five, in a leisurely stroll down the faint overgrown tracks of the road that led to the southerly parts of the plantation land.

Darby looked with a vague stirring of revulsion at the hulking ruin of the outermost barn, and the area behind it. where he had received an edifying lecture on the nature and behaviour of hounds, that last night at Chinaberry, when his childhood came to an abrupt end. The barn existed now in a skeletal remnant only, and its yard had been utterly eradicated; Darby was relieved, as he walked past the place, that it did not look the same, and that recollections did not rush back upon him with a horrible sense of reality.

They went on past the south fields, all standing idle, empty and desolate. The road turned westward a half mile south of the house, as Darby remembered, but now ended immediately. They continued on a narrow path that led past a forlorn and abandoned relic, the overseer's house. It was nearly fallen down, crumbling slowly under the combined assault of time, the elements, and creeping undergrowth.

Darby had lost no time in questioning Julia on the Willard affair, and she had substantially verified the information provided by Ely Griffith. Satisfied that this burdensome worry had been lifted from his conscience, Darby gratefully pushed all thoughts of the old overseer out of his mind. The old ruined dwelling was identified for Trav's curiosity – then they went on, with no further mention of the Willard subject.

The strollers followed the path as it penetrated and wound through the forest. At length they emerged from the dark green of leafy shade, and paused at the edge of the little forest-enclosed meadow, on the opposite side of which stood the squatter's cabin.

Darby gazed at the scene before them for a moment, and said, 'Somethin's different here. Somethin's missin'.'

'Yes,' said Julia. 'Something's missing.'

Darby frowned suddenly as the realization struck him. 'The chinaberry tree,' he said. 'It's gone.'

'A casualty of war,' Julia said. 'Confederate troops camped here once, and the area was shelled by a Federal gunboat. The chinaberry tree took a direct hit.'

The others followed as Julia went to the centre of the clearing and stood by the shattered stump of the tree, jutting like a gaunt, ancient bone of a dinosaur, its base half hidden in high weeds.

'The great losses of war are thoroughly documented, and grieved over,' she said. 'But there is no earthly way to calculate the infinite *small* losses.'

She smiled suddenly, looking at Darby. 'There are victories, too, though, and survivors.' She gestured toward the cabin.

There were subtle differences in the cabin's appearance, Darby noticed. The roof, already a ruin in earlier years, was now entirely gone. The forest had encroached, had come in closer; the meadow was not as large as it had been. Behind the cabin, a tall loblolly pine that had been nonexistent or too small to notice in earlier times now rose to impressive dimensions, and spread ragged branches over the open roof area of the little structure below.

Moses chuckled in gentle scorn, and grinned. 'That ol' house ain't nevuh gon' fall down,' he said. 'It's too ugly to die.'

Trav and Luanna joined in light laughter at the old man's humour; Julia smiled in permissive acceptance of it. She knew that no one loved the old cabin as she did. She took Darby's arm, and they went toward the little house. The others followed.

At the doorway, before they stepped inside, Darby said, 'Watch out for the ha'nts, Julia.'

Her quick secretive smile suddenly reminded him of Julia the girl. 'The ha'nts have missed you, Darby,' she whispered. 'Almost as much as I have.'

Inside the cabin, Darby was struck by the same eerie feeling of immense enclosed silence that had always impressed him so strongly when he was a boy. Under their feet, and adding to the sense of hush, was a thick carpet of pine needles, instead of the bare hard-packed earthen floor that he remembered.

He pointed out to Trav the Greek inscription on the rough log wall, and ran his finger lightly over it, and was awed again with the wonder of its ageless endurance. *God Bless This House.*

He turned to Julia with a questioning look. 'Julia, I was wonderin' about Cap'n Andrew –'

She shook her head. 'He never came back. We've never heard from him again.'

'I'm sorry.'

Julia refused to mourn. 'Uncle Andrew has been so awfully busy, sailing the high seas, fighting off fierce pirates and battling storms – he's just lost track of time. Someday he'll remember, and come back.'

'Sure.' Darby smiled with her. 'Someday he's gonna come and take you for a ride on his beautiful ship, jus' like he promised.'

'You, too,' she said.

In the afternoon they walked down the road through the willow thicket, to the river, because Darby and Trav wanted to take care of the task of unloading and cleaning out their skiff.

Luanna immediately discovered the name on the side of the boat. 'What's this – *El Bandido Moreno?*' she asked.

'That's a name Trav stuck on me in our early days, down in Santa Fe,' Darby answered.

'All I did was introduce him to the modest pleasures of cards,' Trav said. 'How was I to know he'd turn into a fiendish addict?'

Darby rolled his eyes skyward and spoke in the impassioned tones of a country preacher. 'Sisters and brothers! Let me warn you against the poisonous sin of card playin'! It will corrupt your souls, and turn you into monsters with hairy faces!'

'Even worse,' said Trav, 'it might bring you into possession of things you'd be better off without.'

'Amen!' Darby said.

Trav continued: 'That's what happened to Darby. I felt sorry for the poor lonely waif, so I invited him to sit in on a game with a couple o' cowboys – just a friendly little game, you understand, nothing serious.

'Well, right away the innocent beginner is an instantaneous card shark, and cleans out everybody, wins all the money in sight. Finally one o' the cowboys puts up his beautiful brand new Colt revolver, with jewel-studded holster – and damned if Darby doesn't win that, too.

'The cowboy accused Darby of cheating at that point, and made some unsportsmanlike comments about his ancestry.'

'I thanked him cordially,' Darby said, 'and offered to plug him between the eyes with my new pistol.'

'Well, Darby took to wearin' that big shiny revolver,' Trav went on. 'He thought it gave him a certain dash and style. To my way o' thinkin', he tended to swagger a bit.'

'I wasn't swaggerin', Trav,' Darby protested. 'I was *limpin'*. The damn thing pulled me over to one side.'

'Anyway, one evening about a week later I was sittin' in a little cafe called Pancho's, waitin' for Darby to meet me, and I was tellin' Pancho and some other fellows about Darby and his new toy. And in a few minutes who should walk in but the cowboy from the card game. He spotted me right off, and came over and asked me where my African partner was. He said he'd been thinkin' about that little game, and he'd decided he was goin' to get his gun back, one way or the other. Well, I looked at this fellow, and I did some fast thinkin'. He was known to be an expert shot, and he was in an ugly mood. And Darby – my pal Darby didn't know which end of a gun the bullet comes out of.

'So I went all solemn and seriouslike, and I said, "Friend, I wonder if you have any idea how lucky you are to be alive and well at this moment."

'The cowboy said, "Huh?"

'I said, "Friend, is it possible you don't know who my partner is?"

'He looked at me kind of half-dumb and half-worried, and said, "Who is he?"

'I said, "My friend, I'm sorry I neglected to warn you that day when you were playin' cards. You came close to eternity on that occasion, dear friend, oh, so very close. If you only knew –"

' "All right!" he yells. "Who is he?"

'Pancho and the others were all gathered around, listenin'. I got up real close to the cowboy, and in a fearful whisper I said, "My dearly beloved friend, the African – is *El Bandido Moreno!*"

'The cowboy frowned at me, and squinted his eyes, and looked around at the other men. They were all starin' at him with dark ominous looks on their faces.

' "*El Bandido Moreno*," he snorted. "I never heard of 'im."

'I stepped back and staggered a little, as if I couldn't believe my ears. "You're tellin' me you've never heard of *El Bandido Moreno?!*" I squawked. I started laughing.

' "Did you hear that?!" I said to the others. "This poor fellow's never heard of *El Bandido Moreno!*"

'The other men started laughing, too, and we all just stood there laughing, all except the cowboy. Then Pancho turned serious, and reached out and put a hand on the cowboy's shoulder, and said, "If you have never heard of *Moreno*, *Señor*, then all I can say is, your ignorance will lead you to your doom. I feel very sorry for you, *Señor*."

'The cowboy looked around from one to the other of us, tryin' to decide whether to call our bluff or not. And *then* – guess who walked in?'

'*El Bandido Moreno!*' Luanna squealed.

'Right. He walked right up to the cowboy, very casual, and said, "Care for a little card game, pal?"

'The cowboy looked at him for a minute without answering. Then he smiled, a nice polite smile, and said, "No, thanks. I got to be movin' on." He gave us all a quick nod, and walked out.'

Darby took over the commentary. 'I couldn't figure out what the hell was goin' on, and they kept me wonderin' for a while, before they told me. After that I stopped wearin' the damn gun – got rid of it, in fact. But it was too late – my reputation was made. From then on, every time I walked into Pancho's Café everybody would throw up their hands and holler, "Help! It's *El Bandido Moreno!*" and dive for cover. Then they'd all come crawlin' out, laughing fit to kill. Funniest joke they'd ever heard.

'After we left there we didn't get back to Santa Fe for two years, and when we did, we walked into Pancho's, and damned if everybody in the place didn't throw up their hands and holler, "Help! It's *El Bandido Moreno!*" and dive for cover.

'I've been stuck with that little ceremony around there ever since.' Darby shook his head, chuckling. 'Funny thing, we never did see that cowboy again.'

CHAPTER TEN

After finishing their work they beached the skiff, tied it safely up out of the water, and started back up the road through the willow thicket.

Luanna manoeuvred herself into a position next to Darby as they walked, and tried with childlike eagerness to prolong the storytelling mood. 'Tell us more, Darby. What did you do after that?'

'Well, after that we went back to Big Bend,' Darby said. 'And you've heard about our little unpleasantness there. Then we went west again with a big wagon train of emigrants on their way to Oregon – but along the Snake River, where the trails divide, half of 'em peeled off for California instead. The big rush was in that direction then, 'cause the gold fever was on. So we headed down that way, too – figured we'd pan us a million dollars' worth o' the yellow stuff in a few months, and retire.

'When we got there we saw it wasn't quite that simple. The best of it was already over, and the best wasn't very good. Two or three hundred men went broke for every one who succeeded. It wasn't hard for an old card shark like me to see that the odds weren't right. So we drifted on back to work on the trails. In a few years we started workin' on some big ranches in the Sacramento Valley. We made good wages, but we spent it as fast as we got it. Seems like we were awful restless – always driftin', driftin'.'

'But didn't you find any gold?' Luanna asked.

'Naw.'

'None at *all?*'

'Well – one piece,' Darby conceded. 'Show 'em our gold piece, Trav.'

'What d'ya mean, *our* gold piece?' Trav snorted. He reached inside his shirt and pulled out a thin chain, suspended around his neck. Attached to it was a beautifully polished nugget.

Luanna came to him, took it in her hands and examined it closely, fascinated. Julia and Moses, too, came close to see.

'Oh-h-h-h,' Luanna breathed, transfixed with admiration. 'You *found* this?'

Trav grinned. 'Oh, no! Darby won it in a card game, off an old prospector.'

Julia and Moses turned away, laughing, as Luanna stared at Trav in astonishment. 'If *he* won it,' Luanna said, 'why do *you* have it?'

' 'Cause he's too dumb to know when to quit. I won it off him in another game, a week later.'

'Tha's all right,' Darby said. 'I'm jus' lettin' him hold it for me. I'm gonna get it back, one o' these days.'

At the place where the path up the western side of Indian Hill began, Moses left them, saying his old legs did not take kindly to climbing. The others went up the path following its devious way through the willows and out onto the piney hillside above, and on toward the spring-fed pool, halfway up the slope.

Luanna ran on ahead, leaving the others behind, her tan young legs flashing with supple grace. When the strollers arrived at the crest of the little ridge, where the pool came into view a short distance beyond, they saw the girl with her skirt pulled up above her knees, wading in the rippling water, and smiling at them with an unaffected sparkle of joyousness.

They stopped and admired her, like parents watching a pretty child.

'I speak with the authority of an expert,' Trav said. 'And I'm prepared to stake my reputation on the judgment that Luanna is the prettiest girl on the river for five hundred miles in either direction.'

'On behalf of the Douglas family I thank you for the compliment, Mister Travers,' Julia said smiling. 'I'm sure your reputation as an expert is well-deserved.'

Trav walked down toward the pool and climbed on the slope above and beyond it, examining the source of the spring with scientific curiosity, and glancing occasionally at the girl in the water with an earthier interest.

Julia sat on a grassy knoll under a tree, and Darby sat at her feet. For a few minutes he dug aimlessly in the ground with a stick, frowning in thought.

'Luanna's mother was Josie,' he mused.

'Yes,' Julia said.

'And her father – was your father.'

'That's right.' The answer came without hesitation. 'When Luanna was a little girl Papa wanted to give her to me, saying it was to make up for my losing you. In later years he actually felt bad about all that unpleasantness, you see.

'But I said no, I didn't want her. I told Papa I would never own another human being, ever. He tried to insist, said I was being silly and spiteful. But I absolutely refused.'

Julia smiled faintly, in remembrance. 'It was sad – Papa never could quite make me out. Neither could Mama, of course. But she gave up on me very early. Papa at least kept *trying* to understand me.'

'What happened to Josie?' Darby asked.

Julia did not reply for a moment. When she spoke her words were hesitant. 'Well, we – we lost her.'

She saw that Darby was watching her, waiting for more information. She went on, dredging up painful memories with reluctance.

'I was living in Memphis, with my Aunt Amelia, when Papa died. Mama had been in ill health for several years, and I knew she wouldn't be able to manage alone. I came home immediately, prepared to stay. When I got here I found Mama had done two things with commendable efficiency, in spite of her condition. She had made all the funeral arrangements for Papa – and she had sold Josie and Luanna to a passing slave trader.'

Julia turned intense eyes on Darby. 'That was the completion of something that had been developing for a long time – my permanent alienation from Mama.

'Of course it couldn't have come as a great surprise to Josie – she always knew how Mama hated her. But, poor little Luanna – she was only eight years old!

'Mama wouldn't listen to my protests. "Surely you didn't think I was going to keep that *whore* under my roof an instant longer than necessary, did you?" she said to me.

'I said, "Mama, that's an outrageous, hideous thing to say! Josie was no whore, Josie was a slave woman. A *slave woman* – don't you understand that?!"

'Mama looked at me with tears in her eyes, and said, "*You* don't understand, Julia. You don't know the loneliness and misery and humiliation I've had to endure all these years, because of that woman. Surely you couldn't expect me to *keep* her?"

' "But what about Luanna?" I said.

' "And surely you wouldn't want me to separate mother and child, would you?" she said.

' "No, I wouldn't, Mama," I said. "Even though you didn't hesitate to separate families when you sold off Grandpa Gates's people, at Maywood. You might at least have waited until I got here. Josie was my dear friend, and Luanna – Mama, how *could* you?! Luanna is *my sister!*"

'Mama rose up out of her sickbed and came at me, and tried to scratch my face. I had to tear myself away from her – she was like a wild woman.

' "Don't you ever call her that!" she screeched at me. "Don't you *ever* say that again!"

'I looked her straight in the eye, and I said, "I hate you for this, Mama. I hate you for what you've done." Then I left the room.'

Julia stared at her hands in her lap during a long moment of silence. 'I'm sorry I spoke to her like that. She didn't live very much longer.'

She lifted her gaze, with anguished eyes, toward the summit of Indian Hill, on the north slope of which lay the Douglas cemetery. Her face was calm then, as she looked down the slope before them, and watched the beautiful brown girl playing in the water.

'Poor Mama,' she sighed. 'She couldn't change what was. Luanna *is* my sister.'

From the pool Luanna called. 'Darby! Come and cool your feet – the water's perfect!' Her voice was vivacious and lilting.

Darby waved to her and smiled. 'In a minute,' he called. He sat still, waiting for Julia to continue. 'What did you do?'

'Thank God, my kind and wonderful friend, Charles Hollingsworth, was with me, and two other good people from the abolitionist group in Memphis. Moses described the slave trader to us, and told us he had seemed to be heading downriver, toward Vicksburg and Natchez. We left early the next morning to go after him.

'We found no trace of him at Vicksburg, so we kept going. At Natchez we were told that he had been there, but had continued on to Baton Rouge. We went on.

'In Baton Rouge we found Luanna in a slave market. She was alone. She had been separated from her mother after the first day or two, she told us, and didn't know what had become of her. The child was tearful with joy to see us – she was hungry, dirty, and thoroughly terrified. And you can imagine my *own* joy.

'We haggled with the slave market proprietor like fish-wives, trying to get the price down. Finally we bought Luanna for two hundred and fifty dollars – just about all the money we had among us.

'Sometimes I tease Luanna, saying I wonder if she's really worth all that much money.' Julia smiled as her eyes followed the girl splashing in the pool. 'She's worth all the world to me – she's the only kin I have left.'

'But you never found Josie?' Darby asked.

'It was hopeless.' Julia shook her head. 'She was gone.'

There was a squeal from Luanna, and a loud splash; she had fallen in the water, and was completely immersed. Trav scrambled down from the hillside above, to help her, but she was on her feet immediately, and came out of the pool, laughing. The others laughed with her, seeing there was no harm, and she walked up the slope toward Darby and Julia, dripping, and enjoying the attention.

'Luanna, darling, must you be so careless?' Julia's tone was motherly.

'You know how children are,' Darby remarked to Julia, teasingly, and Luanna playfully flipped wet hands at him.

Trav had followed the girl up the slope, and he and Darby now gazed in open admiration at the bountiful contours of Luanna's full young body, outlined with vivid clarity against her thin wet-clinging cotton dress.

Luanna saw the admiring appraisals, and accepted them with obvious relish. Julia, also, saw them. She got to her feet.

'Come along, young lady,' she said, and took Luanna by the hand. 'We'd better get you home to change. You'll catch cold.'

There was an outcry of protest from the men.

'She can lie in the sun, and dry,' Darby suggested.

'And we'll give her a rubdown,' Trav said. This brought a laugh from Darby and Luanna.

Julia did not join in. 'We have to get back,' she said crisply. 'We have chores to do.'

'But you said this was a holiday,' Luanna complained.

'Darby and Mister Travers will expect supper on the table this evening, holiday or not.' She glanced toward the men. 'You and Mister Travers can take your time, Darby. Will you excuse us?'

Julia started back down the path toward the road, leading Luanna by the hand. The girl followed along quietly, like an obedient child, turning once to smile and wave to the two men, before she disappeared from their view.

After they had gone, Trav reclined on the grass near Darby. 'What a girl,' he said, after a moment. 'She sure does have a fine pair.'

'Pair o' what?' Darby said. 'Legs, breasts, or eyes?'

'Take your pick. They're all fine.' Trav gazed thoughtfully down toward the pool. 'But, you know – I don't think Miss Julia likes us to admire her housemaid too much.'

Darby twisted around to look hard at the other. 'Now, just a minute, pal. In the first place, Luanna ain't exactly a housemaid. She's Julia's half-sister.'

'Yeah, I figured that,' Trav said, without surprise. He laughed softly. 'Quite a nice little arrangement Papa Douglas had goin'. A light-skinned missus upstairs, and a dark-skinned one downstairs. He must've been a tired but happy man.'

'And in the second place,' Darby said, 'Julia doesn't consider Luanna *or* Moses servants. She thinks of herself and them as three close friends who live together, all exactly equal.'

Trav looked at Darby with sly amusement playing on his face. 'You really believe that?'

'Damn right I do.'

'Didn't you see the way Julia took Luanna's hand and led her off home like a naughty child? D'ya think there's any doubt in anybody's mind around here about who's in charge?'

Darby laughed, with a trace of annoyance. 'C'mon, Trav, that ain't fair. Julia *is* Julia, that's jus' the way she is. Moses and Luanna are free people – they can go anytime they feel like it.'

'Go? Go where? They got no place to go – and they're prohibited by law from movin' about freely, anyway. No, Luanna will never get away from here unless a knight in shining armour comes along and carries her off. And to do it he'd have to fight somethin' more dangerous than a dragon. He'd have to fight Julia.'

Trav stretched out on his back in the grass and gazed skyward with a beatific smile on his face. 'But, by golly, what a prize,' he murmured. 'It would be worth fightin' Julia and a dragon both.' He grinned at Darby. 'One at a time, of course.'

Darby gave his partner a cold contemptuous look, and got to his feet. 'Let's get back to the house,' he said brusquely, 'and see if we can make ourselves useful.' He started off down the path, without waiting.

In the evening the little group sat again on the front steps of the house, and listened for a while to the secret night-songs of frogs and crickets, and enjoyed the coolness. It was the second time they had done this, and already it seemed an old and comfortable habit. Moses brought out his banjo again, and this time Luanna crooned to his accompaniment – an old lullaby, gently rendered in a vibrant, velvet-soft contralto.

Julia and Darby fell into a pleasant mood of reminiscence, and talked in low relaxed voices of nice moments from the far past – small, trivial treasures, that floated up to the surface of memory.

At length Julia straightened with a sudden impulse, and said, 'Darby Rutledge. That's a fine name. I like it. It's so good to have you here again.' She leaned over and put an arm around Darby and hugged him briefly. 'I'm proud to know you, Darby Rutledge.'

She got up and moved across to Trav, who was resting on one elbow on the opposite side of the steps. Julia extended her hand to him. 'I'm proud to know you, too, Mister Travers.'

He shook her hand and said dryly, 'Jus' call me Trav.'

Julia was seized with an upwelling of enthusiasm. She walked around the bare yard before the steps, clasping and unclasping her hands.

'Just think, Darby! How remotely improbable it was that you would survive, after running off into this ruthless world, as pathetically ill-equipped as you were. How improbable that we *both* survived, and have come together again. Doesn't that say anything to you, Darby? Doesn't that *tell* you something?'

She came and stood before Darby, and took both his hands in hers. Her eyes shone in the darkness.

'It means that some powerful, mysterious force is on our side – call it God, or fate, or whatever you like. We are whole once more. Our little family is complete, Darby, now that you are here. Together, all of us together – Mister Travers, too – we can do the impossible. We can give Chinaberry a new life!'

Darby gazed up at her in the silence of fascination. It was the same feeling he had known as a boy, when she had tried to plant some exciting treasure of knowledge in his undisciplined head.

Trav's intent gaze was fixed on her also, as he leaned forward. 'Uh, Miss Julia,' he said quickly, 'I don't think you quite understand. Darby and I aren't *stayin'* here. We're just visitin'.'

Julia looked at him blankly, as if unable to comprehend.

'Not staying?' She turned her eyes on Darby. 'Not staying, Darby?'

Trav went on hastily. 'We have an option on some land in California, y'see. It's a beautiful piece of property – we were lucky to get hold of it. We're goin' to start a ranch, soon's we get back.'

There was no visible response to this information. Trav smiled, and went on.

'We've been planning this for a long time – savin' our money, and lookin' forward to it. It's goin' to be great, havin' our own place, after workin' for years on other people's places.'

Julia was staring at him, stony faced. He appealed directly to her. '*You* can understand that, Miss Julia – you love *your* place.'

'Yes,' Julia said bleakly. 'Of course – I understand.' She sat down again on the steps.

Trav laughed nervously, fighting against the void of quiet that had descended. 'Pretty soon we'll be a couple o' rich cattle barons.'

'Ever thought of bein' a *cotton* baron, Mister Travers?' Luanna asked quietly.

Trav shrugged. 'I don't know anything about cotton. I'm a western man, not a plantation man.'

Julia gazed at Darby with veiled, solemn eyes. 'Are *you* a western man, Darby?'

He was picking aimlessly at the sole of his shoe; he removed a small fragment of dried mud from it and threw it across the yard. 'I been knockin' around so long,' he said, 'I don't know *what* I am.' He did not look at Julia.

After a moment Julia straightened with a sudden upturn of her irrepressible spirits. She reached out and patted Darby's hand, and smiled gently. 'Well – it's good to have you here for a while, anyway.'

Trav quickly tried to help the fluttering revival of cheerfulness. 'Naturally, we'll expect all of you to come and visit us on the ranch someday.'

'Thank you, Mister Travers,' Julia said. 'That would be nice.'

She got to her feet. 'I seem to be unusually tired tonight. If you-all will excuse me – I think I'll go to bed now.' She moved past the others on the steps, acknowledged their goodnight-sayings with a nod, and went into the house.

Conversation had died. Moses strummed his banjo and sang softly – an ancient melancholy chant-song of mingled hope and despair, born in the dark recesses of slave quarters long ago.

The others listened in gloomy silence.

CHAPTER ELEVEN

Beginning the next day the visitors abandoned their idleness and set themselves a schedule of activity. A conference was held to consider the staggering number of tasks that needed attention on the place; projects were suggested, priorities discussed, argued, and tentatively determined, and work begun.

Trav and Moses formed a team and set about the job of dismantling the useless and rotting ruin of one of the old barns, to clear the area and prepare for the hoped for eventuality of a new structure. Darby, with his greater experience in shop work, undertook a refurbishing of the meagre contents of Moses's dilapidated tool shed. Rusty axe blades were cleaned and sharpened; broken handles replaced with sturdy new ones, cut from hickory limbs; harnesses repaired, in anticipation of the day when mules, ploughs and wagons would again be part of the plantation's equipment.

Several days were spent in an almost feverish dawn-to-dusk dedication to labour. And Julia watched it all, and saw form, order and progression begin to take shape and emerge from stagnation and rubble, and felt within herself a stirring of excitement that she hardly dared acknowledge to herself – though she expressed it readily and in glowing terms to the others – and nursed a quiet hope that the nadir of the troubled history of Chinaberry had at last been reached, a turning point passed, and the long uphill climb to recovery begun.

Then it was Saturday, and in the afternoon, by deeply ingrained tradition, there was a sharp diminishing in the level of human industry and the expenditure of energy, and an indulgent languor settled over the premises, a calm that would last until Monday. For a little while each person sought his own preference in leisure; it was a time of welcome rest, and a brief renewal of private thoughts in solitude.

Moses went off to the river, on a fishing expedition. In his little skiff he would expertly plumb the murky backwaters, following the labyrinthine contours of cays and inlets, seeking out the fat lazy catfish that lurked there, silent and hidden. He did this often; it was the form of relaxation he loved best, and, besides, provided a much needed and highly valued dietary supplement. Both Trav and Darby declined with smiling thanks Moses's invitation to join him – maybe next time, they said – having recently endured long days in the cramped confines of their own skiff.

Julia and Luanna turned their attention to the pursuit of special personal interests. Julia set forth in sunbonnet to the corner of the vegetable garden that she had set aside for flower culture, there to prune and pamper her prized rose bushes. Luanna sat at the kitchen table – the kitchen being the only room in the house that contained table and chairs – and spread an enormous half-finished quilt before her, and busied herself with needle and thread and enthusiasm on some tiny details of its vast kaleidoscopically colourful patchwork pattern. Darby retreated upstairs for an afternoon nap.

Only Trav, whose restless spirit usually derived from leisure more tedium than enjoyment, found himself temporarily without a source of diversion. He walked with Moses to the river and saw him off and wished him good fishing, strolled back toward the house, stopped for a few minutes in the enclosed stillness of the willow thicket and watched the secretive black-and-yellow-flashing play of a pair of warblers, returned to the house and paused briefly in the shade of the sycamore tree, finally wandered up to the front steps and sat down and gazed up the slope of Indian Hill, across the road.

Presently his mind began to work. It was necessary, he told himself, to establish a timetable. There was a question to be settled: how long would he allow himself and Darby to remain there, before insisting that it was time to leave? The exact length of their stay was a subject that had never been properly discussed – an omission that he now saw was a serious mistake.

Clearly, Julia's immediate assumption had been that Darby was no mere visitor, but a prodigal son returned home. She had been genuinely distressed a few evenings ago – and at the same time, he thought, calculating in conveying a pathetic impression – on hearing that their plans were to return to California. She had not put up an argument, and Trav had been relieved at this – but now he was beginning to have apprehensive second thoughts.

Julia Douglas was not going to give up without a fight on

something she wanted very badly – he knew enough about that frail blonde woman's miraculous history to be sure of that. And she wanted Darby intensely, that was certain. What impelled her to this want – whether simply a wish to collect manpower for the operation of the plantation, or some mysterious subliminal love-attraction for him who had been a childhood plaything – he could not tell. Probably a little of each. She needed manpower, obviously. It was equally obvious that she held for Darby a tender fondness that pictured him still as a pet, rather than a man.

A tender fondness – he grimaced – that was a woefully inadequate description of Julia's feeling for Darby. Rather a deep, fierce, tenacious attachment, a possessive – *that* was it; the quality of the lady of Chinaberry that made Trav feel threatened by her. Possessiveness.

He saw his own position as quite a simple one. He was welcome to stay there because he represented manpower, of course – and, no doubt, because a willingness to stay on his part would fairly well seal Darby's entrapment.

Was that the right word, entrapment? He wanted to be fair – but he could see it no other way. Julia was already well along in some plot to achieve her objective, he was sure, and she would be skilful – and every day they stayed increased her chances for success.

A fixed timetable – a firm departure date that couldn't be altered, that would permit no procrastination – that was the only defence.

Besides, damn it, there were practical considerations. It was now close to the end of June; it would be prudent to depart by mid-July, in order to have ample time to clear the western mountain passes before first snowfall. Also, they would have to purchase horses somewhere, for the overland trip – that might prove to be a time-consuming chore.

Decision came swiftly: they would leave in three weeks, if Darby was agreeable. Decision expanded, and grew firmer: He, Trav, would stay no longer than three more weeks, regardless of developments. With this resolve came a sense of improved control. He felt much better. With nothing stirring, he began to find the quiet of the summer afternoon intoxicating. He leaned back on his elbows and yawned, and thought of stretching out in the shade under the sycamore.

He was mildly startled to discover Darby standing beside him; he had not heard the other man come out of the house or cross the veranda. He looked up and said, 'Hey – thought you were takin' a nap.'

Darby sat down. 'Couldn't sleep.'

'Too hot?'

'Things runnin' through my mind.'

'Like what?'

Darby glanced up toward Indian Hill, his face intent with thoughtfulness. He looked at Trav. 'Let's take a walk, want to?'

Trav did not particularly want to. 'What you got on your mind, pal?'

'I want to show you somethin',' Darby said. 'Somethin' beautiful.'

Trav nodded. 'Couldn't say no to *that.*'

They walked down to the sycamore tree by the front road, crossed the road and followed a little path that led across an empty field to the base of Indian Hill. Darby led the way, then, climbing with the path in a meandering way up the steep south slope of the hill, to the top.

The grassy quarter-acre of the rounded summit was enclosed in a natural horseshoe effect, with forest growth on three sides, but opening southward to a wide view over the flat green low-lying plantation land, and the great river on its western border.

Darby stood on the south edge of this summit clearing, and Trav came up beside him. A gentle breeze came and went, teasingly, intermittently ruffling the hot afternoon air. Several towering castles of cumulus floated in space, miles above them to the south and west, their great snowy stratospheric heights laying broad blotches of dark shade across the land far below, and over the sheen of the river surface.

'You see that curve of the river, way down yonder?' Darby said, pointing. 'Chinaberry land extends all the way down to there. And over that way –' He scanned the horizon to the southeast, peering through a soft diffusion of sunlight and distance. 'Well, you can't even make out the boundary in that direction. It's a mighty big piece o' land. A tremendous piece o' land.'

'Yeah,' Trav said, without expression.

'And all goin' to waste. Ain't it a shame?'

Trav looked hard at his companion, and didn't answer.

'And look down there, Trav.' Darby's eyes had dropped to a lower angle, to the house and its surroundings, below them.

From that viewpoint the dismal condition of the roof, with gaping holes among the broken and dilapidated old wooden shakes, was glaringly evident.

'That house was built about sixty-five years ago, and it's still solid,' Darby said. 'But you can see it needs a lot o' work. Look at that roof! You know, I think we got our work priorities mixed up, Trav. We got to get busy on that roof, real soon.'

Luanna came into their view. She came out of the back of the house, carrying two empty pails, and walked down a broad pathway that bisected the vegetable garden. She was heading for the well, which was located near the front road on the opposite side of the garden area, a hundred and fifty yards from the house. She moved with languid, unhurried deliberateness, in keeping with the mood of the lazy afternoon. The men watched her from the hilltop.

'What a pleasure,' Trav murmured.

'Why didn't she tell me she needed water,' Darby grumbled. 'I'd have brought it for her.'

'The way she moves,' Trav said. 'I don't know what it is – it's just a pleasure to watch.'

'Trav, we got to do somethin' about that well.'

'What's the matter with the well?'

'It's in the wrong place – too damn far from the house.'

'Wonder where she got that pair.'

Darby's face went grim with annoyance. 'Which pair you referrin' to *this* time?'

'Those eyes. Those unbelievable almond eyes.'

'Her mama had eyes like that. People used to say Josie was part Indian, or part Chinese – I don't know what all they said. It was a mystery.'

'I figure Luanna's blood is half white, half Negro, and half mystery,' Trav said.

'That's three halves.'

'Right. She's a woman and a half.' Trav chuckled in appreciation of his own wit.

'Seems to me like you're gettin' to have a one-track mind,' Darby snapped. He walked away a short distance, and stopped, and gazed again down at the house below.

In a moment Trav followed. 'And it seems to *me*,' he said, 'you're gettin' a little bit grouchy.'

Darby smiled faintly. 'Unintentional,' he mumbled.

'What's the matter, pal? Somethin' botherin' you?'

'Naw – I was jus' thinkin' about that well problem. Moses tells me there's plenty of underground water, all over the place – no damn reason under the sun why a new well couldn't be dug, up closer to the house. Moses says he remembers Julia's papa talkin' about doin' that, thirty years ago. Jus' never got around to it – too busy havin' parties, I guess. Back in those days there wasn't no shortage o' help, o' course. Inefficiency jus' didn't pose any problem. Now it does.'

Trav listened gravely, studying Darby's face.

'Speakin' o' problems,' he said, 'I'd like to talk to you about one *we* have.'

'Go ahead.' Darby was ready to listen.

'The earth goes on turnin', as you know. And the seasons continue to evolve and progress, flowin' one into the next in their slow deliberate pace, just as they've always done. You know that.'

'And?'

'Accordin' to my calculations, we can only afford to spend about three more weeks here, at the outside. Your plans are jus' gettin' too damn elaborate, son. We ain't got *time* to do all the nice things you're talkin' about.'

Darby's smile was gentle. 'Aw, c'mon, Trav. Loosen up a little. For once in our lives, we're workin' for an unselfish purpose, helpin' other people. Why not jus' pitch in and enjoy it? It'll do you good.'

'You were gonna show me somethin' beautiful,' Trav said dryly. 'Where is it?'

'There!' Darby flung his arm toward the lush spreading land below them. 'Right there, if you'll only jus' look!'

He pointed off to their left. 'Look yonder, Trav, jus' for instance. See those three fields over there? Those are the northeast fields – they're the finest on the place. And, Trav, the finest fields on *this* place is as fine as you can get.'

'I don't follow you, Darby,' Trav said. 'You practisin' to be a salesman, or somethin'?'

'Moses tells me those fields haven't been planted in seven or eight years. They're just achin' for a crop.' Darby's eyes measured the far dimensions of the land. Excitement shone in his face. 'You know somethin', Trav? I bet we could do wonders here, if we put our minds to it.'

'God damn!' Trav growled. 'Here it comes – I might've known it.'

'If we jus' had a mule and a plough, Trav, jus' *one* mule and a –'

'We don't *need* a mule and a plough! We're gonna be ranchers, not farmers!'

'Yeah, but listen, Trav –'

'Yeah, but *you* listen. We got our life savings tied up in a piece o' land in California. You gave me your word that if I came here with you we'd go right back, you wouldn't get involved. And now I'm findin' out how much your word is worth. It's worth about as much as a pile o' cow crap!'

'Christ,' Darby muttered. 'Look who's grouchy now.'

'I can see what's happening. I can see it clear as day, and I don't like it.'

'What's happenin', Trav?'

'The mother hen is gathering you under her wing – and you're turning into one o' her baby chicks.'

Darby laughed soundlessly. 'That's plain ridiculous, Trav. If you don't *like* Julia, that's your privilege. But you got no cause to go insultin' people –'

'Three weeks,' Trav said. 'We're leavin' here in three weeks – or *I* am, with or without you. I'd appreciate it if you'll let me know as soon as you've made your decision.'

They glared at each other, tense and bristling, and, it seemed to Darby, across a cold windswept distance. Darby's expression softened; he spoke with conciliatory gentleness. 'Let's not be this way, Trav. I was only daydreamin': It didn't mean a thing. Forget about it.'

From far below Julia called, her voice floating up the hillside faintly. 'Darby!' She stood under the big sycamore by the front road, and waved. 'Come on down.'

Darby returned the wave. 'Be right there!'

He moved toward the path down the slope, paused and glanced back at Trav. 'Coming?'

'Later,' Trav said, and when Darby continued to stand looking at him, added, in a fair imitation of a drawling southern accent, 'Hop to it, boy. Yo' mistress done called you.'

For an instant Darby's eyes flashed in anger. Then it was gone, covered by an easy amiable smile. Darby tossed his friend a quick jaunty salute, turned and went down the hillside.

CHAPTER TWELVE

When Trav came down off the hill ten minutes later and approached the house, walking with the unhurried aimlessness of one who has no particular destination or purpose in mind, Darby and Luanna were with Julia in the rose garden. Julia was evidently showing the others the blossoming radiance of her favourite bushes. All three waved to Trav, and motioned for him to join them.

He shrugged inwardly and said to himself, what the hell, might as well pitch in and enjoy it, as Darby suggested. For three weeks, he thought. For three weeks I'll relax and enjoy it. He started toward the rose garden.

Suddenly Julia put down her trowel and came rapidly out of the garden toward him. He stopped, seeing her approach, and in that instant became aware of a faint sound far off, to his left. His mind immediately identified the dull thudding of a horse's hooves on dirt. He looked down the little road that led into the plantation lands from the east, and saw a man on horseback approaching. The horse plodded along at a slow sleepy pace in the afternoon heat, but in the profound quiet the gentle sound carried clearly across the distance.

Julia stood in the front yard, shaded her eyes with her hand, and studied the approaching horseman intently. Trav observed her curiously. From a greater distance she had heard the sound of the horse sooner than he.

Luanna and Darby had followed Julia out of the garden.

'Who is it, Julia?' Luanna asked. Her voice was hushed, and strained with a touch of anxiety.

Julia turned, performed an exaggerated sigh of relief, and smiled. 'It's all right,' she said. 'It's Mister Hodges.'

Trav, watching, saw Luanna reflect the other woman's feeling of relief that the visitor was identified, and friendly. The state of siege continues, he thought. How long will they have to go on living this way? But – he realized with a mild shock – this arriving stranger would be the first human being, other than Darby and the three residents of Chinaberry house, he had seen since crossing the river from Tolliver's

Landing – that was almost a week ago. Isolation breeds suspiciousness, undoubtedly. He remembered the wary hostility with which he and Darby had been greeted initially. Suddenly it seemed more understandable. Suddenly it seemed perfectly natural.

While they waited for the visitor to cover the remaining distance, Julia explained hastily to Darby and Trav: 'George is a fine man, and a dear, dear friend. He's with the New England Freedman's Aid Society, working to provide schools and teachers for black children – for emancipated people of all ages, in fact. He's doing wonderful work, under the most difficult conditions imaginable.'

Trav glanced at her and saw that her eyes were shining with the animated excitement that periodically seized her. It was a look that he had learned to recognize. She broke off and hurried down to the road to meet Hodges, waving to him as he came nearer.

George Hodges was a paunchy, sandy-haired man, about fifty years of age, with a wide ready smile that was plainly visible before he came close enough for conversation. Julia stood in the middle of the road and greeted him with effusive cordiality, held his horse's reins while he alighted, and kissed him on the cheek.

'I'm so glad you came, George,' she said as she led him toward the others. 'I have a special treat for you – two, I should say. First of all, I want you to meet a new friend we've gained.'

To Trav's surprise Julia led the visitor directly to him.

'Mister Robert Travers, from California – I'm sure you'll find him as interesting as we do.' Julia smiled from one to the other. 'Mister Travers, Mister George Hodges.'

Trav extended his hand, and said easily, 'Glad to meet you, George,' and got his second surprise when Hodges spoke.

'It's a pleasure to make yo'uh acquaintance, Mistuh Travers. Welcome to the South.' The deep slow speech was native southern.

The handshake was vigorous and firm, the eyes steady, free of deviousness. Trav liked the man instantly. 'Thank you,' he said. 'Jus' call me Trav.'

Hodges turned to Luanna, who was standing expectantly at his elbow. 'Luanna, my dear, how are you?' He regarded her with a fond smile, and kissed her lightly.

Julia took Hodges by the arm and led him toward Darby. 'The second special treat, George,' she said with subdued excitement. She explained Darby's identity to Hodges, who reacted with engaging interest, and exclaimed with astonishment and gladness at the news of his miraculous reappearance. He pumped Darby's hand enthusiastically, as if they were long separated friends, at last reunited.

'You see why I'm glad you came, George,' Julia said. 'Besides the principal reason, of course, which is that I'm always happy to see you, good friend.' She hugged his arm, and smiled warmly up at him.

'By the way,' he said. He turned to his horse, loosened a leather strap behind the saddle, and brought down a small clothcovered basket, and held it out to Julia. 'Sarah's been putting up preserves from morning till night, for weeks,' he said, smiling broadly. 'She sends you-all some samples.'

Julia accepted the gift with unaffected delight, peeked under the cloth and admired the basket's contents extravagantly, and passed it to Luanna for her inspection. 'Your Sarah's so *good*, George. Please give her our thanks, and our love.' She clung to Hodge's arm and pulled him toward the house. 'Come in and rest, now, and have a cool drink of water.'

Darby took the visitor's horse, leading it around to the back of the house for watering. Hodges called thanks to him, and beamed a smile at his hostess.

'My goodness, Julia!' he admonished, chuckling. 'You always act as if the King of England had arrived, whenever I stop by to say hello.'

'No indeed, I don't,' she laughed lightly. 'No king would receive half so cordial a welcome here.'

Hodges offered courtly assistance to Julia up the veranda steps, holding her hand, with his other arm lightly around her waist. She accepted the courtesy with a grateful smile, and leaned on him delicately.

Trav was wryly amused at this, remembering that he had seen Julia glide rapidly up and down those steps many times with perfect ease, unassisted.

Trav, in fact, found himself watching Julia closely and constantly, with a strange mixture of conflicting feelings. She performed in the role of hostess, he noticed, with a degree of charm and graciousness that would have done credit to a lady of nobility, despite her condition of severe poverty. It was clear that with Julia social polish had never been a case of *couldn't*, but merely of *wouldn't*. Trav realized that his admiration for the lady's mettle was growing, grudgingly but steadily, hour by hour. And it made him uneasy. For there was no denying that she was his adversary – the most formidable adversary, he ruefully acknowledged, of his life.

They sat in the dining area, relaxing with informal ease in Moses's rough handmade chairs, and sipped their cool drinks of water, the traditional potion of hospitality in the rural South. Darby came in presently, and again received warm thanks from Hodges for taking care of the horse. They chatted about trivialities for what seemed to Trav an inordinately long time; finally he determined to direct the conversation into some meaningful channel.

'Miss Julia tells us you're with some New England society or other, teachin' school for freedmen,' Trav said to Hodges. 'With that in mind, I frankly had expected to hear you speak in northern accents, rather than southern.'

Hodges smiled. 'Yo'uh confusion is perfectly understandable, suh. You might imagine that teaching black folks to read and write is not exactly a typical occupation for a native white southerner, eh?' His ready laugh boomed out.

'George is hardly a typical southerner,' Julia said. 'Just the same, he's typical of a certain *kind* of southerner. The kind that sees there's an enormous amount of work to be done, and has rolled up his sleeves and begun, regardless of the opinions of others.'

'That describes you, my dear, much more than me,' Hodges said, and beamed at Julia.

Then his face grew quickly serious. 'But it's foolish to talk of the typical southerner. There is no such thing.' He glanced at Trav. 'Could you describe the typical westerner, Mistuh Travers?'

He gazed fixedly at Trav as he continued. 'It is most unfortunate – it is a tragic thing – that people outside the South have a lurid picture in their minds of the white southerner. A cruel, grinning, cold-hearted ruffian, brandishing a murderous whip, with his foot on the neck of the prostrate black man. I have to protest, suh, that's not typical either.

'There are many decent people in the South – more than any of us know, I think – who earnestly desire to see the black people somehow admitted as worthy members to the society of man.

'Both of us – Julia and I – belong to that group, each in his own way. The difference between us is that, before the war, I could nevuh decide what ought to be done about the problem, so I didn't do anything. Miss Julia, heah, as you undoubtedly know, nevuh had any trouble deciding what to do, and she went about doing it, years ago, with utter disregard for her own safety.'

'You're being unfair to yourself, George,' Julia said. 'It was easy for me to think of something to do. I inherited slaves – I simply set about freeing them.'

'Easy to think of it. Doing it was something else altogether.' Hodges frowned solemnly, in thought. 'Frankly, I was nevuh entirely shuah that what she was doing was exactly the *wisest* thing,' he said to the others. 'But I nevuh ceased to admire her fo' doing it.'

'Your teachin' work, Mister Hodges –' Darby said, leaning forward. 'I'd like to hear more about that.'

'Good!' Hodges reacted with enthusiasm. 'That affords me the opportunity to open the subject I wanted to discuss with our gracious hostess.' He glanced at Julia, then turned to face Darby.

'Outsiders might imagine that the former slaves are all happy as can be, now that they're emancipated. Nonsense, of course. We all know that the vast majority are in no way equipped by experience or training to be independent self-supporting people. Naturally, one of the most pressing needs is education, something that was forbidden fruit in the old days – as you're aware, no doubt.

'Well, the society I'm working with is just one of a number of philanthropic organizations active throughout the South, trying to help fill that need. It's a fine movement, doing worthwhile work, and I'm proud to be associated with it. Besides,' – he smiled ingratiatingly – 'it helps pacify my guilt feelings about not doing *anything*, all those years.

'But our existence has been precarious. We've depended heavily on the support of the Freedmen's Bureau – that's the Federal agency that provides aid to the emancipated people, you know – and the Bureau has been hovering on the verge of extinction. President Johnson has recently vetoed the bill passed by Congress extending the Bureau's life, but our friends in the North are quite optimistic – they're expecting the veto to be overridden.'

Julia made her own characteristically optimistic prediction. 'It *will* be overridden,' she said firmly. 'I'm absolutely sure of it.'

'In any case,' Hodges said, 'we push on. We have a little one-room building in Hanesville, kindly donated by some friendly folks over there, which we've converted into a big classroom. Last winter, our first year of operation, we had a capacity enrolment, and come this fall it's going to be much heavier, I know.

'We're busy right now building on an extension for additional classrooms, so in that respect we'll be in fair shape. Where we'll be hurting is in our desperate need for teachers.'

At this point Hodges shifted his gaze and directed his words to Julia.

'That's mainly why I'm here today, dear lady, to remind you once again that I am counting heavily – nay, I am praying – that you will see your way clear to come and join us in the fall.'

All eyes turned to Julia. She seemed momentarily flustered.

'Well – I thank you, George. And you know how deeply I admire what you're doing, and how very much I'd like to be a part of it.'

She got up, and began to walk about the room restlessly.

'But, you see – there's a dream I'm nursing in my head – or I suppose some people would call it an obsession. I want to resurrect Chinaberry. I want to pull it up out of the muck and mire, somehow, and make it go again. In an entirely different way from before, of course, but I want it to live again. I don't know what it is, really – possibly I'm impelled by some sort of guilt feelings myself – some deep-down subconscious guilt over the knowledge that I am at least partly responsible for Chinaberry's ruin in the first place.

'I don't know what it is – I only know I have my heart *absolutely* set on doing this. And I'm afraid it will tax the energies and endurance of all of us to the utmost. Our capacities are extremely limited, you see, more so than it may appear. Darby and Mister Travers are being enormously helpful while they're here, just *enormously* – it's unbelievable what they've accomplished in just a few days – but they'll be leaving soon, they'll be going back to California. There's really only Luanna and Moses, and me.'

'I understand your feelings for the place,' Hodges said, in a kindly voice. 'But is it more important than our cause?'

'No, of course not. But it's – right now it's the most important thing in the world to me.'

'Julia – you spent years fighting for freedom for the slaves. You were the one who was in there fighting when most of the rest of us who shared your beliefs were too cowardly or too uncertain of ourselves to move a muscle or open our mouths. Now that that primary goal is achieved, surely *you*, of *all* people, are not going to give up the fight – surely you know that the war is only half won?'

Julia looked away from him, defensively. 'I'm tired, George,' she said weakly. 'I've done my share. Somebody else will have to carry on the fight.'

Hodges regarded her gravely. 'That's uncharacteristic of you, Julia,' he said.

'Is it? Really?!' Julia's voice rose shrilly, and a sudden anger burned on her cheeks. 'Do I have a reputation for such superhumanly saintly, noble, self-sacrificing goodness that for once in my life, when I want to pursue a small *personal* desire, rather than some shining ideal up there in the sky, everybody must look at me with sad reproachful eyes and say, "That's uncharacteristic of you, Julia"!'

Hodges gazed at her, and his eyes were sad indeed, but innocent of reproach. 'I'm sorry, Julia,' he said gently. 'I didn't mean it that way. I apologize.'

Julia came to Hodges impulsively, and put her hands on his shoulders. 'Forgive me,' she half-whispered. 'Forgive me, George. That little outburst *was* uncharacteristic of me, I sincerely hope.'

Hodges chuckled good-naturedly, and reached up and patted her hand. 'Think nothing of it, my dear. My fault entirely. I've been accused, among other things, of being overly persistent – and I suppose it's true.' He smiled toward Luanna. 'I even had the temerity to believe I'd be able to persuade *both* of you to come and work with us this year.'

'Oh, I'd *love* to do it, Mister Hodges,' Luanna said eagerly, then subsided quickly, remembering what Julia had said. 'But, with our burden of work here, and all –' She added, with instinctive modesty, 'Of course, I don't have the experience Julia has.'

'Well, we'll just have to wait and see what happens,' Julia said briskly. 'Other possibilities may open up for us. Perhaps –' Her eyes searched the room, as if seeking a solution to the problem. She carefully avoided looking at Darby or Trav. 'Perhaps our little family will grow. Who knows?'

'*I'm* not pregnant, Julia,' Luanna said innocently. 'Are you?'

An outburst of laughter released all tension, and the mood of genial relaxation returned. Soon there occurred a certain social ritual, refined by generations of use and permanently set in traditional form, and performed with exquisite grace.

'You'll stay for supper, of course, won't you, George?' Julia said, to begin it.

Hodges played his part and declined with thanks, saying he had to get back to Hanesville before dark.

Julia disposed of this trifling ploy with ease. 'It stays light very late, this time of year. Besides, we'll have supper early.'

Hodges protested that it would be an imposition. His protestations were protested in turn.

'You *must* stay,' Luanna declared. 'Moses has gone fishing, and when Moses goes fishing he always comes back with enough fish for a whole regiment.'

Hodges admitted to being strongly tempted. Further urgings, and the visitor's sham resistance crumbled. This settled, the conversation again wandered off and lost itself among pleasant trivialities.

Presently there was a shout from Moses outside.

'There!' Julia exclaimed. 'Moses is back with our supper already!'

They looked out and saw him approaching, grinning broadly, and holding up for display a string of plump gleaming catfish. There were gasps of delight and admiration.

Trav started for the door, saying, 'I'll go help him,' and went out. He crossed the back veranda and went down the steps quickly, and started across the yard toward Moses. As he went his face was grim from the thoughts that churned in his mind.

Dear God, I can't believe it. She couldn't have staged that touching scene – there is no way she could have planned it, no way she could have gotten word to Hodges, directing him to show up at this perfect time and provide her with a convenient sounding board to play her sad song upon, and wring our hearts. Wring Darby's heart – that's the point.

He suddenly remembered foolish, pompous old Junior Tolliver, fixing him with baleful eye and muttering, 'She's a witch – she is *no mortal human.*'

Trav smiled without amusement, and mumbled softly to himself, 'You ain't so foolish, Junior.'

His smile softened and brightened as he went forward to greet Moses and admire his catch.

The supper was pleasant, the company relaxed and congenial. Hodges grew lyrical in praise of the delicious catfish, and entered into a lengthy technical discussion with Moses on the fine points of fishing methods. Later he declared to Trav and Darby that he was eager to hear something about life in California.

They obliged him to the extent of relating a few carefully chosen, light, harmless anecdotes.

Hodges probed with intelligent questions. What, for instance, were the prospects for freedmen to settle in the West?

'Good,' declared Trav without hesitation, then added, trying to be honest, 'Well, it won't be perfect, human nature bein' what it is. But, relative to other regions, I expect it to be fairly good.'

'I've been a harness-maker, a trail driver, a ranch hand, and a plain ol' drifter,' Darby said. 'I've had a few troubles, but no more than most people, I reckon.'

'Really?' Julia said quickly. 'What about Mister Rutledge's property, in Big Bend?'

'Well –' Darby shrugged. 'Outside o' that –'

'Darby was cheated out of some property in Missouri, that rightfully should have been his,' Julia explained to Hodges.

Darby cut it short. 'Let's not go into that. It's a long dreary story.'

'It could've happened to *me*,' Trav said. 'Could've happened to anybody.'

'It was a freak thing, anyway,' Darby said. 'And outside o' that, I really can't complain too much.'

'You've been incredibly lucky, Darby,' Julia said. 'So far.'

'He's got the kind o' luck *I* need in a partner,' Trav said. 'When we get back to California we're goin' to start our own ranch, Darby and I.' He looked at Hodges, but his words were meant for Julia.

'I feel confident that any man of intelligence, talent and energy, like Darby, can make a good life for himself there – I'm confident enough that I don't hesitate to tie my own future in with his.'

Hodges listened with eyes narrowed in contemplation. 'A black ranch hand may have very little trouble,' he mused. 'A black ranch *owner* might have an altogether different set of experiences, don't you think?'

'Well – I suppose so.' Trav tried to remain casual, to avoid sounding defensive. 'There are all kinds o' people there, good and bad, jus' like anywhere else. But it's a free and open society, and a *young* society – it hasn't had time yet to become hidebound, and set in its ways.'

'Any particular reason to suppose that it won't?'

'There's a *chance*, that it won't. That's the best any of us can do in this world – take our best chance.'

Hodges nodded, without conviction.

'I feel confident,' Trav repeated, firmly.

'I wish you both luck,' Hodges said.

The visitor took his early departure – with elaborate apologies for having to do so – to cover his return trip before the long lingering summer twilight faded. His goodbyes were prolonged and fervent. He urged Darby and Trav to take the time to come and see him, and visit the school, before departing for the West. They promised to make every effort.

Julia walked with him to the front road and waited there with him until Moses brought his horse. She held the animal's reins while Hodges mounted.

'Now don't be angry, Julia,' he said, beaming down at her from the saddle. 'I'm going to dare to mention the subject once more. I will not give up hope that you will find a way to come and work with us this fall. We *need* you. You and Luanna both.'

Julia's smile was bright, and there was a hint of cunning in it.

'I shouldn't be at all surprised if it works out, George,' she said. 'Somehow I have a feeling – well – you may be sure I'll do my very best.'

Hodges chuckled, and leaned down to pat Julia affectionately on the cheek. 'Your best, dear lady, is plenty good enough for me.'

He waved to her, wheeled the horse and waved to the others on the front veranda steps, and slapped his mount into a brisk trot down the dusty road.

CHAPTER THIRTEEN

In the morning – Sunday – Trav was downstairs at an early hour. He went out onto the back veranda and sat down on the top step, and breathed deeply of the fresh morning coolness; the heat of the day had not yet begun to build. Moses was already at work with a hoe, he noticed, far down in the vegetable garden. Trav watched the old man thoughtfully for a few minutes, then got up and strolled in that direction.

Moses straightened up from his work and leaned on his hoe. He gently rubbed the small of his back with his free hand, and grimaced in discomfort. When he noticed Trav approaching, the grimace was instantly replaced by a smile.

'Mornin', Trav!' he called out cheerfully.

'Mornin', Moses. Where's an extra hoe? I'll help you.'

Moses shook his head vigorously. 'No, no, no – you jes' keep me company, an' I'll be grateful.'

Trav sat down on an old log section nearby, and Moses went on with his hoeing.

'I noticed you rubbin' your back,' Trav said. 'You troubled with backache?'

'Got a touch o' rheumatism, I reckon. Or maybe it's lumbago.' He glanced at Trav with a quick grin. 'Better jes' call it a touch of old age.'

'Well, I've been told that a certain blonde lady insists upon a condition of exact equality among you folks. And yet I notice you doin' most o' the hard work around here – especially in the garden. How come?'

Moses leaned on his hoe again and looked at Trav, and his eyes crinkled with amusement.

'I'll tell you how come. It's 'cause I don't 'low them women to fool around in my garden. They can pick, but *I'll* do the tendin'.'

'Oh, I see – it's your own decision.' Trav felt slightly foolish.

'Tha's right. Them women ain't worth a nothin' in the garden, I can tell you. 'Specially Julia. Luanna ain't so bad, but Julia! Lawd, I have to chase her out o' heah! Why, not long ago I came out jes' in time to stop her from prunin' my tomato plants. She was gon' *prune* my tomatoes! I said, "Lawd, Little Missy, them tomatoes ain't roses! Get on away from heah," I said. "Go fuss with yo' rose bushes, and leave my vegetables alone!" '

Moses's stout frame shook with mirth. 'I sweah, Julia's got a lot o' talents, but this ain't one of 'em!'

He stopped short, and squinted up into the morning sky. 'My goodness, that ol' sun's gon' heat up good an' proper today, I can sho' tell.' He walked over and sat down next to Trav, mopping his brow. 'Guess I'll rest awhile.'

'Good idea.'

From their seat on the old log the two looked out over the neat rows of garden plants.

'You evidently know what you're doin' here,' Trav said. 'You sure got a nice garden. Soil's very fertile, I suppose?'

'I tell you,' Moses said with solemn gravity. 'What you do is, you dig a little hole, drop in a seed – and jump back!'

He laughed – and Trav was affected by the old man's simple hearty good humour, and laughed with him.

They sat for a moment, quiet, placid and relaxed.

'Sho' wish we'd git some rain, though,' Moses said. 'Seems like we ain't had a good rain in a month o' Sundays.'

After another moment Moses said, very casually, without looking at the other man, 'You don't like Julia very much, do you, Trav?'

Trav was jolted by the unexpected question – inflected like a statement of fact.

'You got the wrong idea, Moses. I like Julia fine. In fact I think she's a mighty fascinatin' woman. That's what scares me.'

'Scares you?'

'Darby and I were just on the verge of somethin' good back in California. We were just about to make somethin' of ourselves, after years of wastin' time. I'd hate to see Darby get sidetracked now. But when I see Miss Julia in action –' Trav shook his head glumly. 'I got a feelin' she's gonna have her way.'

'What's her way, Trav?'

'Why, she's plottin' to keep Darby here. It's plain as day.' He frowned at Moses, and the old man gazed back stolidly. 'Ain't she, now? Be honest.'

'She can't keep him heah, 'less he wants to stay. He's a grown man, a free man. He can do what he wants.'

Trav nodded, with a wry smile. 'That's what you'd think. That's what *I'd* think. But I don't think that's what Julia thinks.'

Moses shrugged. 'You make her sound like a spoiled and wilful child.'

'Well, now, is that so far wrong?' When Moses didn't answer immediately, Trav pressed him. 'Come on, think back. Wasn't she always?'

'Wilful, sho' she was. Spoiled, no. That word nevuh came close to describin' Julia. Even when she was a little child, she felt uncomfortable about bein' in the class of special privilege. She always tried in every way she could to close the distance between herself and us black folks.'

Moses gazed absently off across the field, his mind set to musing.

'From the time she was old enough to walk Julia always went her own way, thought her own thoughts, and spoke her own words. Everybody else heah at Chinaberry, black or white, was jes' ordinary – I mean they was jes' what you'd expect 'em to be, fo' theah place and time and condition o' life – no mo' and no less. But Julia – she was a constant, everlastin' astonishment. A real, live, genu-wine *individual*.'

The old man glanced at Trav, smiling. 'I ain't the right one to question about Julia's faults. She's got her faults, no doubt about it – everybody does. But don't ask *me* about 'em. The worst *I* can think of to say about Julia is things like – she ain't a very good gardener.'

He got to his feet and picked up his hoe. 'To me, she's the closest thing to a livin' breathin' angel that evuh walked the earth.' He returned to his work.

Trav watched him in silence for a minute, and then said, 'All right, Moses. I stand corrected.'

Moses's good humour burst forth again in a bright smile. 'No, Trav, *I'm* the one needs correctin'. I got no business lecturin' you.'

In a few minutes Julia came out of the house, and started toward the chicken yard. She waved to the men in the garden and called out cheerily, 'Good morning, Mister Travers. Morning, Moses.'

Moses worked his way down a garden row, deftly chopping out unwanted weeds from among his vegetable plants.

Then he shifted to the next row and worked his way back.

'Tell me somethin', Moses,' Trav said, as Moses drew near again. 'How long do you think I'd have to stay around here before the ladies stopped callin' me Mister Travers?'

Moses pursed his lips and frowned in deep thought, 'Oh, I'd say – 'bout ten yeahs.' He grinned when he saw Trav's look of consternation. 'Southern women ain't unfriendly, Trav, they're jes' formal. An' they can't be hurried. You got to git used to that. It don't mean nothin'.'

Moses hoed another row, and returned.

'Well, let me ask you somethin' else.' Trav tried again. 'And I hope you don't think this is a funny question –' He got up and came closer to Moses, frowning, trying to choose his words carefully. 'Were Darby and Julia ever – lovers?'

Moses threw back his head and cackled with laughter.

'It was a funny question,' Trav muttered.

'Lawd, Trav! In the old times, slave boys didn't go 'round makin' love to their masters' daughters, no suh! Not even *that* slave boy and *that* master's daughter!'

He eyed Trav with sudden shrewdness. 'You mean to say, in all yo' yeahs togethuh, you ain't nevuh asked *Darby* that?'

'Sure I have – he told me the same thing you just said. Just thought I'd seek another point of view.'

Moses chuckled softly. 'But I'll tell you this –' He turned suddenly serious. 'It hurt me to lose Darby, an' it hurt me even more to see Julia's grief. But in a way, down deep in my heart, I was glad. If Darby hadn't run away – them two would've come to a bad end.'

The old man shook his head, and his eyes were solemn. 'A very bad end.'

Darby had slept late. He came out of the house and sat down on the back steps, yawned, and blinked in the morning sun. Listlessly he waved to Trav and Moses in the garden, and they returned the greeting. Trav, observing him, thought, Darby and I are not used to this domestic life. It's a little strange to sleep under a roof again – even a roof with holes in it. It'll make us soft and lazy if we're not careful.

A few minutes later Luanna came out of the house, and walked past Darby, smiling at him as she went down the steps. From that distance Trav could make out few of the words spoken, but he watched, fascinated, as a graphic pantomime scene was played.

Darby called to Luanna as she started across the yard. She stopped, and Darby got up and went to her. There was a brief conversation; he asked her something – she replied, pointing toward Indian Hill. After a few more words they began to walk together in the direction of the front road. Julia came into the picture, returning from the chicken yard. She put down the implements she was carrying, and hastened after Darby and Luanna, calling to them. The three stood together for a few minutes near the front yard, in a three-way conversation.

Then Julia took Darby's arm and pulled him back toward the house. She said something laughingly to Luanna over her shoulder, and Darby twisted around to cast a lingering look at the girl. Luanna managed a wan smile as she watched the other two walk away from her. Then she turned quickly and went on alone toward the front road.

Trav watched the girl until she was out of sight, admiring again the tall figure, the long legs, and the graceful movement of her walk.

Then he noticed that Moses was watching *him*. He grinned, sheepishly, and Moses grinned back, in universal male understanding.

'She's a good lookin' girl,' Trav said.

'Sho' she is,' Moses agreed.

'But, Moses – did you see that little performance just now?'

Moses' face turned blank. 'Yes, I saw it.'

'And you still can't find any fault with Julia, besides the fact that she's a rotten gardener?'

'No,' Moses answered without hesitation. 'I don't blame her none. Whatevuh little crumbs o' happiness she can salvage in this life – will be lots less'n she deserves.'

The old man went back to his hoeing, having dispensed with the subject, and Trav shook his head in mild astonishment. He walked along the garden row next to Moses.

'Uh – where do you suppose Luanna was goin'?' he asked, after a moment. He tried to sound only casually interested.

'Oh prob'bly up to the pool. She's jes' like a little kid – she spends every minute she can playin' in the water.'

'How about yourself? What about free time for you?'

Moses glanced up, amused again, seeing that Trav was still exploring the equality question. 'Every few days, whenever I feel like it, I take off and go fishin'.'

'But that's work. You're providin' food for the table.'

'Pshaw!' Moses laughed in soft scorn. 'That ain't work, that's the way I enjoy myself. Besides, I can catch all we can eat in an hour – I did yesterday. But usually I'm out from sunup to sundown.' His eyes twinkled, as he winked at Trav. 'My frien', you got to figure out how to take all day doin' somethin' that ought to take an hour!'

Moses's hearty laugh rang out again, and Trav smiled – but his thoughts had strayed; his eyes drifted off toward the front road. Luanna had disappeared.

'Up to the pool, eh?' he mused.

'Ain't no use, Trav,' Moses said, reading his thoughts. 'That gal's got her mind on Darby.'

'If that's true, then that gal's well on her way to gettin' herself hurt.' He looked hard at Moses. 'Ain't that right?'

'I 'spect so,' Moses conceded.

'Well then – in view o' these conditions – don't you think it would be kind, generous and noble of me to do whatever I can to take her mind *off* Darby?'

Moses pondered the question carefully. 'I don't think you can do it,' he said. 'But it's worth a try.' A faint smile drifted across his face.

Trav gave the old man a playful punch on the shoulder. 'See you later, Moses.'

He started away, and Moses called after him. 'Oh, Trav –'

Trav stopped.

'Don't forget what I told you – southern women can't be hurried.'

Trav grinned and nodded. He turned and walked rapidly away toward the front road and Indian Hill.

Moses watched him go, with a look that was old, wise, detached, and, still, gently amused. Then he turned back to his work.

CHAPTER FOURTEEN

Trav walked up the path on the west side of Indian Hill until he reached the crest of the little ridge, halfway up, from which point the pool came into his view, a short distance down the gentle slope on the other side. There he paused.

Luanna was standing in shallow water at the lower end of the pool, near the point where it emptied into the tiny brook that drained it. Her skirt was pulled up to a level midway between knee and thigh, and tucked in at the waist. Her bare legs glistened with sun and water. She stood quite still, with head bowed, her eyes intently probing beneath the surface of the softly moving cloudy-greenish element around her, searching.

Trav stood for a moment gazing down at the girl. What's she looking for, he wondered. Tadpoles? Crawfish? Or something secret and imaginary, that only she knows is there.

Moving with quiet stealth, he crept a little way down the slope toward the pool, and sat down under a slender pine tree. He would watch her for a few minutes in silence; she would see him shortly, and he would smile and say something clever and gallant about what a charming picture she made.

She did not raise her eyes; for several minutes her concentration remained fixed on her search. Suddenly her hand darted into the water and made a capture. She straightened, and stood examining some small creature in the palm of her hand, and was absorbed for a while in the joys of curiosity and wonder. At length she held her hand out over the water, opened it, and allowed a tiny frog to leap back to its natural habitat and scurry to safety in the depths.

Trav smiled, watching the girl. She *is* like a child, he thought. A child of nature – innocent, guileless, unspoiled, as cleanly transparent as the sunlight that sparkled on the water surface, one of the three remaining inhabitants of an estate that had been envisioned by its architects as a mighty social and economic institution enduring into succeeding centuries – possibly one day this simple brown girl, unconcernedly catching frogs in a forest pool, would be the last surviving descendent of the Douglases of Chinaberry.

She had walked out of the pool now, on the far side. She was still unaware of her audience.

Trav's attention wandered for an instant only. When he looked at her again she had slipped her blouse off over her head, and draped it on a nearby bush. Her skirt followed, and was neatly hung over a low branch. Only thin white cotton panties remained, and these she pulled off with a quick downward movement. Then she turned back to the pool, and stood ankle-deep at the edge, poised like a nymph, and as nude, preparing to plunge into the cool rippling water.

Trav sat staring, stone-still and breathless. He was amazed at the quickness with which the girl had undressed; he was stunned by the tawny loveliness of her nudity – and paralyzed at the thought that his presence, discovered now, would brand him in her eyes as a lewd and juvenile jokester, beneath contempt.

Two observations – one of the circumstances, and one of the vision before his eyes – competed for attention in his agitated mind: what rotten luck – and what a gorgeous body.

Don't look up, he said to her mentally. Dive in. Go ahead, dive.

Luanna stood at the edge of the pool, indecisive. She lifted one foot and waggled a toe on the surface, making a light splash.

Silently Trav pleaded for action.

Go on, dive in. If you'll only dive, I can be back over the crest of the ridge by the time you come up and open your eyes. Then everything will be all right. Go on, don't be a coward. Dive.

She was a coward. She waded cautiously forward until she stood knee-deep in the pool, then leaned forward and dabbled her hands playfully. Slowly she moved forward into deeper water, scooped it up in her hands and splashed it on her throat and shoulders, and let it run in gentle trickling rivulets over her large firm breasts and down her belly, and lifted her face toward the sky, eyes closed, with a soft faint smile of blissfulness. Little waves lapped caressingly around her hips.

Trav sat smitten, frozen, suspended in a hypnotic spell. He tried to tell himself to look away, but dismissed the idea as useless, and stared. Mental discipline seemed to slip away – he no longer cared greatly whether she saw him or not.

Please, don't dive just yet. Let us linger in this condition for a delicious moment, while I drink it all in.

Perversely, she dived – or flopped, and struck the water awkwardly, with an enormous splash.

Instantly Trav was on his feet and flying back up the slope. He dove over the crest and hit the ground and lay still. The sound of the girl's continued splashing reached his ears. He breathed a sigh – he had escaped.

He rolled over and got to his feet, and crept soundlessly down the path a short distance, then turned about and came back up again, whistling. At the top of the crest he called, 'Luanna?' and looked down toward the pool. She was very still in the water now, submerged to her neck. She gazed up at Trav with a blank expression.

He came down toward the pool, smiling at her, looked closer, and said innocently, 'Oh – I didn't realize – excuse me.'

'That's all right,' she said coolly. 'If you'll just go back over the ridge for a minute, I'll get dressed.'

'Oh, you don't want to get out yet,' he said pleasantly. 'You look so cool and comfortable.' He sat down on a small rock, a discreet distance from the pool.

'I *do* want to get out,' she said.

'In a minute. I want to talk to you first.' He crossed his legs and settled himself comfortably.

Luanna idly ruffled the surface of the water with her finger-tips, and flicked a spray of droplets at an insect that buzzed close to her.

'I didn't notice you being eager to talk a minute ago, when you were here,' she said.

Her remark was so casual that it took Trav a moment to react. His jaw dropped, and a look of astonishment came over his face.

'You mean – you knew I was there all the time?!'

'No,' she answered frigidly. 'I knew you were there when I came up from my dive and saw you disappearing over the ridge.'

He felt foolish – crushed, like a small boy caught in mischief.

'I was jus' watchin' you play in the water – I was plannin' to speak to you in just a minute. I didn't know you were gonna take your clothes off, now did I?'

She did not respond. Her fingers traced light patterns in the water

'Aw, listen,' he said. He tried to sound appealing. 'I'm sorry. It was unintentional, believe me.'

'What did you want to talk to me about, Mister Travers?' Her voice was stonily impersonal.

'Well – let's see – I wanted to ask you a couple o' things. First, I'd like to know how you'd feel about it if I suggested to Julia that she give up this place as a lost cause, and all of you come to California with Darby and me.'

She stared at him, dumbfounded. 'Mister Travers, there is no possibility on *earth* that Julia would consider such a wild idea.'

'That's not what I asked you. I want to know how *you'd* feel.'

'Julia will never leave Chinaberry – there's just no point in discussing it.'

'You're still not answering my question.'

'I won't leave Julia.'

Trav shook his head, his lips grimly compressed. 'Once a slave, always a slave,' he muttered.

'Will you please go away so I can get out now?' Luanna said sharply.

'I wonder where you get all that dumb loyalty,' he said, without moving. 'Do you really think it's a *virtue?*'

'Julia is my sister, Mister Travers. I owe my life to her. I promised to help her bring this place back, and I'm goin' to keep my promise.'

'That's a bunch o' reasons,' Trav said. 'All bad.'

'May I get out of the pool now?!' She slapped the water impatiently, and her voice rose in anger.

Trav studied her for a moment. Then he leaned forward and began to unlace his shoes.

'You know,' he said, 'for years I've searched all over the West, lookin' for the woman who was *just* the right woman for me.'

He pulled off one shoe, and started on the other. 'I've looked everywhere – in every town, on every trail, in every trading post.'

Barefoot, he stood up and unbuttoned his shirt.

'Mister Travers, what are you doing?!' Luanna demanded.

'I've looked in every boarding house and every burlesque show – I've even checked the brothels.'

'Are you coming in swimming?!' Her voice was shrill with alarm.

'I'm comin' in the water,' he said, tossing his shirt aside. 'But swimming is not uppermost in my mind.'

He began to unclasp his belt.

Luanna's eyes flashed defiance at him. 'All right, I'm gettin' out!' she snapped. She waded clumsily into shallower water, toward the far side of the pool, and Trav's eyes lingered on the surface as her body slid up and into view, smooth and gleaming with wetness. She stepped out onto the grassy bank and quickly ducked behind a bush and reached for her clothes.

He was as quiet and quick as a cat – he went around the pool, and she didn't know he was coming until he grasped her wrist and pulled her around and up close to him.

'Let go of me!' she hissed.

He held her close and tight, with her breasts pressed against his chest. 'I've looked everywhere,' he said, his mouth almost on hers. 'And where do I finally find her? In Mississippi, in the middle of a frog pond!'

She struggled. 'Mister Travers –! Let me go!'

Her efforts were lacking in wholehearted determination, it seemed to him. 'Jus' call me Trav,' he murmured, and kissed her.

He thought he felt her resistance diminishing, and he sought to consolidate his gains by slipping an arm farther around her, with his palm in the small of her back. His other hand slid down and covered a breast.

With a sudden surge of exertion she gave him a mighty push. It took him by surprise; he staggered backward, twisted and teetered on the edge of the pool, with arms flailing – and struck the water with a sharp splat. He emerged choking and sputtering, wiping water from his eyes, and looking around in dull astonishment. Luanna was already half dressed.

He dragged himself out to dry land on the other side of the pool, and stood for a moment brushing and rubbing uselessly at his dripping pants. Then he walked back to the rock where he had left his shirt and shoes and lay down flat on his back in the grass, limp and panting, as if exhausted.

'Ah, me,' he said. He gazed up at the lacy top of a pine tree sweeping the morning sky. Calm returned.

'Now then, Mister Travers,' he said to himself. 'Let us review the events of the last minute or so, and determine, if we can, just where we went wrong.

'Let's see – southern women, we've been informed, are not unfriendly, but they *are* formal. There we have it – very likely we neglected some small but crucial gesture of formality. Possibly we should have bowed from the waist and said, "By your leave, madam," before we handled the lady's anatomy. And another thing, Mister Travers. We were cautioned that southern women can't be hurried. We were not only told that, we were reminded of it pointedly. There is absolutely no excuse for our having ignored that important information – I can't think what came over me.'

He sighed, and put an arm under his head for a pillow. 'I must say, though, had our informant wished to be *really* helpful, he would have warned us that southern women, besides bein' friendly and formal and unhurryable, are also strong as bulls.'

Luanna's face entered into his view of sky and treetops. She was fully dressed, and she looked down at him with soft concern.

'Are you all right, Trav? I hope I didn't hurt you.'

Her quick switch from defiance to gentleness struck him as funny, and he laughed. 'I'm fine. I always talk to myself in moments of stress.' He smiled up at her. 'Besides, I'm makin' progress. You jus' called me Trav.'

She sat down on the rock beside him. 'Don't ever try that again, please,' she said gravely.

He sat upright, his eyes suddenly earnest. 'Let's play that scene again, Luanna – I did it all wrong. I'll go back down the path and come up again, and you take your clothes off and get back in the water –'

She laughed, her eyes dancing with merriment.

He saw that she was willing to slip right back into a warm, easy, natural relationship, and felt a glow of success, and of relief. The damage he had done was not serious. He reached cautiously for her hand, and she let him take it.

'I didn't say it right, but *what* I said was true – about lookin' for the right woman for myself. You're the one, Luanna. I'm sure of it. And I'm not just after a little temporary fun. I'd like to take you back to California with me.'

She blinked, and looked at him curiously for a moment, as if unsure of his meaning. Slowly she shook her head. 'No, thank you. I won't be a white man's toy. Temporary or otherwise.'

'If a marriage proposal will make any difference, you've got it. I'd be very pleased to marry you.'

'I won't be a white man's concubine, either.'

'Wife. The word is *wife*.'

'Concubine,' she said stubbornly. 'That's what your rancher friends in California would call me.'

He snorted. 'That's foolish. You're mostly white yourself. About eleven sixteenths, I'd say.'

'When it comes to racial matters, Mister Travers, people aren't much interested in fractions. Five sixteenths black is black.'

He started to reply, but she rushed on.

'Don't try to tell me that people in California are any more interested in that kind of arithmetic than people in Mississippi.'

A trace of coldness had returned to her voice. She withdrew her hand from his.

'I should've been satisfied with a *little* progress,' he said gloomily. 'We're back to Mister Travers again.'

'I'm sorry.' The gentleness was back in her voice. She reached out and touched him lightly on the shoulder. 'I thank you for askin' me – I feel honoured, truly I do. But it's not possible. I'm very sorry.'

He lay back on the grass again and gazed up at the treetops.

'You're a nice girl, Luanna, but you've sure got rotten reasons for things. You have to devote the rest of your life to Julia because you're related to her, and she rescued you from the slave market once. And you can't marry me because some bigots in California might not approve.'

Luanna's head was bowed. She studied her hands in her lap. 'That's not the real reason I can't marry you,' she said weakly.

'Of course not. I know that. Your heart would like to belong to another, wouldn't it?'

'I guess so.'

'Somebody I know, I'll wager. A good friend o' mine, in fact.'

She nodded.

He came up on one elbow, and looked closely at her.

'Then let me give you some friendly advice. You've got to start showin' a little spunk. You've got to start speakin' up, lettin' people know that you're a person with wishes and hopes and desires, jus' like everybody else. You've got to develop a little wilfulness, a little stubbornness – a little bitchiness, for God's sake. You've got to *fight* for yourself. You've got to stop bein' so damn *nice.*'

She sat very still and quiet, studying his face.

'And you know who you've got to fight, don't you?'

She continued to gaze at him, without speaking.

'You know damn well who,' he said.

'I can't,' she whispered. 'I just can't.'

He nodded. A thin, cynical smile crossed his lips.

'In that case, sweetheart, you ought to reconsider my offer. We'd make a good pair, you know – we have a lot in common. Julia's gonna beat the hell out o' both of us.'

The girl's sombre eyes held on him for a moment longer. Then she stood, took a deep breath, and looked around at the quiet pool and the green wooded hillside.

'My, it's a pretty day,' she said.

'All right,' Trav said. 'Don't listen. But don't say nobody ever tried to help you.'

She smiled down at him. 'Come along, little boy. We'd better get you home to change. You'll catch your death of cold.'

She walked up the path toward the crest of the ridge, and Trav sat up and looked after her, and shook his head glumly.

'What a waste,' he muttered under his breath.

She stopped and looked back and smiled again. 'Coming, little boy?'

He got up slowly, and reached for his shoes and shirt.

'Yes, Mother,' he said, and followed her up the path.

CHAPTER FIFTEEN

During their light noonday meal Moses announced that he was going down to the river in the afternoon and work on his skiff.

Julia laughed at him gently, and said, 'Moses scrubs and polishes that old skiff as if it were the finest craft on the river.'

'It might jus' be,' Darby said. 'Except for *El Bandido Moreno*, of course.' He shot a sly grin at Moses.

'We'll have a race one o' these days,' Moses cried boisterously. 'Then we'll jes' *see* which one's best!'

'You're on!' Darby laughed.

Trav said, 'I'll bet on *El Bandido* – on one condition.'

'What's that?' Moses said.

'That *you* row *El Bandido*, and Darby rows *your* boat.'

Moses threw back his head and shook with laughter. 'Oh, no you don't!' he boomed at Trav. 'You ain't gon' git me to risk my life in that ol' broken down Arkansas scow!'

Darby glared at him in mock outrage. 'What's wrong with *El Bandido?*' he demanded.

'Well, fo' one thing, that crazified name. Skiffs ain't got no business havin' names in the fust place. But if a skiff's got to have a name, it ought to be somethin' like – Miss'sippi Belle.'

This brought a roar of scornful laughter from Trav and Darby. Moses went on, undaunted.

'I'd hate to be a bandit if I had to depend on that mouldy old tub to make my getaway in!'

The three men went out presently, continuing their noisy discussion of the relative merits of skiffs.

When they had gone Julia looked at Luanna with shining eyes, and said breathlessly, 'Isn't it wonderful, Luanna? How long has it been since there was laughter and merriment here?!'

Trav and Darby sat on the front veranda steps. The humid stillness of the southern summer afternoon was a heavy opiate that drugged them and nade them drowsy. They were silent for a while. Then Darby spoke, without looking at his companion.

'What happened this morning? Did you fall in the pool?'

Trav had been surprised earlier, when he and Luanna had returned to the house. His pants had been damp still, and he had been prepared for questions – but nothing had been said. He looked quickly at Darby now, again mildly surprised.

'No, I didn't fall in the pool,' he said, 'Luanna pushed me in the pool.'

Darby glanced curiously at Trav, and looked away again. 'How did you, uh – how did you do with her?' He seemed embarrassed by his own inquisitiveness.

'What makes you think I was tryin' to, uh – *do* with her?'

'I got eyes. I ain't blind.'

'Oh?' Trav affected more surprise. 'That's good to know – I was beginnin' to wonder about your vision.'

Darby pursued the question. 'So, how did you do with her?'

'She pushed me in the pool, that's how I did with her.'

Darby grinned. 'Good.'

'Thanks.'

'I'm not overjoyed to see you chasin' after her body. She ain't just another one o' your common ordinary western bordello gals, y'know.'

Trav's eyes opened wide in astonishment. 'Hey –' he breathed. 'You were right – you're *not* blind.' He scowled suddenly, and poked a finger at Darby. 'Let me tell you somethin', old friend. I wasn't just after the body, I was after the girl. I'm not blind, either – I know a jewel when I see one.'

'So you thought you'd just quietly appropriate it, huh?'

'Didn't see *you* makin' any moves in that direction. No sense in *both* of us bein' stupid.'

'So I'm stupid,' Darby said peevishly.

'You act like it. Lettin' what's-her-name lead you around by the nose.'

Darby bristled. 'I'm not lettin' anybody lead me around by the nose!' For a moment he glared belligerently at Trav. Then he looked away, and went on in a conciliatory tone. 'But, look – it's none o' my business, about you and Luanna. I wish you the best o' luck.'

'Forget it. My luck's already run out.' Trav leaned close to Darby and spoke in a low voice. 'Listen. The girl's a peach, and she's ripe for *you* to pick – nobody but you. If you had good sense you'd grab her and run, before what's-her-name knew what happened.'

'Her name's Julia,' Darby snapped. 'Cut that out!'

'When are you gonna make a decision, Darby?' Trav's voice went hard. 'What are you gonna *do*?'

'I don't know!' Darby flung himself off the steps and stood for a moment in the yard, gazing down toward the front road. 'I need time to think.'

'That's a damn good idea,' Trav said quietly. 'Think.'

'I'm goin' for a walk. See you later.' Darby started toward the front road, stopped after a few steps and looked back at Trav, and smiled softly. 'Be patient with me, pal,' he said. He went down to the road and walked eastward, away from the river.

Trav watched his friend until he was out of sight. Then he leaned back on his elbows and stared at the white and brown trunk of the big sycamore tree, at the front of the yard.

'Ah me,' he sighed.

Julia came out of the house, stood still on the veranda, and looked around. 'Where's Darby?' she asked quickly.

'Went for a walk,' Trav said.

'Oh –' She gazed off down the road, frowning. Anxiety touched her voice. 'I hope he doesn't go far.'

Trav twisted around and looked up at her curiously. 'Darby's been around quite a bit, Julia. I doubt if he'll get lost. Actually, he's a big boy now.'

She gazed down at him with an expression that was strangely blank. She forced a light laugh. 'I didn't mean to sound like an old fuss-budget,' she said. 'It's just that – well, it's not altogether safe for him to – to wander about freely, alone. He might – there are people who might be inclined to –'

'Oh, yes –' Trav caught her train of thought finally. 'Ely Griffith warned us about that, I recall.' He smiled placidly. 'I wouldn't worry if I were you. Darby's amazingly adept at takin' care of himself. Besides, he wasn't goin' very far.'

'All right, then.' She seemed to be reassured. 'I was going to ask him to do me a small favour, since no one else is here – Luanna's gone off to the pasture to see about the cow –'

Trav got to his feet, and bowed with elaborate gallantry. 'I'm at your service, madam. Small favours or large – just ask.'

'Thank you, sir,' she smiled. 'I wonder if you'd go down in

the garden and see if you could find me a nice big ripe tomato. I need it for a dish I'm preparing for supper.'

'Let's see, now,' he pondered. 'Tomatoes are those round red things, right?'

She laughed – a light, easy, charming laugh, and her eyes sparkled.

He was surprised, and slightly annoyed with himself, to feel a tingle of pleasure at her lively response to his feeble little joke. He saw that she was one of those women who had the trick of making the dullest man feel like a paragon of wit. His admiration for her was growing constantly, he knew – and he was appalled to realize that he was being affected by her charm, in spite of his efforts to remain detached.

He went down the steps and off toward the garden, calling back to her, 'I go in quest of the rare and exotic fruit of the jungle! I shall not return empty-handed!'

Julia stood for a few minutes on the veranda, to enjoy a soft breeze that stirred the stifling air. Then she turned to go back inside, but paused, as she noticed Moses emerging from the willow thicket, coming up the road from the direction of the river.

Odd he should be returning so soon, she thought – then she saw that someone was with him, walking a few paces behind – a white man. The stranger was elegantly dressed, in a spotless white suit, and his face was in the deep shade of a wide brimmed hat. Julia studied him for a moment, and recognized him. She moved to the top of the veranda steps and stood quietly waiting.

Moses came across the yard, ahead of the other man, and on his face was the look of impersonal official dignity that he used to wear, long ago.

I haven't seen that look in years, Julia thought. The face of the butler.

Moses stopped a few feet from the steps, looked up at Julia, and announced with ceremonious pomp, 'Miss Julia, ma'am, Mistuh Ramsey is heah to see you.' And from one eye, out of the blank expressionless mask that his face had become – came a quick wink. He turned and walked away, heading back to the river.

Julia came down the steps, smiling, and extended her hand. 'It's nice to see you, Philip.'

'Julia –' he breathed. He swept his hat from his head and took her hand. 'Julia, I can *not* believe it! Is it possible that after all these yeahs, and all we've both been through, you can still be so lovely?!' He stared at her, enchanted.

She regarded him with a bemused expression, and stood still and permissive while he kissed her hands, one after the other. When he turned them over to kiss the palms, she withdrew them.

'What have *you* been through, Philip?' she asked lightly.

'My Lord, Julia, the waw! What we've *all* been through. I virtually had to mortgage my soul to obtain a presidential pardon and regain possession of my plantations!'

'I'm so sorry to hear that,' Julia said gently – but her serene expression failed to reflect deep sorrow. 'Come inside, and have a cool drink of water.'

'Thank you, my dah'lin',' he said with a smooth smile. He took her hand and placed it over his arm, and escorted her up the steps and into the house.

Philip Ramsey was tall and handsome, in the conventional way of tall handsome men. At thirty-seven he was still trim, and his clean-shaven face retained much of the pink, open, innocent look of boyhood, but was fleshed out somewhat – a detail that added a much needed touch of maturity to his appearance.

He stood in the middle of the converted pantry, the combination kitchen and dining area, and looked with eyebrows uplifted in astonishment at the homemade furnishings.

Julia said, 'Do sit down, Philip,' and went to get his drink of water. She betrayed no hint that she was aware of the crudity of the accommodations, much less offered any word of apology for them.

Philip sat down gingerly on the edge of one of Moses' handhewn chairs, and allowed his eyes to follow Julia's movements with minute attention. She brought the water, and sat down opposite him.

'I must say you're looking well, Philip,' she said chattily. 'How are things at Graystone?'

'As good as can be expected, under the circumstances – which is to say, not very good at all. Recovery, I feah, will be agonizingly slow.' He sipped at his water daintily.

'Things are no bettuh at Briarhaven,' he went on. 'I cling to the hope that we'll be able to keep both places runnin' somehow – but it's far from certain. If we can, it will only be at the cost of a rather severe personal sacrifice.'

He looked at Julia with drooping, melancholy eyes, and

sighed. 'We're bein' forced to live apart, you see. Dorothy is managin' Briarhaven herself, while I look after Graystone.'

'Oh – that's unfortunate.'

'Thank heavens Dorothy has a good head for business mattuhs, unlike all the othuh Wards – *and* unlike most women –' He chuckled softly. 'Otherwise, we'd be sunk.'

'Are things really all that desperate?'

'You can't run a plantation without a labour fo'ce, Julia,' Ramsey said gloomily. 'Now that we have no slaves, and very little ready cash for *hirin'* hands, what's to be done? We're tryin' a sharecroppin' arrangement, but it's very discouragin'. The Nigras simply won't work. They're so hopelessly entranced with the idea of freedom – the po' simple souls think that bein' free means bein' free to live in idleness.'

He stopped short, and smiled at her indulgently. 'But I almost forgot – no need to expect sympathy from *you* about the loss of our slaves, eh, Julia?'

'No, Philip. No sympathy. But I *will* offer advice. I think you should sit down and talk to yourself very seriously about the relative importance of things. Wouldn't it be better to give up one plantation, rather than sacrifice your marriage?'

He gazed at her longingly, and a limp insipid smile played about his lips. He sighed again. 'I just can't get ovuh how lovely you are, Julia. Hardship seems to have refined yo'uh beauty.'

She smiled faintly, acknowledging his admiration without interest. Poor Philip, she thought. He's been here five minutes, and already I'm bored with him.

'When I heard you'd come back, my dah'lin', I wanted desperately to get ovuh heah to see you,' he went on. 'But I was just leavin' fo' Washington – the business about obtainin' presidential pardon, you know.'

'Yes.'

'I felt the only way to handle the mattuh was just to *go* theah, and take care of it personally. Otherwise, they say, it takes forevuh!'

'I imagine.'

'Naturally, I couldn't very well avoid bein' classified, as they put it, as a landowner in one of the states lately in rebellion, et cetera, whose property value is twenty-five thousand dolluhs or more. What a bothuh!'

Julia tried to look sympathetic, but her face betrayed faint amusement as she listened. 'But what a charming way to remind me that you're a wealthy man, Philip.'

'No, really, Julia!' he protested. 'That's the way it's spelled out in the president's amnesty provisions. You must be familiar with it. Didn't you have trouble with that also?'

'None whatsoever. Chinaberry was completely gutted, as you know, and not worth nearly that. Besides which, of course,' – she glanced at him impishly – 'I was known to be a loyalist.'

She got up and reached for his cup. 'Luanna made a lovely cake for Sunday dinner. May I give you a piece of it?'

'Who's Luanna?'

'My –' She caught the word *sister* before it came out, and quickly swallowed it. 'That is, a girl who lives here with me.'

'No, thank you, dah'lin'. I'll have some more watuh, though, if you please.'

As she started to move away he caught her hand and pulled her toward him, and looked up into her face with pleading eyes. 'Don't be unkind, Julia. I'm prepared to be helpful to you – tremendously helpful, in all sorts of ways. And you cannot deny that you need help.'

'We're managing here quite well, thank you,' she said stiffly, and pulled away from him and went back to the kitchen area.

He got up and followed her, and stood behind her, gazing hungrily down at her hair and shoulders. He leaned down and kissed her with a feathery touch of his lips on the curve of the neck.

'Don't' Philip,' she said softly.

'Julia, dah'lin',' he murmured close to her ear. 'I'm mad about you, always have been –'

'Please, Philip. Behave yourself – you're a married man.' She turned and handed him the refilled cup of water.

He took it and set it down, and clasped her at the waist, with both hands. 'Julia – come and live at Graystone.'

She looked at him wide-eyed, in genuine astonishment. 'Philip Ramsey! I've known you since we were children, and that's the first time you *ever* said anything that surprised me!'

'That's because you nevuh paid attention when I talked to you!'

'Whatever can you mean, come and live at Graystone?! I'm sure Dorothy would be delighted with *that* arrangement!'

'I wasn't bein' – quite frank, before, about Dorothy,' he

said forlornly. 'The reason she's livin' at Briarhaven is because we are, shall we say – estranged.'

He looked at her with pain shining in his eyes, and Julia was struck with the odd thought that Philip would have made a fine actor.

'I'm sorry to hear that,' she said.

'The children are all with Dorothy, naturally – except our oldest, who's in school in Natchez. I miss the children terribly, of course. But Dorothy –' Again the heavy sigh. 'I'm afraid our marriage was nothin' more than a makeshift affair, at best. I think she's always known that I married her only because I couldn't have you.'

'Really, Philip!' Julia laughed scornfully. 'That's too absurd!' She tried gently, without success, to disengage herself from his grasp.

'Julia, listen to me.' His voice took on urgency. 'It's not too late for us. This is our best time of life, anyway, and you're so beautiful, so desirable –' His lips sought her neck again. 'I love you madly, madly –'

'Stop it – stop it now!' She tried to twist away from him, but he pulled her closer.

'Come and grace my bed with your beauty, Julia, and I'll be your slave –'

'You know I don't approve of slavery, Philip.'

Her flippancy enraged him. He seized her shoulders in a grip so ferocious that it made her gasp.

'*You* stop it!' he shouted, his voice quivering with fury. 'You've teased and tormented and made fun of me all my life. I have loved you, I have offered you my devotion – and you have laughed, and spat upon it with contempt! I have gazed in your eyes with longing, and all I've evuh seen theah is that damned everlastin' look of *amusement!*'

She strained against his grasp. 'Let me go, Philip! Let me –'

'Julia, I will not *stand* for it any longer!'

'Please, Philip! You're hurting me –!'

He covered her mouth with his own.

Trav stood in the doorway, observing. He cleared his throat loudly, and said, 'Excuse me.'

Philip whirled, releasing Julia, and glared at the intruder. Julia drew back and smoothed her hair, and struggled to regain her composure.

'Who are you?' Philip blurted. 'What do you want?'

Trav walked unhurriedly into the room and held out a large ripe tomato to Julia. 'Madam, I bring you the produce of the warm fertile earth.'

'Oh – thank you,' Julia said, and took the tomato. 'That's beautiful.'

'Best I could find.' Trav glanced at Ramsey. 'In some cultures, I hear, they call it the fruit of love.'

'Julia, who is this man?' Ramsey demanded.

'I'm sorry – Mister Ramsey, Mister Travers.'

Trav extended his hand. 'Jus' call me Trav,' he said genially.

'How do you do,' Ramsey muttered. The handshake was perfunctory.

'Sorry I took so long,' Trav said to Julia. 'But I noticed you had company, so I figured, why interrupt?' He looked at Ramsey again, and smiled.

'Well – that was thoughtful of you, Mister Travers.' Julia stole a sly look at him; somehow she was sure he must have been standing on the back veranda for a long time, listening – not so much reluctant to interrupt, as waiting for just the right moment. For the first time she felt a stirring of appreciation for his wry sense of humour.

'Mister Travers is from California,' Julia said to Philip. 'He's – he's here on a visit.'

'I see,' Philip said. He eyed Trav coldly.

Trav looked from Philip to Julia. 'Listen, I hope I didn't walk in on anything of major importance,' he said innocently, 'If I did I'll be happy to leave –'

'Oh, not at *all*, Mister Travers,' Julia said hastily. 'Mister Ramsey's an old family friend – he just stopped by to say hello. He's our neighbour at Graystone, the plantation just south of here.' She smiled placidly at Philip. 'I don't know whether I've mentioned Graystone to you, Mister Travers. It's a beautiful place. Really, you ought to see it –'

'Excuse me, Julia,' Ramsey said stiffly. 'I'm sorry to rush away like this, but I really must be goin'. My boatmen are waitin' at the river. Mustn't keep them waitin' too long, you know – have to treat Nigras with consideration these days, or they get surly.'

He retrieved his hat from the table where he had left it, and turned to Trav.

'Pleased to make yo' acquaintance, Mistuh –'

'Travers.'

'Mistuh Travers. I hope you enjoy yo' visit.'

'Thanks,' Trav said heartily. 'I'm sorry I spoiled yours.'

Ramsey paused and looked at Trav with closer attention. 'How long will you be in the South, Mistuh Travers?'

Trav shrugged. 'Hard to say, exactly.'

'What did you say yo' business was?'

'You might call it – prospectin'.'

'Prospectin'?'

'For business opportunities.'

Ramsey's narrowed eyes signalled suspicion. 'Well, I must tell you you've come to the wrong place,' he said abruptly. 'Theah's precious little opportunity in the South today, even fo' southerners. None whatevuh fo' outsiders.'

'I'd like to discuss that subject with you,' Trav said. 'Mind if I walk along with you to the river?'

Ramsey regarded the other with a blank expression, and shrugged. 'If you like.'

He glanced at Julia, and looked back to Trav. 'I'll be with you in a minute, Mistuh Travers. If you'll excuse us –'

'Sure.' Trav turned and went out to the back veranda.

Philip and Julia looked at each other for a moment in awkward silence. He took a tentative step toward her.

'Julia – I'd like to apologize for my – my uncouth behaviour,' he said meekly.

'Forget about it, Philip.' She smiled. 'It was nothing.'

'I kissed you,' he said. 'That is very much more than nothin' to me.' He took another step toward her, and she moved back.

'I want you to know that my invitation is permanently open, Julia. It will stand as long as necessary, until you finally come to realize what *I've* known fo' twenty yeahs – that we belong togethuh.'

'Well – that's kind of you, Philip. I thank you.'

He extended his hand to her. 'Well then, goodbye fo' the present, Julia.'

She shook hands, but stood far back from him.

'Come to Graystone, my dah'lin',' he said, in a dramatic whisper. 'Anytime. I'll be waitin' fo' you.'

She made an effort to keep the sound of impatience out of her voice. 'Thank you again, Philip. Goodbye.'

When Ramsey came out of the house Trav got up from where he was sitting on the veranda steps. As the two men started to move away Darby appeared around the corner of the house, and approached. He stared in frank curiosity at the stranger.

'Daniel,' Trav said quickly, 'see what you can do to help Miss Julia in the kitchen, while I escort this gentleman to his boat.'

Darby grinned, and shuffled his feet. 'Yas suh, boss. I'se sho' gwine do dat.'

Trav shot a sharp look at him that said, *Go easy on that phony act, you ham.*

Ramsey cast a brief uninterested glance in Darby's direction. For an instant their eyes met. Then Ramsey turned away, and walked rapidly toward the front road.

Trav hastened after him.

CHAPTER SIXTEEN

Darby went into the kitchen area where Julia was at work, with her back to the door.

'H'lo, Julia.'

She turned quickly, and greeted him with eagerness. 'Oh . . . Darby! I'm so glad you're back!'

'Back? I haven't been away.'

'You really shouldn't wander off by yourself, you know.'

He frowned at her. 'I didn't *go* anywhere – jus' down the road a piece.'

'Did you have a nice walk?'

'Um.' He sat down at the table across the room and put his feet up on another chair.

She went on with her cooking preparations. After a moment she shot a sly glance at him and said, 'Did you see the man outside?'

'Yeah. Who *was* that?'

'An old admirer of mine. Philip Ramsey, from Graystone.'

'Oh.' He didn't seem much interested. He leaned back and locked his hands behind his head. 'Where's Luanna?'

'Gone to fetch the cow from pasture. Why?'

'Jus' wondered.'

After another minute she looked across at him curiously. 'Aren't you interested in hearing about Philip Ramsey?'

Darby shrugged. 'Not particularly. He and I never became fast friends, for some strange reason.'

Julia smiled. After a calculated pause, she said, 'He kissed me.'

'How romantic.'

She gave him a playful, pouting look. 'Well – I thought you'd be jealous.'

'Of *him?!*'

'Is that so ridiculous? He asked me to come and live at Graystone.'

When he didn't reply immediately she looked around at him, and saw that his expression was thoughtful and sombre. 'Well, don't you think that's *funny?*'

'To tell the truth,' he said slowly, 'I suppose you could do worse.'

Her hands froze at her work. She turned a stricken look on him. 'Darby! You're joking, aren't you? Would you really have me do that?!'

He grimaced in protest. 'No, Julia, I wouldn't have you do that. But what's the future here for you and Luanna, with Moses the only man around? Moses is very old.'

She turned away from him and bowed her head. 'That's why I was so happy when I thought you'd come back. . . .' Her voice grew faint, and trailed off.

Darby got up slowly and went across the room and stood next to her. She was mixing dry ingredients in a bowl, and did not look at him.

'Ah, Julia,' he said gently, 'let's not be like this.'

She looked up and gave him a quick smile. 'I'm sorry. Silly of me. Would you bring me a dipper of water, please, Darby?'

He brought the water and held it out to her.

'Pour it in,' she said.

He dumped it into the bowl. It splashed.

'Gently, Darby!' She laughed, and patted his cheek. 'You men are such roughnecks!'

She worked the material in the bowl, while he stood beside her and watched with boyish curiosity.

'What's it gonna be?' he said, and stuck his finger in the bowl for a taste.

She slapped his wrist lightly. 'Keep your fingers out. Look but don't touch is the rule around here.' She smiled up at him, and went on with the work.

Presently his attention drifted away from the food bowl, and onto the woman. He stood gazing down at her slender shoulders, and luxuriant yellow hair, which was bound up high on the top of her head. Little wisps of hair that had escaped the binding curled in delicate ringlets at the nape of her neck.

'I like your hair this way,' he said.

'It's for coolness.' In a moment she glanced up at him and said, very casually, 'Of course, what I said a minute ago doesn't apply to *me*.'

'What?'

'Look but don't touch. That applies to the food, not to me.'

'Oh.' He ran a finger lightly around the curls at the base of her neck, then let his hand drift down over her opposite shoulder to her upper arm, and come to rest there.

'I can't get over it, Julia,' he murmured. 'When we were fourteen I thought you were as beautiful as a human creature could be. I was wrong. You're even more beautiful now.'

She stopped working and turned a little toward him. Her face was grave, unsmiling. 'Are you happy, Darby? I mean are you happy being here with me?'

'Of course I am. I jus' wish it could last forever.'

'*I'm* not happy, Darby.'

'Why not?'

She moved closer to him, and put a hand on his shoulder. 'Because it *could* last forever, but you want to go away again. And because we can never be together.'

'We're together all the time, Julia.'

'I mean alone together. I want to be alone with you, Darby.' Her hand crept up on the back of his neck. '*Really* alone.'

He gazed at her fixedly, and laughed an uneasy little laugh. 'Julia – you bewitch me, you know. Always did, even when we were children.'

'I'm glad.' Her intense eyes moved up close to him, and her hand crept farther up the back of his head, exerting a slight pressure toward her. 'I have no other power over you anymore. Thank God I still have that.'

Then her moist lips parted and came toward his and covered them, pressing hard, and her arms wound tight around his neck. His hands hung helplessly in the air for a fleeting moment of surprise, then came down and covered her back and pulled her close against him. She breathed a long soft yearning sigh and rotated her mouth hungrily on his, and sighed again with greater joy as she felt him responding, his breathing become heavier, and his strong hands roam eagerly over her back from shoulders to waist to buttocks, and back again. After a long time she turned her head and stood with lifted face and closed eyes while he dropped tiny kisses like rose petals on her eggshell ears and slender neck.

'Julia, Julia. . . .' His voice was husky, low, and trembling. 'Oh, God, it's crazy, Julia. It cannot be. . . .'

'Oh, yes, yes, it *can* be,' she whispered fervently. She held his face in her hands and smiled up into his eyes. 'It can be, and it *will* be.'

But gently he pulled back out of her clinging arms, and

moved away from her, and she stood reaching after him. Across the room he leaned against the wall next to the back door, and gazed soberly out into the blazing afternoon light.

'Trav didn't want me to make this trip.' He spoke softly, as if to himself. 'He thought it would be a big mistake. And over the years I've discovered Trav's very seldom wrong.'

Behind him he heard her voice, also soft, dripping with scorn. 'Trav, Trav, Trav . . . he's so wise, wise, wise. . . .'

He glanced around and caught her eye. 'I know,' he said dryly. 'You don't like Trav.'

And she replied with a vehemence that surprised them both. 'That's not true!' She flushed, became momentarily flustered, absently patted her hair. 'Mister Travers is a fine man. I know very well what a wonderful friend he's been to you –'

'And always will be.'

'Of course. But now I think he's leading you down a primrose path –'

'Oh, Julia!' He turned impatiently away and stared out the door again.

'Darby – when we were young, wasn't I your friend?'

He did not look at her. 'The best, Julia. The best I ever had.'

'You trusted me, didn't you?'

'Always.'

'Then trust me still, Darby. I know what's good for both of us.'

He turned his eyes back to hers, and found them pleading. 'We are good for each other,' she said simply.

He smiled. 'I'll never *not* trust you, Julia.'

Her own bright indestructible smile shone through immediately. She reached for her mixing bowl, and held it out to him.

'That's better. *Now* you can taste.'

He didn't move. His eyes wavered. 'Excuse me, Julia – I jus' saw Luanna comin' up the road, with the cow. I'm gonna go help her – I'll be right back.' Instantly he was out of the house and down the back steps, and bounding across the yard.

Julia hurried to the door and called after him. 'Darby, that's ridiculous, she doesn't need . . .'

He was running at top speed down the south road. And from a distance Luanna, bringing the cow, waved to him.

With a bleakness in her eyes Julia turned back to the kitchen and went on with her work.

The cow stopped in her tracks at the man's approach, rolled her massive head from side to side in mute alarm, and suddenly bolted to the right, toward an open field, ignoring Luanna's efforts to head her off. The girl stood at the side of the road, uselessly swinging a stick that she carried, and waited for Darby. He came up to her smiling broadly, unperturbed at the disturbance he had made.

'Hello!' he called. 'I came to offer you my more or less invaluable assistance.'

She laughed lightly. 'Well, you came at exactly the right moment – somebody just scared off the cow.'

'Dastardly deed!' he exclaimed. He took the stick from her. 'But do not despair, Señorita. I, *El Bandido Moreno*, have come to the rescue!'

He bounded after the cow, waving the stick in the air, and the animal, having come to a stop a short distance away, tossed her head and broke into a loping run, heading across the field toward a wooded area on the far side.

Darby chased the animal with comical ineptitude, hollering, 'Halt! Whoa there! Here, Bessie, here!' The cow offered an occasional hoarse bellow in reply, as she wheeled and turned to avoid her pursuer. Luanna followed some distance behind the chase, watching nervously, torn between concern and amusement. She was not familiar with Darby's expertise at handling cattle, gained from years as a trail rider and ranch hand; she did not dream that his clumsy, ineffectual efforts were deliberate.

The cow came to a halt at last, exactly according to Darby's plan, on the edge of the woods at the far side of the field. He walked up to her slowly and spoke to her in soothing tones.

'There, Bessie, there now. Easy, girl.'

The big bovine eyes rolled apprehensively, but the animal stood still, and Darby patted her gently on the neck.

'That's a good girl, Bessie. Settle down, now.'

The cow recognized authority, and did as she was told.

Luanna came up, and stood watching. She said, 'Her name's not Bessie, you know. It's Lulu.'

Darby recoiled. 'Yeah. And I been wantin' to have a serious talk with whoever's responsible for *that*.'

'I'm responsible,' she said. 'What's wrong with it?'

'It jus' won't do, that's all. Lulu ain't no name for a cow. That's a name for a painted whore in a western bordello.'

Luanna smiled. 'I wouldn't argue with an expert,' she said. She moved to a tree nearby, and sat down in the shade beneath it.

Darby took hold of the cow's great head and lifted it, and looked into the big brown stupid eyes. 'I know one when I see one,' he said. 'And I can tell you for a fact – this ain't no whore. This here's a respectable cow, and her name is Bessie.'

'Why Bessie?' Luanna said. 'Bessie's so ordinary.'

Bessie – or Lulu – began placidly nibbling at weeds, and Darby left her and went toward Luanna, and lay down in the grass beside her.

'Of course it's ordinary – that's the point. Cows *are* ordinary. And they ain't overly smart, either. They can be led astray easily. You can ruin a good cow with the wrong name.'

She laughed at him with gentle scorn. 'Pshaw! You sound like Moses, makin' a fuss over the name of your skiff.'

'*That* was a joke,' Darby said stuffily. '*This* is serious. You give a nice sweet innocent cow a name like Lulu, and first thing you know she'll be slippin' off to town, battin' her eyes and wigglin' her hips at every bull on the streets.'

'Wish she would,' Luanna said. 'We could use some calves around here.' She giggled and brushed his nose playfully with the end of a weed stalk. Darby grinned, sneezed, grabbed her hand and took the weed away.

He came up on one elbow and studied her face closely, until she said, 'What's the matter?'

'It's uncanny,' he said. 'Your eyes really *are* exactly like your mama's.' He lay back, his mind drifting off into thoughts of Josie.

'Your mama was a beautiful woman, a good, good woman. She always treated me nice – sorta looked after me, without lettin' it be seen that she was doin' it. I used to tease her, and torment her a lot – I'm sorry about that now. I guess secretly I always thought of her as my mama.'

Luanna looked at him with solemn gravity. 'Does that mean you think of me as your sister?'

'Lord, no!' he blurted, and rolled up to a kneeling position and gazed into her eyes, alarmed and frowning. 'At least I don't *think* so.'

He leaned forward and kissed her. It was a light, gentle kiss, but lingering, and she sat very still, neither responding nor resisting.

He sat back on his haunches and smiled at her. 'That didn't feel like kissin' my sister,' he said. 'So much for *that* theory.' Then his smile vanished. 'On the other hand, I didn't notice you vibratin' with passion. Let's try that again.'

He rocked forward, put a hand on her shoulder, and planted a second kiss on the full soft lips. And for a breathless moment – so brief a moment that it seemed to him a dream-like flash of time – the girl's response blossomed forth warm and eager and unexpectedly ardent. She pushed her body toward him until her prominent breasts brushed tantalizingly against his chest. Her mouth opened fluidly; her teeth touched his teeth, her tongue caressed him lightly in the mouth. His hands moved over her, seeking to pull her down onto the ground and into his arms –

Then it was over. She broke off the kiss with a sudden compulsive twist of the head, and rolled away from him. He reached for her, clutching frantically, and found only air. Instantly she was on her feet, and looking down at him with a composure that he found incredible. He poised himself in a half crouch, staring.

'We've got to be goin',' she said matter-of-factly. She picked up the stick that Darby had thrown aside, and started toward the cow. 'Get along, Lulu.'

Obediently the cow moved off.

'I mean Bessie,' Luanna added. She smiled toward Darby. 'Are you comin'?'

Darby sat back under the tree and continued to stare at her. 'God!' he breathed. 'I can't believe you! Weren't you *here* just a second ago? Weren't we *kissing?* Didn't you *feel* anything?!'

She looked at him with cool quiet eyes, and made no answer.

'You must have felt *something*, damn it. Nobody could kiss somebody like that and not feel it.'

Her eyes fell away from his. 'We've got to go,' she said weakly. 'Julia will be wonderin' what happened to us.'

Darby remained where he was, observing her. 'Why are you afraid of me, Luanna?'

She didn't answer. She turned her head to look toward the cow, and vaguely waved the stick in the animal's direction. Then she looked back at Darby again.

'Julia will be waitin'.'

'Yeah,' he said quietly. 'That she will.'

Luanna prodded the cow along, and paused a short distance away and looked back at him once more. 'I thought you were here to help me,' she said.

He sighed, got to his feet, and followed her. 'Here I come, Sis,' he sighed.

When they got back to the house Julia was sitting on the rear veranda steps. 'What took so long?' she said. She sounded a trifle cross.

'Bessie ran away,' Darby said. 'But I caught her, and I've corrected her problem. You won't have any more trouble with her now.'

'You mean Lulu? I didn't know she *had* a problem.'

'Bessie. The *former* Lulu. It was a simple case of confused identity.' Darby sat down on the steps beside Julia. 'She'll be all right, now that she has a decent name.'

'Darby decided her name should be Bessie,' Luanna said.

'Ain't no cow gonna behave properly with a name like Lulu,' Darby said scornfully.

'No cow will behave properly with a name like Lulu,' Julia said.

Darby looked at her blankly for a moment before he realized she was correcting him. He shook his head sheepishly, and smiled.

'I never was much good with grammar, was I, Julia?'

'It's never too late,' she said pleasantly. 'We'll work on it together.' She patted his hand.

Luanna moved past them up the steps, and went into the house.

Moses and Trav returned from the river together when the sun sank low, and Trav announced cheerfully that he'd had a rewarding afternoon. Moses had taught him much about the care and maintenance of skiffs, and he'd had an interesting chat with Philip Ramsey.

'Not a bad fellow at all, Ramsey, when you get to know him.'

'Really?' Julia said with an arch look. 'I must try to get to know him sometime.'

During the evening meal Julia was chatty and vivacious, and told stories of mischievous exploits that she and Darby had concocted when they were children.

And Trav watched her with his unrelentingly suspicious eye, and saw it all as part of her calculated plan – but helpless to resist her light, witty charm, he was swept along with the others in the mood of nostalgic pleasure.

Afterward they sat in the coolness on the front steps, as was their unvarying custom, and watched the blue-to-burgundy-to-black progression of the gathering darkness. Moses stood in the yard and sniffed the air carefully, and studied the sky.

'Rain comin'?' Luanna asked him.

'Not that I can make out,' he said. 'Ain't had no decent rain in days and days. Hope we git some soon.'

'Better hope it holds off a while longer, till we get that roof job done,' Darby said.

Moses shook his head. 'Can't hope *that*, Darby. Garden's more important than the roof.' He went back to the steps and picked up his banjo and sat down, preparing to play.

Julia watched him thoughtfully. 'Moses, I was just thinking – maybe tomorrow you could make a trip across to Tolliver's Landing and pick up a few items at Mister Griffith's store. I have a short list of things I need.'

'Sho' will,' Moses said casually, and strummed his banjo.

'I'll go with you, Moses,' Trav said, and added, to Julia, 'You jus' give *me* your list. I've been wantin' to make a contribution, anyway.'

Julia gave him a small smile. 'That's kind of you, Mister Travers, but not necessary. The work you've been doing is a tremendous contribution.'

'By the way,' Trav said. 'I should have mentioned it sooner – when we were there before Ely sent you his kindest regards. I got the feelin' he has a very soft spot in his heart for you.'

Julia smiled gently. 'I think secretly Mister Griffith has always held decent convictions – or, at least, has decent instincts. Unfortunately, he's never had the courage to match.'

'Hey,' Luanna said brightly, 'why don't we *all* go tomorrow – make an excursion of it?'

'We ain't got time for excursions,' Darby said impatiently. 'We got to get goin' on fixin' that roof.'

'I would like *you* to have a treat, anyway,' Julia said to Luanna. 'I want you to take two dollars out of our cash box, and buy yourself something pretty.'

'So, how many are goin'?' Trav said. 'Can we all squeeze into one skiff, or shall we take both?'

'Well, actually –' Julia said quickly. 'Somebody ought to stay here and take care of things. And that will be me, I think.'

'Oh, Julia!' Luanna said in annoyance. 'Take a holiday, for once!'

'The cow and chickens don't take a holiday,' Julia said. 'They have to be looked after.'

'That's not fair,' Luanna said glumly.

'Nonsense!' Julia said. She reached for Luanna's hand and gave it a little squeeze. 'You go and buy yourself a nice piece of cloth for a new dress. It's a dull life here for a young girl – the change of scene will do you good.'

Luanna appeared unconvinced. Julia laughed lightly and said, 'I don't mind not going, really – you know I've never liked riding in skiffs. Besides –' She looked at Darby, and her eyes met his and held them. 'Maybe somebody will volunteer to stay and keep me company.'

Darby looked at her steadily. 'I'll keep you company,' he said. He smiled suddenly. 'You can keep *me* company, while I split shingles.'

Trav noted Julia's long weighted gaze, holding on Darby. Then he glanced at Luanna, and saw on her face a look of shrivelled emptiness.

'Well, hell!' he blurted. 'Darby's right – we ought to get movin' on that roof. Why don't we forget it for tomorrow, and all go some other day?'

Julia turned an uneasy look on him. 'We're badly in need of some staples from the store,' she said hurriedly.

There was a short silence.

'We'll go,' Luanna said. Her deep solemn eyes were fixed on Julia. Then she looked at Trav. 'In one skiff. Just you and I and Moses.'

It was settled. The silence descended again. On the far side of the steps Moses pretended to be absorbed in fussing with his banjo.

Julia looked up at the sky and breathed deeply of the soft night air. In a moment she turned to Moses.

'Play us a merry tune, Mister Musician,' she said. 'I feel happy tonight.'

CHAPTER SEVENTEEN

The sun had climbed high in a bright cloudless sky, portending another blindingly hot day. Luanna and the three men walked down the front road toward the river; Darby would accompany them to the landing, and return.

Luanna's mood was determinedly sunny and cheerful. She joked with the men, and laughed readily, and speculated, with a mischievous sparkle of eye, whether she should confine her flirtations at the store to old Oscar, the black employee, or work on Mr. Griffith himself.

Work on Ely, Trav advised her. Always aim for the top.

As they moved through the willow thicket a colourful butterfly fluttered across their path, and Luanna gave a little cry of excitement and ran down the trail ahead, in pursuit of it. Her companions watched her, each with his own personal variety of male admiration.

'Seems like she comes into her own when Julia's not around,' Trav remarked.

'Well, it's funny about them two,' Moses said. 'Julia's always been high-powered with men, but nevuh very popular with women. I think it's 'cause she shines in company, puts othuh women in the shade. Now, Luanna's 'bout the only woman I evuh saw that don't *mind* that. She's content to sit quietly in the background, an' let Julia be the centuh of attention. Seems to me like tha's one o' the main reasons Julia's so attached to her.'

Trav threw a quiet, bemused glance at Moses. That, he was sure, was the closest the old man had ever come to finding a flaw in the character of Julia Douglas.

At the river Trav gallantly handed Luanna into the skiff called *El Bandido Moreno*. Moses expressed a reluctance to risk his life in 'that ol' Arkansas scow,' but climbed in, rolling his eyes heavenward and calling on the angels to watch over him.

Darby pushed them off and waved to them as the skiff glided outward, and called to Trav: 'Keep an eye on that girl. Don't let her get too chummy with those dirty-minded white men.'

Luanna gazed back at Darby across the widening stretch of water, and her eyes were sombre. She waved to him.

'Have a good day,' she called.

When Darby emerged from the willow stand on his return to the house he saw Julia sitting on the front steps, waiting for him. For a moment he stood still and gazed at her. Her hair was bound up high on her head again, and she was wearing a thin sleeveless cotton dress, one he had never seen before, that left her arms and shoulders bare. The dress was bright yellow. He went up to her and stopped, and they looked at each other in silence.

'Well,' he said finally. 'Here we are.'

'Yes. Here we are.'

He sat down beside her on the steps and they were quiet for a while longer, gazing down toward the big sycamore tree by the front road. Except for a few listless twitterings of unseen birds, the morning was lifeless, the air heavy and still.

'What shall we do?' he said.

'What would you *like* to do?'

He pondered, and studied the sycamore. 'Well – guess I ought to get busy splittin' those shingles for the roof, huh? Want to come and watch me work?'

She looked at him with an expression that was cunning and secretive, and made no answer.

He frowned. 'Julia, you better be concerned about that roof –'

'Darby?' Her voice was as soft as the summer air. 'Do you remember the last day we spent together? Before you went away?'

'Of course I do, Julia.'

'Do you remember – all of it?'

'Every bit.'

She put her chin on his shoulder. 'We were such poor innocents, weren't we? So ignorant . . .'

'*I* was. You were my teacher. You knew everything.'

'We were searching for something, Darby. In our blind, childish, clumsy way, we were searching. . . .'

'What were we searching for, Julia?' He waited for her answer; he was the pupil still, she the teacher.

A dreamy smile played on her face. 'We were much too foolish to know. And I'm not sure we're yet wise enough. But I want to try again. Don't you?'

His face was troubled. 'I'm afraid, Julia.'

'Of me?'

'*For* you. For myself. For both of us.'

'Maybe you would rather have gone with the others to Tolliver's Landing.'

'No. I want to be with you.'

'But you're afraid.'

He smiled his little-boy smile, and shook his head. 'Scared to death.'

'Oh, Darby!' She laughed gently, and rubbed his cheek with a finger. 'Don't be like that!'

He made a sudden show of jauntiness. 'All right, Miss Julia, ma'am. You've always been in charge o' things – so tell me what we're gonna do today.'

'I'll tell you what we're *not* going to do today.' She went on rubbing his cheek. 'We're not going to split shingles.'

He laughed, and shrugged helplessly. 'Well, what then?'

She put a finger to her lips and gazed thoughtfully into space. 'I think – today we'll pick wild grapes by the river.'

He grinned at her, and said, in the dialect of his boyhood, 'Heah I is, Miss Julia. Ready to go!'

She brought forth a small basket, already neatly prepared, from the kitchen. 'There's a pail for the grapes inside,' she said. 'And a picnic lunch for two.'

He looked at her in genuine astonishment as she handed him the basket. 'Well – you're mighty efficient, I must say.'

'Of course,' she murmured. 'I *believe* in efficiency.'

They walked arm in arm in a leisurely stroll down the road toward the southerly part of the plantation land, going past the remains of the old outbuildings, past the empty fields, and on to the sharp right turn in the road that led past the overgrown ruins of the overseer's house. And as they retraced the route of countless childhood excursions, remembered and unremembered, a mood of quiet nostalgia crept over them, and crowded their minds with the dim dreamy flickerings of ancient images.

Passing the old abandoned house of the overseer, Darby approached it, and peered into its dark, silent, cave-like interior. Quickly he returned to Julia, waiting at the road, and they walked on.

'After your papa discharged Mister Willard, did you ever see him again?' he asked.

'Never, I'm happy to say!' she answered with a laugh. Then she added, more soberly, 'I've seen Gene once or twice, though.'

'Gene?'

'The son. You remember that strange little boy?'

'Oh – yeah.' Darby's memory retrieved a shadowy picture: a small boy, perhaps six years old, climbing idly on the gate of the overseer's front yard, and peering at passersby with a baleful glare that was chillingly incongruous with his age.

'Where have you seen him?'

'Oh, around – once or twice,' she answered vaguely. 'He's a troublemaker.'

'In what way?'

'Oh – I don't know.' She seemed reluctant to talk about the subject she herself had brought up. 'He's a Confederate deserter, and the leader of a gang of hoodlums. Petty thieves, that's all they are. Disgusting.'

Darby thought about this. 'But if he refused to fight for the Confederacy – maybe that means he's on our side.'

Julia threw back her head and laughed. 'Oh, Darby, no! His kind don't desert out of *conviction.*'

Darby frowned at the ground as they walked, and continued to ponder. 'I wonder how a man gets to be –'

'Oh, fiddle-faddle!' Julia shook him by the arm and smiled up at him. 'I refuse to talk about nasty things! This is our day together, and I want it to be the nicest day ever.'

They went on to the end of the road, where the cool green forest began. He followed behind her, then, as they threaded their way along the narrow path that wound through the woods.

And as they walked Darby found himself watching the woman ahead with a fascination that grew on him relentlessly. That astonishing yellow dress – uncannily reminiscent of the one she had worn on their final day together as children, two decades before, except that it was simpler, thinner, more clinging, and more revealing of the lithe body underneath – how did she come by such a dress? It had a daring provocative style not usually associated with the well-born southern lady – on an ordinary woman, Darby mused, it would probably look vulgar. On Julia – enchanting.

His eyes followed the smooth liquid movements of her hips, the graceful twist of the supple waist as she edged past branches on the narrow path, and the delightful games of mottled light and shadows played by the sun and the foliage upon her bright hair and bare arms and shoulders. As he watched he realized with surprise, and a little catch of excitement in his throat, that there was no underwear beneath the dress, that under the flimsy yellow fabric was the lovely cream-smooth body – and he felt a stirring of the tremulous weakness that had seized him the day before, in the kitchen, and knew that the bewitchment was inexorably growing, and couldn't – wouldn't – be stopped.

At a certain grassy spot in the woods Julia paused and waited for him to come up to her. 'Do you remember this place, Darby?' Her smile was soft and beguiling.

He glanced around briefly. 'No, not especially. Should I?'

'Fie on thee!' She scorned him with a little laugh. 'This is the spot where we lay on the grass, and you asked if you could see me.'

'Oh – Lord!' He shuddered with mortification, remembering the painful awkwardness of that childish moment when he had dared to be bolder than he had ever been before in his life, and ask her for that which he thought to be the ultimate treasure. He grinned sheepishly at her. 'Have mercy, Julia! Try to forget that, will you?'

'I should say not! That was lovely – one of the nicest things that ever happened to me.' She took his arm again, and they walked on.

Presently they stood on the edge of the little meadow deep in the forest, and looked across at the old cabin, slumbering in its age-long solitude.

Darby chuckled. 'Amazing! What keeps that ol' pile o' logs from falling down?'

'You know, Darby . . .' Julia fell to musing. 'Wouldn't it be fun if we could fix it up, put in a floor and a roof, and make it habitable?'

He gave her a disapproving frown. 'Are you crazy?! You need to worry about gettin' the *real* house fixed up.'

'Yes,' she said meekly. 'It was just a thought.'

They went across the clearing and entered the silent old ruin, and by unspoken agreement sat down on the rough weathered planks of the wall bench, as they had done many times in the past. The almost unearthly stillness of their surroundings entered into their minds and became part of them. They were quiet for a long time.

Then Darby whispered, 'Are you listenin' to the silence, Julia?'

She smiled and nodded.

After a while he spoke, in a voice subconsciously softened by the tranquility of the mood.

'Everything seemed strange to me, Julia, comin' back here. Familiar, but different, and – strange.'

'Even me?'

'Even you – at first. Not any more. Right now, this minute – everything's good, everything's natural. I feel – right at home.'

She smiled at him. 'Twenty-one years,' she said dreamily. 'Where did they go? It's as if they never happened.'

'Sometimes I wonder, Julia. What would've become of us, if I hadn't gone away?'

'If you hadn't gone away ...' she echoed faintly. 'The large directions of life are governed by little ifs.'

He looked at her curiously. 'Julia – how come you never married?'

Unexpectedly she giggled. 'The fellow I liked jilted me, and ran off to Missouri and California.'

'Seriously, Julia –'

'Seriously, Darby, I've just been too busy for marriage. There's been the garden club, and the sewing circle, and the literary society, and the endless social responsibilities of a southern lady – you just can't imagine!'

He looked away with a resigned smile, seeing that she would not discuss the subject. 'Well, then, tell me about Charles Hollingsworth.'

'I thought you heard all the gossip about me from the gentlemen at Tolliver's Landing.'

'Trav heard the gossip. I'd like to hear the truth.'

'The truth is that Charles Hollingsworth was a kind, gentle, sweet-natured, soft-spoken man – so much so that people often made the mistake of thinking he was not altogether masculine. But he was. He was lion-hearted in courage, and incredibly brave. He had lofty ideals, and he pursued them steadfastly, and never wavered. He belongs in that rare small group of quiet heroes, like your Mister Rutledge.'

Her gaze drifted off into the distance, as she looked back across lost years. 'He was a warm and wonderful friend. And he was my lover. I suppose we would have married, had he lived.'

After a pause she looked at Darby. 'I loved him dearly. Almost as much as you.'

Darby shrugged, and said, 'Well, you couldn't make me jealous with that Ramsey fellow, but now you've succeeded.'

She put a hand on his shoulder, leaned toward him, and caressed his cheek with her lips in an airy-soft kiss that made his heart flutter suddenly – but when he put out his hand to touch her she had drawn back.

'Don't be jealous, Darby. Don't ever be jealous. You are one of the lucky people of the world. It is for others to be jealous of you.'

They deposited their picnic basket in a cool dark corner of the cabin, and continued on down the little path through a tangle of jungle growth, until they stood on grassy banks, with the river stretching in a wide shining sheet in the sunlight before them. Then Darby led the way a short distance upstream and away from the river again, and skirted an inlet where a small brook babbled, committing its modest contents to the waters of the world. Soon they gazed up into the dark green canopy of a huge and ancient cottonwood, which stood as Darby remembered it, creaking and groaning from the weight of a vast multi-tentacled vine that wound itself from the shady base to the sunlit top, sixty feet from the ground.

Julia turned to Darby with a little gasp. 'We forgot the pail!'

Darby gave her a smug smile. 'That's all right – we don't need it.' He climbed a few feet into the vine, pulled down a handful of low-hanging grapes, and brought them to her.

'Oh!' Her eyes opened wide with surprise. 'They're hard as rocks!'

He laughed at her gently. 'Lord, Julia, after all these years – you *still* don't know when the grapes get ripe!'

She gave a little shrug of helplessness. 'You see what you did, when you ran away? You went off and left my education incomplete.' She came closer to him, and her hand crept up his arm. 'I wish you wouldn't leave things unfinished like that.'

They hovered, motionless – her lips drifted slowly up toward him – and Darby felt his breath catch involuntarily, and knew that he trembled on the brink of a great height.

The moment was shattered by the deep vibrations of a steamboat whistle, hurtling across the treetops from the river.

Julia was wide-eyed immediately. 'Downriver – it's mine!' she shrieked.

Darby shouted, 'Upriver! Mine!'

They scrambled back to the river as fast as they could, leaving the two giants of the forest, the cottonwood and the grapevine, locked in their mighty decades-long death struggle.

Julia was right; the steamboat, standing far out in mid-stream, was moving with the current down toward the great ports to the south. They stood for a moment watching it.

'What was the score, you remember?' Darby asked.

And Julia, the inventor and arbiter of all games, replied without hesitation. 'Twenty to nineteen, your favour. Now we're even.'

'One more, and you win the longest-adjourned contest in history,' he said.

She threw him a saucy look. 'Maybe I'll let *you* win, for a change.'

He shook his head, and smiled down at her. 'No, you win, Julia. That's the way it always was, and that's the way I like it.'

They walked along the edge of the river, and Darby took off his shoes, rolled up his pants legs, and waded in the muddy shallows along the shore. Julia sat down on the bank and smiled, watching him. He took off his shirt and tossed it carelessly toward the dry ground near Julia – and it fluttered through the air and fell short, partly in the water.

Julia leaned forward and retrieved it, scolding him. 'Darby, don't be careless!'

He scooped up water in his palms and threw it overhead, and stood grinning as it rained down upon him. Julia squealed and moved back when some of the man-made precipitation fell on her.

'Come on in, Julia!' he called to her, and she smiled and shook her head – then suddenly changed her mind.

Swiftly she discarded her shoes and tucked her skirt up, and reached for his extended hand, holding on to him for balance, and giggling in girlish delight as the tepid brown water flowed over her feet and the cool mud oozed between her toes.

They waded in the water like children, hand in hand, and watched for the instantaneous darting of small fish, and the comically frantic tail-wagging of fat round tadpoles. Something large thrashed in the water suddenly, a few yards away, and Julia gasped and clung to Darby with a tremor of fright.

He held her, and said soothingly, 'Don't let a little ol' catfish scare you,' and gazed at her wonderingly, remembering that she was afraid of nothing.

She looked up at him, then, with a strangely shy smile, started to speak, and stopped. Her look turned to a stare. He saw her moist lips part slightly, as they had in the kitchen the day before, and move almost imperceptibly toward him again. That was all the warning – there was no time for thought or reaction – the long hungry kiss began again, this time deeper, more furious, more overwhelming by far than before. She breathed with passionate expansion, and her breasts beneath the thin cotton dress pressed themselves against his bare chest so insistently that he could feel the hard rising nipples, he could feel tiny goose bumps on her arms around his neck, and a quivering far down inside her, and he knew she felt the strong uncontrollable pulsing from his loins, for she pushed herself upon him and rubbed with a voluptuous undulation of her hips – and all the while spoke to him in an intimate wordless murmur that made his heart race. . . .

The warm water lapped softly around their ankles. For a wild moment he felt that he was sinking, that he was standing in quicksand, and that the day was turning by some horrendous miracle into night. The spell passed – suddenly Julia was leading him by the hand, smiling back at him, out of the shallow water and onto the land. A small cloud had floated across the sun, putting a shadow on the river.

When they were on the grass again she stopped him and held him in a loose embrace, her grey eyes soft and smiling, and said, 'Picnic time. Hungry?'

He stared at her dumbly.

They walked back to the cabin in silence, Julia leading him by the hand as if showing him the way. She spread the contents of their picnic basket in the shade of the cabin while Darby sat with his back against the cool log wall and watched her with profound wonder.

She handed him a sandwich, laid the open palm of her hand on his bare chest, and spoke for the first time in minutes. 'Goodness! We left your shirt by the river.' Sly amusement glimmered in her eyes. 'What *could* we have been thinking of?'

They ate little, and with little interest. The silence between them grew heavier, and was charged with a taut electric excitement that each felt, and knew was shared by the other. Afterward Julia put the food basket away and lay on her back in the grassy shade, and stretched languidly. 'Time for nap,' she murmured. Darby came and lay on the grass beside her. She smiled at him, and closed her eyes.

The humid drowsiness of early afternoon crept over the forest, and brought a stillness deeper than that of morning or of night. Once in a while, from far off to the northwest, a faint distant rumble of thunder sounded – otherwise the day was as quiet as if all human life and the workings of nature everywhere had ceased.

When Julia opened her eyes Darby was lying on his side gazing at her.

'Can't sleep?'

He shook his head.

'Neither can I.' She rolled onto her side to face him.

A gentle breeze that smelled of rain brushed the trees of the forest, stirred the foliage lightly, and touched them with a hint of chill.

'Guess I ought to go get my shirt,' Darby said.

'No.' Julia put her hand on his arm and let it glide up and around his shoulder. 'Don't need a silly old shirt.'

The thunder rolled across the sky, somewhat closer now, more demanding of attention. The day was darkening from a towering thunderhead, building gradually to the west, across the river.

'It's gonna rain,' Darby observed.

'Moses said it wouldn't,' Julia countered.

'Mother Nature can change her mind without notifyin' Moses.'

'We can always go in the cabin.'

'Sure.' He grinned. 'We can always go in the roofless cabin.'

Logic was useless; the soft grey eyes held him irresistibly. 'Darby – there's something I wanted to tell you. Lately I've been thinking a lot about Josie, remembering something I learned from her. When she was nursing Luanna I used to sit with her for hours, and we'd have long talks. She was not exactly a happy person, but she was content, she was truly content. I couldn't understand how that was possible – she knew how wrong it was, the way my father owned her, and possessed her body by command. But she told me she experienced deep joy with my father. When she was with him she felt important, she said, she felt – valued. I was very young, and I couldn't comprehend that – all I could see was that if something was wrong it was totally wrong. But later I understood. It had nothing to do with race, or slavery. The truth is that in his own way my father loved Josie deeply. And she loved him.'

Darby was entranced, but mystified. 'Why are you tellin' me all this?'

'Because I want to feel that way with you.' Her hand moved with hypnotic gentleness up and down, up and down, on his arm and shoulder, and her voice became as caressing as her hand. 'I want to be possessed.'

He searched her face, and shook his head faintly, in wonderment. 'I'm jus' not sure about you, Julia. After all these years – I'm not sure you're real.'

Her soft smile was a mixture of sweetness and guile. 'Wait – there's something else I wanted to tell you. I used to have a secret dream, when we were children. A game I played, all by myself.'

'Secret? I thought I knew all your dreams.'

She shook her head. 'Not this one. Late at night, in my bed, I'd pretend you were a fierce African warrior, a tribal chieftain, and I –'

'Julia!' He grimaced, starting to protest.

She shushed him with a finger on his lips. 'And I was your captive slave.'

'*You?!*' He stared at her, incredulous. 'You, a slave?!'

'Everybody was deathly afraid of you, even your own warriors, you were so fierce. Everybody but me. *I* wasn't afraid. I liked being your slave.'

He laughed aloud, in scorn. 'You're crazy, Julia. Jus' plumb crazy. . . .'

'Darby –' Her voice was suddenly earnest, her eyes held him with a bright intensity. 'If you could only know – it was the most exciting thing I've ever felt, imagining myself being summoned to your tent, and going willingly, eagerly, knowing you were going to use my body for your pleasure – it was the wildest, most delicious thrill I've ever known.'

He stirred restlessly, and moved as if to turn away, but she clutched his arm and held him.

'It was so exciting, I used to lie in my bed and tingle all

over, just thinking about it. I used to take off my nightgown and lie naked and caress my own body, and imagine it was you, the warrior chieftain. . . .'

He was transfixed, wanting to tear himself free, yearning to hear more.

'And to this day, Darby – in all the years since then – I've never had a real-life experience nearly so marvellous as that imagined one.' Her arm was around his neck now, pulling him gently, inexorably, toward her. 'I want to recapture that thrill, I want to feel it again – this time, *totally*. I want you to possess me.'

'Julia, you don't –' His voice was faint and faltering. 'You don't know what you're sayin'. . . .'

'Let's stop pretending, Darby. We've always belonged to each other, as long as we both can remember.'

'I'm not pretending. I'm bewitched, and I know it. But –'

'But you're holding back from me.'

'You're jus' not thinkin' beyond this moment, this day –'

'Oh, my Darby . . . my dearest! I've been thinking about this day for twenty *years*, never daring to dream it would really arrive. Now it's here. Let's not hold back, let's give ourselves to each other, the way it was always meant to be – please?'

He came up on an elbow and leaned over her, looked down into the burning grey eyes, and thought that he was gazing into a depth so vast and infinite that he could dive into it and fall forever, never rising. Another part of his consciousness followed the caressing movement of her hand on the bare skin of his back and shoulder, as soft as the feathery touch of summer air.

Her body strained upward toward him in anticipation. He was rigid, breathless, suspended between rising desire and a mysterious terror.

'Julia. . . .' he whispered hoarsely, and shook his head in a last desperate effort to retain his reason. 'What's to *become of us*?'

The moist lips beneath him parted, trembled, and touched his. 'Take me, Darby,' she whispered. 'Use me for your pleasure. . . .'

And desire rose like the ocean at floodtide, drowning all terror and reason alike. He came down to her and covered her lips, knowing that he was bowing to an immutable law of nature, as far beyond human control as the great glowering thunderhead moving slowly over the river. He put a hand behind her shoulders and pulled her toward him, and she responded with a murmur of sweet yielding, her slender arms sliding around his back and holding him in a bondage that was soft as silk and strong as steel. A tremor coursed through his sinews with spasmodic violence, like a flash of pain. He crushed her hard against him, and his hand roamed over her body, slid under the yellow dress, and, finding there no encumbrance of underclothing, moved up along the smooth free curve of the hip and around the thigh, finding the secret places, caressing tenderly, caressing constantly. . . .

He saw himself as if in a dream, from a distance. He was on his feet and lifting her, and marvelling at the lightness of his precious burden, and the ease with which his physical dominance, once unleashed, had taken possession of them both. He felt himself carrying her into the cabin, and standing there in the deeper shadows, holding her and kissing her with a devouring eagerness, as she lay trembling and helpless in his arms.

He set her gently on her feet then, and she stood with eyes closed, swaying slightly, while he held her with one hand and with the other unbound her hair, and let it fall through his fingers in yellow profusion over her shoulders. With his hands on her hips he slid her dress easily upward and off over her head, and dropped it to the ground.

Serenely nude she stood, still swaying slightly, and glowing with expectancy. She filled his eyes with unbelievable wonder – a beautiful, wild, wanton creature. And a stranger.

The day had grown menacingly dark; the giant thunderhead now rolled over them. As he took a step back from her a startling flash of lightning glared and crackled in the air, and thunder broke resoundingly and close, shaking the ground. Her eyes were open wide now and staring at him fixedly, and he stared back, panting, stunned by the power of nature in the sky and in his own body.

He unclasped his belt and struggled out of his clothes with a rough impatience, and saw her gaze fasten on his dark powerful horizontal-thrusting masculinity. She held out her arms to him, and pulled him toward her with her yearning eyes.

Overhead the storm loomed and rumbled and threatened, and the day grew darker, and darker still.

Her waiting arms encircled him. One of his hands moved

around the graceful curve of her back beneath the flowing hair, and the other took into its gentle holding a soft rounded breast. Their bodies merged and sank together to the ground.

She lay on the carpet of pine needles, and he kissed her pale throat, shoulders, tender pink nipples, caressed with his lips the length of the lovely fragile body to the down-soft pubic cushion, while she arched her back and thrust herself toward him, digging her fingers frantically into his shoulders, and crooning a soft sound that was not language but more eloquent than language.

At length she pulled him over her with a pleading urgency, locked him in her arms and between her slender legs and enveloped him in warmth and sweetness.

'Take me, take me. . . .' she whispered again, and a tiny sob caught in her throat as he pushed himself with infinite loving tenderness into her.

Another flash of lightning – and in the brief garish illumination he saw her shining face clearly one last time before all sensations were lost in the central supreme sensation. The thunder exploded; his heart pounded; in his ear Julia's crooning gradually grew and deepened, finally rose to a tremulous wail of joyousness – and all the sounds pulsed and echoed hopelessly in his mind.

Nature paused, and waited. They mounted together to the ultimate rapturous climax, fighting for breath, their mouths and bodies and beings locked together, and clinging to each other as if to life itself.

Then at long last, when they lay still and spent, the world moved on; the rain fell, with surprising gentleness, filtering quietly down through the multilayered pine branches above, and into the waiting earth below.

CHAPTER EIGHTEEN

The visitors to Tolliver's Landing were ready to depart for home when the storm broke. They took shelter under the eaves of the landing warehouse and waited until the peak of the downpour had passed, then launched their skiff for the return crossing while large gentle raindrops were still speckling the water with ringlets.

The thunderhead had delivered less than it had threatened; the shower had been vigorous for a few minutes only, dwindling rapidly as its lofty source slid across the sky and over the river. Its dying drizzle drifted shimmering down through sunshine, slanting in from the west under the edge of the cloud. Soon the last drops vanished, and by the time the travellers landed on the east bank of the river the sun was bright and unobstructed, with nothing remaining of the atmospheric disturbance but a bright green glisten on wet foliage, and the feeble rumble of thunder rolling distantly off toward the east. The warm earth was already steaming itself dry.

Moses, who had been elated at the prospect of a thorough drenching of his parched garden, grumbled and complained, and declared that the storm was a shameless fraud.

They beached their skiff, shouldered the provisions they had bought, and walked up the little road – dusty before, now damp and sticky – through the willow thicket. When they reached the house they found that Julia and Darby were not there.

'Wonder where they went,' Trav said, as he helped Luanna unpack kitchen supplies.

'Probably to their old favourite playground,' the girl said. 'The squatter's cabin.'

Trav went to the back door and gazed off down the road toward the south area. 'Maybe we should walk down there and meet 'em.' He glanced quickly at Luanna, to note her reaction.

'No,' she said bluntly. 'We shouldn't.'

Luanna bustled about the kitchen, making preparations

for the evening meal. Moses hurried off to see about the cow and chickens – he said nothing, but it was clear that he guessed the animals had not been seen to that day.

Trav tried to help Luanna in the kitchen until she laughingly chased him out, saying that he only got in the way. Then he wandered out onto the rear veranda, and sat down on the top step. He fixed his gaze down the south road, and waited.

He saw Darby and Julia when they were a quarter of a mile away, walking arm in arm, and coming toward the house at a languidly slow pace. As they came nearer he observed them carefully. He noted that Julia clung to Darby's arm, and looked at him almost constantly. Even at that distance he could see that her face shone with a special light. And her hair, usually bound in a prim bun, was flowing loose behind her shoulders.

It's not much, he thought – but it's enough. The question that had burned in his mind all day seemed to be answered with startling clarity. He got up and went inside, and climbed the stairs to his room.

Darby found him there, stretched out on his bedroll, staring at the ceiling.

'H'lo, Trav.'

Trav looked around quickly, as if surprised. 'Hello, there!' he said cheerfully. 'How was your day?'

'Very good. How was the trip?'

'Fine.'

Darby sat down on the floor next to his friend. 'Trav –' he began, hesitantly, but got no further.

'I'm afraid Luanna didn't have a good day, though,' Trav went on. 'And I guess it was my fault. I amused myself sendin' ol Junior Tolliver into spells of outrage by escortin' Luanna in and out like a high-born lady, carryin' things for her, buyin' her refreshments –' He laughed wickedly. 'You should 'a' seen Junior simmerin' – I thought he was gonna boil over!'

His laughter died quickly. 'But the whole thing made Luanna miserable, I'm afraid. Poor kid. She deserved a better holiday than that.' He shook his head glumly. 'She deserves a better life than this.'

'Trav, Julia wants to talk to you.'

'That so?' Trav yawned suddenly, and stretched lazily on his bedroll. 'Maybe later, huh? That was a tiring trip today. I feel like grabbin' a nap.' He yawned again, and rolled over on his side, his back toward Darby.

After a moment of hesitation, Darby said, 'Sure, Trav.' He got up quietly and went out.

The evening meal was eaten early, and in comparative silence. The sporadic conversation was trivial and half-hearted, when it occurred. All faces were blank and guarded. Julia, ordinarily the initiator of conversational topics, was unusually, unnaturally quiet. Her hair was again tied neatly in its bun, behind her head.

Afterward, when they assembled on the front veranda for their customary evening hour of relaxation, the western sky was still bright with the sinking sun. Julia sat on the top step and gazed up at the shadowy bulk of Indian Hill, across the road. Abruptly she announced, 'I feel like taking a walk.' She got up and glanced around at the others. 'And I'd like some company,' she said. 'Not too much – just a little. Any volunteers?'

'Choose somebody,' Darby told her.

'All right. I choose Mister Travers.' She went down the steps, turned and looked back at Trav. 'Will you come, Mister Travers?'

He leaped to his feet. 'I'd follow you, Miss Douglas,' he proclaimed theatrically, 'to the ends of the earth!'

'I don't intend to go *that* far,' she said with a vague smile. 'Just to the top of Indian Hill.' She started toward the front road, hesitating long enough for Trav to come up beside her.

The others sat quite still on the steps, watching them go, each wrapped in private thoughts.

They climbed the little path that meandered like a length of twisted thread up the south slope of the hill. Julia walked with astonishing rapidity, so that Trav was forced to scramble to keep up, and there was neither time nor breath for talking. She did not slacken her pace until she stood on the summit, and turned bright sparkling eyes on Trav as he came up to her, puffing heavily.

'It's wonderful up here,' she said, and her voice was vibrant with exhilaration. 'It's my second-most favourite place.'

She lifted her face to catch the soft air-stirring of dusk, moving invisibly across the hill from the southwest. 'Mm-m-m. Feel that nice breeze!'

'And the first?' Trav said.

'What?' She looked at him blankly.

'Your *most* favourite place.'

'Oh –' She smiled. 'The squatter's cabin, of course. I've always had a secret desire to live there myself. Ever since I was a little girl I've envied the people who built it, whoever they were. They may have been poor, but they surely must have had a bountiful plenty of warmth and love.'

'How do you know? Maybe they got on each other's nerves.'

'Pooh, Mister Travers! You have no instinct for the romantic.' Her scorn was joking, and she tossed a quick smile at him before turning away. She walked a short distance to a grassy knoll, spread her skirt carefully, and sat down.

He watched her, and saw that she expected him to follow. What am I in for? he thought. What does she have in store for me, from her clever bag of tricks?

She smiled at him again, and patted the grass beside her – an invitation.

Whatever it is, it'll be high-class. She's no junk dealer. If I was sane I'd get the hell out of here right now.

He went and sat beside her.

'I guess I ought to thank you,' he said. 'It's very flattering to be chosen as milady's walking partner.'

'Well – there was something I wanted to talk to you about.'

'So I heard.'

There was no urgency. She smoothed her skirt again, with elaborate care, and brushed a fallen leaf away, then gazed placidly toward the colourful sunset sky. Finally she turned her eyes full on him.

'I want to offer you a business proposition, Mister Travers.'

'We came all the way up to this beautiful spot to talk *business?! Now* who has no instinct for the romantic!'

'I'm sorry – I used the wrong expression.' She laughed lightly. 'Besides – this involves a great deal more than business.'

'Well, I'm listening,' he said.

She turned a little more toward him, and spoke with sudden seriousness.

'As you know, I want very much to revitalize Chinaberry, and make it flourish again. Not like before, of course – the old plantation system is gone forever, and good riddance. I'm thinking about something quite different. A sort of – colony, a kind of loose family, and a place where people of all colours and both sexes can live together in peace, with mutual love and respect.'

Trav listened with studied attention.

'Now, we need many things,' Julia went on. 'We need money, we need equipment and supplies, we need people, we need time – most of all we need people. Not just *any* people, of course. *Good* people.'

She paused and took a deep breath before continuing. 'Darby has decided to stay.'

She paused again, and glanced nervously at Trav, as if expecting an emphatic reaction. He remained silent.

'For just a year, to help get us on our feet. That's a wonderful beginning, but it creates problems, too. Darby is distressed, worried that you'll feel betrayed. He doesn't want to lose your friendship, and I don't want that to happen, either. He needs you.' She gazed at him with piercing intensity. 'We all need you.'

Trav pursed his lips thoughtfully. He said nothing.

'So, what I'm proposing –' She shifted her position once more, to face him more directly. 'I'm proposing that you and Darby *both* stay – permanently – and assume joint ownership with the rest of us. If you agree, I'm prepared to deed one fifth share of the property to you.'

She stopped; Trav continued to maintain his silence. She continued. 'The five of us are a cross-section of black and white, male and female – I think we'd make a good nucleus of the kind of free idealistic communal life –'

'Uh, Miss Julia –'

Trav stirred for the first time, and Julia stopped short and waited, without breathing.

'You say you're prepared to deed one fifth of the property to me. What does Darby get?'

'Why, he gets one fifth also. My plan is that all five of us would share equally. It would be like a – like a company, with each member having a twenty per cent share.'

Trav leaned back on an elbow and looked up at her quizzically. 'You spoke of it as the idealistic communal life, what you have in mind. That's interesting – I *have* noticed that you're an extremely idealistic-minded person.'

'Yes, I am,' she said readily. 'If being discontented with

this grossly imperfect human society, and wanting to create something better is idealistic, I am indeed.'

'Now me, I'm more the realistic type,' Trav said. 'And I like to consider things from a practical angle. For instance, when I walked back to the river with your neighbour Philip Ramsey yesterday, I took the trouble to ask some practical questions – and I got some solid practical answers.

'By the way – I think you're makin' a big mistake, not takin' Ramsey seriously. He's basically a decent fellow, considerin' everything. And, he's got a lot of high quality stuff up here.' Trav tapped his forehead.

Julia forced a weak smile. 'We seem to be digressing, Mister Travers.'

'Right. Well, one o' the things Ramsey told me was that the bottom has dropped right out o' plantation property value hereabouts, now that the slave labour force has been eliminated. His own place, Graystone, is just hangin' on by a thread. And, he pointed out, this is in spite o' the fact that Graystone's in good physical shape – it's been lived in, maintained, used, and cared for, without interruption. Chinaberry lay here for years, neglected, abused, and overgrown. In Ramsey's opinion, Chinaberry is virtually beyond bringin' back.'

For an instant Julia's eyes flashed anger, but quickly cooled. 'That, Mister Travers, is *perfect* nonsense.' Her voice was calmly controlled. 'The Chinaberry land is no less rich than it ever was before –'

'It's not a question of the quality of the land, dear lady. It's a question of the *value* of *property*, of *economic feasibility*. In Ramsey's opinion –'

'In *my* opinion, sir, Mister Ramsey's opinion is entirely irrelevant. And it seems to me that we continue to digress.'

'I think not.' Trav raised himself closer to Julia. 'The point is that you're askin' for a total, long-range commitment, and offerin' in return twenty per cent of what appears to be more or less nothing.'

Julia folded her hands in her lap and gazed serenely off toward the sunset. 'My, my – you certainly *did* have an interesting chat with charming Philip, didn't you? Would it interest you to know that charming Philip has tried all his *life* to get his hands on this property, which he describes to you as practically worthless?'

'Yes, we discussed that, too.' Trav smiled faintly. 'My

impression was that he's not so much interested in gettin' his hands on the land, as he is in gettin' his hands on the lady who owns it.'

Julia sniffed. 'He's a liar. He's a buffoon, a lecher, and a liar. What other fascinating morsels of misinformation did he favour you with?'

'One more. I'd heard a little about the Black Code laws – the various restrictions on the emancipated people. Ramsey acquainted me with a detail in those laws that I *hadn't* heard about. It seems that black people are allowed to own land *only* in incorporated towns. In other words, they are not permitted to own *agricultural* land. That bein' the case, Miss Julia, what becomes of your plan to bestow shares of ownership on Darby, or Luanna, or Moses?'

He watched her carefully, with narrowed eyes. This will destroy her position, he thought. This will cut her down. But her cool steady gaze told him he was wrong.

'Why, that's easy, Mister Travers. I will simply *do* it, that's all. The law you mention was an irrational act, adopted in a moment of panic. It is foolish, illogical and altogether indefensible from any point of view.'

'Just the same, it's –'

'*And*,' Julia went on firmly, 'it's completely unenforceable. It will be stricken from the books within a year or two at most. Meanwhile, I'll make whatever agreements I choose concerning my property – personal agreements, just between us few. There's no difficulty there. My friends trust me, Mister Travers.'

Trav nodded. 'Sure they do. And I don't blame 'em for that. But they'd be fools to believe that because somethin' is plainly wrong, it'll automatically be corrected soon. That's your idealism again, Miss Julia, foggin' up your vision.'

Julia sighed. 'I take it, Mister Travers, you're not interested in my proposal.'

He did not answer immediately. Restlessly he shifted his position. After a short pause he said, 'I'd like to make you a counter-proposal.'

She looked at him with quick curiosity.

'I'd like to propose that you write off Chinaberry as a lost cause, sell the land for whatever you can get, and come to California with Darby and me. All of you. If we put our combined energies into the ranch, we'd have somethin' goin' that really has a *future* to it.'

'I don't consider Chinaberry a lost cause, Mister Travers.' Her voice was soft, but as chilling as a glacial wind.

Trav slumped in discouragement. 'What do you think is more important, Julia – land, or people?'

'Why, people, of course. But without roots people have no – no identity. Chinaberry is part of me – and it's part of Darby, too.'

'That so? Let me tell you somethin' about Darby that *I've* noticed. He's different from you or me – and I don't mean colour. Me, I take an idea like freedom for granted – never give it a thought – 'cause I've always had it. But Darby – there's never been a day I've known him that he hasn't taken his freedom out and held it in his hand like a precious stone, to feel it, admire it, and thank God for it. Never a day – except the days he's been here.'

Julia was rigid. 'What do you mean by that?!'

'That you're takin' his freedom away from him again, as surely as if you were turnin' the clock back twenty-one years.'

Her eyes glowed dangerously. She got to her feet, and turned to him with a face hot with anger. 'That's a cruel, a despicable thing to say, Mister Travers. I don't take people's freedom away. I was setting people free here long before it was legal or safe to do so!'

'I know that, Julia, and I give you full credit for it. But with all your talk of roots and identity and idealism and what-not – you're entanglin' two nice people named Darby and Luanna in your private web of dreams, so they have no chance for any identity of their own.'

Julia's breath exploded in exasperation, and she turned away from him as if to leave and return to the house. Then she stopped, came back and stood before him, and spoke with a calm deliberation that was controlled by an intense effort of will.

'Mister Travers, I began fighting the battle for a better kind of life when I was fourteen years old, and I've been at it ever since. There were others like me in the South – I make no claim to uniqueness. But we were few – we couldn't accomplish anything significant. It took a terrible war, that left everybody, friend and foe alike, desolated, to do what nothing else could. It cut the festering poison out of our bodies with a bloody sword.'

She paused, trembling imperceptibly, and fought to tighten the grip on her control.

'Please understand me, Mister Travers. We were horribly wounded, but we *are* recovering. After all those years of pain and struggle, we stand at the beginning of a new time, when the odds no longer seem hopeless. At last we have a chance to build a good life. And *now* – you say toss it aside, and call it a lost cause!'

She pulled herself up, straight-backed, to her full height, her eyes bright with passionate certainty. 'And I say you're ignorant, Mister Travers. I'm sorry for you, you're so very, very ignorant.'

She turned away from him, and he sat motionless, gazing in wonder at her stiff slender back.

How can anybody who looks so frail be so invincible? He shook his head, bewildered, and got up and went toward her. From directly behind her he spoke with as much gentleness as he could command.

'You're messin' my life up good and proper, lady. But I've got to admit I'm almost enjoyin' it. There's somethin' about you. . . .'

She turned toward him quickly, and saw admiration shining openly in his eyes. She extended a hand toward him, tentatively.

'Is there any way I can reach you, Mister Travers?' she said pleadingly. 'Is there *anything* I can do to make you think differently?'

He looked at her in silence for a moment, and the silence was heavy with conjecture and unspoken meanings.

'Well –' he said slowly. 'You might try jus' callin' me Trav, for a change. And if that doesn't help,' – his words lingered on his tongue, as he studied her – 'you might try lettin' your hair down. That seemed to work like a charm on Darby.'

Still she refused to be ruffled. Her gaze remained steady, and intensely grave. 'Do not joke with me, please,' she said. 'I would make love to you right here on the grass if I thought it would change your mind.'

He took a step closer to her. 'Now that's an idea I find extraordinarily attractive.'

Casually he slid his arm around her waist and pulled her up to him and kissed her. She accepted him passively, offering neither resistance nor response.

He continued to hold her close, and spoke directly into her ear. 'That's amazing. You didn't put a thing into that, and it wasn't half bad. If you tried just a little, you could probably make me forget every other woman I've ever known.'

She pulled back and looked into his eyes. 'Possibly I could make you forget. But could I make you *stay*?'

He released her now, and stepped back. 'You know, you baffle me a tiny bit, ma'am. You're not all of a sudden madly in love with me – how come it's so important to you that I stay?'

She answered without hesitation. 'Because you're a superior person, and we need superior people. You're highly intelligent, extremely capable, of excellent character, and you have good sound attitudes – for the most part.'

He grinned. 'Do that some more – it feels good.'

'Besides which –'

She was coming to the real reason now, and he waited, sure that he already knew it – but her candor startled him, nevertheless.

'If you'll stay, Darby will, too.'

'I thought that was all settled – he *is* staying.'

'Only for a year. He has no intention of giving up the idea of that ranch in California with you.'

Her voice went low, weighted with determination. 'That's not good enough,' she said. 'I want him for life.'

He stared. 'You don't baffle me, lady. You absolutely dumbfound me. But I'll give you credit again. You're honest. That's damn certain, you're honest.'

He began pacing up and down before her, and went on, speaking more rapidly.

'Well, let's explore your plan in greater detail. I'm the practical type, remember – things have to be spelled out for me. Now, as I understand it, you'd have us all livin' together in beautiful, boundless love. And, naturally, love includes sex, right? So how would it work, exactly – would you make love to Darby in the morning and me in the evening? Or vice versa? Or would we have you on alternate days – or every other week, maybe? And who'd make love to poor Luanna? I'd gladly volunteer, but she'd only want Darby, and that'd make *you* jealous. What about Moses, where does *he* fit in? I suppose he could keep score –'

'Please forget about it!' Julia snapped. She turned her back on him. 'I'm sorry I said anything – I don't know why I even tried to talk to you at all. I want this thing so much, I – I suppose I'm trying too hard. . . .' She walked a few steps away from him, and stood with head bowed.

'Well, you don't need to worry about it,' he said quietly. 'You'll succeed, all right. In a few days you've managed to rope Darby in for a year. In a year there's no way you can fail to trap him for good.'

'Trap?!' She threw the word back over her shoulder. 'I appreciate your delicate terminology!'

'What would *you* call it? You're offerin' him two irresistible lures, both worthless. You're offerin' him twenty per cent of land he's not legally entitled to own, and you're offerin' him the chance to pick up where he left off twenty-one years ago, and go right on bein' your devoted slave.'

She whirled on him, and her eyes pierced him with burning fury. 'Mister Travers, I think we should stop wasting our breath on one another. I have absolutely *nothing* else to say to you – now or ever!'

'Well, I –'

She had tossed her head like an unruly colt and bolted away, starting down the path toward the house.

'– guess you're right,' he finished lamely, to empty air.

The dusk had deepened to near-darkness when Julia came down off the hill. She crossed the front road and walked rapidly toward the house, where Darby, Luanna and Moses were sitting on the front steps, waiting.

As she came near Darby searched her face, and saw that it was grim, and set in stone. He slumped. A wave of depression rushed over him. Julia walked past the people on the steps without speaking, and went into the house. Luanna got up quickly and followed her, saying, 'Julia, wait!'

Darby and Moses sat motionless, watching Trav saunter unhurriedly down the hill slope, cross the road, and come toward them. His expression was casual and placid, and told them nothing. He stopped at the foot of the steps, and he and Darby gazed at each other in silence.

Trav glanced toward Moses. 'Play us a sad tune, Mister Musician,' he said, and sat down heavily on the bottom step.

'What happened, Trav?' Darby said at last.

Trav remained silent another moment before answering.

'Miss Julia and I had us a nice, civilized, friendly, what you might call man-to-man talk. And we found that, while we disagree on a few insignificant trifles, we see exactly eye-to-eye on one central fundamental issue.'

'Which is?'

'That I've worn out my welcome here.'

After another short pause, Darby said, 'Is that all you're goin' to tell us?'

'That about sums it up, I think.'

'Well, since you won't tell us, let me see if I can piece it together. First, she told you I had decided to stay awhile.'

'Not *first*. But she did get around to it.'

Darby put out his hand and laid it lightly on Trav's shoulder. 'I'm sorry about that, Trav. I should've talked to you about it myself. I wanted to tell you this afternoon, up in the room –'

'That's all right, forget it,' Trav said. 'I pretty well knew what you wanted to say – I jus' didn't feel like hearin' it, right then.'

'And it looks like you didn't feel like hearin' what Julia had to say jus' now, either. She asked you to stay, didn't she? Practically begged you, in fact. Even offered you a partnership in the place. You turned her down cold, didn't you?'

'Yep. Even threw in a couple o' nasty little insults, to seal the bargain.'

'I'm sorry you did that.'

'So am I. Wasn't very sporting.'

'I mean I'm sorry you turned her down.'

'I was out o' line, insultin' her, that's a fact. Had no right to do that.' Trav sighed dejectedly. 'We've been playin' a little game all along, Julia and I – and she's beaten me hands down. I ought to have the decency to be a good loser. I'll apologize to her, before I go.'

Darby glanced at his friend with quick anxiety. 'Go?'

'Before I leave, in the morning.'

'Trav, you're not – you're not *leavin'*, are you? So *soon?*'

'Sure I am. First thing in the morning.'

'Aw, but Trav –'

'I told you, I've worn out my welcome – nothin' left but shreds and tatters.'

Trav got to his feet, and went up the steps. 'Guess I'll start puttin' my gear together. Want to be ready for a quick start in the morning.'

At the doorway he paused and glanced back. 'I'm goin' to sleep early. Try to be quiet when you come in, will you?'

He went inside, and Darby and Moses listened to the slow ascent of his footsteps up the stairs. After a moment Moses picked up his banjo and strummed softly, absently, without meaning. Darby stared at the ground, and his face was so bleak and desolate that Moses tried not to look at him.

CHAPTER NINETEEN

Morning brought a high thin cloud cover, a delicate cotton gauze blanket that spread over the sky and filtered the ferocious rays of the sun, and made them benign.

When Darby came downstairs he found Moses and Luanna in the kitchen. Luanna was preparing breakfast.

'Julia sleepin' late?' Darby asked.

'No, she went out early,' Luanna said. 'Went to take Lulu to pasture. 'Scuse me – Bessie.'

She glanced at Darby and started to smile, but he did not look at her.

'Thought you usually did that,' Darby said. He sounded cross.

'Oh, we change around. Julia wanted to go today.'

Darby frowned. 'We'll jus' have to go and find her. Trav will want to say goodbye.'

He sat down at the table with Moses, and Luanna poured coffee for them both.

'Darby, Julia said if Trav should leave before she gets back, we should tell him goodbye for her. She wishes him good luck.'

Darby glared at her. 'Sure. I bet she does.'

'She does, Darby. She meant it. She just didn't want to – talk to him any more.'

They ate in strained silence. Afterward Luanna began kitchen cleanup, and Moses sat at the table with Darby for a little while, in unaccustomed idleness.

'How does he feel?' he asked. 'T'ord *you*, I mean.'

'Don't know.' Darby shrugged. 'He wouldn't talk to me any more last night, when I went upstairs. Pretended to be asleep. It was the same when I got up this mornin'.'

'He won't be angry with you, surely,' Luanna said earnestly. 'It's Julia he blames.'

Darby stared at the table top. 'She wouldn't even say goodbye,' he muttered. 'That's the first time I ever saw Julia's beautiful manners fail her.'

'Nev' mind,' Moses said gently. 'It's jest as well. Her and Trav done said all they had to say, and tha's that.'

The old man shook his head and gazed absently out through the back door at the hard grey light of morning.

'Somethin' jes' ain't right about this world,' he said slowly. 'The Lawd makes such a *few* good people. One heah, one theah – jest a few. Ain't it sad when two o' them rare good people meet up – and then can't git theah heads togethuh 'bout things?'

They lapsed into glum silence.

After a moment Moses said, 'Well, work ain't gon' git done with me sittin' heah.' He pulled himself up with an effort. 'When Trav's ready to go, I'll be in the garden.' He went out.

Luanna went quietly about her work. She turned her eyes often toward Darby, with long looks, as if she wanted to say something comforting to him. He took no notice of her.

Soon they heard Trav coming downstairs. He came into the kitchen, carrying his canvas travelling bag and bedroll, said, 'Good morning!' with beaming cheerfulness, and set his things in a corner.

Luanna went toward him, smiling. 'Good morning, Trav. Sit down – I'll fix you some breakfast.'

'Thank you, my love.' He grinned and winked at her, and sat down. He glanced across the table at Darby.

'Well, I'm off, lad,' he said heartily. 'Any parting words of advice?'

Darby gazed at him somberly. 'Have you thought of what it's like on the Santa Fe road in midsummer?'

'Yep. Thought of it. So I figured I'd angle up to the Platte River and take the northern route. Smart?'

'A little less dumb. But not smart. Smart would be to stay here for the winter, and start back in the spring.'

'Ah, my boy,' Trav smiled. 'I want to be in California in the winter, 'cause that's when you get your best work done. Don't you remember those crisp, cracklin' bright winter days? By spring I expect to have a barn and corral built. This time next year, I'll be grazin' my own cattle.'

Luanna set his breakfast before him. Trav smiled up at her and said, 'Thanks, beautiful.'

'*Your* cattle?' Darby said quietly.

'My cattle, our cattle – that's up to you, pal.'

Luanna had sat down between the two men. Trav ate in silence for a few minutes, then glanced up at Luanna.

'By the way,' he said, 'if you can get packed in half an hour, it's still not too late to take me up on my offer.'

Darby shot a quick curious look at Luanna. She stirred uncomfortably, and said nothing.

'Uh – should I leave you two alone?' Darby asked.

Trav leaned back in his chair and laughed. 'Hey, have we ever had any secrets from each other where women were concerned?' He leaned forward and punched Darby playfully on the shoulder.

'I asked Luanna to marry me,' he said. 'And she turned me down.'

Trav finished his last morsel of biscuit and drained his coffee cup, and noticed that Darby was studying him closely.

'If you don't believe me, ask her,' Trav said.

Luanna got up and brought the coffee pot and filled Trav's cup, then sat down again.

'But, bein' a man of vast patience and understandin',' Trav went on, 'I thought I'd give her another chance, seein' as how women have been known to change their minds.'

Luanna smiled at him, but the brightness was faint and fleeting. Her eyes became solemn again immediately.

'I appreciate it, Trav,' she said, almost in a whisper. 'But I can't.'

'All right,' he said casually. 'Fifty years from now I don't want to hear about you complainin' you never had a chance to get away from here.'

He gulped his coffee, and looked from one to the other of his two silent companions.

'What a couple o' long-faced sticks-in-the-mud!' he said. 'I'm goin' back west, where the company's livelier.'

He got up and went to the corner and picked up his bedroll. 'Where *is* everybody?' he asked suddenly.

'Moses is in the garden,' Darby said. 'And Julia, uh – Julia had some chores to do. She said to tell you goodbye – and she wishes you the best o' luck, the very best in the world.'

'Nice,' Trav said dryly.

Darby got up and took Trav's canvas bag, and hoisted it to his shoulder.

'I'll walk you to the river,' he said, without looking at Trav.

When Moses saw them emerge from the house he put down his garden tools and came toward them.

'I can't believe it,' he said to Trav. 'It don't seem right fo' you to up and go, jes' like that.'

Trav smiled softly. 'It's the only way, Moses.'

Moses glanced up toward the cloud cover above. 'Rain's comin'. Fact is, I think we gon' be in fo' a spell of it. Maybe you bettuh wait till it blows ovuh.'

'I figure I'll get rained on two or three times 'tween here and California,' Trav said with a chuckle. 'That don't mean a thing to an old trail rider.'

Moses shook his head, and his old face sagged. 'I sho' do hate to say goodbye.'

'Don't do it. Not yet, anyway. I'd like to have you cross the river with me, and bring the skiff back.' Trav grinned at the other man. 'If you don't mind ridin' in the old Arkansas scow jus' once more.'

Moses would not banter. 'Well, all right,' he said lifelessly. He took Trav's bedroll and said, 'I'll load this for you and git the skiff ready.'

He went off toward the front road, and Darby followed him, saying, 'Wait, I'll go with you, Moses.'

Trav turned toward the house, and saw Luanna standing on the back veranda. He waited. She descended the steps and came toward him. 'I'll walk you to the front road,' she said.

They walked together slowly to the front of the house, and across the yard to the road.

'Nice of Darby to go on ahead,' Trav said. 'Guess he thought I might like to plead my case with you one last time, in private.' He smiled at her. 'Don't worry. I won't.'

At the front road they stopped and stood under the sycamore tree.

'I'm sorry, Trav,' Luanna said. 'I'm sorry about everything.'

'Don't be. Jus' remember what I told you. Bein' a quiet little kitten is very nice, but you can sure get left out o' things that way. Try bein' a tigress for a change. You've got claws – use 'em.'

She looked at him in silence for a moment, her large eyes grave and thoughtful. Then she smiled and held out her hand to him. 'You've been a good friend, Trav. Thank you. I hope we meet again.'

'I'm countin' on that. But it's all up to you, so – get to work.'

He looked back at the house, its dilapidation painfully evident in the cloudy grey morning glare, but its lofty dimensions graceful and imposing still.

'Funny,' he said softly. 'I never thought I'd be sorry to see the last o' this old place. . . .'

He turned back to Luanna. 'Well –' He kissed her lightly on the cheek. 'Good luck, sweetheart.' Then he stepped out onto the road, gave her a little salute and a jaunty smile, and walked rapidly away toward the river.

She stood watching him, and when he turned to look back from the edge of the willow thicket, she called out, 'Good luck to *you!*' and waved to him.

In the middle of the willow thicket he found Darby sitting on the side of the road, waiting.

'Hey, thanks for waitin' up,' he said, and came up to Darby and sat down next to him.

'And thanks for givin' me one last word with Luanna. No use, though. That girl's gone in love with somebody else. Wish I knew who the blind insensitive clod was – I'd bust him right in the mouth.'

'Trav –' Darby groped for words, shaking his head in a turmoil of frustration. 'This is – this is crazy, Trav.'

Trav looked at him solemnly, without answering.

'I mean, you're jus' gonna go away like this, and – we ain't even had a chance to talk.'

'Let's talk now,' Trav said. 'What do you want to talk about?'

'Well – how about my share o' the ranch?'

'What do you want to do about it?'

'Count me in, Trav. You take sixty-forty on it, 'stead o' fifty-fifty, on account o' havin' to do the first year's work by yourself. Would that be all right?'

'Don't worry about *that*. I thought maybe you'd want me to buy you out altogether.'

'Hell no, Trav. I said count me in. I mean it.'

Trav smiled. 'Better get goin',' he said, and got up.

Darby rose and grasped his friend by the arm. 'You don't think I'm comin' back, do you?' he said sharply.

'I jus' like to look at a situation, and consider all possibilities.' Trav's voice remained calm and even.

'Well, it's pretty clear what you see in this situation. You see a dumb, simple-minded black fool, in love with a high and mighty white goddess. So the simple-minded fool lets the goddess take over his life, his independence, his manhood, his everything. That's the picture you've got, right?'

Trav smiled slyly. 'Not half bad, for a wild guess.'

'That's phony, Trav. That ain't the way it is, at all.'

'No?'

'No. What we have here is a brave, lonely, courageous, tired woman who ain't young any more, tryin' to accomplish somethin' worthwhile against hardships that jus' won't quit – and hopin' to salvage somethin' for herself out of a busted-up life. She needs help – she needs it bad. And I owe that woman more than I could ever hope to repay, if I spent the rest o' my life workin' at it. So, I'm gonna devote a year to helpin' her, and pay off just a tiny little bit o' that debt.'

He fixed an intent look on Trav that pleaded for understanding. 'That's it, Trav. I swear, that's all there is to it.'

Trav nodded. He put his hand on Darby's shoulder. 'All right, pal. I'll take your word for it. You ought to know.'

They walked on to the river.

Trav was carrying on an amiable, mostly one-way conversation as they approached the landing, where Moses was waiting by the skiff.

'My plan is, I'll spend today gettin' some horses lined up, and stay overnight with Ely Griffith, then head out west early tomorrow mornin'. Ely offered to put me up whenever I came back through, and he told me he knew where I could get a couple o' good horses for a fair price. You know, the more I see of Ely, the more I like him. He's a pretty nice old gent.'

'He offered to put you up,' Darby mused. 'You already had this quick getaway planned when you were there the other day.'

Trav smiled wryly at Darby's suspicious frame of mind. 'I've got a surprise for you. He offered to put us *both* up.'

As they came up to the skiff Moses said, 'You want me to row, Trav?'

'No thanks, Moses. I'll take it over – it'll be all yours comin' back.'

Trav scowled at the skiff, and gave its prow a gentle kick. 'I'll be glad to get rid o' this ol' wooden horse, and get on a live four-legged one again.'

He turned to Darby. 'Well, pal –'

'You write, you hear?' Darby said brusquely. 'I want you to keep me posted on how things go. *Every* little thing.'

'Sure I will. You, too.'

There was a short pause.

'Trav, you – you ain't goin' away mad at me, are you?'

'Hell, no!' Trav chuckled.

'I mean – is everything all right?'

'Everything's fine. And to show you I mean it –' Trav reached under his shirt and removed the thin chain from around his neck, and held it up. The gold nugget twisted and swung, and glinted dully in the pale light.

'I have a present for you.' He thrust the necklace into Darby's hand. 'Try to hold on to it this time, will you?'

Darby looked at it for a moment without speaking. 'Thanks,' he said finally, in a weak voice.

'And tell Julia for me –' Trav hesitated. 'Well, tell her thanks for the hospitality, and – tell her I'm sorry we couldn't be friends. *That* would have been nice.'

'Yeah. I'll tell her.'

They stood and looked at each other awkwardly.

'So long, pal.' Trav held out his hand.

'Good luck, Trav. See you next year.'

They shook hands – a firm, brisk clasp – and both turned away quickly, not trusting themselves to prolong the moment. Trav got in the skiff and took up the oars while Moses pushed it off, then scrambled aboard. Trav pulled on the oars, and the skiff moved out.

Darby walked slowly along the bank, watching. When the boat was fifty yards out he cupped his hands over his mouth and called, 'I'll be waitin' to hear from you!'

A moment later he shouted, 'You be careful, now!'

Trav nodded and waved each time – and then he was beyond voice range.

Darby walked a few steps to the rotting remains of the old Chinaberry landing, and sat down. He locked his arms around his drawn-up knees and sat motionless, his eyes on the receding skiff, until it became a tiny bit of flotsam, far out in the broad stream. Idly he picked up a few pebbles, and tossed them one by one into the water. The skiff was gone, then, out of sight – and he sat and stared out across the empty river.

The girl came up behind him as silently as a figure in a

dream, and knelt and reached around him with both hands, and put her fingers over his eyes.

He froze for an instant. 'Who's that?'

'Guess,' she whispered.

He pondered. 'Gimme a hint.'

'Well – it's *not* Julia.'

He pondered still. 'Doggone! I jus' can't figure out who it could be.'

He grasped her wrists and pulled her hands off his eyes and turned to look at her. His face registered amazement.

'Well, I declare! It's Mister Douglas's *other* little girl!'

She sat down beside him. 'I was watchin' you,' she said, 'and I could see you were feelin' sad. I was hopin' I could cheer you up a little.'

'Thanks.'

'Don't be sad, Darby. You'll be with your friend again before long.'

'It ain't only that.'

'What else, then?'

When he didn't answer immediately she said, 'Is there anything I can do?'

He shook his head. 'The trouble is – I don't think I can live up to Julia's expectations.'

'That's what we all work at, all the time – livin' up to Julia's expectations.'

'But it's different with me. Julia must 'a' created an imaginary Darby in her mind, durin' the years we were apart – and I got a feelin' her imagination ran away with her. I'm just afraid I can't be all she wants me to be.' He glanced at Luanna, then looked away. 'You don't understand.'

'Yes I do,' she said gently. 'I'm not so dumb.'

He smiled weakly, but his face became sombre again immediately. 'I don't know exactly what to do about it, Luanna. I'd hate to hurt Julia in any way – but I want to do somethin' about *you*.'

She looked at him in mild surprise. 'Am *I* complicatin' your life, Darby?'

'You're damn right you are.'

'Maybe I should've taken Trav up on his offer. It would've simplified things.'

'Well, you could never do better than Trav, I can tell you that.'

He paused suddenly and gazed at her wonderingly, as if

with a new stirring of awareness. 'But I'm glad you didn't.' He took her hand. 'I want you with *me.*'

She smiled – a smile of inexpressible sweetness, he thought – and said, 'Then that's all that matters.'

He leaned toward her, searching her eyes. She hesitated, then made a slight, shy responsive move. Their lips came easily together in a tender, lingering kiss. Gently he pulled her a little closer – and she melted into his arms, and the kiss became abandoned and ravenous. His hands moved eagerly, lovingly, over the soft warm curves of her body, and brought from deep within her a delicious murmur of acquiescence. For a long while they held each other in the hungering embrace. Then her lips were against his ear – she bit him playfully on the earlobe and smiled an intimate secret smile that he could feel without seeing.

'This is all that matters,' she whispered.

Reluctantly he pulled back, and looked at her with pain in his face. 'No, Luanna. There are other things that matter.' He sighed despondently, and gazed with brooding eyes at the quietly lapping water at their feet.

'I've got myself into a damn pretty mess.'

She took his hand and held it in her lap. 'Don't worry about it now. Things have a way of workin' themselves out, I always think. Let's see what tomorrow brings.'

He raised his eyes to hers, and shook his head gently in a wonderment of admiration. Her serenity, her cheerful reasonableness, seemed to him as soothing as a heavenly balm.

He leaned forward once more, touched her cheek with his hand, and kissed her on the corner of the mouth. 'You're beautiful, Luanna,' he said simply. 'You're beautiful, and you're good. And I'm grateful for that.'

They walked slowly, hand in hand, back up the little road toward the house. Before they emerged from the willow thicket they separated, and she walked on ahead.

Darby threw himself immediately into work. He took an axe from the tool shed and went across the east fields to a stand of red cedar, and selected a straight medium-sized tree. When Moses returned from the trip across the river he followed the sound of the ringing axe to the site, and found Darby stripping the felled tree of branches, and preparing to chop the trunk into short sections. Moses gave a shout of enthusiasm, and went to get another axe, and joined in. By midafternoon they had finished splitting the trunk sections into bright slender new shingles, and were starting on a second tree.

Julia and Luanna came to admire the industry, and Luanna set herself the task of arranging the piles of shingles into neat stacks, and bundling them.

Darby looked triumphantly at Julia and announced, 'That house is gonna have the best-lookin' roof you ever did see.'

Julia clasped her hands and beamed with pure happiness.

The workmen did not return to the house until dark, and in the evening, after a late supper, sat still and lethargic at the table, subdued with fatigue. In low voices they reviewed the day's production, and discussed plans for building a tall ladder for easy access to the high steep roof of the house.

Soon Moses went off to bed, saying he could see he was going to be hard put to keep up with Darby's work pace. And Darby sat with the women for a short time only, before he too yawned and stretched and excused himself. 'Got to get choppin' early in the mornin',' he said, and climbed the stairs to his room.

After the supper cleanup was finished Julia and Luanna sat at the kitchen table with sewing baskets, straining their eyes at mending work, under the dim light of a single lamp. They sat in silent concentration for a long time.

Then Julia paused and gazed across the dark room.

'It's incredible, isn't it?' she said. 'It seemed so hopeless for such a long time – but now I dare to believe we may actually have a chance.'

Her eyes shone as she looked at the other woman. 'Isn't it miraculous, Luanna, what a difference it makes having Darby here?'

Luanna answered casually, without pausing in her work. 'Yes indeed, a great difference. In many ways.'

After a moment Julia said, 'Luanna, I was thinking – perhaps we should make some sort of change in our living arrangements. I thought it might be better if we had separate rooms. It would give each of us more – well, privacy. What do you think?'

'Yes, maybe that would be a good idea,' Luanna said placidly. Still she did not look up from her sewing. 'It would certainly make things less awkward for Darby.'

She glanced up then, and saw that Julia was staring at her.

'I mean, it would certainly be easier for him to make a choice.'

'A choice?!'

Luanna put down her work and met the other's gaze headon. 'Julia, you've always believed in bein' open and truthful about things.'

'Yes, I have.'

'Then let me be that way now. The truth is that you and I are –' Luanna had to force herself to go on. 'We're what you might call – rivals.'

'*Rivals!*' The word sounded like a doleful bell tone, as Julia repeated it. She sat with her hands lifeless in her lap, her work temporarily forgotten. After a long silence she said, 'Has Darby – has he expressed any – feelings toward you?'

'What he has expressed to me –' Luanna spoke slowly, searching for appropriate words '– has been nothin' but hopelessly mixed-up, tormented confusion. He's wretched over Trav's leavin' and torn between loyalty to you and –'

'And love for you?'

'No, no, it's not as simple as that. He's just – in torment, that's all. It hurts me to see it.'

She turned earnest, troubled eyes on the other. 'It just makes me wonder, Julia – are you sure it was *right* to persuade him to stay here?'

Julia gazed at the girl for a moment, then turned her eyes back to her sewing basket, and resumed her work.

'I must say,' she sighed, 'I thought I was too old and wise to be taken by surprise like this. My goodness! – I don't think I could ever possibly get used to the idea that you and I are – *rivals*.' She uttered the word with an almost audible shudder, as if it were an obscenity that should not be mentioned in polite conversation.

'It's certainly the last thing *I* would wish on us,' Luanna said.

Julia stared unseeing into a far corner of the room. 'This is strange,' she said softly. 'It's not like me to feel unsure of myself. Perhaps it *wasn't* right to keep him here.'

She lifted her eyes and reached for Luanna's hand.

'Promise me one thing, Luanna. Whatever develops – you and I are friends, we are sisters, and we will love each other dearly, always.'

'Oh, I promise, Julia. I do!'

Julia smiled and squeezed Luanna's hand, and her eyes glowed with renewed optimism, as if another difficulty had been efficiently disposed of.

'Let's go to bed now,' she said. 'We've got to get an early start, too. Exciting things are happening at Chinaberry!'

The sisters put away their sewing baskets and took the lamp and tiptoed quietly, arm in arm, up the stairs.

CHAPTER TWENTY

The night was still and stifling, and heavy with a clinging humidity. Moses slept restlessly, turning and fussing in his bed, troubled by the familiar aches of stiff old bones and sinews. Hours passed, as he dozed and woke, and dozed again. Toward midnight a waning moon climbed above the flat eastern horizon, but the thin gossamer cloud cover that had lain across the sky since the previous morning trapped and absorbed its light, so that it touched the dark earth with illumination too feeble to be detectable by human eyes.

A faint sound floated in from some distant source across the dim night landscape beyond Moses's window. It intertwined itself accommodatingly with fitful dream-images in his mind, drifted away, and returned. Slowly it grew stronger and more distinct, more persistent, and finally obliterated the dream altogether and penetrated a higher level of consciousness.

Moses sat up abruptly, wide awake, and listened. Then he reached hurriedly for his clothes.

By the time he got a lamp lit and started for the front of the house, Julia and Luanna were coming down the stairs. They went outside and stood at the top of the veranda steps and peered into the darkness down the front road to the east, toward the sound. Nothing could be seen but a single faint light, swaying and bobbing as if suspended in the night air, several hundred yards away. But the sound was now clear and unmistakable – the pounding pulsation of horses' hooves, beating the dirt road.

Moses stared sullenly at the light as it drew nearer. 'It's that gang,' he muttered.

'Damn!' Luanna said, between clenched teeth. 'Why can't they leave us alone? They *know* we haven't got anything worth stealing!'

They stood for a moment in silence and indecision. Then Julia put a hand on Luanna's arm.

'Wake Darby, and warn him,' she said. Her voice was low and urgent.

Luanna turned and disappeared into the house.

Julia continued to stand beside Moses, watching the approaching light. Without looking in her direction Moses said quietly, 'Go on in the house, Little Missy. Git on upstairs.'

She went, and Moses stood alone on the veranda and held the lamp high, waiting for the invaders. His face was grim; his dim old eyes smouldered with a deep stubborn defiance.

There were six men – five on horseback and another in the driver's seat of a small flatbed wagon, on which a lantern hung, and swung precariously, as the vehicle bounced with reckless abandon over the rutted old road, and turned circling into the yard of Chinaberry house. The horsemen swarmed into the yard in a noisy, dusty cloud of shouting and the stamping of unruly steeds. Outwardly they were all cut from the same cloth – unwashed, unshaven, with facial growth that ranged from ragged stubble to full bushy beard, and hair that protruded in rancid stiffness from battered old hats – and they moved amid a constant cacophony of oaths and yells and the loud senseless laughter of roistering comrades-in-adventure.

One rider separated himself from the milling crowd. He was a large, blond, broad-shouldered man with pale blue eyes narrowly set in a florid, beefy face. Though young – not yet thirty – he radiated an air of self-assurance and authority that set him subtly apart from the others. He reined his horse expertly near the foot of the veranda steps, stood in his stirrups, and surveyed his troops like a commanding general.

'All right, settle down!' he yelled, in a booming voice that rolled across the yard and echoed in the hollow chambers of the house behind him. The noise level among his followers diminished sharply.

The leader directed his attention to the driver of the flatbed. 'Billy, bring the wagon on up heah, so's we can unload that thing!'

The wagon driver slapped at his sweating horse with a short whip, and with a series of shouts in a thin high-pitched voice, manoeuvred his vehicle nearer the front steps. The little wagon carried one prominent piece of cargo – a huge trunk, gleaming black, and padlocked.

The commander rasped out more orders: 'Soon's we git unloaded, Billy, you and Lucius hitch the horses an' wagon on down yonder by the well. The rest o' y'all grab holt, heah, le's git this damn thing inside. Come on, goddamn it, hurry up, now!'

The men dismounted, and surrounded the wagon. One of them climbed into it and pushed the trunk toward the rear for the others to reach. It was grasped, slid off the wagon bed, and lowered to the ground with a heavy thud.

'Careful, you clumsy bastards!' the commander bellowed.

Moses stood still and quiet in the doorway of the house, watching.

When Luanna went up the stairs she met Darby emerging from his room.

'Luanna, what the hell's goin' on?' he demanded, and started for the stairs.

The girl grabbed his arm and pulled him back. 'Don't let 'em see you,' she whispered urgently.

'Who are they?'

'It's one of those rovin' gangs of thieves. White trash – human filth!'

Julia came rapidly up the stairs toward them. She spoke calming words, but there was a tremor in her voice.

'Everything will be all right, if we just remain calm,' she said. 'We must try very hard not to provoke them.'

She came directly to Darby, and stood close to him in the darkness. 'You should stay out of sight if you can. There's no need for them to know about you.'

'I don't understand, Julia. What am I supposed to –'

'If they *do* find you, play dumb. Don't talk any more than you have to. Above all, don't tell them your name.'

Darby tried again to protest. 'What am I, some kind o' criminal? I've met up with rowdies before, I can take care o' myself –'

'Sh-h!' Julia shushed him. They stood for a moment listening to the sounds of raucous voices below, and heavy footfalls on the veranda steps.

'These aren't just ordinary rowdies,' Julia whispered. 'The leader of this gang is Gene Willard.'

Darby went momentarily rigid. 'Willard,' he murmured. Something terrifying stirred deeply within him, and clutched at the pit of his stomach with a chilling grip.

The trunk was lifted off the ground and brought up

clumsily, with bellows and curses, onto the veranda. Then the two men assigned to the task gathered the horses, tied the reins to the back of the wagon, and drove off down the front road toward the well, by the far corner of the garden.

The burly blond leader had dismounted and taken the lantern from the side of the wagon, and now went up the steps and started into the house.

Moses stood in the doorway, blocking his path. 'What is it you want, suh?' he asked quietly.

The big white man stopped and stared. It was the first notice any of the gang had taken of Moses. The leader squinted and stooped slightly, to bring himself down to Moses's level. He peered into the man's face.

'Hey, what's yo' name, darky?' he said abruptly.

'My name's Moses, Mistuh Willard. You know me, suh.'

'Yeah, I know ya!' Willard grinned. He threw back his head and laughed loudly, and turned to his companions behind him.

'Hey, looka heah, men!' he yelled. 'This old barn's jest about to fall down, but Miss Julia's still got her goddamn fancy butler!'

The other men responded with an uproar of laughter, and Willard beamed at them. He turned back to the man in the doorway.

'Moses, my man,' he said, affecting a pompous tone, 'announce me to Miss Julia, if you please. Tell her her true love's done come to see her!' Appreciative laughter arose again from the men behind Willard.

Moses stood his ground, stern-faced. 'This ain't no proper way to act, Mistuh Willard, comin' 'round disturbin' people in the middle o' the night. I'm surprised you nevuh learned no bettuh mannuhs than that.'

Geniality drained away from Willard's face. His voice became flint-hard and quiet.

'I ain't got time to fool with you, darky. You git out o' my way, now, or we'll drag you outside and tie you to a tree and peel the skin off yo' back.'

Willard pushed his bulk into the doorway. Moses edged back slightly, but continued to block the other man's path.

'Mistuh Willard, suh, you ain't got no right –'

'Move, goddamn you!' Willard exploded, and pushed Moses back with a vicious thrust.

The old man staggered, and fell against a wall.

Willard stepped into the house, and his companions followed. They stood in the entrance foyer while Willard held his lantern high, and peered into the dim interior of the great empty main room, beyond the open archway to their left.

Willard nodded, looking pleased. 'Yeah, this'll do fine.' He turned to the man at his elbow, a swarthy, grim-faced man with thick black hair and beetle brows.

'All right, Clayton, you and the boys git the trunk in heah.'

Clayton turned to a tall lanky man with deep cavernous eyes and a full beard, who was standing directly behind him. 'Come on, Ham. Take holt o' one end,' Clayton said, and went out, and Ham followed.

Willard's remaining companion was a balding man, of slight build, with a tendency to paunchiness. In his forties, he appeared to be the oldest member of the gang. He looked around furtively, and edged closer to Willard.

'Hey, uh, Gene – what you got in that trunk?' His voice was low and confidential. 'You can trust *me*, Gene.'

'When everybody's heah we gon' have a little meetin', Tucker. Then you'll find out.'

Tucker grinned. His large round eyes gleamed with curiosity. 'Somethin' special, huh, Gene?'

Willard looked mysterious. 'You're damn right it's special.'

Ham and Clayton brought the trunk inside, edging forward slowly, with Ham carrying the front end, and backing up in short, laborious, awkward steps.

'Put it in the big room, theah,' Willard barked. 'Up against the long wall.'

A moment later he bellowed in anger, when Ham allowed a corner of the heavy trunk to crash into a side of the archway.

'Careful, goddamn it! That trunk's worth thirty dolluhs!'

A flickering of light at the top of the stairway caught Willard's eye. He looked up and saw Julia slowly descending the stairs, carrying a lamp. She gazed down at Willard with an icy haughtiness.

'Well, well! Miss Julia, honey!' Willard boomed. He handed his lantern to Tucker, and bounded halfway up the stairs to meet her.

'Hot damn, ain't you the good looker!' His eyes roved over her in insolent admiration. 'I done come to see you, honey. Come heah an' give yo' sweetie a great big kiss!'

She shrank back from him, her eyes flashing hostility. 'Gene Willard, what is the meaning of this?'

Willard's face clouded in a playful pout. 'Sweetie-pie, ain't you glad to see me?' he whined. This brought a sniggering laugh from Tucker, in the foyer below.

'How dare you invade my home?' Julia demanded.

'Ain't no invasion, honey. We jes' want to borrow yo' big front room fo' an hour or so – we gon' have us a little business meetin'. That room's had so dang many fancy social events, I thought it'd be jes' the place fo' *our* little ceremony. Only thing is, I want you and yo' niggers to stay upstairs and don't come down till we tell ya, on account o' this heah meetin's real *secret*.'

Julia glared at the man, her face set in defiance. 'Some day, Gene Willard, order will be restored, and trashy people like you will no longer be allowed to –'

'Who you callin' trashy people?!' Willard's eyes turned mean; he dropped his playful manner instantly.

'You're mighty proud o' this ol' broken down, moth-eaten place heah, ain't you, my fine lady? I guess you don't remembuh who made Chinaberry into a prosperous plantation in the first place, do you? You think yo' daddy did? No, ma'am. *My* daddy, tha's who!'

He advanced slowly up the stairs toward Julia, and she retreated before him.

'My daddy toiled and sweated and broke his health, drivin' the lazy niggers on this place, makin' the wealth so you lordly Douglases could live in luxury. And what thanks did he git? Tried to stop a runaway slave one night, and the black bastard came near to killin' 'im. And what did yo' daddy do to show his appreciation? Dismissed 'im! Threw 'im out in the cold!'

His hard blue eyes, squinted half shut, impaled Julia with hatred. 'Trashy people, huh? Well, jes' look at yo' fine plantation now! I tell you, a Willard wouldn't *live* in a rotten mouldy dump like this!'

The other two men had come in, returning from securing the horses. All five of Willard's followers stood in the foyer now, staring silently up at the confrontation on the stairs.

Julia had retreated to the upper hallway.

Willard glared up at her, breathing heavily. 'Now git to yo' room, and stay theah!' he yelled.

He turned and stomped heavily back down the stairs, and

at the bottom noticed Moses, still standing near the front door. 'And you, darky! Gimme that lamp, and git upstairs!'

Moses silently handed his lamp to Willard, and started up the stairs.

Willard glowered, and shouted, 'Move yo' ass, goddamn it!' and kicked at Moses as the old man went past him.

Julia took Moses's arm as he came up to her on the upper landing, and guided him without a word toward the large room, the former study, at the front end of the hall.

Willard swaggered into the cavernous main room downstairs and stepped over to the trunk, which had been placed, according to his instructions, against the long interior wall. His followers milled about aimlessly, awaiting orders.

'Horses watered and secure, Billy?' Willard addressed the man who had been the wagon driver.

Billy was short and stubby and round-faced, with small, beady, constantly shifting eyes. He was near thirty, but his face reflected the blank transparency of a mind that had ceased to develop twenty years before.

He nodded eagerly to Willard. 'Yeah, Gene! All done, Gene!'

'All right, you and Lucius look through the back o' the house and see if you can find any furniture you can drag in heah. I need a table.'

Lucius, in his early twenties and the youngest member of the group, was plump, pudgy, and pink-cheeked. He picked up the lantern and started obediently for the dark recesses of the house.

Willard continued to bark orders with military efficiency. 'Clayton, you and Ham git upstairs and look around, see if you can find anything valuable.'

'We went ovuh this damn place befo', Gene,' Clayton growled. 'Ain't nothin' heah, you know that.'

'Look ag'in. We ain't been heah fo' months.' When Clayton failed to move promptly, Willard raised his overpowering voice. 'Go on, goddamn it, don't stand theah arguin' with me!'

Clayton shrugged. He and Ham went out.

'Tucker, go down to the wagon and git the hammer and chain, and nail up Miss Julia's room. We got to make shuah they don't come spyin' on us.'

'Right, Gene.' Tucker grinned again, and glanced at the

trunk. 'Must be sump'm *mighty* special,' he said, and went out.

Billy remained; he had not followed Lucius in search of furniture. He moved soundlessly toward Willard, and hovered at the big man's elbow. 'Hey, Gene,' he whispered. 'What you got in that trunk?'

Willard turned on him. 'I gave you an orduh, goddamn it!' he roared. 'Now git!'

Billy got.

Willard turned and gazed at his trunk. He bent close and examined the corner that Ham had struck against the archway. When he saw that there was no damage, he straightened and patted the trunk affectionately, and smiled with satisfaction.

'Special,' he mumbled softly. 'Goddamn right.'

With a clamour of bangs and scrapings Lucius and Billy brought the table from the kitchen into the front room, went out and returned with the chairs, along with much boisterous merriment over the crude homemade furniture.

Lucius sat down heavily in one of Moses's chairs, and a leg collapsed. Lucius tumbled onto the floor, and Billy screeched with laughter. Lucius scrambled up, seized the broken chair and smashed it against the wall. It came apart in an explosion of pieces that flew in all directions. Billy's laughter grew apoplectic. Willard relaxed his grim commanding visage briefly, and chuckled.

'All right, now git upstairs and help Ham and Clayton make a search,' Willard told them. 'Must be *sump'm* valuable around heah.'

In a few minutes Tucker returned to the house from the wagon, carrying a short length of chain and a hammer. At the foot of the stairs he stopped, and stared upward.

Ham and Clayton were descending with a black man between them, holding their captive firmly by the arms. It was not the old man, the former butler – but a younger one, whom Tucker had never seen. He stood aside as the others came down the stairs and went past him, then followed them into the front room.

Willard glanced briefly at the prisoner, and scowled at Ham and Clayton. 'You stupid bastards, I said look fo' sump'm *valuable*. I didn't say bring me a stray nigger!'

'Jes' wait a minute, Gene,' Clayton said. 'Theah's sump'm peculiar 'bout this 'un. He talks funny – he ain't even southern.'

A noisy flurry of footsteps down the stairs brought Lucius and Billy bursting into the room.

'Look what we done found, Gene!' Lucius said excitedly. He and Billy dumped their findings on the table – a leather wallet, a gold nugget necklace, and a holstered revolver.

There was a hush as the men stared in wide-eyed fascination. Willard picked up the necklace and held it high. Six pairs of eyes intently followed the slow turning of the nugget on the chain, and admired its luster.

The prisoner took advantage of the moment to glance quickly at each man in the group. One by one, he mentally took their measure.

'Hot diggety dog, ain't that sump'm?!' Billy exclaimed. He beamed proudly at his companions, and said, 'We found it. Me an' Lucius, we found it.'

Willard put down the necklace and picked up the wallet. He opened it, and the other men, watching closely, caught a glimpse of a substantial amount of money. Willard closed the wallet immediately, and looked at the initials on the outside.

'D. R.' For the first time he looked directly at the black man.

'What's yo' name, boy?'

'Ross,' Darby answered readily. 'Daniel Ross.'

'Wheah you from and what are you doin' heah?'

'I work for a white man from California. I been travellin' around with him.'

'What white man? Wheah is he?'

'His name's Mister Travers. He ain't here right now – he's gone visitin', 'cross the river someplace.'

'You got employment papers?'

'No. We don't have nothin' like that in California.'

Willard stared intently at Darby for a long time. He gestured toward the things on the table. 'This stuff belong to yo' employuh?'

Darby hesitated for an instant. 'No. It belongs to me.'

'To *you?!*'

The men surrounding the prisoner exchanged significant looks.

'Damn – he sho' *does* talk funny,' Tucker muttered.

'He don't even say *suh* to people!' Lucius said, half in awe.

Willard picked up the revolver. He pulled it out of its holster, examined it, and found that it was empty of ammunition.

All eyes were now riveted on the weapon, in a new round of admiration.

'Goddamn, that's a beauty!' Ham said.

'Me an' Lucius, we found it,' Billy said quickly. 'Lucius, he found the necklace, but I found the gun. I found it myself.'

Willard put the pistol down and stepped around the table and stood in front of Darby. 'Don't you know it's against the law fo' niggers to carry guns in this state?'

'I wasn't carryin' it,' Darby said. 'It was stashed away.'

'Don't gimme no sassy answer,' Willard said grimly. 'You must 'a' carried it when you *brought* it heah.'

Darby shrugged. 'It's only a souvenir. You notice it wasn't even loaded.'

Willard studied Darby in silence for a moment longer. Then he turned to the other men and rasped out an order. 'Take 'im upstairs and put 'im in with the others. Tucker, take the chain and lock 'em in. Hurry up, now, we got business to 'tend to.'

'Can I have my things back?' Darby said.

Willard glared at him. 'You can't have nothin'. This stuff's stolen property.'

'Yeah,' Darby said dryly. '*Now* it is.'

Without warning Willard advanced and laid a smashing blow across Darby's face with the back of his hand. Darby rolled with the blow expertly, minimizing its effect, and lunged toward Willard. He was immediately pinioned on both sides by Ham and Clayton.

'Git 'im out o' heah!' Willard bellowed.

Ham and Clayton hustled the prisoner out and back up the stairs. Lucius picked up a lamp and went along, and Tucker followed with the hammer and chain.

'Goddamn sassy-ass bastard!' Willard muttered, as he watched them go.

The heavy door at the front end of the upper hallway was swung open, and Darby was given a push that sent him sprawling onto the floor of the room.

Tucker stuck his head in, looked around, and noted the room's occupants. 'Is this heah everybody, Miss Julia? Ain't nobody else on yo' place, is theah?'

Julia moved toward the man, her eyes fixed on him intently. 'You look familiar, sir. I'm sure I should know you. May I ask your name?'

Tucker ignored the question, as she had ignored his. 'Now y'all behave yo'selves, you heah?' His eyes flitted nervously around the room once more. Then he withdrew hurriedly, slammed the door shut, and set to work immediately to secure it.

He looped the chain tightly around the great brass doorknob, pulled it taut to one side, put a nail through the end link and hammered it into the wall. The door was immovably closed.

The people in the room listened to the noise of the nailing, and then to the heavy thudding of boots along the upper hall, dying away, as the men went back down the stairs.

After a moment Darby muttered, 'They took my things.'

Julia clasped her hands together and began to pace, slowly. 'It's very important that we remain calm and quiet,' she said. 'They're just petty thieves, nothing more. They won't hurt anyone, if we don't provoke them.' After a short pause, she added, 'Everything will be all right.'

It sounded more like desperate hope than statement of fact.

CHAPTER TWENTY-ONE

The meeting was called to order by Tucker.

'All right, settle down, now! Quiet!' he screeched.

The unruly gangmen jostled each other, seeking advantageous positions, and settled themselves in a semicircle. Ham utilized one of Moses's chairs; the others, disdaining them, sat on the floor. Order prevailed eventually.

'Call the roll, Tucker,' said Willard, who remained standing, with Tucker.

Willard's lieutenant barked out the men's names, receiving a careless response of 'Heah,' after each.

'All present, Gene,' Tucker reported, and took a chair.

Willard stepped forward and stood before the assemblage. All faces were upturned toward him in an expectant hush.

'Now men, I know you got questions on yo' minds. You're wonderin' why I called this meetin' so sudden-like. You're wonderin' why we came way out heah to this ol' tumble-down place to have it. And you're wonderin' what I got in heah.' Willard patted the lid of the massive trunk, behind him.

'Well, the answer to all them questions has to do with one and the same thing. This heah's a special, important meetin', and it has to be held in a quiet out-o'-the-way place, 'cause it's secret – and I mean *secret*.'

He allowed himself a short pause, for effect. 'So befo' we go any furthuh, you got to take the oath o' secrecy. Stand up and raise yo' right hand.'

He raised his own right hand, and the others scrambled noisily to their feet and followed the example.

Willard stared at a point in space and recited in dramatic tones: 'I sweah I will hold all things I see and heah this night in sacred secrecy, and will nevuh divulge no word nor hint of these proceedin's to no human soul, except a fellow initiate, on peril of my very life.'

He fixed his audience with a fiery glare. 'Say, "I sweah!"'

They repeated, in solemn unison: 'I sweah.'

'Take yo' seats, and pay attention,' Willard said sharply.

'This is a serious mattuh. You men have been chosen for a very high honour.'

Willard took a key from his pocket and bent to the padlock on the trunk. Necks craned forward, as the men watched. Willard removed the lock and placed his hand on the trunk lid – but did not lift it. He turned toward his audience again.

'As you know, men, I jes' recently got back from a trip up to Tennessee. Went to visit some relatives, I told you, remembuh? Well, I ain't got no relatives in Tennessee, men. I went to see some important people about a very important organization they got goin'. This organization, I can tell you fo' a fact – is gon' be the thing that saves the South.'

Another dramatic pause. Willard's audience was breathless and still, completely captured. He lifted the trunk lid, and all necks stretched forward again. The lid came up a few inches only; Willard reached inside and brought forth a thin book, and dropped the lid shut. He held the paper-bound volume close against his chest, and his audience fidgeted in unrelieved curiosity.

'Now men,' Willard continued – and his voice took on a heavy solemnity – 'I have heah a book, that is prob'bly one o' the greatest books evuh written. Someday, I predict, it will be on the shelf of every decent, God-fearin' home in the land, alongside the Bible. It's a bible itself, in a mannuh o' speakin'.'

He glanced down at the book with a look of reverence.

'Now, I was allowed to purchase this little book. And it came deah, I can tell you – this copy is one o' the very few in existence, so far. I was allowed to have it only aftuh takin' a sacred oath o' loyalty, and a solemn vow to protect these pages' – he gripped the book fiercely, in both hands – 'with my life.'

Billy could stand it no longer. 'What is it, Gene, what *is* it?'

'Hush up, Billy!' Tucker snapped.

Abruptly Willard whipped the book around and displayed its cover. The men squirmed forward and squinted to see; hands reached out for it.

'Lemme see!'

'Closuh, Gene!'

'Give it heah!'

'Don't touch it!' Willard hissed at them, and the hands fluttered down. Willard obligingly held the book out farther.

The men stared at a pen-and-ink drawing of a man – a ghostly, hooded, incorporeal being – on horseback. Horse and rider were draped in a flowing white robelike covering that melded them into a single entity. The skull and crossbones, that ancient symbol of the mysterious, the menacing, and the occult, was emblazoned on the tall hood of the human figure. The rider guided his charger not over the ground, but seemingly through the night sky, floating in a black background void of space. In one upraised hand he brandished his combination holy relic, battle standard, and emblem of conquest – a flaming white cross.

Beneath the drawing was an enigmatic, cabalistic symbol:

* * *

The men examined the artwork in gaping silence. Only Billy dared ask a question.

'Gene, what's them funny lookin' little stars, underneath, theah?'

'That,' said Willard, 'stands fo' the lettuhs K, K, K.'

Tucker gasped in sudden recognition. 'God-a-mighty! It's that, uh –' he groped for the name – 'what you call it – Ku Klux!'

Willard withdrew the book safely to his chest. 'Men,' he announced, in heavy solemn tones, 'tonight we form a den of the Ku Klux Klan.'

The men stared, silent and motionless, their faces slack with awe.

'The Ku Klux!' Lucius breathed.

'The Ku Klux!' Billy repeated, his eyes wide with excitement. 'Hot diggety dawg!' He frowned suddenly. 'What the hell *is* it?'

'You ignoramus!' Tucker snapped. 'It's an outfit that goes around preservin' law and orduh.'

'It's sump'n like the White Camellias, down in Louisiana, ain't it?' Ham said. 'I got a cousin b'longs to the Camellias.'

'Wait a minute!' Clayton rasped. 'We don't give a damn 'bout law and orduh. We're outlaws.'

'Not any mo', we ain't, Clayton!' Willard boomed. He opened his book, taking on the appearance of a backwoods preacher searching for a text. 'I'm gon' read you sump'm – then you gon' know exactly what it means to be a membuh of the Klan.'

He cleared his throat elaborately, and read, in a voice that vibrated with piety and dignity:

'"*This is an institution of chivalry, humanity, mercy, and patriotism, embodying in its genius and its principles all that is chivalric in conduct, noble in sentiment, generous in manhood, and patriotic in purpose.*"'

Willard closed the book and gazed at his audience. 'We can comprehend the purpose,' he said. 'But do we comprehend the spirit?'

He opened the book again, to the first page. 'Listen,' he said, almost whispering. 'Meditate. And comprehend the spirit.'

He read – or rather declaimed, and his eyes burned with evangelic fervour.

'"*What may this mean,*
That thou, dead corse, again, in complete steel,
Revisit'st thus the glimpses of the moon,
Making night hideous; and we fools of nature,
So horridly to shake our disposition,
With thoughts beyond the reaches of our souls?"'

A profound silence followed. The men sat spellbound, speechless with wonder.

Then Billy provided the only possible response: 'Hot diggety dawg!'

Willard abruptly tossed aside the cloak of mystical reverence, and took on a brisk businesslike manner.

'Now, the first thing we got to do is elect officers. The book don't say much about how to conduct elections, so I reckon we'll jes' do it the fastest way.' He fixed Tucker with a stern look and said ponderously, 'Tucker, I heahby elect you Grand Magi. That's second in command.'

Tucker accepted the high office with a solemn nod. Clayton emitted a low scornful snort.

'Clayton, you're elected Grand Monk,' Willard said. 'That's third. Tucker is second on account o' he's got seniority.'

Clayton's scowling expression remained unchanged.

Willard continued: 'Ham, you're elected Grand Exchequer. You're in charge o' the funds. The finances.'

Ham nodded gravely. His long lean frame straightened slightly with pride.

'Lucius, you're elected Grand Turk,' Willard went on. 'And Billy, you're elected Grand Scribe.' He paused, thoughtfully. 'Wait a minute.' He opened the book, and consulted it, frowning.

'No, that won't do,' he mumbled. 'The Grand Scribe has to be able to read and write.'

General laughter erupted – in which Billy's own moronic cackle rang out loudest.

'Billy, you be Grand Sentinel,' Willard said.

'What's sentinel, Gene?'

'Guard. You're in charge o' the Grand Guards.'

Billy beamed with joy. 'Hot diggety dawg!'

'All right, that's about it for the present,' Willard said, and added, offhandedly, ' 'Cept fo' the head man – the Grand Cyclops.' He looked at the Grand Magi. 'You're second in command, Tucker. You got any suggestions fo' Grand Cyclops?'

Tucker looked around in befuddlement for a moment before he realized what was expected of him. 'Oh, yeah, uh – I reckon I suggest *you*, Gene.'

'I accept,' Willard said quickly. 'That takes care o' the elections.'

'Seems kinda funny, Gene,' Ham said. 'We got a wagon-load o' officers, but no men. Ain't we gon' have no men?'

'Sho' we are. Soon's we recruit some ghouls. Regular membuhs are called ghouls.'

'Ghouls!' Billy shrieked with laughter. Several other men permitted themselves discreet snickers.

'Quiet, goddamn it!' Willard growled. 'This heah's serious business!' He stepped to the trunk and put his hand on the lid. Instantly necks craned again; attention was riveted.

'Now, men,' Willard announced. 'One o' the most important things about bein' in the Klan – the uniforms.'

He opened the trunk wide. It was filled to the top with garments of pure snowy white, neatly folded. Eyes bulged, and jaws dropped, as the men stared at the dazzling finery. Willard reached in and lifted out a robe, and held it aloft with one hand; with the other he displayed a hood, on which the skull and crossbones symbol was crudely embroidered in black.

'Hot diggety dawg!' Billy gasped.

'Them's beautiful, Gene,' Tucker pronounced solemnly.

'This one's mine,' Willard said. He pointed to a series of black stars embroidered down the front of the robe he held. 'This heah indicates the Grand Cyclops. But we got enough uniforms heah fo' 'bout thirty membuhs, and since theah's only six of us so far, I reckon you can take yo' choice.'

Willard stepped back. 'So y'all come forward and choose yo' uniforms.' He lifted a precautionary hand. 'But do it in a dignified and orderly mannuh.'

Pandemonium followed.

CHAPTER TWENTY-TWO

Moses and Luanna sat on the floor of the front room upstairs, with their backs against the wall, the lamp on the floor beside them. Though the closed and boarded room was stifling, they sat close to the lamp, as if they derived some subtle comfort from its feeble light.

Julia slowly paced the length of the long room. The ancient floorboards creaked softly under her feet.

Darby crouched by the door, with his ear pressed against it. 'I can jus' barely hear 'em,' he said. 'But I can't make out what they're sayin'.'

In a moment he got up and moved to the centre of the room, and stood there with his eye roving thoughtfully around the gloomy prison cell. Then he went to the wall facing the front of the house and examined the boards nailed over the windows, pulled at them, tested their strength. They were immovable, the old nails rusted in place.

Julia came toward him. 'That's not the way out,' she said quietly. 'The way out is my father's old secret passageway, back there.' She pointed toward the far rear corner of the room.

Darby stared at her for a moment, comprehension lighting his face. 'Yeah!' he breathed. 'I forgot about *that*.'

'The boards over it don't seem terribly strong,' Julia said. 'I think you and Moses could pull them down.'

Darby went quickly to the far end of the room to investigate. Shortly he returned. 'We can do it if we have to,' he said. He sat down next to Luanna.

'They'd hear the noise,' the girl said.

'Besides,' Moses said, 'that ol' stairway is rotted, sho.' We'd break our legs tryin' to go down it.'

'We can do it if we have to,' Darby said again.

'Well – let's try to be patient for a little while,' Julia said. She resumed her slow pacing.

Moses glanced up at her and said, 'Sit down, Little Missy. You makin' me nervous with all that walkin' to and fro.'

Julia started to sit down, but thought better of it. 'It makes *me* nervous to sit still,' she said crossly, and went on pacing.

Order had returned to the big room downstairs. Long white garments were strewn in disarray on the table, and draped over the open trunk. Six robed and hooded figures stood in resplendent dignity – five in a group, facing their leader. After a brief inspection of his troops, the commander nodded his approval.

'Fine,' he said, his voice muffled under the hood. 'Y'all look jes' fine.' Willard walked slowly back and forth before the group, and proceeded with the programme of instruction.

'Now, men, theah's one thing you got to learn, and learn good. This heah's a secret society – and I mean *secret.* Don't you *evuh* forget it. Befo' you can even *talk* to anybody on Klan business, you got to be absolutely *shuah* he's a fellow membuh. You do this by usin' the Identification Code.'

He thumbed rapidly through his little book. 'It works like this – Tucker, come up heah and go through it with me.'

Tucker came forward, and Willard handed him the book, opened at the proper page.

'It's all written out heah, see? Now you read the part o' the First Man.'

Tucker held the book close to his hooded face, and studied it. He read: ' "*Halt! Who goes theah?*" '

'A friend,' Willard responded.

' "*Friend of what?*" '

'Justice and Mercy.'

Tucker studied the text. ' "*R—A—I—N,*" ' he read.

Willard answered: 'C—L—O—U—D.'

In a quick aside to the others he explained. 'We spell out the code word, y'see? Our code word is *raincloud.* Then we know each othuh as fellow Klan membuhs, and can talk freely – but not until then. Cleah?'

The students nodded.

'That'll do, Tucker.' Willard took the book from Tucker, faced the class, and pointed a stern finger at each man in turn.

'Men, yo' shoulders are now burdened with a great responsibility. From now on it's gon' be yo' duty to preserve and protect the ideals of chivalry, humanity, and patriotism, jes' like it says in the book.'

His narrowed eyes bore into his listeners. 'And y'all know what that means, same as I do.'

The class members gazed thoughtfully back at their instructor.

'Why, sho' we do,' Clayton said quietly. 'It means keepin' the niggers in theah place.'

Willard smiled. 'I see we comprehend the spirit.' He began to pace again, very slowly. 'Well, then – does anybody know of any niggers that need instruction in the mattuh o' keepin' in theah place?'

'Sho' do,' Clayton said. His eyes drifted up toward the ceiling. 'An' he ain't far away.'

Darby, listening at the door again, moved back when he heard the heavy footsteps coming up the stairs and approaching along the hallway. The chain lock was wrenched out of the wall with a screech, the door was flung open, and several robed and hooded men entered. The man in the lead, who carried the lamp, stepped aside, while the next two moved forward swiftly and seized Darby, pinioned his arms expertly, and rushed him out, before there was time for words or reaction.

Julia was upon the other two immediately, breathing fire and fury. 'You beasts! How dare you! What are you trying to–'

The fourth man lunged suddenly and gave Julia a shove backward. 'Hush up, woman!' he rasped.

'Easy, Lucius,' said the man with the lamp. 'Le's go now.'

'I'm jes' gon' git this heah othuh lamp,' Lucius said. 'We need some mo' lights downstairs.' He went across the room and picked up the lamp that was on the floor between Luanna and Moses. Then he paused, standing above the people on the floor, and stared down at Luanna.

'My, my,' he said softly. 'That's mighty tenduh lookin' dark meat!'

Luanna froze, and stared at the floor.

'C'mon heah, Lucius!' the first man snapped. 'We ain't got time fo' such as that!'

Lucius turned away reluctantly. In the doorway he paused and looked back at Luanna. 'I'll see ya latuh, honey!' he said. His lewd grin was as apparent as if his face had not been hidden under the hood. He went out.

'Now y'all be nice and quiet, and you won't git hurt,' the first man said, and went to the door.

Julia followed him.

'I know you, Mister Tucker,' she said, her voice calm and firm. 'I remember you now. I remember your parents, from when I was a child. They were in this house as guests, on several occasions.'

'You're mistaken, ma'am,' Tucker said hoarsely. 'You got me mixed up –'

'You come from a good family, Mister Tucker. How is it possible that you choose to associate with such vile, contemptible –'

'Now, you got the wrong idea, Miss Julia!' Tucker's voice rose in vigorous protest. 'We ain't hoodlums, or anything like that. We're membuhs of a responsible political organization.'

Julia's eyes drifted disdainfully over the man's long ungainly white robe.

'Is *that* your badge of political responsibility, that bedsheet you're wearing?'

Tucker made indignant noises. 'Now, look heah –'

'And why do you have that pillow case over your head, Mister Tucker? There are no mosquitos in here. Or is it because you're ashamed for anyone to look you directly in the eye?'

'Go ahead and make fun, Miss Julia. Someday you'll thank us. It's the duty of people like us to *protect* people like you!' Tucker hastily backed out of the room.

The door was slammed shut, and the chain nailed back in place. Footsteps receded in the hall, and down the stairs, and all was quiet again.

Julia stood still in the darkness. At her side she suddenly felt Luanna's presence. Their hands groped for each other; they clung together for a moment, each silently trying to fight off the inexorable welling up of fear.

From across the dark room came the soft rasping sound of a match being struck. The women turned, almost startled. Moses's old lined face was an ancient African mask in the faint flickering light, as he bent over a candle, bringing it to life.

The women came toward him, drawn to the tiny light as if it were a blazing torch of hope.

'Where'd you get the candle, Moses?' Julia asked.

'Out o' my pocket,' he said casually. 'You'd be surprised, the things I carry in my pocket.'

Laboriously he got to his feet, picked up the candle, and held it out toward Luanna.

'Hold the light fo' me, honey,' he said. 'It's time I started workin' on them boards ovuh the passageway.'

CHAPTER TWENTY-THREE

In its lively history the spacious main hall of Chinaberry house had served many purposes. It had been a stage on which were performed both elegant public ceremonies and intimate family affairs. It had been a ballroom and banquet hall; a scene of weddings, funerals, and christenings; a billeting for soldiers; a shelter for vagabonds; a refuge for fugitives. On this night it had already filled one novel function – that of classroom. And now, with no modification, still another, stranger one.

It became a courtroom.

Eugene Willard, Grand Cyclops, judge, and prosecuting attorney, placed the evidence – the wallet, the gold nugget necklace, and the pistol – on the table, in a neat row. He gazed at the prisoner, standing before him at the opposite end of the table, flanked by the Grand Monk and the Grand Exchequer, who stood ready to apply any physical restraint, or persuasion, that might be needed. On either side of the table stood the Grand Magi and the Grand Turk, stiff and straight, like sergeants at arms. All the gangmen were attired in their stately white robes, their faces concealed beneath their hoods; all, with their ghostly staring eyeholes below the skull and crossbones, looked exactly alike to the captive, except the Chief Inquisitor himself, who seemed to claim a higher degree of celestial significance with the row of black stars embroidered on his judicial gown.

'Now, then,' Willard began, addressing the prisoner. 'What did you say yo' name was?'

'I said it was Daniel Ross.'

Willard remained benign. For the moment he chose to ignore the hard edge of belligerence in Darby's voice.

'And you're from California, you say.'

'That's what I say.'

'Git around a hell of a lot, don't ya? Quite the travellin' man.'

Darby stared sullenly at the questioner, and said nothing.

Willard pointed to the things on the table. 'And you claim these heah articles belong to you. That right?'

'They belong to me, yes.'

'Why, sho' they do,' Willard said pleasantly. He picked up Exhibit A. 'And heah's yo' initials right on the front o' this pocketbook. D. R. That proves it's yo'rs, don't it?'

'It don't necessarily prove anything,' Darby said wearily. 'But they *are* my initials, and it *is* my pocketbook.'

'That's fine. Thank you fo' straightenin' us out on that point.' Willard smiled under his hood. 'But wait a minute.' He opened the leather case and extracted the money, and waved the bills before the court.

'We have heah exactly one hundred an' twenty-three dolluhs. It's been counted.' He gazed around at his associates. 'Gen'lemen, have any o' y'all evuh heard tell of a nigger that had a hunnerd an' twenty-three dolluhs?'

No one had.

'Well, now, Gene,' Tucker, the Grand Magi said thoughtfully, 'maybe in California it ain't unusual at all fo' a nigger to have that much money. We don't know how it is in California.'

'Christ!' groaned the Grand Monk, Clayton.

Lucius, the Grand Turk, snickered.

'Maybe you're right, Tucker,' Willard conceded. To the court at large he said, 'The statement of the Grand Magi will certainly be taken unduh consideration.'

With a deft movement Willard had reached under his robe and deposited the money in a pocket. He now put the wallet back on the table and picked up the gold necklace. He held it high, and allowed it to swing gently, suspended from his fingers.

'Purty, ain't it?' he said to the court. 'Now what can we tell from this? Anybody evuh heah of a nigger ownin' a gold necklace?'

Laughter, from beneath several hoods.

'Still, who knows – maybe in California, eh, Tucker?'

He deposited the necklace in his pocket, with the money, and picked up the gleaming pistol.

'Now, what can we tell from this?'

'That's illegal, no goddamn question about it,' declared the Grand Monk.

The Grand Magi attempted to enter his standard objection. 'In California, everybody prob'ly carries –'

'To hell with California, Tucker!' the Grand Monk snarled. 'This heah's Miss'sippi, and in Miss'sippi it's against the law fo' a nigger to go armed!'

'Tha's right, goddamn it!' the Grand Exchequer agreed, and the Grand Turk added his support to the majority view.

The Grand Cyclops nodded sagely. 'You're right, gen'lemen. You're absolutely right.' He gave Tucker a long look.

Then he put down the gun and picked up the wallet again. 'Now, gen'lemen, lemme call yo' attention to this heah article one mo' time. I looked it ovuh while y'all were upstairs, and I found sump'm real interestin'.'

He opened the wallet and displayed it in all directions. 'Looks empty, don't it? But look heah –' He flipped open a hidden compartment, and exposed a folded piece of paper.

Darby's eyes narrowed as he watched. His lips were compressed, his face set in grim silence.

'Well, what have we heah?' Willard's tone reflected only innocent curiosity as he extracted the paper and unfolded it.

'We have heah, gen'lemen, a deposit receipt from a bank in Sacramento, California. It's fo' the sum o' six hunnerd and forty dolluhs. And it's made out to somebody by the name of –' He read, enunciating carefully – 'Darby Rutledge.'

Willard gazed placidly around the court, and allowed the heavy silence to take its effect.

'Darby Rutledge,' he repeated. 'Gen'lemen, do any of you think it's a little bit peculiar that somebody named Daniel Ross is carryin' a bank deposit slip that's made out to somebody named Darby Rutledge?'

Several silent nods of hooded heads provided an affirmative answer.

'And, gen'lemen, do you find it a mite peculiar, as well, that Darby Rutledge, whoevuh he is, and this heah Daniel Ross, jes' happen to have the same *initials?*'

'Peculiar as hell,' the Grand Monk affirmed.

'*Damn* peculiar!' the Grand Exchequer declared.

Willard leaned forward, his hands on the table, and fixed his eyes on the prisoner. 'If you're Daniel Ross,' he growled, 'who is Darby Rutledge?'

'I am,' the prisoner answered immediately. 'I go by that name in California. It's my business name.'

'Yo' *business* name?!'

Uproarious laughter erupted in the court.

'Sho' it's his business name!' the Grand Turk cackled. 'An' his business is thievin'!'

The laughter rose to a higher pitch. The Grand Cyclops was permissive for a moment, then rapped on the table and called for order.

He pulled himself up to his maximum height, and intoned in the ponderous voice of judgment: 'Prisonuh, you are charged with bein' in this state illegally, without employment. You're charged with travellin' unduh a false name. You're charged with bearin' arms, in cleah violation o' the law. And you're charged with possessin' stolen property. Klansmen, you will now delivuh the verdict. All those –'

'Guilty!' the Grand Turk screeched.

'Cut out the oratory, Gene,' the Grand Monk blurted. 'Let's lick 'im.'

'Jes' hold yo' horses, goddamn it!' Willard thundered. 'This heah's gon' be done accordin' to lawful and propuh procedure!' The Chief Justice adjusted his hood, and proceeded. 'Now, Klansmen, delivuh the verdict. All those believin' the accused guilty, signify by sayin' "aye".'

The shout arose in unison: 'Aye!'

'Innocent, signify by sayin' "no".'

Willard looked directly at Tucker. There was silence.

'Can *I* say somethin'?' the prisoner asked.

'Shut up!' roared the judge. 'Prisonuh, you are heahby found guilty as charged, and sentenced to ten lashes fo' each charge. That's forty lashes. Klansmen, take the prisonuh out and prepare to administuh and sentence.'

The men on either side of the prisoner grasped him by the arms, and were suddenly thrown back.

'Just a damn minute! Don't *I* get a chance to speak?'

'Take 'im out!' Willard bellowed.

The Grand Monk and the Grand Exchequer seized the prisoner on either side and hustled him rapidly out of the room, in a flurry of grunts, growling oaths, and thudding boots. The Grand Sentinel followed, dancing excitedly at the heels of the other men.

'Billy!' Willard called sharply.

Billy stopped in the doorway and looked back.

'Not you. You go on down to the well and stand guard ovuh the horses and wagon.'

Billy whined in protest. 'Aw-w-w! How come I have to miss all the fun?!'

'You're the Grand Sentinel. It's yo' duty.'

Billy took up the wagon lantern and stomped out, muttering darkly. Only the Grand Magi remained in the room with his leader.

Willard removed his hood and wiped his brow. 'Goddamn! Gits hot unduh theah!' he mumbled. He turned to the other man.

'Tucker, go on down to the wagon with Billy and git the whip and the rope out o' the strongbox. Theah's a brand new rope in theah, ain't nevuh been used.'

Tucker pulled off his hood. He gazed at Willard with a hard, troubled frown. 'You shuah 'bout all this, Gene?' he said quietly.

Willard's answer was calm and patient. 'Ain't but one thing worse'n a white carpetbagguh, Tucker. That's a black one. This heah Daniel, or Darby, or whatevuh his name is – he's the kind o' nigger we *don't want* in the South.'

'We didn't *prove* nothin' on 'im, Gene. I ain't too shuah 'bout it, myself.'

Willard scowled, and stepped close to his chief assistant. His voice became low and ominous. 'Theah's sump'm *I* ain't too shuah about, Tucker. I ain't shuah I did the right thing makin' you second in command. I ain't absolutely positive you're *with* us.'

Tucker stared at his chief. His mouth twitched; he shook his head timidly, and smiled. 'Aw, pshaw, Gene! Don't git to thinkin' *that* way. I was jes' – I was jes' speculatin', that's all. I'm with you, one hunnerd per cent.'

'All right.' Willard clapped his lieutenant on the shoulder. 'Go git the rope and the whip.'

'Right, Gene.' Tucker started for the exit.

'And leave the speculatin' to me,' Willard said.

'Yeah. Right, Gene.' Tucker glanced back over his shoulder, laughed nervously, and hurried out.

Willard watched the man go, and his brow was pulled tight with thought. After a moment he picked up one of the lamps and started for the arched doorway, then paused and looked back. One other lamp remained in the room, set on the floor in a corner. Willard's eyes drifted over the disarray of the scene – one chair overturned, another dismembered, its parts creating a clutter; the Klan garments strewn about, like the aftermath of orgiastic revelry. In the midst of the dishevelled piles of cloth in the open trunk lay the bible, the precious book of by-laws. It'll be safe here, Willard thought, and started to turn away.

He paused again. Something was tugging at him, nibbling gently at the bottom of his mind – a tiny phantom thought, or shred of memory, or something, elusive and secretive – that he could not quite identify. He tried to grasp it, to hold it still for examination, his frown deepening from the irritation that mental exertion always brought. For an instant he almost captured it, caught a glimpse of it as it scurried away.

'Darby. . . .' He heard himself mutter the word softly, as he stared at the floor. 'Darby – where the hell have I heard that name before?'

His store of memory yielded nothing but the tantalizing question itself; the shadowy phantom remained concealed.

Willard disliked puzzles. He shook his head impatiently and went out.

Darby was rushed across the yard to the sycamore tree by the road, and pushed up against it, with his back to the trunk.

'You stand right theah and don't move,' Clayton ordered. He whipped off his hood and wiped his damp brow, and muttered, 'Can't breathe unduh this goddamn thing!' He flung it aside.

Ham and Lucius took the cue, and emerged from their head coverings with relief.

'Well, what are we waitin' for?' Clayton said. 'Somebody go git the rope and the whip.'

'We're waitin' fo' Gene,' Ham said. '*He* gives the orduhs.'

Clayton glared at the tall bearded man. 'Yeah? What are *we* supposed to be, flunkies?'

Darby had resumed his study of the robed men, looking from one to the other, listening, and trying to appraise each one individually. A gleam of hope sprang to his mind.

There's dissension in the ranks, he told himself. It's time to start talkin'.

'You gents ought to think real long and hard about this,' he said casually. 'My boss'll be back any time now, and he'll have some friends with him. They'll be pretty mad, and when that rough crowd gets mad, there jus' ain't no tellin' what might –'

The men were looking at Darby with empty expressionless faces.

Lucius suddenly giggled. 'Don't he talk funny?'

No good, Darby thought. He tried another tack.

'You're interested in punishin' thievery, I take it. Fine. But, hell, you got the wrong man. Your leader took my hundred and twenty-three dollars and put it in his pocket – not to mention my gold necklace. Now ask yourselves this question, gents – how much o' that money d'ya think *you'll* ever see?'

For a moment the men were suspended in a thoughtful silence.

'That's a point, by God,' Clayton said quietly.

'Why, you son of a bitch,' Ham muttered.

Clayton whirled on him.

'Hey, hold it!' Lucius yelled, and grabbed at Clayton.

Ham smiled down into Clayton's fierce scowl. 'I meant *him*,' he said, jerking his head toward Darby.

'*You're* supposed to be in charge o' the goddamn money,' Clayton snapped. 'How come *you* ain't askin' that question?'

'Don't worry,' Ham said. He continued to smile. 'I aim to.'

Tucker came down the front steps of the house and walked rapidly off in the direction of the well. Then Willard came out of the house and down the steps, carrying one of the lamps, and approached the men under the sycamore tree.

'Tucker's gone to git the rope and the whip,' he said. 'And I want you men to be careful with our brand new rope. It's got to last awhile –'

Ham had moved up close to Willard. 'Hey, Gene, what's gon' happen to that hunnerd 'n' twenty-three dolluhs you got in yo' pocket?'

Willard looked at him in genuine surprise. 'What d'ya mean?! It goes in the official expense fund, naturally.'

'But I thought *I* was the ex-check – whatevuh you call it,' Ham said.

'Yeah,' Clayton said. 'How come Ham ain't holdin' the money?'

Willard snorted with irritation. 'Because, goddamn it, I ain't had time to take care of every little piddlin' detail – what the hell are you gittin' at, anyway?!'

'See what I mean, gents?' Darby said.

Willard moved toward him, muttering. 'Shut yo' mouth, you bastard!'

'What expense fund you talkin' 'bout, Gene?' Clayton persisted. 'You nevuh mentioned no expense fund befo'.'

Willard turned on his questioner. 'Goddamn it, Clayton, use yo' head! You know how much I paid fo' them thirty sets o' robes an' hoods? Dolluh and a half apiece! Forty-five dolluhs!'

'That's a hell of a lot less'n a hunnerd an' twenty-three.'

'That ain't all! Think o' the trip to Tennessee! The book cost me twenty dolluhs, jes' by itself –'

'What about the gold necklace?'

'That *plus* the money won't covuh my expenses!' Willard's patience ran out. 'Goddamn it, have I asked you fo' a contribution, Clayton?'

'No, but I'd like to see it all written down, facts an' figures, on a piece o' paper –'

Willard put his lamp on the ground and advanced, thrusting his face close to Clayton's. His low even voice took on the cutting edge of controlled fury.

'I don't have to account to you, Clayton. Not fo' a goddamn thing.'

Tucker had come back without reaching the wagon, hearing the sounds of anger. He and the other men formed a silent ring of spectators as Willard and Clayton stood toe to toe, locked on each other's glinting eyes.

Darby watched closely. Now, he thought. Then: No, wait. Maybe it'll get better. Maybe they'll fight.

The antagonists held their positions, silent, tense and motionless, like panthers poised for the kill. The other gangmen watched and waited with animal-like passivity, ready to pledge their loyalty to a new leader, or reaffirm their allegiance to the old one.

Then Clayton backed down. 'Naw, Gene, you don't have to account to me.' He shuffled his feet in the dirt; his eyes dropped away from Willard's. 'I didn't mean nothin'.'

It ain't gonna get better, Darby told himself. It's got to be now.

He bolted.

'Git 'im, git 'im!' Willard screamed.

They rushed in a yelling stampede after the fugitive.

Darby bounded across the road, clearing it in two leaps, and headed for Indian Hill. At the base of the hill he ran into an unexpected tangle of low growing vegetation, stumbled in the darkness, and tried to change direction. Clayton caught him from behind and pulled him down. As he fell Darby spun in the air and delivered a sharp blow to the side of Clayton's neck that stunned the man and left him momentarily limp on the ground.

Darby struggled to rise – but the howling mob was upon him.

In the far rear corner of the room upstairs Moses struggled with the boards that covered the ancient secret passageway. In spite of the self-imposed restriction of working in silence, he had managed to pry several boards loose, but most were maddeningly stubborn. Luanna held the candle while Julia stood by, watching.

Then they heard the sounds of voices from the front of the house.

'They've gone outside,' Julia said. She moved swiftly down the length of the dark room, and peered through a crack in the front window boards. Moses went on working.

Presently the voices in the yard below grew louder.

'What are they doin', Luanna called, in an anxious whisper.

'I can't see much,' Julia answered. 'They have Darby with them – but they seem to be arguing among themselves.'

In a moment Willard's cry of alarm rang out: 'Git 'im, git 'im!' It was followed by hoarse shouts, and the sound of sudden commotion.

Without stirring from her observation post Julia called out excitedly, 'Darby's running! He's running away!'

Luanna and Moses turned and stared in Julia's direction. They waited, hardly daring to breathe, for more information. When none came, Luanna set the candle upright on the floor and ran to the front windows and searched for a crack in the boards.

By the time she found one Julia had turned away from her own. Her face was twisted in anguish.

'They're beating him! Oh, my God, they're beating him!'

Luanna looked briefly, then put her hands over her face and groaned softly.

The women came together instinctively, clasped each other, and moved away from the windows, as if to escape from the sound.

At the other end of the room Moses crouched by the old closed passageway, and listened. In his long, comparatively placid life he had heard the sounds of beatings a few times; he recognized them easily, even at a distance, through boarded windows.

He nodded. 'They're beatin' him, all right.'

He turned grimly back to his work. His hands were trembling – and were useless now anyway, against the boards that were stuck fast. He picked up a loose board and, using it as a lever, began to attack the unyielding ones with energy that was fed and renewed by anger. Sweat rolled from his face as he laboured. He made no further attempt to keep his efforts quiet.

And while he worked he muttered softly, under his breath, punctuating each straining effort with a corresponding syllable.

'The goddamn . . . yellow-bellied . . . shit-ass . . . sons o' bitches. . . .'

It was the first profanity that had passed his lips in thirty years.

CHAPTER TWENTY-FOUR

The fight lasted five or six minutes, during which the Klansmen made an interesting discovery concerning their uniforms. The beautiful flowing robes restricted arm and leg movements infuriatingly, reducing efforts at combat to clumsy ineffectual flailings. Thus, despite their overwhelming numerical superiority, the gangmen found themselves absorbing almost as much punishment as they were able to mete out. One by one they withdrew long enough to fling their uniforms furiously aside, then returned to the battle.

Willard circled the action, yelling encouragement to his troops, and hurling frenzied oaths, like stones, at the head of their solitary opponent.

The force of numbers inevitably prevailed, and resistance ceased. Darby went down to stay, and the gangmen stood over him proudly, like victorious gladiators, panting, and each one nursing private bruises that he would not have cared to acknowledge.

They half carried their victim back to the front yard, and pushed him up against the sycamore tree again. Several hands held him – primarily to hold him upright; he was clearly incapable of further escape efforts. His limp body sagged against the tree trunk, his head lolled drunkenly to one side. Blood flowed freely from his mouth, and down his forehead and into his eyes.

The man before him grasped him by the cheeks and held his head forcibly straight.

'Listen, nigger,' a voice said, 'jes' fo' that little trick, yo' sentence is doubled. Now you git *eighty* lashes.'

Darby heard the words without fully comprehending their meaning. He pondered dully. The voice he had heard had a strange hollow ring to it, as if reaching him from a great distance, across a void. He made a concentrated effort to focus his eyes on the speaker.

It was Horace Willard, the overseer.

'No. . . .' Darby sighed, and looked away. 'No, it can't be. . . .'

'Tucker!' Willard shouted. 'Wheah's the whip?'

'I, uh – I ain't got it yet, Gene,' Tucker said, sheepishly.

'Goddamn it, Tucker!'

Billy had come up from his guard post at the well, to watch the action. 'I'll bring it, Gene!' he piped, and scampered away.

'Bring the rope, too!' Willard yelled after him.

Darby's head cleared slightly. He looked again. The man standing before him was Willard the younger. It was Gene Willard, still attired in his ceremonial robe.

'Who appointed you?' Darby said huskily.

'What's that?!' Willard snapped at him.

'Who elected you sheriff? Where'd you get the authority to put people on trial? Who chose you to be chief magistrate, judge and jury of all the courts?'

Willard delivered a back-handed slap across the prisoner's bloodied head.

Darby's mind spun. Something inside him said, *Shut up, you fool. Don't make it worse.* Something else said, *What the hell – one more lick or two won't matter.*

'I told you before, gents,' he shouted at the men behind Willard, 'you got the wrong party. The thief among you is your own bully-boy leader –'

Another blow from Willard, in the other direction. Darby's head snapped back against the tree, and sank to his chest. He panted heavily. He blinked and squinted, trying again to clear his vision. The ocean roared in his ears.

From somewhere out beyond the roar he heard the powerful voice, booming, 'Billy! Hurry up with that whip!'

Darby's mind wandered in a grey swirling mist. Briefly the mist parted; he caught sight of a few fragments of lucid thoughts, and formed a resolve.

Eighty lashes. Did somebody say somethin' about eighty lashes? In my shape that'll finish me off, sure. Might as well go out fightin'. Trav would be proud....

With the ultimate effort of will he tightened every muscle and summoned the last ounce of his drained energy into a tense explosive bundle, and hurled himself forward.

Moses grunted and strained, and pulled at the last board that blocked the passageway. It resisted with all its perverse inanimate might, then came loose, with a protesting screech from bending nails. Now, one final effort, applied to the door, held by hinges frozen by years of rust and disuse – the door resisted in turn, quivered, creaked and groaned, and gave way. The air from the dense blackness of the narrow passage below and beyond smelled of ancient mouldering dungeons.

'I'll go first. Y'all stay close behind me,' Moses said to the women. 'Gimme the candle, Luanna.'

'Listen, both of you,' Julia said. Her voice was low, steady, and urgent. 'When we get downstairs, go outside and sneak around toward the front. Keep out of sight, and watch for a chance to help Darby somehow. I'll go in the front of the house and – perhaps – create some sort of – disturbance, or something.'

Moses gazed intently at her for a moment, frowning.

Impatiently she urged him on. 'We must hurry, Moses. Hurry!'

He shook his head. 'I don't know what we gon' do,' he said. 'But all right, le's go do it.'

He took the candle from Luanna, and entered the narrow, steeply descending stairway, groping cautiously with his feet for solid footholds on the rotted old steps, and brushing at cobwebs that formed eerie silver patterns in the candlelight.

Luanna went second, one hand on Moses's broad shoulder before her, the other tightly clasped to Julia's hand behind.

Willard whirled, his eyes wide with surprise. Then the breath went out of him, and he bent over clutching his belly where Darby's blow had landed. He sat on the ground, groaning softly, while his comrades converged on Darby and forced him down. Clayton leaped on the prone figure and sat astraddle, and brought his fists down again and again from the top of his reach, dropping them like sledgehammer blows on the flesh beneath him.

'Attaboy, Clayton,' Willard grunted. 'Give it to 'im, give it to 'im good.'

Just before his mind closed down Darby had one last thought, a fragmentary image that flitted like the silent wing-beats of a bat from the recesses of his memory.

That look of slack-jawed surprise on Gene Willard's face – it had borne an incredible resemblance to the look on the face of the overseer that night years ago, in the instant before being rendered serenely blank by the swift descent of a barnyard shovel. . . .

Willard pulled himself back to his feet, and stood gazing down at the unconscious man. He kicked, testing, and his boot made a satisfying thud against Darby's ribs. The prisoner lay still.

Billy returned running from the wagon, carrying a length of rope and a coiled whip.

'We don't need the rope now,' Willard told him. 'Jes' gimme the whip.'

'Hey, Gene,' Tucker ventured, 'ain't he – uh, ain't he had enough by now?'

'The sentence ain't been carried out yet, Tucker.' Willard's reply was patient but grim.

He uncoiled the whip and snapped it expertly in the air once or twice. The other men moved back a few paces.

'Hold it a minute, Gene.' It was Clayton this time.

Willard turned a sardonic look on him. 'Don't tell me *you're* going soft, Clayton!'

Clayton's hard eyes entertained no such possibility. 'It don't make sense to whup a nigger that's out cold and can't *feel* it,' he said. 'Ain't wuth the work. He won't even yell.'

A faint grin twisted Clayton's stiff grimy face. 'It ain't no fun if he don't yell, Gene.'

Ham, Lucius and Billy all nodded and mumbled assent, allowing this to be an excellent point.

Willard considered it. 'I reckon you're right.'

Clayton turned to Billy and snapped an order. 'Billy, bring a bucket o' watuh from the well.'

'Wait a minute,' Willard said. He bent over the man on the ground, and observed him closely. 'I think he's comin' 'round.'

Darby stirred, and groaned softly.

Willard stood directly over the prisoner, watching him. When he saw the eyelids flutter open, he spoke.

'On yo' feet, boy.'

Julia stood at the far dark end of the great hall of Chinaberry house. She looked down the length of the room, and was momentarily immobilized with astonishment at the litter of robes and hoods, draped over the huge open trunk and strewn on the table and chairs. The trunk and the table formed the shadows of hulking giants on the bare walls and ceiling, projected from the pale glow of the solitary lamp that had been left behind, standing on the floor in one corner.

Julia looked, and felt as if she'd never seen this room before.

Silently she moved across the floor to the high front windows, nailed closed with boards, like the windows in the front room upstairs. Again she found a small crack in the rough surface that gave her a narrow view of the yard, and stood with her eye glued to it, trying to make out the actions of men whose dim figures were barely visible in the feeble half-light outside.

When she saw the still, crumpled form on the ground she put her hand to her mouth and bit her knuckle to prevent herself from crying out.

He reached, he groped, grasping for something solid to steady himself against, and climbed slowly and laboriously up from the total black of oblivion into murky greyness. Silence gave way; the ocean roar returned – and with it, searing pain.

And down through a long steep echoing tunnel the voice of Horace Willard, overseer, floated to him, saying, in its flat chilling twang – *On yo' feet, boy.*

He seemed to hear it repeating, louder, and then over and over again, reverberating off the dank stony walls of the tunnel, and pounding in his ears.

On yo' feet boy.

Then the tunnel opened and widened, and high walls and a ceiling came up and locked themselves in place above him.

He was sitting on the floor in the upstairs hallway with his back against the wall, outside Mister Douglas's study. His heart beat wildly, in panic from the imminent presence of some looming peril, unknown but felt.

Then he looked up and saw the broad flabby florid face of the overseer, with its narrow deep-set ice-blue eyes, reptilian in their steady unblinking gaze. The man stood enormously tall, soaring far above him, but the voice was close now, close – revoltingly intimate, inside his head.

On yo' feet, boy.

He was suspended in a frozen moment when time refused to move, but clung with mindless obstinacy to the instant of the utterance of four crude, ominous words.

At last he struggled free. He flung his arm over his eyes and cried out – and time moved on.

He looked again, almost against his will. The inflated face of Horace Willard floated down closer and hovered, filling his vision. He forced himself to grapple again with the intricacies of speech.

'It ain't fair,' he whispered.

'What's that?' a hard voice demanded. The face came closer still, threatening to smother him.

'It ain't far, Mister Willard. I ain't done nothin' wrong.'

The face floated back farther, higher, and smiled. The walls and ceiling were gone; the face glided across the night sky like a ghostly cloud. It spoke – or, strangely, a voice sounded, though the curled lips did not move.

You done got them dogs all riled up, the voice said. *Le's give 'em a little exercise.*

'No, no. . . .' He twisted his head from side to side, trying to escape the disembodied face.

Two things I want you to learn, the voice said. *One is how the dogs work.* Smiling, smiling, the face hung suspended serenely before his eyes. *The other thing is – how unhealthy it is for a nigger boy to git friendly with a white girl –*

He raised his head and stared upward, with wild eyes. 'No, it ain't right!' he shouted. 'Whatever there was between me and Julia wasn't no business o' yours!'

'What's the crazy bastard talkin' about?' someone muttered.

Panting, struggling painfully, he pulled himself up on one elbow. His blurred vision dimly registered the dark outlines of the house.

'I got to say goodbye, Julia,' he called out. 'I got to run away now.'

'He's ravin'. He's out of his head,' someone said.

A shrill moronic laugh rang out.

'Shut up, Billy!'

Julia could hear the voices, faint and muffled, through the crack in the window boards.

'No, Darby, don't talk! Don't. . . .' she whispered. She lowered her head and closed her eyes, and trembled with the intensity of her concentration, trying to communicate with him.

Darby stared at the ground, and clawed aimlessly at the earth with his fingers. He spoke in a low, almost incoherent mumble, and six men stood over him silent and motionless, straining to catch his words.

'I hit Mister Willard with a shovel. Maybe killed him.' His strength failed; he fell back.

'Great God Almighty!' the voice above him thundered.

The face came down over him agaïn, livid, snarling and ferocious. Large hands seized his head and wrenched it upward. He caught his breath in pain.

'What did you say, you bastard?! *What did you say?!*'

The fierce eyes remained fixed like sword points; the lower part of the face twisted into the broad slobbering jaws of a bloodhound.

Darby tried to pull away, but his muscles refused to respond. 'No –' he gasped. 'Don't turn the dogs on me.'

The hands released him abruptly; his head fell back against the ground. He stared into space, found the pale last-quarter moon sailing close to the zenith, and tried vainly to bring it into focus.

'Goodbye, Julia,' he murmured. 'I'm goin' out west and be a free man. I'll see you again someday. I promise.'

He sighed, and closed his eyes.

Willard stood with his feet wide apart, breathing heavily. He lifted his eyes upward, and his face was contorted by the force of a cataclysmic revelation.

'Darby!' he screamed at the night sky. '*Now* I know that name!'

Julia turned away from the window, and stood with her back pressed against the rough boards. Her face was ashen, her heart constricted in her throat.

Willard stalked around the man on the ground, staring down at him. When he turned to his companions they recoiled involuntarily, and shrank back from the wild passion that raged in their leader's eyes.

'This – this was the one!' His voice was husky and thick. 'This was the bloodthirsty son of a bitch that almost killed my daddy – all them yeahs ago!'

The men gaped, paralyzed.

'Jesus Christ, Gene! You don't mean –'

'Goddamn right, I mean! Didn't you heah 'im?! Darby – that was his name, I tell you! That was the bastard's *name*!' He stood over the unconscious man, pointed a forefinger, and bellowed.

'Prisonuh, I heahby charge you with the attempted murder of Horace Willard, overseer of Chinaberry plantation, on the night of the twenty-first of April, in the yeah eighteen hunnerd an' forty-five!'

Darby's head rolled restlessly. Dimly he heard the shouting, but comprehended nothing, and cared for nothing.

'Klansmen, you have heard the evidence from the prisonuh's own mouth! What is the verdict?!'

The frenzied cry arose almost exultantly: 'Guilty!'

'Klansmen, what is the sentence?!'

'Hang 'im! Hang 'im! Hang 'im!'

The savage shouts ripped across the night, penetrated the thick absorbent forest in the distance, rolled up the slope of Indian Hill, and echoed through the dark empty chambers of the house.

Quietly, as if in a trance, Julia moved away from the boarded windows, and stood in the centre of the big room. Her mind reeled with disconnected, fragmentary images that tumbled and spun in nightmarish disorder. She pressed her fingers to her forehead, trying to steady her senses and regain some degree of control.

Her eyes fell on Gene Willard's huge trunk, and the billows of white cloth spilling from it – ordinary cotton cloth, but in that faint light glowing with a curious pristine purity, as though sanctified by the blessings of heaven.

She stepped closer to the trunk, and saw the little book, lying there among the folds. She stared at it, transfixed by the ghostly illustration on its cover – and shivered with a cold mysterious horror. Something tore at her heart, struggled silently within her, lined her face with anguish, and gripped her throat with tension that fought to be released in a scream.

She resisted; she denied it, and permitted herself only a soft whisper: 'Is this how it ends? Is *this* how it ends. . . .'

Then the struggle was over, the tension gone, and in its place, repose – the question answered.

She moved quickly, picked up the lamp burning dimly on the floor, carried it to the trunk – with precise care, as if it were a fragile treasure – and placed it, overturned, in the soft white bed.

Oil dripped, soaking slowly into the porous cotton cloth. The tiny flame flickered, reached out and licked tentatively at its surroundings, found them congenial, and leaped out of the strict confinement of the lamp chamber.

She watched for a moment as the little fire spread and expanded rapidly, seething with the robust zest of appetite aroused. Then she turned and walked without haste toward the far end of the room, whence she had come. Her eyes drifted aimlessly along the bare scarred walls. In a remote dark corner her thoughts paused and dwelled for a moment, in dreaminess.

There, long ago in another life, liveried musicians once sat and played for dancers. Her eyes drifted again; it seemed to her that the gaunt grotesque shadows hanging on the walls and ceiling moved, undulating softly, swaying to the strains of gentle music that was faded and forgotten, and would never be heard again.

The flames were crackling with abandon now, climbing the wall behind the trunk, licking the floor, reaching in all directions for more and more substance to appease their hunger, for anything – rapacious, ravenous, omnivorous.

Julia gazed down the length of the great room once more, her face lit with the cleansing light of fire, and serene. To the house she loved she murmured a last parting word.

'Poor Chinaberry – you lived too long.'

Then she turned away, moved silently toward the rear of the house, and disappeared into the darkness.

CHAPTER TWENTY-FIVE

Gene Willard's eyes flashed like a madman's, and his speech came out thick and furious, and pitched in the shrillness of near-hysteria. His rantings tore at the nerves of his comrades, and stirred them to frenzy.

'Whea's the goddamn rope?! Billy, gimme the rope!'

Billy scurried to pick up the rope from where he had dropped it.

'Now you got it all dirty! It's brand *new*, goddamn it!'

Billy hung his head in shame.

Willard moved about in boiling agitation, exhorting his men to their tasks.

'Take hold of 'im, somebody, drag 'im ovuh heah unduh the tree – come on, you lazy bastards, move!'

Rough hands dragged Darby toward the sycamore tree, while the others fumbled with the rope.

'Grab hold o' the rope end, Tucker, pull it out straight!'

'Wheah you want 'im, Gene?'

'Ovuh theah, below that heavy limb. Hurry up, now!'

The men pulled clumsily, with grunts and oaths, on their limp sagging load.

Willard's attention shifted rapidly back and forth.

'Come on, Tucker, pull on it, straighten it out – not *that* limb, you dumb bastards! The big one! Git out o' the way, Lucius, move back!'

The leader's exasperation rose explosively. 'Son of a bitch! Got to do every damn thing myself! Gimme room, goddamn it!'

The men scrambled in all directions, each trying to play an important role, each getting in the others' way.

'Billy, bring that goddamn lantern closuh! Gimme some light!'

Willard struggled to position the prisoner properly, while continuing to shout orders.

'Somebody throw the end o' the rope ovuh that limb. Ham, you're the tallest, you git busy with that!'

Ham threw the end of the rope upward, and ducked. The

rope descended and draped itself over his head. He tried again, with the same results. In his efforts to evade the falling rope, he tripped over Darby's legs, and fell backward, roaring in anger.

'Jesus! Gimme that, you clumsy fool!' Willard snatched the rope and threw it over the limb – not quite far enough. The stiff new rope curled maddeningly; the loose end remained beyond reach.

'Cheap goddamn rope!' Willard snarled.

At the other end of the rope Lucius worked feverishly, trying to construct a noose. He was sweating, cursing, and botching the job.

'We ain't gon' hang 'im without makin' 'im yell first, are we, Gene?' Clayton said. 'That ain't no fun – a nigger can't yell when he's hangin'.'

'What the hell do you want me to do about *that*, Clayton?' Willard snapped.

Clayton produced a bone-handled knife from his pocket, and opened a long slender blade, honed to gleaming sharpness. He grinned at Willard. 'This'll make 'im yell.'

'How the hell you gon' make the son of a bitch yell, when he's unconscious?!' Ham demanded with loud scorn.

'Pull his pants down,' Clayton said. 'I'll show you how to make a *dead* man yell.' His twisted grin grew wider.

'You bastard!' Tucker said huskily.

Clayton whirled on him. He whipped the knife up to eye level, and squinted fiercely down the blade toward Tucker. 'How would *you* like to yell a little, you nigger-lovuh!'

'Goddamn it, shut up!' Willard thundered. He thrust himself between Clayton and Tucker.

'Clayton, git yo' ass ovuh theah and help Lucius with the noose, 'fo' I knock yo' goddamn head off!'

Clayton snapped his knife closed and did as he was told.

Willard turned, bumped into Billy, and erupted again.

'Git back to yo' post, Billy! You're on guard duty – git back to the wagon!'

'Aw, Gene, how come *I* have to miss the fun?!'

Willard moved toward him, and Billy departed.

Clayton expertly fashioned a noose, while Lucius pulled Darby up to a sitting position, propped against the base of the tree. Clayton slipped the noose over the prisoner's head, pulled it down around his neck, and tugged it tight.

Darby opened his eyes briefly, and looked around without seeing, without comprehension. His head slumped forward on his chest.

Ham strained upward, reaching for the loose end of the rope that dangled over the limb.

Willard urged him on. 'Jump up and git it, Ham. Jump, jump!'

Ham made an ungainly attempt to jump, and came down in a crouch, clutching his back, and grimacing.

'Jump yo'self, goddamn it!' he growled at Willard. 'I got a bad back.'

Tucker tugged lightly on Willard's sleeve, and said in a low voice, 'Gene? Hey, Gene –'

'Git away, Tucker!' Willard yanked angrily on the rope and pulled it off the limb, and prepared to throw it again. 'I got to do every goddamn little thing myself –'

'Hey, Gene –' Tucker was persistent. 'Looka yonduh, Gene.'

Willard glanced impatiently at Tucker, and saw that he was staring in the direction of the house. Willard looked, and froze in his position.

All eyes turned in that direction. A hush fell, as the men stared, open-mouthed and silent.

'Gawd a' mighty!' Ham breathed softly.

Through the cracks in the boarded front windows a flickering brightness was visible, producing a vivid veined pattern against the dark bulk of the house. A stream of ghastly yellow light slanted from the wide front doorway across the veranda, dancing as if to an eerie silent rhythm.

Lucius, standing closest to the house, turned and studied his leader's face carefully, waiting for a reaction.

'The house is burnin', Gene,' he said matter-of-factly.

Clayton laughed softly.

Tucker rubbed his chin and said, 'Ain't that a shame? Somebody must 'a' left the lamp –'

'Jesus God!' Willard bellowed. 'The book! I got to save the book!'

He ran for the house, and crashed into Lucius as he went past. Lucius went sprawling.

'Goddamn, Gene!' he bawled. 'Watch wheah you're goin'!'

Halfway to the house Willard paused long enough to motion frantically to the others. 'Come on, you bastards! We got to save the book!'

The men shook off their paralysis and ran after Willard. Lucius dragged himself up and followed, muttering.

Willard approached the veranda steps at full speed, and took half of them in a single bound. On his second leap his foot came down hard on the top step, and plunged through the old decayed planking. Suddenly he was sitting sideways, in a grotesque position, his right leg sunk to the thigh in the void below the steps. Like a wounded bull elephant, he roared in thunderous fury.

Lucius almost laughed. 'See, I *tol'* you to watch wheah –' He caught himself and swallowed his words, as he saw the rage on Willard's face.

Tucker reached the injured man first, and bent over him. 'You hurt, Gene?'

'The book, goddamn it, the *book!*' Willard screamed, and lunged at him, and Tucker staggered back.

'Nevuh mind me, save the book!'

Clayton and Ham ran up the steps and across the veranda to the doorway, and their faces were immediately lit with the garish glare of an open furnace. They stopped dead in their tracks.

'Go on, damn you!' Willard shouted at them. 'Git in theah and grab the book, 'fo' it's too late!'

The men turned away from the brilliant light in the doorway, and retreated. Clayton stood over Willard and gazed down at him, grim-faced.

'Git it yo'self,' he growled. 'It's *yo'* goddamn book!'

He walked down the steps and away from the house, and Willard stared after him, thunderstruck.

'Help me up, somebody!' Willard gasped. 'Git me out o' heah!'

Ham and Tucker bent over Willard from either side, grasped him by the arms and hoisted him up out of the gaping hole.

Willard staggered onto the veranda. His trouser leg was ripped open, his leg bleeding from a long ugly slash. He was almost speechless with fury as he flung his rescuers back from him.

'You goddamn yellow bastards!'

He lurched toward the doorway, and plunged into the house.

'Gene, you damn fool, come back!' Tucker yelled. He rushed after Willard, but stopped at the threshold. Ham and

Lucius came after him, and the three stood in a huddle and shielded their faces with their hands, and peered through their fingers at the inferno within.

The flames broke through the outside wall at the front of the house.

Clayton went toward the sycamore tree, his squinting eyes fixed on Darby. The prisoner was still propped against the tree trunk, the noose snug around his neck. His head remained slumped forward on his chest. He had not moved.

Clayton strolled leisurely up to the tree and stood gazing down at the unconscious man at his feet. With a casual movement he drew out his knife and opened the blade, and smiled at the soft firm click it made as it fell into place. He drew his finger caressingly along the wicked, glittering edge.

Willard staggered back to the doorway, almost falling into the arms of his comrades. They grabbed him and pulled him out of the house, across the veranda, and down the steps.

Willard groaned softly, and grimaced in pain, dragging his bloody leg.

'Watuh!' he croaked. 'We got to have watuh!'

'I'll git you some, Gene,' Lucius said, and started away.

'Not fo' *me*, you fool! Fo' the fire! Git the bucket out o' the wagon, and whatevuh ones you can find at the well – fill 'em and git 'em up heah! It's our only chance!'

The men stared, appalled by the enormity of the assignment.

'Go, goddamn it!' Willard screamed.

Ham and Lucius ran off toward the well.

Tucker remained. 'You're out o' yo' mind, Gene! It's too far gone, we can't do nothin' –'

Willard clutched blindly at the other man. His eyes were wild and raving. 'I got to save the book, Tucker, I *got* to! I swore to guard it with my *life!*'

'But look!' Tucker waved toward the house. 'You can see, it's too late –'

'Come on!' Willard gasped, pulling at Tucker. 'Le's go 'round the back, see if we can find anothuh way in!'

He wheeled and started to run toward the rear of the house, and collapsed immediately on his injured leg. Tucker moved to help, but was waved off. Willard got up and went on, limping, and Tucker followed him, swearing under his breath.

A pale glow now radiated through fissures in the upper part of the house. The fire had broken through the ceiling of the lower floor, and was invading the darkness of the upstairs with a merciless illumination.

Darby raised his head, and it rolled against the mottled trunk of the sycamore. His blood-caked eyelids fluttered open; he stared dully, without interest, at the legs of the man standing before him, silhouetted darkly in a fitful yellowish light. He caught a glimpse of a glint of steel as the man bent over him, but his mind made no attempt to interpret it, his muscles declined to move.

Then there were other legs – someone else had stepped into the limited range of his dim and cloudy vision. Darby's eyes closed. His head slumped again in weariness and resignation.

Clayton glanced up, startled.

'You son of a bitch!' he exploded, and sprang. His knife flashed in a murderous arc, hovered in the air, and quivered.

Large calloused hands closed around Clayton's throat. He opened his mouth to cry out, and the sound was caught and stifled – his eyes protruded in amazement, then in terror. The knife swung downward, rose and descended again and again. It slashed through cloth, and tore and clawed at flesh – but the angle was wrong, control was missing; it could not find its mark.

Darby's mind wandered in the grey no-man's-land of semi-consciousness. From somewhere above his head he heard heavy breathing, the straining of desperate exertions, and another, horrible, gasping, unearthly sound. He fell over to one side, dug his fingers in the dark ground, and tried to crawl away, moving in agony, inch by inch.

The great sycamore trunk shivered as something was slammed hard against it. The knife quivered again, hanging in the night air; the hand that held it went limp, and opened. The weapon fell to the ground. The tree shook again, and a third time.

The noises diminished abruptly, and ceased. Clayton dangled grotesquely, suspended, his feet supporting no weight. The great rough hands relaxed their grip, and

Clayton crumpled without a sound. His back propped against the tree for a moment, very near where Darby had been – then he slid off onto the ground and lay still, face up.

One side of his head, toward the house, was lit by the glare of flames. The other side, in the shadows, gleamed darkly with oozing blood. His wide open eyes caught the soft reflections of the last-quarter moon, whose tiny rays found their way now and again through the drifting foliage of the tree.

CHAPTER TWENTY-SIX

Ham and Lucius ran as fast as the darkness and uncertain terrain would permit, threading their way through the garden to the well where Billy was posted, guarding the horses and wagon. Unaware of the path that led straight across the cultivated area, they crashed blindly, cursing and stumbling, through corn stalks, bean vines and tomato plants.

When they arrived, scratched and torn, at the well, they were confronted with the muzzle of a rifle.

The Grand Sentinel, resplendent in robe and hood, sighted down the weapon's gleaming barrel, and trained it steadily on the approaching men.

From beneath the hood Billy's muffled shout rang out: 'Halt! Who goes theah?!'

Ham and Lucius stopped in their tracks and stared, dumbfounded. Then Ham recalled his training.

'Friend!' he yelled.

'Friend o' what?!'

Ham looked to Lucius for assistance. Lucius pondered, and remembered.

'Justice and mercy.'

'R—A—N!' shouted Billy.

'That's R—A—*I*—N,' Ham corrected.

Willard came staggering toward them in desperate haste, dragging his injured leg and cursing the pain. He stopped halfway through the garden and stared, aghast, at the scene at the well.

'R—A—I—N!' Billy yelled out.

Lucius responded. 'C—L—O—U—'

'Jesus Christ-all-goddamn-mighty!' Willard screamed toward the night sky. 'You stupid bastards! The watuh, god-damn it, the *watuh!*'

He trembled with rage, but could summon no more strength to vent it. He sank exhausted to his knees beside a cucumber patch, propped his forehead in one hand, and stared at the ground.

The flames built inexorably toward their hellish climax. They climbed, devoured, broke triumphantly through the roof and reached exultantly toward the moon, and spread leaping along the high outside walls, feasting with brutish, gargantuan appetite. The sound, which had begun as a vicious hissing, had now deepened and matured to a horrendous roar. The yellow glare had turned to a blinding white, and painted the surrounding fields, the slope of Indian Hill, and the dark green walls of the forest in the distance with nightmarish illumination and stark quaking shadows.

Willard limped out of the garden area, circling toward the front road, maintaining a respectful distance from the raging fire. His face was streaked with dirt and sweat, and sagging in weariness. He moved with slow lethargic calm; haste was forgotten, defeat recognized.

Shortly Ham and Lucius returned through the garden, each carrying a bucket of water. They found Willard and Tucker standing at a corner of the garden near the road, quietly watching the fire.

Timidly Lucius said, 'We brought some watuh, Gene.'

Willard took no notice of him.

Lucius set his bucket on the ground and joined the silent fire watchers. Ham shrugged, and raised his bucket to his lips and drank with dripping relish.

Willard turned at length and spoke in a voice that was flat and expressionless, and drained of vitality.

'Lucius, you and Ham go git the horses, and tell Billy to bring the wagon on 'round. We bettuh be gittin' out o' heah.'

Ham and Lucius went off, taking the buckets with them.

Willard turned his back to the burning house, and stared glumly off into the darkness. Tucker watched him quietly.

'I'm disgraced,' Willard said. 'I took a vow to protect the book with my life. The book's burned up, and heah I am still.'

Tucker was unmoved. 'Theah must be plenty mo' copies o' the book. I don't see what's so all-fired important about a little ol' –'

'Goddamn it, Tucker!' Willard growled. 'Theah's a hell of a lot you don't see, I notice!'

'It's jes' tough luck, Gene – anybody can have tough luck. You'll have to do some tall thinkin', and figger out a way to explain to 'em how it happened –'

'How it happened!' Willard turned on the other, his fury

reviving. 'Suppose *you* explain it to me, Tucker! How the hell *did* it happen?!'

Tucker regarded his chief with a detached coolness. He did not answer.

'I'm disgraced, Tucker,' Willard said hoarsely. 'I'll be kicked out o' the Klan, shuah.' He turned away, shaking his head in a daze of despair.

Billy drove the wagon along the front road, and pulled it to a stop near Willard and Tucker. He had shed his robe and hood. Ham and Lucius followed along on foot, leading the horses.

Lucius looked around. 'Hey – wheah's Clayton?'

'Prob'bly got yeller and lammed out,' Ham said casually.

'Good riddance if he did,' Tucker muttered. 'I nevuh did trust that bastard.'

Willard limped painfully to the wagon. 'Help me aboard, somebody. I'm gon' ride in the wagon – my leg's too bad to ride horseback.'

'How 'bout the nigger, Gene?' Ham said.

They all glanced toward the sycamore tree, a short distance up the road. The still dark form, lying in twisted repose under it, was barely visible.

'Leave 'im be,' Tucker said. 'He's prob'bly done fo', anyhow.'

'Go and check,' Willard said. 'If he's alive, throw 'im in the back o' the wagon. We'll finish our business with him latuh.'

Tucker started for the tree. A rending, crashing sound from the direction of the house stopped him. All the men turned to look.

A wall had collapsed. A section of the upper floor area, suddenly deprived of support, jutted out over flame-filled space, defying its fate for a few miraculous seconds, then broke loose with an agonizing screech of protest, and thundered down in a mountain of flaming debris.

The inside of the house was exposed – obscenely, like the guts of a maimed and mortally wounded beast. Inner walls, rooms ripped open and revealed, and part of the broad central staircase, were now intermittently visible in a bright forest of tree-high flames.

The men stood staring again at the fire, their fascination renewed by the unearthly sight of the blazing interior of the structure. Billy sat motionless in the wagon, his wide eyes feasting on the sight with an excitement that was half fear and half delight.

'Hot diggety – jes' *look* at what! Wouldn't you hate to be in theah?!'

Willard turned back to the wagon and grasped the side of it and attempted to climb up, but could not raise his injured leg. He grunted with pain and anger.

'Son of a bitch! One o' you lazy bastards gimme a hand heah –'

Something made him stop and look around quickly. The other men were staring up at Billy, a peculiar glassy look in their eyes. Willard was impatient and annoyed. He never paid any attention to anything Billy said – certainly not at a time like this.

'What was that?' he snapped at Billy.

'I said wouldn't you hate to be –'

An extra dimension of meaning to his remark suddenly penetrated Billy's mind. He stopped, gulped, and gaped at Willard with eyes wide, childlike, in horror.

'*In theah!*' He finished in a whisper of awe.

Willard's jaw dropped. For a moment he stared at the man in the wagon before turning his gaze back to the fire. Almost furtively he glanced at his companions, and saw that they were all transfixed with the same thought. They looked dumbly at each other, at Willard, and back at the blazing house. None wanted to be the first to utter the awful realization that had fallen over them suddenly, like the shadow of damnation.

Billy voiced it at last, in his direct, simple, unadorned way. He spoke softly, addressing no one, completing the observation he had unwittingly begun.

'We didn't only burn down Miss Julia's house. *We done burned down Miss Julia.*'

Another section of wall collapsed. The men stood still, rigid as statues, staring.

'God have mercy on us,' Tucker said, after a moment. There was a tremor in his voice.

All eyes drifted away from the flames and came to rest on Willard. He stood rooted, his gaze fixed in the infernal radiance of the blaze.

'It's the curse,' he murmured.

'What's that, Gene?' The men listened attentively, eager for any kind of enlightenment.

'The evil curse on this place,' Willard said solemnly. 'I knew about it when I was a kid. Everybody 'round heah knew 'bout it. The curse o' doom has been on this place evuh since it was built. Now it's come to completion.'

'What kind o' curse, Gene?' Ham and Lucius edged closer.

'The Indian curse, the Indian curse!' Willard spat it out vehemently. 'Every damn thing the Douglases evuh did, they did wrong. The very first one heah – that was Julia's grandpa – went and built his house right at the foot of a hill that everybody *knew* was a sacred Indian burial ground. *That* brought the curse down on 'em – and now they've got their reward.'

The other men turned their gaze on the dark sombre bulk of Indian Hill, across the road. In the eyes of Billy and Lucius there was total belief, and genuine fright; in Ham's eyes, uncertainty and apprehension. Tucker glanced at the hill without interest, then fixed a quizzical look on Willard.

'That's very interestin', Gene,' he said. 'But it wouldn't hold much watuh in a court o' law.'

Willard snorted. 'I don't figger to tell it in a court o' law, Tucker. Fact is, I was jes' thinkin' – we bettuh move our operations somewheah else. Maybe down to the next county.'

Tucker's hard gaze held on Willard. 'If I was *you*, Gene,' he said quietly, 'I'd move cleah on out o' the *state*.'

Willard felt a twinge of uneasiness. There was something different in Tucker's manner – something missing. The fawning, obedient, servile softness that had always made him an easily controllable, therefore reliable lieutenant – was gone.

Instinctively Willard summoned his gift for leadership. This was the essential moment to restore order, discipline, and efficiency – and he moved quickly to do it.

'We'll discuss all that latuh,' he said bluntly. He took hold of the wagon again, and barked his orders.

'All right, men, let's cleah out! Tucker, you and Lucius grab the nigger and throw 'im in the back o' the wagon. Dead or alive, throw 'im in – we can't take no chances. Billy, soon's I git aboard, move the wagon on down by the tree. Ham, gimme a hand heah, to climb in.'

Lucius and Tucker moved off toward the sycamore tree. Ham collected the horses' reins and began to tie them at the rear of the wagon.

Willard snapped at him impatiently. 'Come on, Ham, goddamn it, hurry up!'

Ham snapped back. 'Keep yo' damn britches on, Gene! I'll be theah soon as I secure the –'

'Gene!'

It was Lucius calling, from beneath the sycamore, and the sound of his call rang like a shot.

'Come heah! *Quick!*'

Tucker was kneeling over the figure on the ground. Lucius was standing and gesturing frantically at Willard and the others. His face screamed panic, silently.

Ham ran toward the tree, and Billy leaped off the wagon and ran after him. Willard followed, limping painfully, and muttering curses.

When Willard got there the others were kneeling in a tight huddle. They turned stricken faces up at Willard, their eyes glazed with shock. They spoke in hushed voices.

'It's Clayton, Gene.'

'Jes' *look* at that! His head's all bashed!'

'The nigger's gone. Plumb disappeared.'

'Goddamn! I thought *sho*' we done knocked the life out o' that nigger – but look what he done to Clayton!'

They made room for Willard, who knelt over Clayton and examined him. The others fell silent, awaiting the authoritative pronouncement.

'Son of a bitch,' Willard mumbled. 'He's dead.'

The authority was lacking. Willard looked at the other men, one by one, his eyes questioning. 'He *is* dead, ain't he?'

Tucker stood up. 'He's dead, all right.'

One after the other the men rose, and backed away from the crumpled body of their comrade.

'God a' mighty!' Lucius said breathlessly. 'I don't figger any *two* of us could 'a' whupped Clayton – 'cept maybe Gene. But that nigger got up off the ground half dead, and – and –'

Lucius peered out toward the darkness at the edges of the flickering illumination from the fire.

'Wonduh wheah he went to?' he said uneasily.

'Don't worry about it, Lucius,' Ham said. 'He's prob'bly halfway to California by now.'

Lucius giggled nervously, and Billy joined in.

'God a' mighty!' Lucius said again. 'What a man!'

Willard spoke in tones of solemn wisdom. 'Now you see

what I mean about the evil curse,' he said. 'It's the curse that done it. Ain't no othuh way in the world you could explain a thing like this.'

'Oh, I don't know, Gene,' Ham said. 'That bastard jes' had a hell of a lot mo' fight in 'im than we knew, that's all.'

'He sho' was one hell of a fightuh,' Lucius said. 'It took all six of us to whup 'im to start with.'

'Four,' Tucker corrected. 'Billy was on guard duty down at the well. And Gene –' He turned his gaze on Willard. 'Gene didn't see fit to join in.'

'Hey – that's right!' Ham breathed, suddenly remembering.

'What the hell d'ya mean by that?!' Willard yelled. 'Look a' my leg! I was hurt!'

'The fight was *befo*' you got hurt, Gene!' Tucker's voice rose to match Willard's. 'What'sa mattuh, you goin' soft in the head now?!'

'But befo' that, I gave the nigger some damn good licks – softened 'im up for ya!'

'Crap!' Ham snorted scorn. 'The only time *you* hit 'im was when somebody else was *holdin*' 'im!'

Willard's fierce glare shifted from Ham to Tucker and back again. The abrupt silence crackled with the menace of another confrontation.

It was Willard who backed off. 'We ain't got time to stand heah arguin' ovuh nothin',' he said mildly.

He glanced down at the dead man. 'Billy, bring the wagon ovuh heah. Le's pick up Clayton an' put 'im in the back. We got to git movin'.'

Billy went to get the wagon.

Lucius picked up something off the ground, a few steps away. 'Hey – heah's Clayton's knife!'

'That explains it,' Ham said. 'The son of a bitch was gon' make the nigger yell, he thought – an' see what he got for his trouble!' Ham laughed soundlessly.

Lucius stepped toward Willard, and asked eagerly, 'Can I keep it, Gene? I found it.'

'Hand it ovuh,' Willard snapped.

Lucius gave up the knife reluctantly.

'Look around and see what else you can find,' Willard told him.

Billy brought the wagon up to the tree. Ham and Tucker gingerly lifted Clayton's body and thrust it into the flatbed, performing their distasteful task as quickly as possible. The cargo struck the wagon planking with a rattling thud.

Billy looked back from the driver's seat and grimaced. 'Ugh! My wagon's gon' git all bloody!'

'Shut up, Billy,' Ham said.

'Goddamn!' Lucius yelled out.

The others turned to see what else he'd discovered.

Lucius screeched in outrage. 'Y'all realize what that son-of-a-bitchin' nigger did?! He stole *our brand new rope!*'

Willard grunted in disgust. 'That ain't the worst thing, Lucius,' he said glumly.

'Jes' think about my book. Even if I wasn't disgraced to lose it, it cost me twenty dolluhs. And the robes an' hoods – forty-five dolluhs fo' *them.* And jes' think about my trunk. That trunk was worth twenty-five, thirty dolluhs, at least.'

'It sho' is a damn shame, ain't it, Gene?' The lowly Lucius shook his head in dignified, comradely sympathy, flattered at being singled out by Willard for an exclusive conversation.

'Christ!' Ham blurted. 'Who gives a goddamn what the trunk was worth?! You *stole* it, didn't you?!'

'And you got the money from the nigger in yo' pocket, Gene,' Tucker said. 'You don't want to forgit that, now.'

Willard turned his weary eyes back to Ham and Tucker. The spirit of rebellion was growing.

'To hell with it,' he muttered. 'Le's git out o' heah.'

He dragged himself to the side of the wagon. 'Come on, Ham. Gimme a boost up.'

It was not an order. It was a request.

'Go to hell,' Ham said. He turned and went to the back of the wagon and mounted his horse.

'Gimme a boost, Tucker,' Willard pleaded. Tucker made no move.

'Lucius, gimme a boost. Come on, y'all, we got to git goin'. If somebody finds us heah we gon' be in big trouble!'

Lucius started to move toward Willard. Tucker raised a hand, and stopped him.

'You mean *you* gon' be in big trouble, Gene,' Tucker said.

Willard stared. 'What the hell d'ya mean?! We're in this togethuh, all of us! Every damn one o' you –'

Tucker waved him silent.

'Lemme tell you sump'm, Gene. We've had a man killed heah tonight. And we've burned up a lady's house, with her inside it. And we're standin' heah listenin' to you tell us it's all the fault o' some damn fool Indian curse, and we're hearin' you jaw about yo' thirty dolluh trunk, and yo' forty dolluh this and yo' twenty dolluh that, and all of a sudden I remembuh sump'm the nigger said a while ago – a question he put – and all of a sudden it seems like he was makin' damn good sense.'

Tucker had approached close to Willard, fixing him with a hard steady gaze.

'The question was, Gene – who appointed you?'

'You son of a bitch!' Willard roared. 'Nobody needs to appoint me! I organized this gang, goddamn it! It's mine!'

'All right, it's yo' gang. And you're welcome to it – whatevuh's left of it.' Tucker turned away.

'Ain't *nothin'* left of it,' Ham muttered darkly.

'Aw, come on, men!' Willard scoffed. He forced a little laugh. 'We jes' had a little accident, that's all –'

'Hangin' a thievin' nigger is *one* thing, Gene,' Tucker said. 'Burnin' a white lady up in her house is somethin' else –'

'*I* didn't burn her up in no house!' Willard screeched. 'It was an accident!'

'You locked her up in theah, didn't you?' Tucker yelled.

'No, I didn't! *You* did – you and the othuhs!'

'You gave the orduh, Gene! It was *yo' orduh!*'

Tucker stalked to the rear of the wagon and swung himself up onto his horse. From that height, garbed in the noble cloak of self-righteousness, he glared down at Willard like an angry god.

'I would nevuh have thought o' doin' a thing like that!' he proclaimed. 'Nevuh!'

'Me neithuh!' Ham declared, with a solemn nod of agreement.

'It was an accident, I tell you!' Willard's voice wavered. 'I didn't mean no harm!'

'Maybe Miss Julia wasn't yo' idea of what a southern lady ought to be,' Tucker said. 'But she *was* a high-born lady.'

'Don't tell *me* about Julia Douglas!' Willard shot back. His eyes roamed wildly, and flashed with a new fury.

'I lived on this place. I've known her all my life. I lived in a little ol' tumble-down shack way back yonduh in the woods, and I watched the high and mighty Miss Julia Douglas traipse up and down like she was Queen o' the May or sump'm – so damn stuck on herself she didn't even know somebody like me was alive – and all the time with her damn sassy nigger boy followin' along at her heels like a puppy dog, thinkin' he was better'n *everybody*, black *and* white!'

'Jes' the same, Gene –' Tucker began.

'You don't know nothin' about it, Tucker! Yo' daddy was a plantuh hisself. You don't know, eithuh, Ham. Yo' folks was pore, but they had theah own place. You don't know what it was like to be a lonesome little kid livin' the way I lived. You don't know what it was like for yo' folks to be livin' in a dilapidated ol' shack stuck off way down in the woods, and a quartuh of a mile away theah's the big house, with fine carriages comin' and goin', and parties and feastin' and merry-makin' day and night, and, and – goddamn! My daddy was the man who *made* Chinaberry's wealth in the first place!'

Tucker and Ham sat on their horses and looked down at Willard from a lofty height of sanctimonious moral superiority. Their faces were stone.

Willard turned to Lucius. '*You* understand what I mean, don't you, Lucius? Don't you understand, Lucius?'

Lucius smiled uneasily. 'Sho', Gene. Sho', I understand.'

He edged away from Willard, and went quickly to his horse, and mounted.

Desperately Willard turned to the man in the wagon.

'Billy –' His voice was almost a whisper – 'Come on, gimme a hand, Billy, you heah? I'm gon' ride with you. Me and you, Billy, we gon' stick togethuh. Come on, Billy. . . .'

Billy gazed at Willard for a moment in silence. Then he twisted in his seat to look back toward the mounted men. With the faultless instinct of a pack animal he identified his new leader, and addressed him.

'What you want me to do, Tucker?'

Tucker snapped an order. 'Move out. Time's awastin'.'

Billy grinned at Willard. 'Be seein' ya, Gene,' he said pleasantly. He slapped at the horse in harness, and the wagon lurched into movement, with Clayton's tethered horse following along behind.

Tucked edged his mount forward and handed the reins of the remaining horse to Willard.

'My leg's busted, Tucker,' Willard whimpered. 'I can't git on. I need help, Tucker.'

'You was gittin' around pretty spry up to a few minutes ago,' Ham said.

Willard kept his entreating eyes on Tucker.

'You're a fair-minded man, Tucker. Tha's the reason I made you second in command – 'cause you're such a fair-minded man.'

'We ain't blamin' you altogethuh, Gene,' Tucker said mildly. 'We jes' think maybe – it'd be a good idea if we didn't ride with you no mo'.'

Willard shook his head, unbelieving. 'It ain't fair, Tucker. I didn't mean no harm. It ain't fair.'

Tucker turned to the men behind him and said, 'Le's go.' He spurred his horse away, following the wagon down the road eastward into the darkness.

'If I was you, Gene,' Ham called out, 'I'd go into hidin'.' He moved his horse out quickly, forcing it to a gallop.

'Wait!' Willard yelled. 'Come back!'

He wheeled to face the last man. 'Lucius, wait! Help me!'

He received only a quick wave of a hand as Lucius's horse bounded past him and away after the others.

Clutching the reins of his own horse, Willard hobbled to the middle of the road and peered in the direction of the departing men, his former followers.

With all the vocal power he could muster he hurled a screaming curse at them: 'May you fry in hell, you goddamn double-crossin' bastards!'

He looked down at his injured leg. It was caked with blood, stiff and useless. Groaning and grimacing with pain and prodigious effort, he pulled himself slowly up into his saddle, and sat for a moment gazing at the back of his horse's head, exhausted and panting. Sweat rolled off his brow. He threw a last quick glance toward the burning house.

Then he turned his eyes back to his mount, and addressed his final remark to the animal, in a soft and piteous whine.

'All I meant to do was *pester* Miss Julia a little bit, and hang her pet nigger,' he said. 'I didn't mean no *harm.*'

He slapped his horse into action and moved off down the road. When he had gone a hundred yards he was out of the contracting circle of fire illumination and swallowed into darkness, and the sound of his horse's hoofbeats died away.

What remained was the steady crackling of the fire – and it was diminishing rapidly. The peak of the intensity of combustion had passed; the last stages would progress routinely to a quiet conclusion.

One final section of wall, toward the rear of the house,

steadfastly maintained its upright stance for a while longer. Then it came down, hissing and spitting in defiance, and buried layers of dying ashes beneath white-hot fresh rubble.

At length the seething mountain of ruin lost its passion and became quiescent. The glaring light dimmed, turned to orange, to sullen red – and the cool darkness of the natural night crept slowly and silently back in again, closer and closer. The night's orgy was over, the feasting done.

Nothing was left but tall blackened brick chimneys, standing like dead sentinels, uselessly guarding the smoking desolation at their feet.

CHAPTER TWENTY-SEVEN

The crescent of the fourth quarter moon had slid across the zenith and down the western sky. Its faint light, filtering through a feathery thin overcast, laid a sheen of pale grey over the broad reflective surface of the river, but on the land was lost, absorbed by the dull brown-green of the fields and forest.

From the place where Chinaberry house had stood, the smouldering remains of the fire radiated a glow so feeble that the sycamore tree by the front road was no longer touched by its light. All was tranquil.

Something moved in the darkness on the east side of the house grounds. A man walked along the lane there, going toward the front road. His movements were heavy and sluggish. At the intersection he paused and looked in all directions as far as his eyes could penetrate the gloom. He listened intently, holding his breath. Then he walked very slowly and cautiously down the front road and approached the sycamore tree, now standing in meaningless solitude in the empty front yard of a house that was no longer there. He circled the tree once, inspecting the ground beneath its overhang, and around its trunk. He stood still and looked again in all directions, listening. The dying fire rubble made a gentle slumbering sound, which blended harmoniously with the soft peaceful night sounds of nature.

He was satisfied. Moving a little more quickly now he crossed the road and made his way the short distance to the base of Indian Hill, and began to climb its narrow winding path.

Halfway up the slope he paused again, and scanned the darkness ahead. He saw what he was looking for – a still figure, sitting quietly on a hillock of grass at the top of the path, the pale drawn face barely visible in the faint moonglow. He went on.

Julia looked at him with a soft smile as he came up to her. 'H'lo, Moses.'

He gazed down at her with a look of long-suffering patience. 'Well – you sho' do lead a body a merry chase.'

'I'm sorry,' she said meekly. 'I just felt like – disappearing.'

He sighed wearily, and sat down near her.

'How did you know where to find me?' she said.

He chuckled gently. 'Don't I *know* you, Little Missy? Didn't I raise you from a pup? Ain't but two places you go when you want to be by yo'self – tha's the squattuh's cabin, and the top o' this ol' hill. You ain't at the cabin, I know. I jes' come from theah.'

'Moses –' She put a hand on his arm and searched his face earnestly. 'How is Darby?'

He frowned thoughtfully for a moment before answering.

'Can't tell for shuah. Luanna says he ain't hurt too bad, but I don't know – he looks terrible to me. I found some clean rags and a bucket fo' watuh in the barnyard, and took 'em to her, and she's washin' his wounds and makin' bandages, jes' like a reg'lar nurse. Darby squirms and groans, but he ain't come around yet – least not while I was theah. Luanna says he's gon' be all right. She keeps sayin' it, jes' like she knows what she's talkin' 'bout.'

He sighed again, shaking his head. 'I trust her, I reckon. She's a good nurse – always was.'

He looked at Julia quickly, moved by a sudden recollection. 'You 'membuh that time I was bad down with my back?'

'Mm-m,' Julia smiled faintly. 'Luanna was just a little girl – but she was the only person you'd allow near you.'

She raised a hand and ran it playfully through Moses's grey hair. 'You were cross as an old bear.'

'Well, anyway, Darby's in good hands now,' Moses went on. ''Course, Luanna was worried about you, too – didn't know wheah you was. I tol' her don't worry, you was all right, safe and sound. I wasn't real shuah 'bout that, but I figgered she didn't need to have *that* worry, 'long with lookin' aftuh Darby.'

She was silent; after a moment he looked at her and saw that she was gazing down the slope at the great awful black stain on the earth, studded with the jewels of orange and red embers, where the house had been. When she looked at him again her eyes were glistening.

'It's gone, Moses,' she said softly. 'Chinaberry's gone.' Her voice was flat and lifeless. She stared at him for a moment, as if wondering if he could comprehend that which she found incomprehensible – then quickly turned her face away.

'Go ahead, Missy, have yo'self a good cry,' he said. 'You'll feel lots bettuh.'

She shook her head vigorously, without speaking.

Moses patted her lightly on the shoulder.

'Funny thing,' he said. 'You nevuh was much fo' cryin'. I 'membuh, when you was a little biddy girl, and fell down and skinned yo' knee or sump'm, you'd bite yo' lip till it bled, 'fo' you'd cry.'

Moses knit his brows in thought, plumbing deeper into remembrance. 'I b'lieve the only time I evuh 'membuh you out and out cryin' was when Cap'n Andrew went away.'

She smiled faintly. 'I cried when Darby went away, too,' she said. 'But you didn't see me then.' She composed her face with care, and looked at him squarely again.

'I was tough when I was younger. I guess I'm not quite so tough anymore.'

'Oh yes you are, Missy. You're as tough as you evuh was. We've been through a good deal of adversity in our days, you and me, and we've always prevailed. And we gon' prevail agin. You'll see.'

She managed another weak smile, taking childlike encouragement from his optimism.

'You think so, Moses?'

'I *know* so.'

'How do you know it?'

'I know it the same way Luanna knows Darby's gon' be all right – 'cause theah's some things you jes' *got* to know, so you can find the strength to go on and do what has to be done, to *make* 'em so.'

'Luanna feels that way, too?'

''Course she does. Everybody does, that has a yearnin' in theah hearts to find some little bit o' happiness in this life, 'fo' they're dead and gone.'

'Luanna's – she's in love with Darby, isn't she?'

He gazed at her, and his words were slow and careful.

'Little Missy, them two people b'long togethuh. Luanna ain't jes' nursin' an injured man. She's nursin' the brightest hope she evuh had fo' her own life – the *only* bright hope.'

Julia was leaning close, listening raptly, and watching the old man's face as he spoke.

'Thank you, Moses,' she whispered. Impatiently she

brushed away a stray tear. 'Thank you for always being there, watching me, and guiding me.'

She got to her feet, and bent to take his hand and help him up. He rose with difficulty, slowly and stiffly.

'You're exhausted, I know,' she said. 'But there's one more thing that needs to be done –'

'Don't worry 'bout it, I know what I got to do,' he said.

She looked at him gravely. 'I hope you'll go across the river to Mister Griffith's house and catch Mister Travers, before he departs.'

He grinned at her. 'That's it. I'm glad to see we're thinkin' the same way.'

'I'd come with you if I could be of any help –'

He allowed himself a soft laugh. 'Little Missy, in a skiff you ain't no mo' 'count than you are in a vegetable garden – and that ain't no 'count a'tall.'

'Well then, I'll stay here and wait for you. But please hurry.'

'You come on down the hill now,' he said. 'I'll walk you to the cabin. Then I'll go.'

She shook her head firmly. 'Luanna's in charge there. She's a good nurse – you said so yourself – she doesn't need me. Besides, there isn't time for that.'

'Well, at least come on down to the cow stall. I'll fix you a pile o' hay in the corner, and you can git a little sleep.'

'No,' she said. 'I'll stay right here.'

'This ain't no place –'

'This is where I want to be.'

He frowned, and sighed with resignation. 'All right. Ain't no use o' me standin' heah arguin' with somebody that's stubborn as a mule.'

He started down the path. After a few steps he turned and looked back at her.

'I was wonderin', Missy – would you care to tell me how that fire started?'

She shrugged vaguely. 'I haven't the slightest idea how it started.'

He stood gazing up at her, his eyes narrowed shrewdly. 'So, you wouldn't care to.'

She said, 'Don't you think you ought to hurry? It'll be light soon. Mister Travers will be getting ready to leave.'

He nodded. 'I'm goin'. I'll be back as soon as I can.' He turned and went down the hill.

Julia watched him, more imagining his dim figure in the darkness than seeing it, until he had reached the front road and gone away down it in the direction of the river. She let her eyes rest for a few moments longer on the fire-ruin below, then lifted them across the quiet night sky, and breathed deeply.

After a time she started to make her way cautiously down the path toward the bottom of the hill.

CHAPTER TWENTY-EIGHT

In the little forest clearing near the southern end of the Chinaberry lands a faint light shone. From within the squatter's cabin a pale glimmer outlined the gaping doorway and window space, giving the ancient structure the unaccustomed look of habitation. A short stub of wax – what remained of the candle that Moses had carried down through the dungeonlike blackness of the narrow old stairway in the big house – was glued by its own drippings to a small flat rock set in the centre of the cabin room, on the spongy pine-needle floor.

Near the wall opposite the doorway Darby lay stretched on his back, his head and upper body elaborately bandaged. What was exposed of his face was bruised and swollen. His eyes were closed, and his chest rose and fell in laborious breathing.

Luanna sat with her feet tucked under her, cradling the injured man's head in her lap. She studied his face intently, watching for any signs of change in his condition. With her fingers she stroked his head lightly, careful to avoid the places of injury.

He stirred slightly and opened his mouth as if to speak, and Luanna leaned down close – but he was still again.

The girl sighed deeply, and allowed her tense body to sag under the weight of exhaustion – still she held Darby's bandaged head in her lap, and stroked his cheek with a featherlight touch of fingertips. At length she dozed, and awakened with a start, and dozed again, fitfully. Outside, the soft sounds of the forest night droned with endless mesmerizing monotony. The measures of time were hopelessly lost.

Darby roamed in the depths of the dark pool of unconsciousness, straining upward, yearning for air and light. He felt himself gaining buoyancy and rising slowly, and saw a delicate shimmering on the upper side of the surface, enticingly close. He reached for it, and with a surge of will broke through.

He awoke. He opened his swollen eyes and looked straight up, blankly, registering nothing, and closed them again with a frown of pain.

Luanna watched him, hardly daring to breathe. 'Darby?' she whispered.

He stirred restlessly, turned his head from side to side, and opened his eyes again. This time he brought the girl's face above him into focus, and saw her smile. He gazed up at her in wonder.

'Luanna. . . .'

'Yes, Darby. I'm here.'

He started to move, but stopped, wincing with pain.

'Luanna, I –' Speech came only with excruciating effort. He lifted a hand and reached for her, and she grasped it and held it tight. He searched her face beseechingly.

'Stay with me, Luanna.'

'I will, I will, Darby. I'm right here, don't worry.'

He closed his eyes and appeared to sleep. In a moment he opened them again with a start. His hand gripped hers fiercely.

'Luanna, last night –'

'Yes, Darby?' She bent closer, for his voice was feeble.

'Last night I had a dream,' he said.

She waited. There was a long pause before he spoke again.

'It was a terrible dream. I dreamed that Chinaberry was burnin', burnin' – all covered with fire.'

His eyes wandered feverishly, without seeing, over the dark log walls of the cabin, and the network of pine branches above that formed its natural roof. At length he found Luanna's face again, and fixed on it, unwaveringly. With a visible effort he recovered his thoughts, and went on.

'We were standin' in the fields, you and me, and we saw the fire, the awful yellow light pourin' out o' the house. We jus' stood there, watchin' it, for a long time. You started cryin', and wringin' your hands, and you said, "What'll we do, Darby, what'll we do?"

'I took your hand and I said, "We got to run away from here, Luanna. We got to run away as fast and as far as we can go."

'You pulled away from me and said, "No, no – we can't!" I said, "We got to, Luanna, we *got* to."

'So we ran together through the woods, and it was so dark we couldn't see anything, we couldn't even see each other – but all the time we could hear dogs yelpin' somewhere behind us. I said, "Come on, Luanna, hurry! Run faster, faster!"

'You started to cry again, and almost fell down, and said you couldn't run no more, and said I should go on without you. But I grabbed you and pulled you along, and we went stumblin' on through the darkness.

'Finally we came to the river. Mister Rutledge was there, and he put us into his boat and started to row. I thought the water was goin' to come up through the bottom of the boat and drown us, and I kept holdin' on to you as hard as I could.

'Then I heard Julia callin'. I looked back toward the shore, and I could still see Chinaberry house, all ablaze, flames leapin' to the sky. And right in the middle of 'em, Julia. She was standin' at her bedroom window upstairs, and she was callin' to me, sayin', "Come back, Darby, come back! You belong to me, come back!"

'I yelled to Mister Rutledge to go back, I had to save Julia – but he jus' looked at me with mournful eyes, and said, "Too late, too late!" – and went right on rowin'.

'Julia kept callin' to me – even after I couldn't see the house no longer I could still hear her callin', callin' – her voice was so pitiful it made my heart want to break. I tried not to hear it anymore – I tried to stop up my ears.'

He gasped for breath; his eyes burned with a frantic light. He gripped Luanna's hand so tightly that it hurt.

'Then you held me close to you, and you rocked me in your arms like a child, and stroked my head with your cool hands till everything was quiet.'

He subsided, and lay still for a moment. Suddenly he tried to raise himself. He reached up with his free hand, groping, slipped it around the girl's neck and pulled her down toward him.

She made a sound like a faint sob and clasped him, enveloping his bruised and bandaged head in her arms, and pressing his face against the soft cushion of her breasts.

'Luanna. . . .'

'Hush, now,' she murmured. 'Put it out of your mind. Everything's all right.'

He clung to her. 'Stay with me, Luanna. I need you.'

'Yes, Darby, yes. I need you, too.'

'Don't go away from me, ever.'

'No, Darby, I won't, I promise. I never, never, never will. Go to sleep now.'

Her voice cooed with the soothing gentleness of a dove's song. She rocked him tenderly, cradling his head, and her tears fell on his chest.

A few feet away the little candle, reduced to melted nothingness, faltered, recovered, sputtered, and held on tenaciously to its final flickering moments of life.

The earth had turned; shadows had moved and shifted, the moon had set. A soft, almost imaginary tint of light touched the sky to the east.

And at the empty open window space of the old cabin Julia's bright eyes, gazing in, hovered there for a moment longer, then floated away, and were soundlessly swallowed in the forest gloom that was slowly turning to misty early morning grey.

CHAPTER TWENTY-NINE

When daylight came the towering column of grey-black smoke that had boiled up invisibly in the night sky above Chinaberry was gone, with nothing but wispy disconnected fragments smudging the blue space of day, and drifting peacefully off toward the southeast.

And on the river Moses's little skiff cut the water, heading for the Chinaberry landing.

As he pulled on the oars Trav twisted in his seat often, watching the delicate floating remnants of smoke on the southeastern horizon. They looked so harmless – yet they touched him with a chilling intimation of reality, which he had not been able to feel fully when listening to Moses's disjointed, nightmarish tale.

Moses slumped now in the bow of the craft, mute and motionless in exhaustion, and grateful for these few minutes' rest, with his work accomplished.

Trav aimed the skiff toward the point where the *El Bandido Moreno* was moored, manoeuvred it broadside against the bank, and leaped out. Moses came to life and stepped out also, taking charge of the lines and motioning Trav to go on ahead. Trav walked rapidly away up the little road toward the place where Chinaberry house should be.

In the willow thicket he lost sight of the high traces of smoke in the sky – and at the same time was engulfed in the vivacious glittering chatter of morning birdsong. The feeling of foreboding faded; he felt himself tempted by the irrational hope that the whole thing was a stupid mistake – or a bad joke. He hurried on.

When he emerged from the willows he stopped abruptly, and sucked in his breath. The reality was complete. Around the base of the charred black chimneys, grotesque in their frozen vertical rigidity, the dead ashes lay like an ugly wound on the land. The horror struck him with the force of a physical blow across the chest. Death is never so hideous, he thought, as when exposed to the merciless mocking light of morning sun.

At first he did not notice Julia. Then he saw her, standing a short distance from the ruin, near the side road. She stood tall, straight and serene, poised like a hostess awaiting the arrival of guests. Trav stared at her, and the admiration he had once fought against welled up irresistibly; she was formidable – she was undefeatable. Even now.

Moses overtook him then, and stood by his side and looked across the desolated grounds at Julia.

'Good,' he said quietly. 'She's heah waitin' – don't have to go climbin' that fool hill agin, lookin' fo' her.'

He nudged Trav on the arm. 'You go on. I'll go back to the landin' and bring the skiffs on down to a point close to the cabin, and meet y'all theah.'

Trav turned a questioning frown on the old man.

'You go on with Julia,' Moses repeated. 'I 'spect she'll want to have a talk with you.'

He went back in the direction of the river, and Trav walked on slowly, toward Julia.

She came to meet him, smiling, her eyes shining, her face as tranquil as a summer dream. She held out her hand to him.

'Hello, Trav,' she said. 'I'm glad to see you.'

A cocky, brazen jay capered in the open window area of the squatter's cabin, and squawked raucously at the people inside.

Luanna opened her eyes abruptly, lifted her head and looked around with a quick stab of alarm. She and Darby lay entwined in each other's arms on the pine-needle floor. Her movement disturbed him; he stirred, groaned softly, and woke.

They looked at each other, to search for and confirm the lasting effect of those final quiet moments of the night, before the oblivion of overpowering weariness had enveloped them. The memory was there; they recognized it and smiled, in unspoken reaffirmation.

The morning was bright. Sunshine streamed through the branches of the loblolly pine overhead, and made a lively light-and-shadow pattern on their bodies, and the pine-needle floor around them.

They lay quietly for a few moments, without speaking. Darby's hand moved with a light caress over the girl's arm and shoulder.

'How do you feel?' she whispered.

'Awful,' he said. 'I just spent the night with the most beautiful girl in the world – and I couldn't move a muscle.'

She laughed softly, and pecked his cheek with a playful kiss.

The jay in the window shifted his position to face intruders, scolded noisily, and flew off.

The sound of Julia's voice calling floated across the forest clearing. 'Luanna?'

As Julia and Trav came across the little meadow toward the cabin Luanna appeared in the doorway, and stepped out to meet them. She looked with pleasant surprise at Trav, and held out her hand to him. She saw the anxiety in his and Julia's faces, smiled brightly, and answered their question before it was asked.

'Don't worry. He's all right.' It was a cool confident statement of fact.

Julia hurried past her, and entered the cabin. She knelt beside Darby, and looked at him closely. He smiled up at her.

'How are you, Darby?' she said softly.

His voice was weak and faltering, but his smile held. 'I'm gonna make it fine, Julia. How 'bout you?'

She returned the smile. 'So am I.'

Darby blinked hard when he saw Trav. With a great effort he raised himself on an elbow. His swollen face was suddenly lit with excitement.

'Trav! You came back, you son of a gun! God, it's good to see you!'

Julia retreated to the old wooden bench against the wall, while Trav knelt beside Darby.

'Good to see *you*. I heard you had a bad night.'

Darby tried to sound flippant. 'Nothin' serious. Just a little disagreement with some uninvited guests.' He grinned at Trav. 'Man, you sure picked the right day to clear out!'

Trav looked the injured man over with meticulous attention, prodding him, and inspecting his bandages. Luanna came and sat down beside Darby on the opposite side, and watched.

'I see you've been in capable hands,' Trav said.

'The best.'

They both glanced at Luanna.

'I come from a distinguished medical family,' she said placidly. 'One of my great-grandfathers was a famous African witch-doctor.'

Trav gazed at Darby with sombre thoughtfulness. 'Well,

I'm relieved,' he said after a moment. 'From what I heard, I figured I'd find you in a lot worse shape than this.'

'They were cream puffs, Trav,' Darby said earnestly, 'Softies. I almost handled 'em by myself. Now that you're back, if they show their ugly faces around here again, we'll –'

'Hold it, pal. I'm not back. I'm here to get you. You feel up to travellin'?'

Darby frowned. His voice hardened. 'Damn it, Trav, we've been over all that before. I'm tired o' talkin' about it –'

'But after last night, Darby – maybe you ought to reconsider,' Luanna said. 'Things are different now.'

Moses appeared in the doorway. He walked into the room and looked down at Darby with fatherly concern. 'How you feelin', young fella?'

Darby smiled. 'Hey, how 'bout that skiff race today, Moses? Maybe now you'd have a chance.'

Moses chuckled and glanced at Julia. 'He's all right. Same ol' Darby.'

He turned to Trav. 'I brought the skiffs down heah.' He nodded toward the river. 'Yours is ready, whenevuh you are.'

'Thanks, Moses.' Trav kept his eyes on Darby. 'Well, how about it, pal? Can you walk?'

'I can carry 'im down to the skiff on my back,' Moses suggested. 'Used to carry 'im when he was little – reckon I still can.'

Darby lay back and looked at the cabin wall, and sighed deeply. He muttered, addressing the old moss-grown logs: 'I'm gonna have to start gettin' up earlier in the mornin', looks like. People plan out my life for me while I'm asleep.'

'If we start now,' Trav said, 'we can take the time for you to get a little rest at Ely Griffith's place, before we start west –'

'Wait a minute,' Darby said huskily. 'All of you, jus' wait a damn minute!' He brought himself painfully up on his elbow again, and spoke with deliberate controlled patience.

'I made a promise to Julia. I have no intention o' breakin' that promise –'

'Darby –' Julia spoke quietly. 'You're released from your promise. I *want* you to go. And I want you to leave immediately.'

He gazed across the room at her, and his look was grim with stubbornness and something almost like hostility.

'What d'you want me to be, Julia? You want me to be a yellow cur, and run off with my tail between my legs?'

She waved him silent, and spoke with calm authority.

'Listen to me, Darby. It was wrong – utterly selfish of me – to try to keep you here. It's not safe. Now, more than ever, that's true, and always will be. And I should have known that. Deep down I *did* know it, of course – I just wasn't willing to admit it to myself. My foolishness has cost me dearly, but I'm content. It could have been worse – much worse. I'm just grateful it isn't too late for me to correct my mistake. And you must help me correct it. You must go.' Her voice was suddenly laden with pleading. 'Please, go.'

'What about fixin' up the house, and renovatin' the fields? What about all your plans?'

She shook her head. 'All my plans are changed. The house is gone. Burned to the ground.'

Luanna put a soft hand on Darby's shoulder. 'That part of your dream was real, Darby,' she whispered.

Darby stared, aghast, searching the faces around him.

'Those bastards!' he muttered. 'We'll fight 'em, damn it, we'll *fight 'em* –!'

'No, Darby.' Julia was on her feet, and her voice was imperious. 'You will not. I won't permit it.'

They gazed at each other, each granite-hard, each unyielding.

'I ain't gonna be a yellow cur, even if you want me to be,' Darby said. His words had an edge like steel. 'I ain't goin' away from here and leave you with not so much as a roof over your head. I just ain't, and that's all there is to it.'

Julia sat down on the wall bench again, and folded her hands in her lap.

'It so happens, Darby, that Trav and I had a long talk on our way down here, and we have concocted an entirely new plan.'

Darby's eyes flew suspiciously from Julia to Trav and back again. 'You mean to tell me you two actually *agreed* on somethin'?'

'We did that,' Trav said, smiling. 'And you know when Julia and I agree on somethin', it *must* be a good idea.'

Darby fixed his gaze on Julia, his eyes narrowed in scepticism. 'Well?'

'Well.' She took a deep breath before continuing. 'I've decided to accept Trav's offer to sell out here, and come to California with you.'

Darby went rigid with astonishment. 'Julia – you mean it?!'

'I hope you approve.'

'Approve?! Of course I approve! It's the greatest thing I've –'

He looked at Luanna, and saw that the girl was staring wide-eyed – first at Julia, then at him. Her face was twisted, the troubled surface of a roily pool of conflicting emotions.

Darby reached out and took her hand, and turned his eyes again toward the woman across the room.

'Julia – I got to tell you somethin', before we go any further.' He held the girl's hand tightly, and his voice was low and even. 'Luanna and I – we're gonna get married.'

Julia was ready. She responded cheerfully and without hesitation. 'That's wonderful! *I* approve of *that*, wholeheartedly.'

Luanna gasped soundlessly. Her voice was tremulous. 'Do we – do we have your blessing, Julia?'

'On one condition.'

They waited breathlessly for her to say it.

'That you name your first daughter Julia.'

'Oh –' Luanna's voice caught. She darted across the room and fell into Julia's arms. The sisters clung together, incapable of speech.

Trav turned to Darby. '*Now*, can you walk?'

'I can walk!' Darby laughed. 'I can walk, I can run, I can even dance!'

He started to pull himself up, but stopped, wincing in pain. 'But I can't get up.'

Trav and Moses helped him, and he got unsteadily to his feet, and smiled triumphantly. Luanna came to his side.

'Come on, everybody, let's get goin'!' he shouted. 'You're comin' too, o' course, ain't you, Moses?'

The old man smiled quietly, without answering.

Darby rushed on, churning with enthusiasm. 'Trav, how many horses can we get? There'll be five of us now –'

'Wait, Darby.' Julia rose and came toward him. 'I'm not exactly coming *with* you. Not just *now*. I have to see to disposing of the property first.'

Darby frowned at her. 'Can't you do that by correspondence? Get Mister Hodges to handle it for you, or somethin' like that?'

'No, that's impossible. The plan is that Moses and I will remain here till it's taken care of, then we'll come and join you. Give us – six months, perhaps.'

Darby protested. 'That's crazy, Julia! It'll be the middle o' winter then – you'd have to wait till next spring. And you can't travel alone, jus' you and Moses!'

'I'd like to know why not!' Julia gave a disdainful toss of her head. 'Considering some of the ventures Moses and I have undertaken – I think this would be one of the tamest.'

'You've never made a trip like that. You don't know what an undertaking it is.'

'It's quite simple, really.' Julia's confidence was unshakable. 'Trav has outlined it for me, and I trust his judgment completely. We'll take a steamboat to St. Louis, and another one up the Missouri to Kansas City. From there we'll take the stagecoach to Santa Fe. *That* will be a trial, I'm sure, but we'll manage. And Trav tells me you have friends in Santa Fe who can be alerted to expect us, and who will offer us hospitality. Then we'll send word to you, and Trav will hasten there and escort us the rest of the way himself.'

She smiled. 'You see? Simplicity itself.'

'But what about right now? Where will you go from here?'

'To Graystone. To the Ramseys.' She added hastily, 'Only because it's just downriver – we can get there in ten minutes.'

Darby snorted. 'That lecherous bastard will be pawin' at you before you can get in the house!'

'Oh, Darby!' Julia laughed. 'Dorothy Ramsey is a dear friend – *and* a jealous wife. *She'll* see to it that I'm safe from Philip!'

Julia's manner was smooth and pleasant, as she deftly disposed of Darby's objections, one by one – on the Graystone question, she saw no reason to mention that Philip Ramsey was living there alone, that his wife had departed.

'Besides,' she went on, 'we'll no doubt move in to Hanesville in a few days, and impose upon George and Sarah Hodges, as soon as I can get word to them.'

Darby was not satisfied. 'I don't like the sound of it,' he grumbled.

'Darby, please. Don't worry about me, I'm in firm control.' Julia laid a hand on his arm. 'Go now. It's dangerous for you to remain here an instant longer.'

'It's safe for you and Moses?!'

'That gang will never come back looking for *us*. They *will* be on the watch for *you*.'

'She's right, Darby.' Luanna spoke softly. 'Gene Willard has a special interest in you, we know that. And he's not likely to forget all about it.'

'Well – damn!' Darby continued to frown, his stubbornness holding fast.

'The Graystone landing is less than a mile below here,' Julia said. 'We'll float on down there as soon as you've gone.'

Her eyes entreated him, as she touched his arm again. 'Go, Darby,' she said gently. 'Now.'

He stood mute, gazing at her, knowing that it was useless to argue further.

'We've got two thousand miles to cover,' Trav said. 'Let's get started.'

Darby turned and looked at Trav for a long moment. With Luanna supporting him on one side, he took a hesitant step toward his friend.

'Give us a hand, Trav,' he said.

CHAPTER THIRTY

They stood once more on the banks of the wide river, in the bright morning sunshine. The high cloud cover of the day before was gone without a trace, and was replaced by a blazing sky and baking heat.

Julia stood on a little rise a short distance from the edge of the lapping water.

'No goodbyes,' she said firmly. 'I absolutely detest goodbyes. Besides, it wouldn't even be appropriate – we'll be together again soon.'

Luanna stood before her. 'No goodbyes, Julia. But come as soon as you can, please?'

The women embraced, and held each other close.

'I'll miss you,' Luanna said. 'I'll be lonely for you.'

'Pshaw!' Julia scoffed gently. 'You'll be living an exciting new life. You'll be much too busy to be lonely for me.'

'But I won't know how to do things without you to help me.'

'That's ridiculous! You're perfectly capable in every way. And, you may be sure, when little Julia comes along Aunt Julia will be right there hovering over her, making sure she's brought up right!'

She smiled and gave the girl a last hug and a quick kiss, and squeezed her hand.

'Be happy,' she whispered.

Luanna turned away, and went to Moses, who waited by the *El Bandido Moreno*, ready to help her aboard. Tears stood in the old man's eyes as he opened his arms to the girl, and took her in a long tight embrace.

'I jes' can't help thinkin' 'bout yo' mama.' He spoke softly, close to her ear. 'Josie would be so happy if she could see you this day.'

And then Trav, standing before Julia: 'You might have known it, dear lady – I wasn't gonna let you get away with not seein' me off.'

She managed a wan smile for him, and held out her hand. 'I'm sorry about all that, Trav, truly I am. My – that was only yesterday morning! It seems ages ago. But, anyway – we understand each other now, don't we?'

'Yes we do, Julia.' He stood gazing at her solemnly, holding her hand. 'We understand each other perfectly.'

He leaned forward and kissed her lingeringly on the cheek. 'You're a beautiful person,' he said.

He turned and went down the bank toward the skiff.

Darby came to her then, while the others waited below.

They stood together for a few moments without speaking. Darby swung his eyes down along the bank of the river, where dense vegetation, overhanging the water's edge, began a short distance from them and extended far downstream.

He spoke quietly, musing. 'Right down there somewhere's the place where I got in Mister Rutledge's boat that night.'

'So – we've come full circle,' Julia said. Her voice was dull and drained of feeling.

'I meant to go look for the place – see if I could find it again.'

'You never could. Twenty-one years is a long time. The forest changes constantly. New young vegetation grows up and crushes the old, and grinds it under. That's how life goes on.'

He regarded her curiously. 'But, you know, the area around the squatter's cabin hasn't changed much. The chinaberry tree's gone, and the loblolly pine's grown up next to the cabin – but it hasn't really changed much.'

'Around the squatter's cabin – that's different. That's a special place. It's protected by a charm.' Her eyes were soft and dreamy. 'The squatter's cabin is like – no other place in the world.'

His eyes fell away from hers. 'I should never have come here. I know that now.'

'You're foolish,' she said crisply. 'If you hadn't come here, you wouldn't have Luanna.'

'And *you* wouldn't have –' He gestured vaguely. 'All that's happened.'

'Darby – what happened to the house was the best possible thing for me. It will force me to start living my life for *vital* reasons, rather than for the preservation of a dead and useless relic. And what happened between *us* – that was my own doing, entirely. I always *was* incurably bossy, you know that – forever managing everything and everybody. And I'm much too old to change my ways.'

His eyes remained despondently on the ground.

'I won't have you looking guilty,' she said. 'It's silly and stupid, and I won't have it.'

He looked at her, and smiled weakly. 'Yes'm.'

She put a hand on his shoulder. 'Now go. The others are waiting.'

He faced her squarely and grasped her by the arms.

'Don't fool around, Julia,' he said sternly. 'Sell the property and come to California fast. We'll spend every day jus' waitin' for you.'

'Yes. I'll hurry.'

'Be sure to write. Care o' General Delivery, Sacramento. You got that?'

She nodded. 'General Delivery, Sacramento. Yes.'

'Now don't neglect it, Julia. We expect to be kept informed, you hear?'

'Yes, yes.'

'And, let's see – what else?' He hesitated, frowning in thought.

She put a finger to his lips and stopped him.

'Take care of my little sister,' she said softly. 'Be good to her, and she will make you happy.'

He smiled. 'I will, Julia. That's a promise.'

He pulled her toward him and kissed her gently on the cheek, and cocked his head slightly with a new thought.

'Wouldn't it be nice if Cap'n Andrew came, and brought you to California on his beautiful ship?'

Her eyes glistened, but her smile was bright.

'Dreamer,' she whispered.

'Learned it from you.'

He kissed her lightly on the other cheek, and held her eyes for an instant longer.

'The best of everything I know, I learned from you.'

He turned away, and Moses came up to help him as he limped down the slope.

At the skiff the two men clasped each other in a quick sturdy embrace.

'Never did have our race,' Darby said glumly.

Moses shrugged. 'Some othuh time,' he mumbled.

Darby made a stab at cheerfulness. 'Jus' wait'll you see the ranch land, Moses. You'll like it. You'll become a western man overnight!'

'Sho' I will,' the old man said with a gentle smile. 'Sho' I will.'

'I'm countin' on you, Moses.'

They clung to each other for a moment. Moses swallowed hard, struggling to retain control of speech.

'If theah's a good Lord anywheah up yonduh,' he said at last, in a whisper, 'may He watch ovuh you. All of you.'

Darby climbed laboriously into the skiff.

Trav operated the oars, and turned the bow of *El Bandido Moreno* outward for the last time.

'I'll leave the skiff tied at Tolliver's Landing,' he called to Moses. 'You can go over and get it whenever you want.'

Moses nodded, and waved.

Trav pulled on the oars, and the land fell away rapidly across the swirling sheet of water. Darby and Luanna, huddled together in the bow of the boat, waved to Moses and searched the bank for Julia, but she was not in sight.

When the skiff was a hundred yards out Julia reappeared quietly, and came to stand beside Moses, and waved.

Without looking at her Moses said, 'What did you disappeah like that fo', Little Missy?'

'Afraid I was going to cry,' she answered simply.

They remained standing there waving until the *Bandido Moreno* had slipped far over the bright gleaming surface of the river toward the opposite side, and was obscured in the shimmer of distant heat waves, and lost. When there was no one there to wave to, they turned their backs on the river.

Moses walked to the path that led back in the direction of the cabin, and went ahead of Julia, to push grasping branches aside. At the edge of the forest Julia paused and looked back across the water a last time. The river was empty.

Just as she started to go on, the deep sound of a steamboat whistle rolled up the watercourse, and echoed away slowly. She turned back in eagerness, her eyes searching.

Moses, up the path ahead of her, waited patiently. 'It's jes' an ol' steamboat, Missy. You've seen a million of 'em.'

'Yes. Just an old steamboat.'

She found the tiny plume of smoke, far down to the south.
'Number twenty-one, upriver,' she murmured. 'I lose.'
'What's that?' Moses said.
'Nothing.' She smiled at him. 'Nothing at all.'
He went on up the path, and she followed.

CHAPTER THIRTY-ONE

The forest lay drugged and slumbering in summer heat; small secret creatures of the brush and birds in tangled branches above were still, invisible and silent, as the sun and the temperature climbed higher.

Drained and numb with weariness, Moses and Julia walked in silence and with dragging movements back to the squatter's cabin, and sank down gratefully in the shade with their backs against the cool moss-covered logs of the old cabin wall.

Julia drew her fingers across her damp brow. 'Heat's getting fierce,' she said. 'Funny – I never used to notice the heat when I was younger.'

'Welcome to the old folks' society,' Moses said dryly.

They rested quietly for a few minutes.

'I want to tell you one mo' time, Little Missy,' Moses went on, 'ain't nothin' wrong with a good honest cryin' jag – nothin' at all. Fact, if you feel like havin' one right now, I'll be happy to join in and keep you company.'

She smiled faintly. 'No thanks, Moses. I'm just too tired.'

Their eyes met for a moment, and suddenly they laughed – he in his deep, genial chuckle, she in a girlish giggle.

'Well, don't say I didn't offuh.' He leaned his head back to rest it against the log wall, sighed deeply, and closed his eyes.

He awoke with a grunt, and jerked his head up off his chest and looked around, blinking. Instinctively he glanced up to check the position of the sun, and saw that it was riding near the zenith – something like an hour had passed. Then he noticed Julia standing in the centre of the little grassy meadow before the cabin.

When she saw that he was awake she came toward him, smiling. 'Feeling better?'

He rubbed his face with his hands, yawned mightily, and shook his head. 'Must 'a' dropped off,' he mumbled.

'So did I,' she said. 'Just woke up a minute ago.'

She stood over him and laughed – the light, musical,

careless little laugh that he was used to, that always made him feel good.

'We're a couple of lazybones,' she said.

He shook his head again, this time in slow wonderment. 'I don't know how you do it, Little Missy. You look like you jes' got back from a tea party.'

'No use moping,' she said briskly. 'Too many things to do.'

She sat down next to him. 'You know, Moses, we've done so many things that people never thought possible, you and I – and we're not done yet, I'll tell the world! Whatever we set our minds to, we can –'

'Wait a minute, Missy.' Moses's quiet voice brought her to a stop. 'Befo' you go gittin' all wound up – theah's a couple little things I got to talk to you about.'

She was suddenly meek. 'All right.'

'First thing.' He twisted his position slightly, so that he could observe her more closely. 'You don't really want to go to Mistuh Ramsey's place, do you?'

She laughed again, and patted his hand. 'I *knew* you'd never believe that!' Her voice vibrated with amusement.

'I had to convince Darby that I'd be safe – otherwise he wouldn't go. So I told him I was going to Graystone, because it was the safest-sounding thing I could think of. Of course I neglected to tell him that Philip is living there alone, and is waiting for me, panting passionately.'

She smiled at Moses. 'No, dear friend, I am *not* going to Graystone. I'd rather sleep in the woods and eat roots and berries.'

Moses nodded, with a look of satisfaction. 'Good. That's my Little Missy.'

'What's the second thing?'

'Well –' He pressed his lips together and gazed off into the forest greenery.

'I ain't nevuh criticized you, Missy, and I don't mean to criticize you now. I know you had a tough job on yo' hands, persuadin' Darby to go. But – you didn't have no right to speak fo' me.'

She sat very still as she listened to him, her eyes quiet and grave.

'Y'see, the thing is, Missy – I'm too old and tired to go wanderin' off to some strange far-off place like California. Ain't no sense in me tryin' to start a new life somewheah else

– theah ain't that much time left fo' me. I've lived my whole life heah on the banks o' the Miss'sippi. Good or bad, this is my home. And I'm gon' stay right heah till I die.'

Julia placed a gentle hand on the old man's arm.

'Don't be angry with me, Moses,' she said softly. 'I didn't have a chance to explain things to you beforehand – but I wasn't really trying to speak for you. I wasn't even speaking for myself.'

His face was blank, uncomprehending.

She got to her feet. 'Come here a minute. I want to show you something.' She bent over him, smiling, and took his hand and pulled.

Moses got up, and allowed himself to be led toward the centre of the meadow.

'I found something very exciting a few minutes ago – just before you woke up,' Julia said over her shoulder. She knelt beside the stump of the chinaberry tree, and pulled aside the tall weeds that obscured it.

'Look.'

From out of the base of the old shattered stump a sturdy young shoot pointed toward the sky, reaching upward, searching for sunlight. Along its slender length grew new leaves, in clusters of bright green summer ornament.

Proudly Julia displayed her discovery. 'Can you believe it, Moses? The chinaberry tree's coming back. It's going to be beautiful for us again.'

Moses cocked his head to one side, studying her quizzically. 'What – what are you sayin', Missy?'

She stood before him, with her hands resting lightly on his shoulders.

'Do you think *I* could go traipsing off to some strange faraway place like California? Would I give up, and throw away everything we've worked for all our lives, just because we've had a setback? Haven't we had setbacks before?'

He stared at her, gaping in astonishment. 'You mean – you ain't goin' neither?'

'This is my home too, Moses.' Her voice was quiet and solemn. 'I belong here, the same as you do.'

He stood speechless for a moment, gazing blankly at her. Then his finely tuned sense of practicality asserted itself.

'Tha's fine, Missy – but you ain't *got* no home now. It's nothin' but a pile o' ashes.'

She moved away from him a few steps, and pursed her lips

in thought. Her words came slowly, in careful speculation.

'Moses – how long do you think it would take you to build a new roof on the squatter's cabin?'

His jaw dropped. 'Little Missy, are you tetched in the head?'

'And a floor, of course. And windows, and a door.'

'Yes, you sho' are.' He answered his own question. 'You done gone plumb loony!'

'It's where I've always *wanted* to live, Moses!' She flung her arms out wildly, in enthusiasm. 'You can make two rooms of it, and build on a small addition for a kitchen, and –'

'With what?' he demanded. 'I ain't got hardly no tools. I ain't got no buildin' materials. I ain't got a wagon to haul the buildin' materials I ain't got, and if I had a wagon to haul the materials I ain't got, I wouldn't have a mule to pull it. And if I had all that – theah ain't no road!'

'You have me,' she said simply.

He exploded with a roar of laughter.

She flew to him and grasped him by the arms. 'We can do it, Moses, I know we can! I'll buy all the things you need!'

'What you gon' use fo' money?'

'We'll sell off part of the property – *part* of it, I said. Not *this* part. This is where we'll live.'

Her eyes shone as she swept them around the little clearing, snugly enclosed by the dense protective forest.

Moses' frown deepened as he shook his head in consternation. 'Lord, Little Missy! Pretty soon you gon' have *me* feelin' loony!'

She shook him vigorously. 'Say we can do it, Moses. Please?'

His frown remained stern. 'Now jes' hold on, Missy. Simmer down. We don't know wheah our next meal is comin' from, or wheah we gon' lay our heads tonight. We got to decide what to do right *now*, this minute.'

'You're quite right,' she said, suddenly calm. 'First, I think we should go feed and water the animals.'

'*Now* you're bein' sensible.' He nodded with approval. 'Then I'll pick sump'm out o' the garden fo' *us* to eat – if them hoodlums didn't trample everything into the ground.'

'Fine,' Julia said. 'Then we'll walk to Hanesville.'

He stared. 'Walk to Hanesville?!'

'Unless you have a horse and carriage tucked away somewhere, that I don't know about.'

'It's seven *miles* to Hanesville!'

'That's where our last remaining friend is.'

Moses nodded. 'Mistuh Hodges.'

'George will put us up, and help us with our building plans. He'll even help us do the work, if I promise to teach in his school this winter.'

'*What* buildin' plans? I ain't agreed to no buildin' plans.' His halfhearted grumbling was useless, and he knew it.

Julia placed a finger on her chin and gazed thoughtfully across the meadow at the little cabin. 'It'll be a nice house. A cozy house.'

She turned her eyes back to her companion. 'And, you know, Moses – I think maybe that's what I was always meant to be, anyway – a schoolteacher.'

Moses's frown slowly turned to a sly smile. 'I must 'a' been losin' my grip, sho' – thinkin' you'd give up and run off.'

He chuckled. 'Tha's all right. I got my grip back now. You ain't nevuh gon' fool me agin. Nevuh.'

She returned his smile. 'Shall we go then?'

'Seven miles,' he said with a sigh.

'Seven miles,' she said. 'And we're both utterly exhausted. What do you think?'

He sighed again. Then he winked at her.

'Le's git started.'

They walked back along the path, out of the woods, and up the little road toward the front of the property.

When they approached the barnyard Moses went ahead of her to open the gate. Julia stopped and stared at him, then rushed forward and began to examine his back.

'Moses! I just noticed your shirt – it's all ripped and torn.'

'Ain't nothin',' he said casually. 'I backed into a briar bush last night.'

She inspected more closely, and frowned in concern. 'Goodness! You're all scratched and bloody! These don't appear to be made by briars – they're ugly slashes.'

He scoffed at her good-naturedly. 'Lord help us! Heah we are homeless people, and you're fussin' ovuh a few little ol' scratches!' He pulled away from her.

'Go on, now, take care o' the animals, while I go see what I can find fo' us in the garden.'

When she had finished seeing to the cow and chickens Julia walked on toward the front road. She did not look in the direction of the fire remains, but kept her eyes steadfastly ahead, roaming up the slope of Indian Hill across the way.

Curious how the hill looked so peaceful and pleasant in daylight, she thought, so mysterious and sinister in darkness. It was easy to understand how the old mythology of its evil curse might have come into being.

Moses met her where the roads came together, and ceremoniously presented her with a lusciously ripe red tomato. They sat down in the grass at the side of the road, under the shade of a small tree, and ate. Moses bit into his expertly, without a drop of spillage; when Julia bit into hers, warm juice ran down her chin. She laughed, and Moses laughed with her.

'Reminds me of when Darby and I were little, and stole fruit out of the orchard,' she said.

When they had finished Moses turned to her, watching her closely. 'Well – ain't you gonna look?'

She shot a quick surprised glance at him.

'You ain't once looked at the house.'

'I know,' she said. 'I don't want to.'

'Go ahead. Look one mo' time, jes' to make shuah it's really true. Then we can go on to the next thing.'

She sighed. 'All right.'

She got up and walked a few steps along the front road toward the sycamore tree, steeling herself, and turned her eyes once more on the lifeless, bloated mass of black ruin.

It was alien; it was unreal. Like a photograph depicting the awful devastation of war in some distant place – regrettable, but, after all, disconnected, unrelated to anything familiar, or to any known person.

She knew what had been there – the ambitions and dreams and hard work of her grandfather, James Douglas, and the ultimate result of his labours; the gracious and elegant lifestyle of her father, Reeves; the patiently endured loneliness of her grandmother, Penelope Douglas, who had lived and died pining for her homeland Virginia, but whose devotion to this frontier home never faltered; the gnawing desperation of Margaret, her unhappy mother, the memory of whom, Julia knew, would stab her with remorse and pain at unguarded moments until the last day of her life; the hearty, intoxicating laughter of her mother's younger brother, Andrew, long disappeared into the far reaches of the world's oceans, who spent but a few rollicking days there, and left an indelible impression; the long sullen self-imposed exile that brought the wasted life of her other grandfather, Milo Gates, to a bitter end; and her own toilsome and perilous years of trying to effect a miraculous transformation, to wash away what was evil and preserve what was good – she *knew* what was lost, but she felt nothing. All the ties that bound seemed severed. All that remained was emptiness.

She took a deep breath, and turned dry-eyed back to Moses.

He stood waiting for her with a little yellow ornament in his hand. A buttercup – one of the last bright roadside treasures of spring raiment, persevering on into the long deadening summer.

His eyes glowed with a gentle affection as she came to him. 'You goin' to town today, Little Missy,' he said. 'You got to look yo' best.'

Carefully, tenderly, he placed the flower behind her ear, in her hair, then stepped back and admired the effect.

'Theah!' He beamed with satisfaction. 'Now you're pretty.'

With a flourish of gallantry he offered her his arm. 'Yo' carriage is waitin', Madam,' he announced in his butler voice.

'Thank you, Moses.' She smiled brightly, and took his arm. 'To Hanesville, please.'

Arm in arm, with a light easy jauntiness that scorned their deep fatigue and flung defiance at the gruelling distance ahead, they walked away from Chinaberry down the dusty little road in the bright hot morning sun.

CHAPTER THIRTY-TWO

The wide brick-hard dirt area that spread before Ely Griffith's store at Tolliver's Landing extended westward away from the river as a narrow gravel-bed road, which, beyond the limits of the village, assumed the proud local designation of highway.

It led past outlying farm houses and their surrounding fields of pasture and cultivation – chief among these, nearest the village, being the substantial property of Junior Tolliver, with its low rambling veranda-encircled bungalow, cool and secluded under the protective shade of large oaks and trailing wisteria vines.

Farther out the farm houses became smaller and more isolated, their supportive lands less expansive, and were separated in some cases by wooded areas, in others by forlorn and ragged abandoned fields.

Some four or five miles west of the river settlement the woods on either side of the road became general, and took on the tangled density of virgin wilderness. Soon the highway began to climb a slight, almost imperceptible grade, emerging gradually from the lush bottomland vegetation and winding through scraggly pines for a while until a gentle rounded crest was attained, from which point a traveller might look back over a flattened panorama of treetops and patchwork land to the river, and suddenly become aware of the long subtle rise he had covered. The promontory was almost bare of trees, covered with rolling grass, and exposed to a fierce assault from the sun, but was swept by a constant breeze that moved across the open sky toward the river.

Here, in midafternoon, a little caravan paused for rest.

With Trav and Luanna helping him, Darby dismounted from his horse and hobbled to a shady spot beneath a small isolated tree a short distance from the road, and stretched out on the ground with a groan of grateful relief. His multiple bruises had by now hardened into a stiff painful immobility that he knew would plague him for many weary days and sleepless nights. He smiled up at the girl who sat down beside him, deriving strength from her quiet constant awareness of his needs, her sound instincts as a nurse, her tender, loving, comforting presence.

Trav went to the pack mule and broke out a water flask, and passed it around. Then he took a resting place in another patch of shade a few feet apart from Darby and Luanna, and gazed back down the way they had come. He shook his head and compressed his lips grimly as he considered his bedraggled little company, and the prospects ahead.

In spite of Ely Griffith's friendly assistance, he had not been able to obtain prime horses – nor could they have afforded to buy superior animals in any case, with their funds seriously depleted by the loss of Darby's cash.

Further, the stock in Ely's store, aimed at local and river trade, had been sadly inadequate for their needs on a westerly journey. Except for a few hastily purchased odds and ends of clothing and food staples – and some preserved fruits bestowed upon them by Ely as a gift – they were heading for the long western trails with severely limited supplies.

Nevertheless, Ely had been of incalculable help. He had taken one look at the injured Darby, and with the calm, sure efficiency of one who had practised basic medicine without a licence for thirty years in the backwoods, had taken charge.

He installed the patient on a couch in the rear of the store, cleaned and redressed the wounds, applying salves from his stock of elementary pharmaceutical goods, and giving into Luanna's keeping a generous supply of bandaging material and medications to take along.

He smiled at Darby and said, genially, 'I b'lieve you got yo'self a cracked rib or two, young fella.'

For Trav he wrote on a slip of paper the name of a physician in the next town, twenty miles to the west, along their projected route of travel.

'You take 'im by to see Doc Simmons,' Ely said. 'Doc'll fix 'im up.' He gave Trav a significant look, and lowered his voice. 'And he won't ask too many questions about how he got that way.'

Ely himself had kept up a steady barrage of questions, and had been given a sketchy summary of the events at Chinaberry the previous night. He had been vastly relieved to hear that Julia was unharmed; his face had gone grim at the mention of Gene Willard's name.

'I've heard bad things about Gene Willard befo', but nevuh

nothin' like *this*. That man'll come to a bad end, shuahly – and the soonuh the bettuh, far as I'm concerned. People like him are a disgrace to the South.'

On behalf of all decent southerners Ely had sniffed and snorted with deeply felt moral indignation.

He had locked up the store, sent his employee Oscar off to fetch the local farmer who had horses for sale, and busied himself preparing a meal for the weary travellers. When Junior Tolliver and Jud Watkins had come up the front steps of the store and pounded on the door, Ely had hastened forward and sent them away, saying he had personal matters to attend to – the store was closed. Jud and Junior had stomped off, loudly muttering their protests at the unseemly interruption of their daily social ritual.

Ely had been a friend. Even so, Trav felt, Darby's near incapacitation from his injuries seemed certain to impose a heavy handicap in the form of a drastic reduction in their rate of travel, for days at least, possibly for weeks.

Trav pictured the way ahead – up the great mid-continental slope of limitless prairie and plains and winding river courses, through deep canyons and windy passes, across plateaux and deadly desert wastes of unearthly painted beauty, on through the fissures of the towering Sierra barrier, finally home to the quiet restful brown and olive of the central California valley – he pictured it, and inwardly shuddered at the feeling of endless, exhausting distance.

I never felt this way about travellin' the trails before, he thought. Guess that's the way you begin to notice when you're not young anymore.

He leaned back on an elbow and looked around in the wilting afternoon heat, and observed his motley expedition. One injured man, temporarily helpless; one young woman, inexperienced in travel and apprehensive of every turn in the road; three spindly-legged horses and an elderly asthmatic mule; inadequate supplies and dangerously low funds; and himself, complete with his congenital pessimism.

Very well. They were stuck with it all – except his pessimism. That could be discarded.

He took another look. The supplies could be added to later, as they encountered trading posts along the way, and their meagre funds would be husbanded with miserly care. The animals would have to be coaxed, wheedled, prodded, patiently nursed along every step of the way. They had time

– a good seventy-five days before the passes of the Sierra were likely to become locked in snow. Luanna was bright; she would gain experience rapidly, and with it would come confidence and courage. And in a way it was better that she did not know at this stage what trials she might have to face between here and the valley of the Sacramento – or, for that matter, in the years of the unknown future.

And Darby. He gazed at his bruised and battered friend and saw him whole again, with his vigorous good health and sunny nature fully restored.

It could be done. We'll make it all right, he predicted firmly to himself, and knew that this assessment of their prospects was arbitrary, but had behind it the force of all his past experience.

Then he thought of Julia. Her intentions had been known to him – on their quiet walk together to the squatter's cabin that morning she had admitted him to the intricate deceptions she had planned for the purpose of releasing Darby from his binding sense of obligation to her, and sending him away again, a free man. Now the secret was his responsibility, and his the decision of judgment to determine at what point in the future he would reveal to his friends the truth – that Julia would not follow them to California. She would not live on the ranch, ever, or be an affectionate hovering aunt to children, except in the form of stories constructed from old memories, and told and retold for years, until they took on a still, faded, lifeless, picture-book existence. He was not sure when he would admit Darby and Luanna to this knowledge, but he knew it would not be soon. Probably he would follow a suggestion Julia had made – that he wait until they were solidly settled in the habits, customs and responsibilities of married life – then the news would be more easily accepted.

He tried to visualize the lady of Chinaberry once more – the startling yellow hair, the saucy imperious toss of the head, the bright grey eyes, shining with that indomitable spirit – but it was a dim, hazy picture. His memory of her had already begun to slip into the shadowy dreaminess of a legend. And with that realization came a dull aching sense of an emptiness within him that had not been there before.

Trav got to his feet, stretched, and looked over at his two travelling companions.

'Let's go,' he said, and started for the horses.

'So soon?' Luanna asked plaintively.

'Got to cover ground before nightfall,' Trav said, and smiled at her. 'It's a long way to California.'

Darby got up slowly, leaning on Luanna. They stood together, his arm around her waist, and gazed off across the bright sky to the east, where the great ageless river lay shimmering quiet in the summer afternoon sun.

'Look,' Luanna said. 'You can see Indian Hill from here.'

Darby looked, straining his eyes, followed the direction in which she pointed. He kept his gaze fixed for a long moment on a tiny spot on the distant horizon, a spot so blurred and indistinct as to be hardly above the threshold of vision – yet to his ardent imagination clearly indentifiable.

'Wish we could see Julia,' he said.

Luanna gazed up at him with solemn eyes. 'I saw her,' she said softly. 'She was smilin' and wavin', and she was sayin', "Be happy. Be happy."'

He looked at her and smiled. 'I believe you.'

He pulled her close and kissed her gently, shifted his arm to her shoulder for support, and turned his eyes with confidence westward toward home.

Domina

BARBARA WOOD

Samantha Hargrave grew up in the teeming squalor of Victorian London, a motherless child of the cruel city despised by her harsh father. It was in the crowded streets where the poor lived and died like animals that she first dared to dream her impossible dream: of becoming a woman doctor – and it was there that she first fired a man's heart with longing.

She knew that hers was a special destiny, that she would need all her strength and will to fight against the prejudice which had banished women from medicine. To train as a doctor she would have to leave her friends, ignore her beauty, face the contempt of women and the scorn of men. From the slums of the city and the overcrowded wards of poverty-stricken charity hospitals to the grandeur of society receptions and the cloistered calm of medical school, Samantha fought to win the title of a woman doctor – DOMINA.

GENERAL FICTION 0 7221 9200 2 £2.50